# FIGHTING MAN OR BEAST?

A pair of huge, misshapen hands shot out from within and grasped his neck like the coils of a python. Conan had not even time nor breath to curse as he was snatched inside. And he knew that he was in the grip of no ordinary man. The huge, powerful Cimmerian was being manhandled as easily as a ten-year-old child. Conan's own hands shot out to grip the other's neck, only to discover that the creature had no neck to speak of. Its head seemed to be set squarely upon its hairy, sloping shoulders. He was not certain whether he wrestled with a man or with an ape.

The two struggled in grim silence, rocking around the room, toppling furniture and spilling things. As a vase shattered on the floor, Conan knew that help would arrive for the thing all too soon. Finally, Conan was able to grip the back of the massive head with one hand, the other going beneath the backward-slanting chin. He began to twist the malformed head around as the breath whistled through his own half-constricted windpipe. . . .

# CONAN

## AND THE TREASURE OF PYTHON

BY
JOHN
MADDOX
ROBERTS

A TOM DOHERTY ASSOCIATES BOOK
NEW YORK

CONAN AND THE TREASURE OF PYTHON

Copyright © 1993 by Conan Properties, Inc.

Cover art by Julie Bell
Maps by Chazaud

A Tor Book
Published by Tom Doherty Associates, Inc.
175 Fifth Avenue
New York, N.Y. 10010

Tor® is a registered trademark of Tom Doherty Associates, Inc.

ISBN: 0-812-55000-5

First edition: November 1993
First mass market edition: August 1994

Printed in the United States of America

0  9  8  7  6  5  4  3  2  1

For my stepson John Cameron Alan Mygatt
Adventurer, philosopher, creative genius, victor of many
battles and my valued friend.

# ONE

## The Seafarer

The port of Asgalun sits on a small bay that indents the coast of Shem. It is the only notable port of that pastoral land, the rest being little more than fishing villages. It is a colorful place, as ports tend to be. In the low hills of the upper town stand the fine estates of the wealthy merchants, surrounded by their fine gardens and their well-tended vineyards. In the lower ground of the town proper stand the sturdy stone buildings, the warehouses and inns, the temples and shops that service the inhabitants and the bustling trade of the port.

And then there are the docks. Here are to be found the men who produce the wealth enjoyed by the merchant-princes of the hillside estates and the shopkeepers of the town. These are the polyglot sailors and the hard-bitten skippers who may have lands of origin but whose only country is the sea. Nobody wastes fine architecture on such men. In any case there is no point in erecting splendid buildings on the shore, for any such would be destroyed every few years by the terrifying storms that blow in without warning from the vast reaches of the Western Sea. No, the seaside district of Asgalun is a shantytown of small transshipment warehouses, cheap inns, chandleries, fish markets, and sailor's dives. Since Shem is poor in timber, these low structures are built mainly of wood salvaged from ships wrecked by storms, the nearby rocks, or mere age. This sturdy but pitch-soaked construction material is so combustible that the entire waterfront of Asgalun burns down with some regularity.

Only hard, salty men inhabit such a place. It follows that it is a sensible place to go when one is in search of just such men.

Conan of Cimmeria was bored. A strange peace had settled over the Western Lands. The petty warlords were temporarily drained of cash and energy, hence of ferocity. The lands that were traditional enemies, which was to say all of them, were war-weary and had turned to settling internal problems and re-establishing disrupted trade. Fields trampled by contending armies had to be restored to fertility, plundered cities rebuilt. Professional fighting men were not welcome in lands that had turned from war. Even the chronic civil war in Ophir had shuddered to a halt from sheer exhaustion.

Such dry spells never lasted long. Conan gave this one no more than a year. But a man could starve in much less than a year. For months he had drifted in the central lands—Ophir, Corinthia, and Koth—looking for a good fight. Usually, he traveled by hiring on to a caravan as guard. With so many soldiers out of work, banditry was rife. Conan had turned bandit in the past, but he felt that was beneath him now. He knew, though, that he would turn bandit again rather than starve. His last caravan had discharged its goods in Asgalun, and Conan had ensconced himself at a wharfside tavern called the Albatross to live on his discharge pay and wait for something to turn up. But now his pay had dwindled to almost nothing and there were still no prospects. He knew that, should a pirate craft appear along the coast soon, he would be sorely tempted to join its crew.

In fact, even as he sat at a battered table, staring out through a porthole-shaped window, he saw a strange ship coming into the little bay. As it rounded the northern cape his practiced eye noted the set of its masts and the shape of its sail. Its hull was low, not heavy-laden but built for maximum speed and maneuverability. He could discern little else and soon the sails were lowered on their yards and the long sweeps were run out to bring the ship into harbor. That was a fighting man's craft if ever there was one, and Conan decided to have a few words with its skipper when it should dock. But he was to have a welcome distraction before that should happen.

"These taverns all look alike," said the young woman. She wore a simple gown of blue silk girdled with a golden cord. It passed around her tiny waist five or six times and was tied with an intricate knot, its tasseled ends dangling almost to her knees. Her low boots were likewise worked with golden thread. But it was not her expensive attire that drew the attention of the idlers and ruffians who crowded the narrow streets of the dockside. It was her great and strange beauty. Her skin was utterly white, her eyes huge and so pale as to be almost colorless. Her hair was silver-white and worn long, almost to her waist, and confined only by a golden fillet that circled her temples. In the center of the fillet, above her brows, was a great, smoky opal in a golden setting. Except for the healthy sheen of her skin and hair and her wide, clear eyes she might almost have been an albino.

Ordinarily, a woman so attractive and so richly dressed could not have walked ten paces in this district without molestation, but the villainous-looking men who were on every hand stood well back and offered her no discourtesy. This was not due to any innate good breeding on their part, but because she was not alone. The man who walked to her left intimidated nobody. He was an active, excitable little man who spoke often and quickly, with many gestures. He wore Aquilonian traveling garments of velvet and leather, his sword a short, basket-hilted weapon such as many travelers carried.

The other, who strode behind her, was the one who ensured her safe passage. He was a very tall man, somewhat gaunt but graced with long, powerful limbs. His massive, gold-bearded head was set atop a sinewy neck and his proud, fierce gaze swept his surroundings constantly, alert to any danger. If he wore any armor it was beneath his leather tunic, but at his wide, bronze-studded belt hung the massive sword of an Aquilonian man-at-arms, its blade long and wide, its crossguard a foot in length, its pommel worked in the semblance of a griffon's head. Its grip, long enough for two hands, was of fine sharkskin, once rough of texture and pearl-gray in color, but worn by age, hard use, and abundant sweat to a smooth near-blackness. The mere appearance of the hilt told any experienced fighting man that this was a man to give wide berth. His springy step and lion gaze told them that it was he and no other who had put such wear on the hilt.

"There it is!" said the little man. "The Albatross! See? There is the image of the soaring bird, above that door. The creature is native to the lands south of here. It is the most graceful of creatures in flight, and the clumsiest on land. It is a sign of good fortune to any ship it deigns to follow, and in the accounts of ancient Acheron its sudden appearance inland was a sign of—"

The woman smiled. "Yes, I know that, Springald. But here we do not seek knowledge but a man. And the man we seek should be there on the other side of that door."

"I shall go through first, child," said the huge man. His fingers flexed upon his hilt. Despite the heat of the day, he wore long sleeves of velvet and gauntlets of beautiful, butter-colored leather. He had to duck low to clear the heavy lintel of the door, and he performed the action like a swordsman. He did not bend from the waist, presenting the back of his neck as a gift to any ill-wisher inside. Instead he flexed his knees deeply and went through upright, straightening to his full height the instant he was inside. His eyes swept the room and he relaxed the slightest bit, signaling for the others to come in.

The large room they were in was on two levels. Just inside

the door a bar stretched along the right-hand wall the length of the upper level. On the left a stair led to an upper story. The upper level was perhaps six paces long, then a set of four room-width steps descended to the lower level, which contained many tables and chairs. Set into the far wall were four round windows through which sunlight streamed. Through the windows they could see the sparkling waters of the bay.

There were no more than a dozen men and women in the place, for the hour was yet early. The man behind the bar surveyed his three new customers. At the sight of their expensive clothing and other trappings he sprang from behind the bar, wiping his hands upon his apron and bowing for all he was worth.

"My masters, my lady, how may I serve you?"

"We look for a man. He is a Cimmerian. We have heard that he is to be found here." The big man spoke in clipped tones, as if he knew the value of his words and was loath to waste them.

"Oh," the barkeep said, disappointed. "You mean Conan. He sits over at that table by the window."

"Excellent," said the woman. "Be so good as to bring a pitcher of your best wine to that table, and four cups."

"At once, my lady." The man scurried back behind his bar.

Conan had watched as the three came in. They were unusual figures to see in a place like the Albatross, and he made a quick evaluation of them. From the cut and material of their clothes, they were Aquilonians. The small man looked intense and excitable, but Conan had a feeling he would be handier with that short basket-hilt than most men would think. The big man was impressive. His fine clothes were not the gauds of a dandy but the rich garments of a nobleman. He was clearly a member of the military aristocracy, and his physical address and the condition of his sword proclaimed that he took the military part very seriously. The woman was a puzzle. Her clothing and company were both Aquilonian, but he had seen her extraordinary coloration only among the Hyperboreans. He saw the barkeep gesture toward him and the three came toward his table. Perhaps his luck was about to change.

The three halted by his table. "Are you Conan of Cimmeria?" asked the big man.

"I am," said Conan, neither rising nor offering a seat. It was too early in the proceedings.

"I am Ulfilo, Margrave of Petva in Aquilonia. This lady is Malia, the wife of my brother."

"And I am Springald," said the smaller man, "scholar and teacher of Tanasul."

"We wish to speak with you about engaging your services for a journey we must embark upon," said Ulfilo. The barkeep appeared with the pitcher and cups. He arranged them upon the table, filling each cup, and left, bowing. Now Conan rose and gestured to the other seats.

"Since you are buying the wine, I will be more than happy to listen to your proposal." The four sat and sipped at their wine.

"This is better wine than I've had these last few days," Conan said, understating the situation. "You have my full attention."

"Since reaching this port," Ulfilo began, "we have inquired concerning seafaring men who have experience of the Black Coast. We were told that you are such a man."

"I am," Conan averred. "But there are many others in this port. Ships sail from here every season to trade among the black lands of the south."

"Yes," said Springald, "down to Kush, and even a bit farther south than that. But we need to go considerably farther. We must go many leagues south of the Zarkheba River."

"We heard rumors," Malia said, "that you used to sail in those waters."

Conan paused. "I did," he said, "but that was a number of years ago."

"It is unlikely that the waters or the coastline have changed in the interim," said Springald. "But it is said that very few traders travel so far south."

"One seeking high profit must go where there are few rivals," Conan said noncommittally. The truth was that few except pirates sailed those waters.

"How far south have you gone?" Malia asked.

"Far enough that the rivers and the lands have no names that you would ever have heard. Far enough that a white skin is a thing of marvel." Abruptly, he laughed heartily.

"Why do you laugh, Conan?" asked Ulfilo mildly.

"Something just struck me," the Cimmerian answered. "The folk of those lands thought *I* was white." He thumped the triangle of massive chest exposed by the unlaced opening of his leather tunic. It was as deeply tanned and windburned as his scarred face. "And I burn as dark as a Pict in those waters. What would they think of this lady?"

"They may get that opportunity," she said quietly.

Conan turned serious. "What is your proposal? Those are bad waters and worse coasts for people who have never roamed the hot lands."

Malia studied the man before her. She saw a man who might have been twenty-five years old, or as easily thirty-five. He was big and powerful and exuded the relaxed ferocity of a predator at rest. His tunic was plain, of supple black leather. In deference to the warm climate he was barelegged. Arms and legs alike were knotted with muscle and scarred with many old wounds. His only ornaments were a pair of heavy bronze bracelets. The sword at his belt was long and severely plain, its crossguard and pommel of unornamented steel. An equally plain dirk balanced it on the opposite side. The purse that hung next to the dirk was very flat. He looked competent and formidable, perhaps even a match for her huge and somewhat overprotective brother-in-law.

"We must find a man," said Ulfilo. "He is my younger brother, Malia's husband. He left Petva, our ancestral home, two years ago. The last communication we had from him was sent from Khemi, in Stygia. From there he went south."

Conan took a long drink of his wine. "South of Khemi lies the entirety of the Black Coast. To simply sail south from Khemi in hopes of finding him would be folly. I suggest you wait at home. If he returns all is well. If not, you must give him up for dead.''

"You do not understand," Malia said. "My husband sent the letter from Khemi after a long journey to the south. He returned north and stayed at Khemi only long enough to outfit another expedition, then he sailed south again.''

"If he did that," Conan said, "then he is a man well fitted to thrive in those fierce lands. Why do you not leave him to his activities?" Conan assumed that the man must have become a pirate. If so, the last thing he would want would be to see his family tracking him down. Many a younger son had left home to sail the shark's road. With a few successful voyages he could return home to set himself up as a country squire, spread a few stories about fabulously profitable trading trips to exotic lands, and settle down to a life of utmost respectability after an exciting career of robbery and murder.

"No, we must find him," Malia said. "His letter was most emphatic. He wants us to outfit a ship and find some brave men and sail after him.''

"Are you interested in helping us?" Ulfilo broke in.

"That depends upon a number of things," Conan said. "First, my pay.''

"A thousand gold marks of Aquilonia," said Ulfilo without hesitation. "Payable upon our successful return.''

Conan shook his head. "If you would hire me to help find your brother, I would want to be paid as soon as he is found. I would wish to return immediately, no matter what your plans might be.''

"That is fair," Ulfilo said. "Very well, a thousand marks when we find my brother alive.''

Again Conan shook his black locks. "No. My toil and danger are the same whether he is alive or not. If he is dead, I want to be paid when we find the place where he died.''

Ulfilo glowered but Malia answered: "Agreed.''

"Then that part is settled," Conan said. "Now, where did your brother sail? And what was he looking for, so far south?"

Now it was Ulfilo's turn to shake his head. "Suffice it that he had his reasons."

"I can accept that," Conan said. "But I must know where you propose to look for him."

"You are accounted a bold man hereabout," the woman said.

"Aye," Conan answered, "but no man calls me a fool. And if I am loath to travel blind, you may be assured that you will never get a skipper to risk his ship, or sailors to man it, without some idea of where they are bound. Even high pay will not tempt men into an unknown sea."

They paused for a while, brooding. Springald looked to Ulfilo. Finally, the man nodded. Malia repeated the gesture. The scholar turned to Conan.

"Cimmerian, what do you know of a place called the Coast of Bones?"

Conan sat back, frowning. "An ill-favored place, avoided by even the fiercest of the pirates. It lies six day's sail south the Zarkheba."

"And have you been there?" Springald asked.

"I have," Conan said, "though not by choice. My ship was blown thither in a storm and we had to lay up for a fortnight making repairs. It was not such an adventure as any man would care to repeat."

"And did you see the jagged white rocks that line the shore?" Springald said.

"How could I not? It is they that make navigation so hazardous. From out at sea they look like the bones of a beached animal, and it is from them that the coast gets its name."

"And the green-stained river that empties its sluggish flow into the sea on that coast? Saw you that?" Springald asked eagerly.

"Aye, it's hard to miss. The only source of fresh water in those parts, and even then it's only fresh by comparison with the sea. We had to strain the green muck out of it six times through fine cloth before it was fit to drink, and even then it could be deadly." Conan gave him a suspicious look. "How come you to know of that coast? Oh, this mysterious brother must have written of it in his letter."

"Nay," said the scholar, "that stretch of coast is little known to men of this day, but it is documented abundantly in the writings of the ancient kingdom of Acheron. Why, in the *Voyages of Ahmes the Explorer* alone, the great navigator details fully ten voyages to that coast and others nearby, and the *Annals of the Pilot's Guild of Python* lists twenty-seven—"

"Peace, Springald," Malia chided. She smiled at Conan. "He can go on for hours like this. Suffice it that we are not ignorant of the land, although we have never been there."

"But these are the accounts of many centuries past," Ulfilo said. "What sort of folk inhabit that stretch of coast in this age?"

"That is the worst part," Conan said. "They are a tribe said to be cannibals. I never saw them eat anyone, but they dragged off both living men and dead. We never saw them again, but we heard the sounds the living men made as the demons tortured them night after night. Even if they are not cannibals, I can tell you that they don't like strangers."

"Pardon me, Conan," said Springald, "but might it be that they just did not like the *kind* of stranger you were? Perhaps they had had unpleasant experiences with men resembling you and your shipmates."

Conan glared, then grinned crookedly. "You mean was I a pirate? Aye, it's true. It was long enough ago that no one wants to see me swing for it now. I was younger and less law-abiding then. And I'll admit that some of my shipmates may have been a bit rougher than necessary when they went into the forest foraging."

"Then," Springald said, "is it not possible that they might be less hostile to men who come as peaceful traders?"

"It's possible," Conan said. "But only if you were in a strong party, heavily armed. All the tribes of the coast are predatory, raiding each other and preying on shipwrecked mariners. They need to trade for what they must have and cannot get by raiding, but they are very lacking self-restraint.''

"What does that mean?" Malia asked.

"I mean they may attack traders to take what they want even knowing that it means no more traders will venture to their land for a long time. They have little sense of the future.''

"I know many men who behave that way," said Ulfilo sardonically. "In the civilized lands we call them kings and nobles.''

"True enough," said Conan. "At heart most of us are savages, did we but know it. The difference is that most of us have learned a little restraint but civilized men of power and coastal blacks never have.''

"What are these people called?" Springald asked.

"They call themselves the Borana," Conan answered.

"Ah! There are a people of southern Kush who name themselves the Palana, and in northern Kush are a mountain people known as Fathada. These two peoples speak a closely related tongue, which is a variant of Classical Kushite. Might these Borana be a southern drift of the same people?''

Conan regarded the little man with dawning respect. "That may very well be. I only heard them scream and chant defiance, but the words sounded Kushite to me, and some of my Kushite shipmates said that they might be able to understand the words, if they were spoken slowly and less angrily.''

"Did you travel inland?" Ulfilo asked.

"Not from the Coast of Bones. On other parts of the Black Coast, yes.''

Malia leaned forward. "What is it like inland?"

Conan gazed out the window, as if drawing a picture from past years and faraway lands. "Men speak of the Black Kingdoms as if it were a single land, but it is not. One man sees a little patch of territory inland from a single landing place and thinks he has seen all of the black lands, but that is foolish. What most people hear about are the great, squalling jungles with their swarming beasts and their pestilences, their fierce predators and fiercer men. But that is just the coast. The black lands are not all jungle, but only a small part. Go inland along some of the rivers, especially the Zarkheba, and you can be in the jungle for weeks, some of it so thick you have to hack your way through with bush knives. Other places, a half-day's trek can put you in the mountains where the tiny hunters make their home. In another, two days' journey can put you on a high plateau where trees are sparse and the land is covered with fine grass and the wild game is abundant. In places I've seen herds of huge antelope so vast that all the scribes of Aquilonia could not number them all.''

"Did you ever hear of a two-peaked mountain called the Horns of Shushtu?'' Malia asked.

Conan snapped back to his present surroundings. "Never. What is it?''

She shrugged her shapely shoulders. "Just a landmark mentioned in my husband's letter.''

Ulfilo glared at her briefly, then turned to Conan. "What of it, Cimmerian? Will you be our guide?''

Conan pondered a while. This was a fool's errand if ever he had encountered one. And he had encountered many. The man they sought was probably dead. The coast they wanted to reach was the most hostile Conan had ever visited. On the other hand, the men seemed competent, the woman was beautiful, and most of all, he had no other prospects. An offer he would have laughed at months before had a certain attraction now. He was bored, and if nothing else, this certainly promised adventure. If they should against all odds be successful, a thousand gold marks would keep him for a long time, perhaps until the wars picked up again. And there was the lure of the Black Coast. Once again he gazed out the window, as if peering past the horizon to the huge, unknown land beyond. So much of it lay there, perhaps as much as all the Western and Eastern lands together, most of it never seen by men of his hue. There were wonders there of a sort undreamed of by scholars like Springald. Horrors, too, and in great abundance. And always hardship and fighting, but those were the commonplaces of Conan's life.

"Aye, I'm with you," he said at last. They relaxed and smiled at one another as if all was now settled.

"We haven't been here long," Malia said. "Is there a suitable ship in harbor?"

"No," said Conan. "Not now, and not for the last few weeks. No ordinary merchant craft will do. We need a fighting man's craft and a brave crew and a canny skipper. There are none such in port just now."

Their faces fell. "Then we are in for a long wait?" Malia said.

"Not necessarily," Conan said.

"Don't speak in riddles, man," Ulfilo growled. "Either such a ship is in port, or it isn't. Which is it?"

Conan grinned. "There is none such just yet, but there will be in a minute or two. Ah! She drops anchor!"

"What do you mean?" Ulfilo asked, rising from his seat and stepping to the window through which the Cimmerian gazed.

Conan pointed through the portlike window to where the newcomer now lay a few hundred feet offshore. "There is a likely craft." The other two crowded at the window to see.

"It seems small," said Malia, her confidence slipping.

"Come," said Conan, rising. "We'll go speak to her skipper. And on the way I'll tell you a few things about seafaring in the dangerous waters." The four walked out of the Albatross.

# Two

## The Shipmaster

"That," Conan said, pointing to the craft that lay at rest a hundred paces from the pier on which they stood, "is a Zingaran hull, built in Kordava. It is made for the coastal trade of that land, and is designed to be swift, for near Kordava lie the Barachan Isles, which are rich in pirates. For that reason, these hulls are much favored by the Barachans, the better to catch their prey. You see the rake of the two masts?"

"Rake?" Malia asked.

" 'Rake' refers to the slight backward angle of the masts," Springald supplied. "It is esteemed among seafarers for improving the handling qualities of the vessel."

"Exactly," Conan said patiently. "No ship is built with that rake to the masts. It will always be the skipper who tries out different rakes, and different mast heights, and different sail plans to test his ship's speed and sailing qualities. I can tell by this rake that the skipper is concerned with getting the best speed out of his ship. just before you three came into the Albatross, I saw this ship round the cape and lower its yards. The sails are lateen-style, and very large for the size of the ship. Only an excellent seaman with a well-trained crew can manage such a rig. Else, the risk of capsizing the vessel is too great.''

As they watched, several men climbed into a small boat that had pulled alongside the ship. The boat backed away from the ship and the oars began a rhythmic rise and dip, bringing it closer to the pier with each stroke. The four on the pier awaited its arrival with varying feelings. Within a few minutes the boat was tied up to a ladder that ran down from the edge of the timber pier. Due to the stage of the tide, the men in the boat had to scramble up several feet of ladder to reach the pier. At another time, a simple step over the bulwark would have accomplished the same feat.

The first man off was a burly figure, swathed in a cloak and wearing a broad-brimmed hat on his head. Conan reached down and gave him a hand, hauling the man up the last few feet in a tigerish surge of muscle.

''Thank you,'' said the sailor, raising his face to see his bene-factor. ''How may I . . .'' At the same instant, Conan and the sailor grasped their hilts. Red hair spilled from beneath the brim of the hat and a red beard framed the man's jaw. A grimace twisted his lips.

''Blackhair!'' snarled the shipmaster.

''Redbeard!'' Conan barked. The others were dumbfounded as the two stood like statues, the skipper's sword half out of its sheath. Silently, Ulfilo moved to get between Malia and the two men who stood poised upon the brink of savage bloodshed. Then, slowly, Conan's hand fell away from his grip.

''We are a long way from the Northlands, Van,'' he said.

Just as slowly, the red-haired man resheathed his sword until his hilt clicked against the bronze throat of the scabbard.

''Aye, I can bear the sight of a Cimmerian this far from the halls of my fathers.''

''Feuds are for the homeland,'' Conan said. ''I have even

made friends of Hyperboreans, once I was south of the Border Kingdom. Down here, we are all just northern barbarians.''

''What does this mean?'' Malia asked in a low voice.

''The captain is of the Vanir race,'' Springald said. ''The Vanir and the Cimmerians are hereditary enemies. The Vanir raid the Cimmerians for children to raise as slaves, and the Cimmerians raid the Vanir for revenge and, well, just for the enjoyment of it.''

The shipmaster looked at the others. ''You seem to have business with me. What might it be?''

''Will you come to the Albatross and share a table with us, Captain?'' Ulfilo asked. ''We have need of a ship, and this man''—he gestured to Conan—''tells us that your ship is the sort we seek, and that its skipper and men are likely to be suitable.''

''Aye, and what sort of ship and men might these be?''

''We need a ship that can go into waters where an ordinary merchantman would be as a fat pigeon in a sky full of swift hawks,'' Ulfilo said. ''We seek men who are not afraid to brave the most hostile of coasts. And we seek a skipper who can drive both ship and men.''

The Van grinned. ''The *Sea Tiger* is such a ship, and I, Wulfrede of Vanaheim, am such a captain. As for my men, you had best look and judge for yourselves. Many men would run from the sight of them. If you are such men, you are not fitted for the voyage of which you hint.''

''Then will you join us, Captain?'' Malia said.

He looked down at the slight form and smiled. ''How could I not when the company is so fair? Yes, I'll even sit down and eat with a Cimmerian to hear this. You must have something very unusual to propose.'' Then he looked up at Conan. ''What of you, blackhair?''

Conan regarded him levelly. ''I could choke down a few bites, even with a redbeard. I told them that a ship like yours might well bear the skipper and men they seek. I do not withdraw my advice.''

Wulfrede grinned. "Then let's all be friends, at least until we've eaten and I've heard your proposal. To the Albatross!"

In the tavern platters of food were brought and they all ate while Ulfilo outlined the proposed voyage. The story he gave was identical to that he had given the Cimmerian. Conan listened closely for any difference. He suspected that they were not telling him everything and was ready to pounce upon the slightest discrepancy.

"First let me tell you that I think you are on a fool's errand," Wulfrede said. "But that is not my business. I am sure Conan here has already advised you that you stand very little chance of ever finding this man."

"You are correct," Malia said dryly. "He has so advised us and it is not your business. What of you and your ship?"

"I have sailed three days southward of the Zarkheba, never as far as the Coast of Bones. But you offer good pay, and I was never one to shrink from danger if there was profit to be had."

"What of your crew?" Conan asked.

Wulfrede shrugged. "I shall tell them where we sail, as always. They may sail with us or leave, as is their right. If we are a little shorthanded, we'll pick up men in Khemi or on the coastal islands. It's never a bad idea to have a few native sailors in those waters. They are not as likely to fall to the local diseases."

"Then we are agreed?" Ulfilo said.

"One thing bothers me," Wulfrede said, leaning forward, his forearms on the table and his fingers laced. "This lady. Does she really propose to come with us?"

"I do," she said. "I am not afraid."

"I do not doubt that, my lady," Wulfrede conceded, "but such a voyage is the death of tough warriors and hard-bitten sailors. The sun alone can strike down someone as fair-skinned as you. And then there are my sailors. These are not men of refinement and restraint, and you would be the only woman among them for a very long time."

"I will stay between her and your sailors, Captain," Ulfilo said, his hand gripping his hilt.

"And I," said Conan.

"Perhaps the two of you can protect her," said Wulfrede, "but the men believe that a woman aboard ship is bad luck. While all is well there should be no problem. But if we encounter misfortune, they will look for someone to blame and then we will have our hands full."

"She goes," Ulfilo said adamantly.

"Very well, on your head be it." He sat back. "Now, if we are to go among the natives as peaceful traders, we must have trade goods. I have yet a cargo of tin ingots aboard, to be offloaded here for the bronze foundries. My hold will be empty by tomorrow afternoon and we may take on more."

"What sort of goods should we take?" Springald asked.

"Such things as the coastal blacks need and cannot produce for themselves," Wulfrede said. "That is always the way with trade, if you would have high profit. They do not mine or smelt iron, though some tribes work it tolerably well. So iron ingots are always in demand. You want small ingots, such as are easily worked in a village forge. There is always a market for axes and spearheads, ready-made, and for knives."

"What of swords?" Springald asked.

"They have little use for them along the coast, save the big bush knives that are tool and weapon both. The south is the land of the spear. Copper wire is a regular trade item, and glass beads, trinkets of all sorts, bells, rattles, mirrors, and so forth. And cloth, bolts of it. But buy fabrics of light weight dyed in bright colors. They have no use for heavy woolens. And buy the cheapest cloth you can find. The profit is higher and it makes no difference to the natives. Even the finest cloth deteriorates quickly in that climate."

"This seems like good advice," Springald said. "Conan, have you anything to add?"

"Lay in a chest of good weapons and gauds of higher quality

as gifts for the chiefs. They will expect it and may take it ill if they do not receive things of higher quality than the others get.''

''And for what do we trade?'' Springald asked. ''It is not our reason for going upon this expedition, but we must act the part of genuine merchants.''

''Once again, the only reason to go so far is to find things that men cannot get here, closer to hand. Ivory is the most important single trade item. There is an endless supply of it in the black lands, it occurs nowhere else but Vendhya, and it is prized everywhere. Feathers of the ostrich and other great birds are very valuable, and they pack down well and weigh almost nothing. In some areas you may find pearls, and in a few places the natives find nuggets of gold in the streambeds. These they may save to trade. The hides and horns of some exotic animals can be valuable. If you are learned in the proper lore, there may be many plants and barks that are useful for medicines and dyestuffs, but I have never traded for such. And, of course, there is always a ready market for slaves.''

''No slaving!'' Ulfilo said vehemently.

''Aye,'' Conan agreed. ''I'll go on no slaving expedition.''

''But why not?'' Wulfrede said. ''It is not as if these were our kinsmen. The trade is recognized everywhere, and the beauty of it is that you need not even leave your ship. When they know you have goods to trade, the local chiefs will raid inland for prisoners and bring them right out to your ship.''

''I will have no part in slaving,'' Ulfilo insisted. The others nodded agreement.

Wulfrede shrugged. ''As you will. The *Sea Tiger* is not fitted out for slaving at any rate. We could pack no more than two hundred in the hold, and many would die before we reached a port where they would fetch a good price.''

''We are agreed then,'' Ulfilo said. ''We shall purchase trade goods from the local merchants while you see to the disposition of your cargo. We will begin loading our goods tomorrow afternoon. How soon after that will we sail?''

"As soon as possible," Wulfrede said. "This is the best sailing season, and we should not waste any of it."

"When begins the season of great storms?" Malia asked.

At this Wulfrede laughed heartily. "This shows how little you know of the ways of the sea. It is *always* the season of great storms on the Western Sea. I own that the big blows come somewhat closer together late in the sailing season, but you must always be prepared to flee before the wind at any time." He rose from the table. "And now, I must see to my ship and cargo. If you cannot find enough of the goods you need in this port, do not worry. We can always make it up in Khemi. Here, make sure to lay in the cloth you will need. Stygia makes beads and bangles in abundance."

"And there we may get word of my husband," Malia said. "It was his last port, in the civilized world."

Wulfrede nodded. "Aye, it may be that we shall hear of him there."

Conan rose. "I would see the ship," he said, "and the men."

"Come, then," Wulfrede said. "Although I would think you would rather spend your last hours ashore carousing. *Sea Tiger* will be your home for a long time, Cimmerian."

The two went out into the bright sunlight and walked to the wharf. They found a barge already unloading some of the tin ingots from *Sea Tiger*'s cargo. Wulfrede had a few words with the factor from the bronze foundry and looked over his inventory, checking it against his own bill of lading. When the barge was unloaded the Van and the Cimmerian rode it back to the ship. Conan studied the craft as they drew nearer. Its lines were as fine as he had thought upon first impression, and the hull sported a coat of new black paint.

After the custom of the sea, Conan waited for the Van to board first. "Come aboard, Conan," Wulfrede said as soon as his feet were firm on the deck. Conan then sprang over the rail and gave the vessel a closer look. Its deck was immaculate, scrubbed white with pumice stone. All the metalwork was in good order, the bronze and brass polished bright, the iron carefully painted against rust. He noted some frayed rope twisted around the belaying pins.

"Have you new cordage?" Conan asked.

"No, but I intend to lay in plenty of new rope," Wulfrede answered. "I had planned to make this last until we sailed back to Kordava, but it will not do for a long voyage south. That climate eats up cordage as it does cloth and leather."

"Have you sailcloth?"

"Aye, in the forward locker. Enough to patch these sails and make up two new ones if need be."

"She's a good ship," Conan admitted. "I've never seen better, for this work." He studied the crew, who studied him in return. Half he could identify as Zingarans and Argosseans. A few other nationalities were represented, and the rest belonged to that stateless breed that seemed to have no home except the salty deeps. They were dressed in a variety of clothing, some wearing no more than a breechclout and headcloth in the heat of midday. Every man wore a knife, although he saw no swords, axes, or other weapons. He had no doubt those more formidable weapons were near at hand. The men were scarred and dark-burned, and some were tattooed. He saw some mutilations that might have been inflicted as punishment for crimes, but none were definitely of that nature.

"Open up your ears!" Wulfrede bellowed, as if he needed to be heard over the din of a gale. "All hands come aft!" As the men on deck shuffled aft others came up from below. Last of all came the ship's cook, a wrinkled old salt dressed in a stained apron and a spotless red turban, the sunlight winking from the gold hoops in his ears. The work of unloading went on, this being carried out by port workers and foundry slaves.

"Listen, sea dogs," Wulfrede began. "Our plan was to find a cargo here or nearby and sail back to Kordava by way of Messantia. But something promising has come our way. Some Aquilonian merchants want to hire *Sea Tiger* for a voyage down the coast past Khemi, to trade among the tribes of the Black Coast. You won't have to endure the crowding and stench of slaves; they want to trade for ivory and the other rich goods of the land. We can be down there, do our trading, and be back before the bad weather sets in. And''—he grinned all around— ''they offer three times the usual sailor's pay, in recognition of the hardship. What say you?''

Conan knew that a rough democracy would prevail here in port. That would cease utterly once they were at sea. He could tell that Wulfrede was a masterful captain from the condition of the deck. He saw no slaves or ship's boys on this vessel. The Van got these hard men to do the work themselves, and Conan knew that to be no easy task. A long-armed man of nameless race whose features were those of an ape was first to speak.

''How far south, my captain?'' His near-lipless mouth was exceptionally wide, and his words made the silver ring through his nose bob. Somehow, the effect was not comical.

''South of the Zarkheba,'' Wulfrede said.

''How far south?'' asked the same man.

''Some five or six days south of there.'' This resulted in some muttering. ''What? Do you sea hounds balk at a little southern cruising? You know as well as I: The more remote, the less visited a land is, there are to be found the highest profits.''

''High profits for the merchants, perhaps,'' said the apelike man. ''But the risks are all the same for the sailors!''

''Umu,'' Wulfrede said patiently, ''no man will be forced to sail with us. I am here to give any such his pay. There are more sailors than there are berths for them.''

''My employers,'' Conan said, addressing the crew for the first time, ''are more than merely generous. Besides triple play, they are willing to offer shares in the profits of the voyage. You all know how profitable one of these voyages can be, for those who survive.'' Wulfrede looked at him in surprise, but let him speak as he would.

''I trust no man's generosity,'' sneered the man named Umu. ''Wherefore are these landsmen so generous?''

''They do not wish to have it noised about,'' Conan said, ''but they are scouting new territory for a trading company that has recently been formed in Aquilonia. You all know that Aquilonia is landlocked, but it is a land of rich merchants. The actual profits of this voyage are not truly important, save insofar as they mean more to come for this new company. Why should they not be willing to divide these first profits with you? And, when they form their trading fleet for future voyages, those who sailed on this first voyage will have preferment.'' The men began muttering among themselves.

"Think it over and make your own decisions," Wulfrede said. "You have until we sail upon the morn after tomorrow. I am not afraid to sail undermanned. There are plenty of sailors between here and Kush to fill your berths. As for me, I sail south, with *Sea Tiger* beneath my feet! You are dismissed.'' The men turned and went back to their tasks, talking among themselves in low tones. Wulfrede rounded upon Conan.

"I always knew the Cimmerians were fighting men," said the Van. "I never expected to encounter one who was sly and subtle.''

"The Aquilonians said that they are not interested in trading profits. I do not think they'll object to splitting the gain among the men in return for a docile crew.''

"And this trading company?" Wulfrede asked.

"Who knows?" Conan answered. "If this voyage proves as profitable as I hope, I may form the company myself.''

Wulfrede roared with laughter and clapped Conan upon the shoulder.

"I think you will make a good sailing companion, Cimmerian! A man who is quick with his wits as well as with his sword is more than a whole crew of landsmen. And I can see that you know ships.'' The Van leaned upon the rail and did not look at Conan as he spoke his next words. "Few men sail as far south as you say you have. I've sailed up and down these coasts for many a year, and I have never met a merchant skipper who has been more than four days south of the Zarkheba unless he was blown far south by a storm. And those wasted no time in turning back north as soon as the winds were favorable.''

"It is an unfriendly coast," Conan said noncommittally.

"And yet . . ." the Van said, hesitantly, "and yet there are tales. Tales one hears in the sailor's dives from Kordava to Khemi, tales of the black corsairs. Some years ago they became truly feared when a whole fleet of them united under a woman named Belit, a Shemitish she-devil. She turned the coast of Kush into a slaughterhouse. It is said that, for a while, she had a consort, a man as wild as she was. Little more than a youth, the story goes, but fierce as a tiger, and of a nation nobody of the south knew, a big, black-haired warrior, so they say. Some few got close enough to claim that he had blue eyes. Did you ever hear these tales?" He pretended interest in the unloading of his cargo.

"Drunken men say many foolish things," Conan grumbled. "It is unwise to give much credit to tavern talk."

"Aye, no doubt you are right. What difference does it make now anyway? It was many years ago. The wench was slain and the man . . . well, the man disappeared, no one knows whither."

"That is true," Conan said. "Now, I want to see the rest of the ship."

For the next two hours, the Cimmerian went over every foot of board, every rope and spar, every piece of tackle on the ship. He climbed to the tops of the two masts and even stripped off shirt, trousers, and boots to dive into the bay and examine the condition of the hull underwater. By the end of his tour, he was satisfied that this was a ship fit to make the voyage and return, and able to defend itself against human predators. Its armory was adequate to arm every man with axe or cutlass, and there were plenty of boarding spears, javelins, and bows with their sheaves of arrows. It held the sort of light armor favored by sailors as well. There were steel caps and quilted vests, some of them covered with iron mail lacquered against the damp salt air.

"I will tell your employers that they could not have chosen a better ship," Conan said when he was through.

"I never saw a Zingaran admiral inspect a vessel so thoroughly," Wulfrede said. "By Njord's beard, I certainly never saw one strip to inspect below the waterline!"

"To judge a ship by what shows above the water makes as much sense as buying a horse without inspecting its legs," Conan said. "I've seen many a ship that was all bright paint and polished metal from the waterline up but was naught but a mass of foul weed, barnacles, and rotted, worm-infested wood below."

"You know ships," Wulfrede said. "How well do you know men?"

"Your crew look like experienced sailors, though rogues and honest mariners can be difficult to tell apart, save when temptation comes their way."

Wulfrede showed his teeth in a wolfish grin. "True enough, but it was not of them I spoke. What of these Aquilonians?"

"A good question. Ulfilo is an Aquilonian noble, and they are a hard breed in my experience. The land is rich but it has no natural barriers, so even the rich must know how to fight hard to hold what they have. He seems typical of that breed."

"Aye," said the Van broodingly, "but all is inheritance with those nobles. We Northlanders are different, you know that. All free warriors are equal and the blood ties of family mean everything. We Vanir, you Cimmerians, even"—he spat into the water—"the yellow-bearded Aesir know the value of kinship, and will trail a man over half the world to avenge a slain brother. But the Aquilonians? Only the eldest brother inherits the ancestral estate. The younger ones must make their own way. Who ever heard of such a one abandoning his land to follow a younger brother?"

"It's a puzzle," Conan admitted, "and one I've been mulling over myself. But they hired me to help find the man, not to search out their reasons."

"Aye, but it's a thing to ponder. What of the other two?"

"The one called Springald seems to be the scholar he claims, but the way he carries himself and the condition of his hands make me think that he's a swordsman as well.''

"A bookman and a fighting man both? It scarcely sounds possible, but I'll not question your judgment. And the woman?''

"She's another puzzle. She talks like an Aquilonian, but by her look I'd swear she was Hyperborean.''

"Three odd loons on a madman's quest," Wulfrede said. "What do you think they're *really* after, Conan?''

"They've hired us both to help them find this wandering brother," Conan said. "Since they're paying us, that is what they search for, as far as we are concerned.''

"As long as their money is good, I will accept that," the Van said, dubiously.

That evening, Conan met with his new employers in the dining room of their inn, a far more respectable establishment than the Albatross. To his amusement, their questions greatly resembled those of the shipmaster.

"Conan," Springald said, "we have no experience of the sea, nor of the men that sail thereon. I have spent my life reading of the voyages of the great mariners, but the greatest of book learning is of little account compared with experience. What do you think of Captain Wulfrede, and his ship and crew?''

"I will tell you truthfully," Conan said, "that the ship could not be better for the proposed voyage. And the master and men are such as can sail it to the waters you wish to reach, and bring you back again.''

"You leave much unsaid," Malia commented.

"Then I'll say it. It is no ordinary merchant vessel you are hiring. This is a fighting ship that can carry some cargo. The men all look like good seamen, but every one of them would look at home with a cutlass in his fist. And Wulfrede could never maintain such a fine ship in such excellent condition carrying an occasional load of tin from Kordava to Asgalun.''

"You mean he is a pirate?" Ulfilo said.

"It is not that simple," Conan said. "There are pirates like the black corsairs, and the Barachans, who do nothing else. But the merchant-skippers who sail in dangerous, remote waters are often part-time pirates. When they encounter those who are strong and well armed, they trade for what they want. When people cannot protect themselves or their belongings, the former merchants take what they want without trading."

"These are people without honor," Ulfilo said.

Conan shook his black-maned head. "It is different on the sea. There, men are always alone and in danger. They are always among strangers, and they see things differently. Besides"—he grinned at Ulfilo—"landsmen are not all that different. Did your ancestors buy the land of which you are now lord? I'll wager not. They took it from someone who was weaker."

"You speak insolently, Cimmerian!" Ulfilo said, glaring.

"Now, my old friend," said Springald, his eyes twinkling, "there is much justice in what he says. Our Hyborian ancestors were savages as barbaric as any. Respectability, not to say nobility, comes with separation from the crimes that established them."

"What does this mean?" Malia asked. "Can we trust the man?"

"To do the job you have engaged him for," Conan said, "I think he can be trusted for that. But if great wealth were to be involved, I might not want to turn my back on him."

"Who has spoken of great wealth?" Ulfilo demanded.

"No one has . . . yet." Conan said.

"Then let us keep it that way. We search for my brother, nothing more."

"I am not the one who has difficulty believing that," Conan said. "Wulfrede and his crew may need some convincing."

# THREE
## The Dark City

The wind blew steadily from the north, filling the two huge, triangular sails almost to bursting as the *Sea Tiger* sped southward. With careful attention to every nuance of the wind, Wulfrede constantly saw to the angle of the yards and the tension of the ropes. Sometimes the sails were lashed down almost flat, other times left to billow forth as if they thought to drag the ship along behind them.

It was a much-frequented coast at the height of the sailing season, so they were seldom out of sight of other sails. From time to time a ship would sail in for a closer look, but the sight of the predatory, rakish hull caused them all to veer away in search of more promising company.

Conan was well pleased with the ship and its handling. Although he was not part of the crew, he readily pitched in to haul on a rope or heave at the capstan when a little extra weight was needed. The others voiced their amazement when they felt his power, which seemed like that of five men. A few of the men resented this display of power, foremost among them the apelike brute named Umu. He was proud of his strength, and used it to lord over the others. Although the ship had no officers other than the captain, Umu regarded himself as the head of the crew, and he resented Conan's intrusion. Conan was aware of the resentment, but the man did not challenge him.

That roused Conan's suspicions. Not that the man saw him as a rival, for in the Cimmerian's world that was normal. In the ferocious, undisciplined world of bandits, *kozaki*, pirates, and mercenaries, the strong always dominated the weak, and always there was one who was strongest, who must answer all challenges for domination. Under ordinary circumstances, Conan would have expected a fight with Umu before the third day at sea. Yet the man merely glared and did nothing. The Cimmerian knew that it was not fear that restrained Umu. There was probably little room for such feelings beneath that low forehead. It had to be something else.

Umu's reticence was not the only thing that bothered him. Every one of the sailors had remained aboard, not one of them leaving ship at Asgalun, despite the likely dangers and hardships of the voyage. Why had they all stayed aboard? It was good that such tough, experienced sea dogs manned the ship, but the Cimmerian had little faith in unalloyed good fortune.

"What do you brood about now, Conan?" asked Malia. She had emerged from her tiny cabin to join him upon the ship's diminutive poop deck, which the Cimmerian shared with the helmsman who managed the ship's tiller. Like the other landsmen, she had been stricken with seasickness but she had recovered quickly.

"The sea is ever a dangerous and uncertain place," he said. "You see that little bank of cloud to the southwest?" He pointed to a barely discernible gray bar upon the horizon.

"I see it. It looks innocuous enough to me."

"To you, perhaps, but it could mean a storm, and it could be upon us with the swiftness of a pouncing tiger. One should never underestimate anything at sea."

She laughed. "Conan, you are as gloomy as our captain is cheerful." She nodded to where Wulfrede stood in the waist, driving his men to try yet another arrangement of rope and sail, swearing merrily while the men groaned at his unending fussing with the rig. "Springald tells me that the Cimmerians are known as a sour, ill-tempered race, while the Vanir are both fierce and merry."

"Springald's knowledge of most things comes from books," Conan said. "The Vanir are a cheerful folk, I agree, and never more so than when they are torturing a captive or burning a Cimmerian village to the ground, leading the women and children away in chains. The Aesir are of a similar humor. You have never seen true merriment until you witness a battle between the two. They can laugh at their own dismemberment at such times."

"Your northlands sound barbarous," she said. "Civilized people take such things more seriously."

"And yet you are no stranger to the north, by your look," Conan rejoined. "Your voice carries no trace of accent, but your face and your color say that you are from Hyperborea."

"My mother was a noble lady of that land. Her father fostered her out to the house of a Brythunian border lord with whom he wished an alliance. His son was my father, but I do not remember him. He was killed when the Nemedians invaded Brythunia twenty years ago. My mother and I were taken to Belverus, where she became a concubine of one of the Nemedian generals. My mother died in the plague of five years past. When a handsome young mercenary captain asked for me, the Nemedian was happy enough to give me away. His wife was already jealous of my beauty, as she had been of my mother's. The mercenary was Marandos, Ulfilo's brother, and he wanted me not just as a mistress, but as a wife. We were very happy for three years, before he returned home."

It was not an uncommon story. Even for the wellborn, life could be very precarious in unsettled times. Woman and younger sons were often little better off than commoners, owning no more than their pride of birth.

"And yet he left you to go adventuring south of Kush," Conan said. He did not intend the comment to be as brutal as it sounded.

"He did not desert me. He thought he could repair all our fortunes that way. He—"

"Malia!" It was Ulfilo, emerging from the cramped cabin area below the poop deck. "We have engaged Conan's services as a guide. If you need a confidant, there are others to fill that role. Springald is fonder of talk than is this Cimmerian."

She rounded upon him with anger. "You are my brother-in-law, not my guardian. I will speak with whom I choose!"

"You are in my charge until you may be reunited with your husband, my brother," Ulfilo said. She glared at him for a few moments, then went below without another word.

"Matters touching upon my family are no concern of yours, Conan," Ulfilo said stiffly.

Conan shrugged. "You may trust me or not, as you wish, but before this voyage is over, you may have need of all the friends you can get, Margrave."

"What do you mean?" Ulfilo demanded.

Conan nodded to the waist of the ship. "I think some of those men may have stayed with the ship in hope that your expedition involves more than finding your wandering brother. To them it seems that the love of brothers, even that of man and wife, is scarcely powerful enough to demand devotion of this sort. For a nobleman to leave his lands and travel across half the world with naught but a woman and a schoolman as company strains their sense of fitness. I would even say that it strains mine, save that you have only hired me to find your brother. That is enough for me, for I am not a suspicious man."

Ulfilo compressed his mouth until the skin around his lips turned white. It seemed to Conan that this signified more than anger. It was the perplexity of a man whose nature was essentially open forced to prevaricate.

"You think these dogs could threaten us?" Ulfilo said at last.

"Our situation could prove anything from merely dangerous to desperate, depending upon how many should turn upon us. But it is nothing we need worry about for a while. They will do nothing as long as there is nothing to gain."

"When we reach the Coast of Bones," Ulfilo promised, "then you shall hear more. But it is impossible for me to say more at this moment."

"As you will," Conan said, "but you've no one but yourself to blame if we all come to grief because you must be so damnably tight-lipped!"

Conan was in a somewhat better mood when Springald came up for fresh air. The small man was pale but steady on his feet for the first time since setting sail.

"Ah, my Cimmerian friend, I almost think I will be able to eat something this evening, or perhaps tomorrow."

Conan grinned. "I rejoice to see you almost recovered."

"All my life I have studied the great voyages of the explorers of old. I have lived with maps and charts and the transcripts of logbooks, but never until I stepped aboard this ship had I ever set out to sea. Somehow, the old explorers never mentioned this revenge of the sea gods upon poor landsmen."

"It passes in time," Conan assured him, "and count yourself fortunate. This is ideal sailing weather, and it causes very little rolling of the ship. Had you set out in rough weather, you might have been wretchedly sick for weeks before you became accustomed to it."

"Do not even speak of it!" Springald said. "Let us speak of other things." He rummaged in the large satchel that went with him everywhere. From it protruded scrolls, parchments, and the corners of books. His hands emerged with a book of some antiquity, to judge by the condition of its cover, once of the finest leather, now tattered and cracked, pierced with numerous wormholes.

"This," Springald said, "is the *Chronicle of the Voyage of Captain Belphormis*. He was a navigator who lived some twelve hundred years ago, and he sailed to lands near our present destination.''

''The book is old,'' Conan said, taking it from Springald's hand, ''but it does not look twelve hundred years old.''

''Nor is it. The original, of which no copy is known to exist, was written upon a scroll. The art of making books with leaves is no more than seven or eight hundred years old, although it is my belief that some of the very ancient civilizations had it. Many arts are lost and then rediscovered. Anyway, this copy was made five hundred years ago for the library of King Heptadios of Aquilonia. As you can see, each left-hand page contains the original text in Old Shemitish, while the facing page contains a translation in the rather quaint Aquilonian of that period. According to notes written on the flyleaf, the book had grown decrepit and it was sent to Luxur to be rebound, along with a great many other books, about two hundred years ago. The Stygians are masters of all arts dealing with parchment and bookmaking. After its return, this book was placed upon a shelf in the Royal Library of Tarantia, and I have reason to believe that it sat there untouched until I discovered it five years ago. The damage you see upon the covers dates from that long stay, the result of neglect and the depradations of voracious bookworms.''

''From the language and the captain's name, he must have been a Shemite,'' Conan said.

''Yes, and his ship was the *Ashtra*, named for a Shemite goddess. Would it surprise you to know that Shem was once a maritime nation of great note?''

''It would! The Shemites are a race of shepherds and herdsmen. Even the sea merchants of Asgalun are resident foreigners. There are Shemitish sailors, as there are sailors of every land that has a coastline, but as a rule they shun the sea.''

''That was not always the case. Many centuries ago there was a nation called Ashur, one of several states in what is now Shem. It was small and poor, but it had the only decent harbor along the coast of Shem, where Asgalun now stands. A warrior-king named Belsepa ascended the throne to found the Den Dynasty. He saw that his land was weak but had access to the sea, and he set out to forge a maritime nation. He formed a complicated system of alliances to obtain the things he needed. Shem has no decent wood for shipbuilding, so he traded up the coast in Argos and Zingara for suitable wood. He made lavish offers of pay and cheap land and tax exemptions to lure shipwrights and rope makers and masters of all the other crafts necessary to a seafaring nation. He hired shipmasters and skilled sailors and navigators who knew the arts of cartography and star-reading to train his Shemites in their skills. By the time he died, Belsepa had laid the foundation for a respectable merchant and military fleet.''

"Then his work came to naught," Conan said, "for I've never heard of such a thing as a Shemitish ship. Even the few Shemite sailors I've known have been pirates. The men of Shem are raiders on land, so they take to the same occupation upon the sea.''

"And yet for three hundred years, as long as the Den Dynasty ruled, the Shemites of Ashur were great navigators and they explored many coasts from far north of Vanaheim to the very southern tip of the continent, where they found a cape where the coastline turns to the northeast. One great expedition is said to have reached Vendhya that way, but no reliable record of it has survived.''

"Reach Vendhya by sailing south?" Conan said in wonder. "That must have been a voyage worthy of a hero!"

"It is supposed to have taken three years to sail there and back, only a single ship of the original five making the entire journey. They were great sailors in those days.'' He sighed.

"Anyway," the scholar went on, "there came a time of famine for all of Shem. The crops failed, the grass withered, and the flocks and herds died. Consequently, the people died. Only the maritime nation of Ashur prospered, and this brought about much jealousy. Then Ashur was struck by a devastating earthquake. The other Shemites said that the famine was sent upon them by their shepherd gods, who were angry that Shemites should turn against them and sail upon the sea. The earthquake was the ultimate expression of their displeasure and a call to the other Shemites to take action.

"The earthquake had leveled the walls and much of the city. A horde of starveling Shemites descended upon Ashur and laid it waste, killing all the folk and burning such ships as were left afloat after the earthquake. They also torched the archives that held the ship's logs and charts. Only a very few books and charts of that nation survived, and this is one." He took back the tome. "Belphormis lived near the end of Ashur's ascendancy. This is a record of his voyage to the seldom-visited Coast of Bones."

"How does it happen that this book survived the burning?" Conan asked.

Springald shrugged. "Sometimes there is no explanation of these things save the whim of the gods. After great destruction, odd things come though unharmed. Oftimes great and valuable works will be destroyed, while trifling things survive unharmed. Perhaps the original scroll was stored in a chest in a basement and escaped the burning. Perhaps it was on a ship at sea. Or it might have been bought or otherwise obtained by a traveler and was already in Aquilonian hands all the time of the disasters. Whatever the case, some scholar thought it worth translating and binding in book form."

"And what had this ancient captain to say about our destination?" Conan asked.

"Let me see . . ." Swiftly, Springald flipped through the pages. It was clear that he knew exactly where to look. "Ah, here it is: 'The jagged white rocks being so numerous and so close-set, we spent all of a very anxious day working the ship between them, until we lay at safe anchor just before sunset. We await daylight to go ashore.' Here he records the next day. It begins with a date which means nothing to us, since the dating system used in Ashur has perished and we can only approximate.

" 'At first light we rowed ashore. A party went to the green stream to refill our water casks but found the water much fouled by river weed and it will take much work to purify enough for our needs. The beach is of fine white sand, and narrow. Heavy jungle grows within twenty paces of the high-tide mark.' ''

"Aye, that is how I remember the place," Conan affirmed. "Were the Borana there so many years ago?"

"There is no mention of them. But there were people." He turned over several pages. "Here is the record of the second day of the trek inland: 'Since setting foot in the jungle we have seen signs of human habitation: strange images and fetishes hung from the trees, carved idols of stone and wood, the ashes of fires and so forth, but until today we saw no men. About noon we came upon a party of warriors.' ''

"Why were they traveling inland?" Conan asked.

"Merchant captains seeking new trade often explored to find local people with valuables to exchange." Conan was aware that Springald had avoided the question, but he let it pass.

"He continues: 'These men are not like the coastal blacks we have seen. They are taller men, with lighter skins and different features, wearing much paint on their faces and bodies. Their loins are wrapped in fine cloth of an unfamiliar weave, and they bear wide-bladed spears of good forging. Many of them wear ornaments of beaten gold. Our two black guides displayed much amazement and fear at this appearance and the foreign warriors regarded them with the greatest contempt, although toward us they maintain a stern wariness that is somewhat short of hostility.' '' Springald glanced up at Conan. "You realize that I am translating a bit here. The Aquilonian of five hundred years ago sounds strangely in our ears. I think that my translation is quite accurate."

"And this translated from Shemitish," Conan said. "Think you that *that* translation was accurate?"

Despite his shaky condition, Springald managed a smile. "That is a very pertinent question, my friend. I have never shown it to a scholar conversant with Old Shemitish, but my own admittedly sketchy knowledge of that tongue tells me that it is an accurate translation." He glanced toward the dark cloud which had been so tiny such a short time before. It now colored a quarter of the horizon. In the waist, Wulfrede swore and barked orders. The sailors began to shorten sail. Springald turned even paler at the sight.

"Mitra! Does this mean that we are in for rough weather?"

Conan grinned at him. "Aye. And if you'd keep your books dry you'd best lock them away in your chest. A ship like this is nailed together loosely, so as to give the timber play in rough water. She'll stay afloat when other ships would break apart, but it carries a price. She'll leak like a basket when the water comes down hard."

"Say you so? Well, I have so much to learn." He thrust the book back into his satchel and buckled its flap down. "I trust you will enjoy the storm. I know I shall not." With that he staggered down the ladder.

Conan awaited the oncoming blow with relish, knowing that it was not one of the great, terrible storms. This would be a mere gust, lasting no more than an evening and a night, and allowing him to see how the ship handled when the weather was rough. As he watched the billowing clouds approaching and the sails being taken in, he thought of Springald, and his book.

Conan was no longer the boy who had once cruised these seas with Belit. He had served in many armies and had learned a great many things about the ways of powerful men. He had also learned a bit about written languages. Most of the civilized armies demanded that a man who would hold officer's rank be able to read and write. Springald had clearly allowed Conan to handle his book under the assumption that this barbarian could not read Aquilonian. Springald had been wrong.

It was true enough that the archaic form of Aquilonian in the book had been confusing to Conan, but he had been able to piece together many words, and among them had been a single phrase of three words written in letters a bit larger than the others, as if it had special meaning. It had been: "Horns of Shushtu."

"A little fun coming up for our landsmen, eh, Conan?" said Wulfrede as he leapt from the deck over the rail of the poop, ignoring the ladder that connected the two.

"They'll be sick," Conan commented, "but they'll endure it. These are not like the merchant's factors that sailormen toy with so often. They'll swallow their discomfiture and come back as haughty as ever. You cannot shame the real aristocrats."

Wulfrede nodded. "Aye, I think you're right. That Ulfilo looks like he could be a hard one. And the white wench holds her nose as high as any I've seen. Even the bookman brooks no insolence from the sailors." He paused, then went on in a different tone: "Conan, have you noted the satchel that the bookman carries?"

"I could hardly miss it," Conan admitted.

"I am no scholar, but I am sailor enough to recognize charts and logbooks when I see such."

"Aye, that is what he carries. But then what of that? He is a scholar and what he studies are the voyages of ancient explorers. What else would he keep with him?"

Wulfrede snorted. "Scholars live in their dusty schools and libraries and read about the adventures of braver men. No, a man sets out to sea with a bagful of charts when he is *looking* for something, and it is not just some other man's brother! I tell you, Conan, these Aquilonians are searching for hidden treasure! What else would take a high noble away from his lands to voyage upon unknown waters?"

Now it was the Cimmerian's turn to snort. "Treasure maps! You know as well as I that those things are traded about in every sailor's dive to separate the gullible from their money. I've been offered as many as three in a single evening, in Kordava. I even bought one or two, back when I was too young to know much about maps, or money."

"Would such frauds fool a real expert?" Wulfrede said. "Do you think this Springald would be gulled by the childish maps peddled in ports?"

Conan shook his black mane. "No, I'll own he would not.

But that does not mean that your suspicions are well founded. And even if they search for treasure, surely they do not think they can trek inland by themselves. They would be nothing but dinner for the Borana, if the wild beasts and the great snakes did not get them first.''

''Aye. So just what *are* their plans?''

''I do not know. I know what they hired me for and I intend to hold up my end of the bargain. When we get them to where they want to go, then perhaps we shall see what their true intentions are.''

Then the storm was upon them and they had too much work keeping the ship afloat and on course to waste time and breath in fruitless conversation.

On a beautiful day, as the sun beat down fiercely, the water in which the *Sea Tiger* sailed changed color from blue to deep green, then to muddy brown. The three passengers were on deck and remarked upon the phenomenon.

''What could this mean?'' Malia asked Springald. Conan was amused that she should ask the scholar instead of a sailor. But Springald knew.

''We have entered the effluent of a river. Were you to dip a bucket into that murky fluid you would find that it is fresh rather than salt. Not that I would recommend that you drink of it. From the tremendous extent of this effluent this can only be the Styx, called the Nilus in some tongues, and it is by far the largest river in the world. It drains a whole continent and carries with it all the corruption and waste of that great land. Stygians can drink it, but foreigners who do fall ill of a thousand diseases.''

''Then we must be near Khemi,'' Ulfilo said. All three were fully recovered from their seasickness and were as hale as ever. He turned to the Cimmerian. ''How close are we, Conan?''

''We will be there by mid-afternoon,'' he said somberly. The Cimmerian now wore only the short breeks common to sailors, his feet bare upon the deck. A strip of scarlet cloth tied around

brow and temple served to confine his unruly hair and keep
sweat out of his eyes during the strenuous work of shiphandling.

"You do not seem to relish the prospect," said Springald.

"I do not," Conan admitted. "I dislike Stygia and anything
to do with the place. Its people are cowed slaves and it is ruled
by priests and wizards. The whole nation is unclean."

"But it is the most ancient of lands," Springald said, "the
heir to ancient Acheron and guardian of the mysteries of storied
Python. We Hyborians are mere children compared to the Stygians. Our ancestors were crude barbarians mere centuries ago.
Stygia measures its history in millennia!"

"It is a history of oppression and enslavement," Conan asserted. "Better clean barbarism, however crude, than the lord-
ship of magicians."

"Nonetheless," Ulfilo said, "to Khemi we must go."

Wulfrede joined them upon the poop deck. "You speak of
Khemi? I must tell you that it is no ordinary port. The Stygians
do not like foreigners. Strangers are not allowed in the city after
dark."

"How can they carry on any sort of commerce with such
restrictions?" Malia asked.

"In the harbor is an island called the Tortoise. It is there that
foreign ships and foreign visitors stay. Only under close watch
are some ships allowed to leave the Tortoise to unload at the
wharfs proper. Any foreigner who is found in Khemi after sun-
down is instantly put to death."

"Stygia sounds as unfriendly a land as Conan says," Ulfilo
commented.

"But rich," Wulfrede said. "The kings and nobles of Stygia
were ever a grasping lot, and little of the wealth that has made
its way to Stygia has ever made its way out again. Stygian kings
have been buried with more gold than most kings ever own."
True to the nature of the Vanir, Wulfrede's eyes burned with
excitement when he spoke of great treasure. "Were their curses
not so damnably potent, I'd have led a few Vanir longships to
Stygia years ago, just to go tomb-robbing."

"A pity they are so xenophobic," Springald commented. "I had hoped to take advantage of our sojourn in Khemi to see some of the marvelous sights I have read about. I had even hoped to obtain passage upriver to Luxur, where it is said that the tombs and temples are of a size and splendor to defy imagination."

Malia shuddered. "I think the sooner we are away the better. Let us transact our business, inquire about my husband, and get on with our voyage."

"That is by far the best course," Conan said.

"More than that, the Stygians will leave us little choice," Wulfrede added.

Flanking the muddy flow of the Styx, two craggy headlands of black rock thrust into the sea. The top of each was crowned by squat, black stone castles, some very ancient and abandoned, others very much in use, their ramparts manned and armed with great war engines designed to sink unwanted ships. *Sea Tiger* lowered sails and ran out the oars.

Before they were well past the harbor forts a red-painted craft bearing a ram in the shape of a crocodile's head sped toward them, driven by many pairs of black oars.

"Do they intend to sink us?" Malia said, alarmed.

Wulfrede laughed. "That is just a customs cutter, ugly as it looks. Believe me, if you ever saw one of their war galleys come for us, you'd grab an oar yourself to get away the faster."

The cutter drew alongside in a spray of foam *Sea Tiger* shipped oars as a gangplank was laid between the two vessels. A number of men crossed from the cutter. Most were dark, stoutly built men of the lower classes, but one was a tall man of the ruling caste, his hair and eyes very dark, but lighter complexioned than the others.

"Your license, please, merchantman," the tall man demanded.

"You've seen it often enough before," Wulfrede muttered, handing over a copper disk engraved with hieroglyphs.

"All Vanir look alike to me," the man said. "You could be

any other redbeard." He looked over the passengers as haughtily as if he were a great lord instead of a government functionary. His gaze lingered upon Conan. "What race are you?" he demanded.

"Cimmerian," Conan said. He stood with arms folded, staring down the customs official.

"Never heard of them," the man said. "What is your business here?"

"We sail for the Black Coast to trade for ivory, feathers, and such other goods as we can find," Wulfrede said. "We need to top up our cargo with trade goods here."

"You understand that you can make payment in gold and silver alone?" the officer said.

"Aye," Wulfrede answered. "I have traded here before."

"But foreigners are foolish and sometimes forget," the man retorted. "And there are certain Stygian merchants who are willing to engage in illicit trade with foreigners. Avoid them. Their punishment is severe and would be far worse for you." Now he looked at Malia. "Does this one go to the Black Coast as well?"

"I do," she said. He ignored her, addressing Wulfrede instead.

"She will just die there. You might as well sell her here. Such coloration is extremely rare in this land, and she will fetch a good price."

Malia's cheeks flamed and Ulfilo's hand went to his hilt, but Conan and Wulfrede each laid a firm hand upon his shoulders.

"We shall consider it," Wulfrede said.

"Then turn around to be blindfolded," the official ordered.

"What?" Ulfilo demanded, incredulous.

"It's the law here," Wulfrede said. "One of their pilots must guide the ship into the harbor. The bottom here is a hedgehog of iron-shod stakes and bronze claws. No one from outside is allowed to know where the safe channel is. Every year they change the arrangement of the ship-killers, just in case. To be doubly safe, the slaves who do the work are killed afterward."

They resigned themselves to temporary blindness as the black silken tapes were bound tightly over their eyes. The sailors were treated likewise and had to row blind. For the better part of an hour there was nothing save the creak of oars in the rowlocks and the quiet voice of the pilot, calling instructions. Then the blindfolds were taken from them.

Blinking in the sudden light, they surveyed the harbor. The greater part of the city lay on the southern shore, its temples rearing gigantically behind the low warehouses of the wharfs. On the north side was the military harbor, where a hundred great war galleys lay in the shelter of a massive stone boathouse larger than any palace of another nation.

Before them was the Tortoise, a humped island no more than a hundred paces in extent, crowded with wharfs and an assortment of warehouses, taverns, and business establishments. In its total lack of temples or statuary, it could almost have been a town of another land.

"I leave you here," the official said, walking toward the gangplank. "Obey the law and pay all your fees." With that he left and they all breathed a little easier.

"Never before has a man spoken thus to me and lived," Ulfilo said.

"That would have meant death for us all," Wulfrede said. "There are some men who just have to be permitted to live, I fear."

"When do we go onto the island?" Springald asked.

"I must see to anchoring and making the ship fast," Wulfrede said. "Then we will take the boat ashore."

For the next hour the shipmaster busied himself with securing his vessel, then he ordered the ship's boat lowered to the water. Half the crew would be permitted ashore at a time, the rest to stay and guard the ship. There was little grumbling at this. Khemi was not as tempting a port as many others.

As the ship was secured, Conan scanned the harbor. The great majority of the craft were Stygian river or coastal vessels. There was an Argossean ship, a foul-smelling slaver. Near it was anchored a Zingaran vessel that had the look of a pirate. Pirate vessels were welcome in many ports, so long as they did not come to raid. They usually had rich cargoes to be sold cheaply. Another ship drew Conan's particular attention. It was Stygian-built, but with none of the ornate touches common to that land's naval vessels. It was black-hulled, low and lean, with two masts and a pair of furled black sails. He had never seen such a vessel of Stygian make. It looked new-built, riding at anchor with no sign of crew aboard. He noticed that Wulfrede was studying the vessel as well.

"What make you of that one?" Conan asked.

"I never saw her like. A trim craft, though, and apt for the raider's life, although she lacks cargo space for a merchant-man."

"And she could not hold enough men for a true man-o'-war," Conan said. "I've heard many things of the Stygians, but I never heard of a Stygian pirate, save he was a ruined noble and an exile. What sort of Stygian sets to sea in such a craft?"

"It is a good question," Wulfrede said, "but perhaps we had best avoid the answer."

Once ashore, the shipmaster guided them to a merchant's warehouse where beads and trinkets for the coastal trade were offered for sale. They arranged for several chests to be trans-ferred to the ship, then went in search of diversion.

"A seaman's tavern is not just a place to feed and get drunk. I intend to speak with my fellow captains and question them about the waters to the south. It has been more than four years since I last cruised those waters, and I want to learn what may have changed."

"How long shall we be in port?" Ulfilo asked.

"It is too late today to get much done," said Wulfrede. "To-morrow I must see to provisioning the ship with food and water. Also I must get the goods you just bought stored away, and I need to lay in new rope and sailcloth. We will need more hands to sail in the south, so I must see about hiring some. Let us say, three days from now."

"Excellent," Ulfilo said. "I shall arrange for rooms for the three of us at a good inn."

"An inn with decent bath facilities," Malia said fervently, "and a laundress!"

Wulfrede chuckled. "Enjoy it while you can, my lady. Where we go, you will get a bath when it rains and where cloth rots too fast to worry about washing it."

"All the more reason to indulge myself now." They were walking down a narrow alley between chandler's and cooper's shops. Abruptly, Malia stopped with a shocked indrawing of breath.

"What is it?" said Ulfilo, alarmed.

The woman could say nothing, but she pointed. Something long and glistening was gliding sinuously over the cobbles toward them. It lazily raised a head the size of a small winecask and regarded them with unblinking black eyes as a forked tongue flicked in and out of its lipless mouth.

"Mitra!" Ulfilo cried. "Can that be a serpent?"

"The great serpent of the southern jungles!" Springald said. "Marvelous!"

Ulfilo began to draw his sword but Wulfrede gripped his wrist. "Must I always be preventing you from getting us killed? Many animals are sacred in Stygia, and *all* serpents are the children of Set. These giants are the holiest of all."

"We must not kill it even if it attacks?" Ulfilo said.

"You needn't worry," Conan told him. "Look, you see that great bulge?" About four feet behind the head an obscenely huge lump swelled and distorted the thing's elongated body. "It has already eaten something or someone today. It goes now to lie up in its lair and digest its meal. That can takes weeks. These creatures eat but seldom."

"How did it get to this island?" Malia asked, having regained her voice.

"They are at home in the water as on the land," Conan told her. "The Styx and other great rivers are alive with them."

They watched warily as the creature slid past them, its coils working endlessly until a tiny, pointed tip wriggled its way across the cobbles at their feet.

"How big do they get?" Malia asked in a strangled voice.

"The Stygians claim that they keep growing as long as they live," said Springald. "That one by its length must be about a hundred years old."

"I have seen them much larger, along the Zarkheba," Conan said. "That one was large enough to swallow a man, but down there they grow big enough to swallow horses and buffalo."

The three Aquilonians looked as if they suspected exaggeration on Conan's part, but having seen the monster in the street, they did not question his veracity. After a brief search the three found a suitable inn and left Conan and the shipmaster to find a hostelery to their own liking. They located just such an establishment near the water. The building was set upon high pilings, to stay above the waters of the annual Styx floods. Soon the two had large stone tankards of foamy brown ale set before them. Wulfrede took a long pull at his and smacked his lips.

"Ah, they are arrogant swine and vicious wizards, but the Stygians are the only people outside the northlands who know how to make decent ale."

"They do that," Conan agreed. "They claim to be the first folk to cultivate grain, and that their corn god taught them to brew ale. If so, he's the only worthwhile god they ever had." They ordered dinner and settled down to some serious talk.

"Think you," began Wulfrede, "that our Aquilonian friends intend to laze away here in Khemi, awaiting the hour of our setting out to sea?"

"The thought has occurred to me," Conan said. "This brother wrote them a letter from Khemi, and it seems unlikely that they would pass up an opportunity to make some inquiries about him. If he truly outfitted an expedition here, there should be word of the man, what sort of ship he took south, bearing what goods, what sort of men he hired."

"Aye. Our employers are being cursed closemouthed again."

"There is nothing to stop us from asking questions of our own," Conan said.

"Nor to keep us from maintaining a watch upon those three."

"Spy upon them?" Conan said.

"Why not? These are not our kinsmen. They clearly do not trust us, so wherefore should we trust them? They could get us killed with their distrust so it is only right that we should see what they are up to. I must see to the ship. Can you watch them?"

"Aye," Conan said. "It's no more than they deserve. I, too, dislike being treated like a simpleton who is not to be trusted with too much information."

"So say I." They clanked their tankards together and drank deep.

As the evening wore on, the two conversed with a number of the mariners who came to the tavern to eat or drink. Only a very few were Stygians. Most were sailors of other nations, most of them passing through, some of them using the Tortoise as a permanent or semipermanent base. When they asked after Marandos, all they got were blank looks.

"These men are in and out of this port," Conan said. "We must ask among the chandlers and such."

"The barkeep has been here for years," Wulfrede said. "Let's ask him." So they called the man to their table.

"An Aquilonian noble?" he said. "About a year ago such a man came to the Tortoise, but I know not from what vessel. He was here a day or two, but no more, then I saw nothing more of him. But he outfitted no ship here on the Tortoise, that I can tell you."

"What is that black ship that lies anchored nearby?" Conan asked.

"There is no such ship," said the barkeep in flat tones.

"We take your meaning," Wulfrede said. "Thank you for your aid." When the man returned to the bar Wulfrede said: "Think you the man lied in his letter? Might he just be some

ruined drunkard who wanted his family to think he was pros-
perous?''

Conan shook his head. ''But he said in his letter that he
*wanted* them to come after him.''

''So they say. Have you read this letter?''

''No, nor even seen it. But might the man have outfitted a
ship somewhere else?''

''Where?'' Wulfrede asked.

''In Khemi proper, rather than on the Tortoise.''

''A foreigner do such a thing in Khemi? How could that be?

''How can there be a beautiful black pirate craft of Stygian
make? How can such a ship be anchored not three hundred
paces away and men deny its very existence?''

To that, the Van shipmaster had no answer.

# FOUR
## Black Sails

It was a hot, sultry night. The all-pervading scent of the great river lay over the island like a pall. Conan the Cimmerian stood within an arcade formed by the overhanging second stories of two buildings that faced one another across a narrow street. He leaned with arms folded, back against a wall, motionless as a statue. When need warranted, he had the patience of a hunter, patience he had learned among the crags of his native Cimmeria and amid the forested lowlands of the Pictish Wilderness.

The building he faced was the inn where the three Aquilonians had taken up lodging. During the day there was no difficulty keeping track of them. The island was small and simply by walking among its few, narrow streets he could detect any movement on their part. At night, a closer watch was called for. There had been no action the previous night. The three had remained within, but around midnight a man had arrived, a Stygian wearing a long black coat. He had stayed less than an hour and had left. During that time a light had glimmered

through a window of one of the rooms Conan knew they had
engaged. It was extinguished as soon as the Stygian had left.
Conan had followed the man to the water, where he had entered
a long black boat manned by four hulking, silent oarsman. Satisfied that he would learn no more that night, he had returned
to his own lodgings.

The next day he had made some preparations. He had purchased
a hooded cloak of black silk, such as was common among folk of
all classes here. Silk was amazingly cheap in wealthy Stygia. He
knew that he might need to do some stealthy tracking, so he stored
away his sword and retained only his dirk, sheathed at his broad
leather belt. Thus accoutred and armed, he could move about the
blackened streets silently and unseen.

He moved even deeper into shadow when he saw the door of
the inn open. Three figures emerged; one tall and bulky, one
short and stout, one petite and slender. All three wore cloaks
much like his own. For a few minutes they stood without the
door unmoving. Conan knew the reason for this. Ulfilo, with
his soldier's caution, was waiting for their eyes to adjust to the
darkness outside. Again, Conan felt a grudging respect. He did
not like Ulfilo, but he had to admit that the man was a true
warrior.

The three set out and Conan fell in behind them. He stalked
well back, for a close following was unnecessary. The island
was tiny, and the barbarian's eyes were as keen as a cat's in the
dim light. If nothing else, he could hear them clearly. Both men
wore boots. Conan himself was barefoot for the sake of silence.
He rarely went unshod in cities, but the Stygians were cleanly
to the point of fanaticism, and required that even the resident
foreigners of the Tortoise scrub their streets daily.

The three went the same way as the Stygian he had followed
the night before. When they reached the river, the black boat
was waiting for them. The four oarsmen were there, but the
Stygian was nowhere in sight.

Conan stood within an alleyway as the three boarded the boat.
While they did that, he removed his cloak and rolled it into a

tight cylinder. The fine silk compressed well and he slipped it into a small, tubular sheath of crocodile's gut. The transparent sheath was waterproof. He secured its end and slung it around his neck by a silken cord. Dressed only in his short sailor's breeches he watched as the boat pulled away from the wharf.

When it was well out on the water, Conan ran lightly to the wharf and lowered himself into the water, carefully, so as not to make a splash. The warm waters of the Styx closed around him as he set out after the boat. Keeping his limbs below the water, Conan began a frog-kicking breast stroke that he knew he could keep up for hours.

With his wet black hair plastered against his skull, any watcher who might have seen him could easily have mistaken him for a swimming seal. The boat in which the three Aquilonians rode was not the only craft upon the water that night. There were numerous boats out fishing for the night-feeding fish. These boats bore torches and fire baskets to attract the fish which were caught with nets, hooks on lines, or trained diving birds. The flames dotting the black waters made an eerily beautiful sight. And the Cimmerian was all too aware that he and the fish were not the only swimmers in the water. The great river serpents were out there somewhere, and nearby he heard a thrashing that meant a crocodile had caught something and was savaging it to death.

He ignored the perils of the river and continued to follow the boat. The stolid rowers were not racing across the water, so he had no difficulty in keeping up. They were pulling toward the southern bank of the river, where the temples and obelisks of Khemi bulked in deeper blackness against the dark sky.

As it turned out, the swim was not a great one. The boat drew up to a set of steps that rose from the water and led to the dusky streets above. The boatmen tied up to a great bronze ring set into the river wall and helped the three passengers onto the steps. At the top of the stair, he could just descry a cloaked figure who resembled the Stygian he had seen the night before.

Steps rose from the river every fifty paces or so, and Conan made for the nearest. He rose dripping, like a creature of the river, and sprang up the steps. Just below the crest, he shook his cloak from its sheath, unfurled it with a snap of his wrist, and swirled it over his shoulders, the silk billowing into a great circle before settling over his brawny frame. He pulled the hood over his head and went up the remaining steps to the street. Thus attired, he would pass all but the closest inspection.

Swiftly, he walked toward the other stair and arrived at its crest just in time to see a tiny, unmistakable form disappear into a narrow street. With a grim smile, he followed.

The four ahead of him led him a lengthy trek through the nighttime streets of Khemi. Like many such streets in the greater Stygian cities, these provided a study in contrasts not to be found in the younger, less sophisticated lands of the north and west. Most of the slaves and tradesmen had left, but that did not mean that the streets lacked life. Everywhere were the shaven-headed acolytes of the various temples, their faces skeletal from the prolonged fasting and other austerities required of them. In stark contrast to these were the voluptuous harlots who paraded the open squares naked except for towering, elaborate headdresses in which candles burned to better illuminate their beauty. Masked men from the desert wearing black and white striped robes led their camels toward the markets that would open in the morning, while certain wizened men dressed in ragged brown sacking sold drugs forbidden in every land save Stygia. Mountebanks put trained animals through their paces. Strange, incomprehensible music wafted from doorways that gave access to dim cellars from which came sounds of laughter and screams of terror.

As Stygia's principal commercial port, Khemi was not as priest-ridden as the great ceremonial centers such as Luxur, but that was only by the standards of that nighted land. It seemed to Conan that every fifth building he passed was a temple dedicated to one or more of the many strange gods of Stygia, and they were not yet near the temple district.

He paused as he saw the four ahead of him stop. Their Stygian guide gestured toward a doorway set in the black wall of a three-story building. The three filed in before him, and the Stygian went after them. Conan quickly stepped up to the doorway, just in time to hear it shut, along with the unmistakable sound of bolts being shot home. He stepped back and examined the building. Like most in the city except for the temples, it had a flat facade, and it abutted the buildings to each side. Its facade was heavily carved with scenes from the history, mythology, and ceremonies of Stygia. Over its doorway, slightly recessed from the other carvings, was an oval panel carved with a strange sigil: a wavy-pronged trident enclosed within a crescent moon. If it signified one of the gods of Stygia, it was one of which he had no knowledge.

There were no windows on the ground floor, but each of the two upper floors had three windows. Even as the Cimmerian scanned the building, he saw a glow from within a third-floor window. He looked the street up and down carefully. Two men walked away from him, half-drunk by the look of their walk. They rounded a corner and the street was deserted. Conan ran to the building and began to climb its facade like a squirrel. To one raised in the Cimmerian highlands, where boys climbed the sheer crags for sport and to rob nests of eggs and feather down, the deeply carven wall was as good as a ladder. Stygian gods and goddesses, many of them beast-headed, provided him ample grip for fingers and toes. It was, he reflected, the only favor the gods of Stygia had ever done for him.

Every few seconds he paused and carefully scanned the street below. As long as he kept motionless, he knew he was all but invisible against the blackness of the wall. In motion, he knew that a passerby, glancing idly upward, might espy him moving against the background of starry sky.

When he reached the window, he moved slowly, an inch at a time. He heard voices from within, and he longed to know what was being discussed, but he knew better than to ruin his chances through impatience. He did not try to pull himself over the sill, but rather he climbed up alongside the window until he was like a man standing beside a door, except that, instead of a floor, he had a half-inch of stone beneath his toes. Slowly, he leaned sideways until he could see into the room and hear the voices.

But before he saw or heard anything clearly he was struck by a strong, distinctive odor. He smelled smoke, and it was not the common smoke from firewood, or oily torches or waxen tapers. It was the sharp, unmistakable smoke generated by burning the stems, petals, and seeds of the black lotus. It was the most powerful of the many drugs used by sorcerers to generate the mystic visions they required to aid their spells and help them contact powers beyond the human plane. There was no fresh smoke in the air. This was the residue left by past burnings. To leave sufficient effluvia for a man to smell it outside the building, he knew that the stuff must have been used within, in great quantity, for generations. Black lotus was a tool restricted to the most powerful sorcerers. Lesser men were quickly driven mad by it. The very implications made his scalp crawl.

Within, the three Aquilonians were seated at heavy, carven chairs of dark wood. Facing them across a table was a Stygian, but not the one who had guided them there. He was a near-giant, taller even than Ulfilo and built massively through the shoulders and chest. His long black hair was neatly dressed and confined by a golden band, in the center of which gleamed a golden oval embossed with the trident-and-moon design. His beard was trimmed to a point, his eyes gleaming blackly above high cheekbones. Conan knew from his look that this was a nobleman of the highest caste.

"But what did he *tell* you?" Ulfilo was demanding. He sought to speak with his usual stern authority, but Conan could tell that he feared the man before him.

"That he had come within sight of that which he sought." The Stygian's voice was deep as it resonated from the powerful chest. "That he saw the very sign, in the mountain pass, before his remaining men forced him to turn back."

"How did he look?" Malia asked anxiously. "Did he look well?"

"My lady, he had just returned from a most arduous journey, one that killed almost all of his men and was nearly his own doom. His appearance reflected his experience. And yet he was eager to resume his expedition. Despite his terrible privations, he was not discouraged. Your husband is a man of great courage and determination."

"My brother," Ulfilo said, "is a man driven to dare the greatest perils and take the most foolish chances. Say you that he found what he sought?"

"Oh, yes, he most assuredly won through. The signs he found along the way were quite unmistakable. And yet he lacked the final link in his guiding chain, and the wealth to mount another expedition, wherefore he came to me, and we struck our bargain."

"And this bargain binds us, as well as him?" Ulfilo said darkly.

"That is so." The Stygian slid a heavy parchment across the table. "As you see, your brother bound himself with the most solemn oaths, and this contract is binding upon your family to its uttermost generation."

Ulfilo looked over the document, his face reddening as he did. "This is intolerable! Whatever the possible rewards, he had no right to bind his kin thus!"

"The gods do not concern themselves with the petty legalities of men," the Stygian reproved him. "This is not a legal document for the courts and their contemptible lawyers and judges to prattle over. This is a record of sacred oaths, and its violation is punishable not by fines and imprisonment but by the terrible curses with which the gods chastise oath-breakers."

Ulfilo seemed on the verge of violence, but Springald broke in smoothly. "Good priest of Ma'at, we have no need here for threats and arguments. We all know what the reward of a successful expedition must be. Such wealth is literally beyond comprehension. If we must divide it, what of that? Even a fraction would be beyond the dreams of the greatest Aquilonian noble. I assure you that the terms you provide in this document are more than satisfactory. Let us all deal with one another in good will, without suspicion or rancor.''

The Stygian smiled thinly. ''Your friend speaks with great wisdom,'' he said the Ulfilo. ''With a scholar as wise and learned as he, with wifely love and devotion such as this lady represents, with warrior virtue such as you possess, how can your expedition fail?'' If there was mockery in his voice, he masked it well.

''How, indeed?'' Springald said.

''Are you satisfied with the ship and crew you have obtained?'' the Stygian inquired.

''The ship is a good one,'' said Ulfilo, ''and although we know little of the sea, the men seem to be good and capable seamen. The captain is a half-pirate of the Vanir, and all the crew look like cutthroats, but I suppose one hires no man for an adventure like this on the basis of his sweet disposition. I think they will do. Our guide for the first stage is a Cimmerian adventurer who knows the coast.''

''A Cimmerian?'' the priest said sharply.

''Aye, a great black-headed rogue named Conan. He is a mercenary and a one-time pirate by his own admission, and I doubt not every sort of bandit and outlaw as well. He would probably cut our throats in our sleep if he thought he could gain by it, but I keep a close eye on the fellow.''

''I do not agree with my friend's assessment of the man,'' said Springald. ''He is a hard man who makes his way alone in a hard world. It would be unusual if such an adventurer lacked a few rough edges. But I think he is trustworthy, and a man of honor after his barbarous fashion. He will be of great aid to us as we make our trek inland.''

''As you will,'' the priest said. ''I can supply you with some men, servants of my own who would look after my interests and yours as well.''

Ulfilo was about to bark out something, but Springald said swiftly: ''Oh, we do thank you, friend Sethmes. However, were we to show up with your men our captain would grow instantly suspicious. He has authority in all things concerning the manning and running of his ship. I fear we must decline.''

"Have it as you will. When do you sail?''

"Perhaps tomorrow," Ulfilo said, "if our captain has transacted all his business. The next day, certainly.''

"Ah, friend Sethmes," Springald said hesitantly, "the, ah, 'link' of which you spoke just now, might that be made available to us?''

Sethmes spread his hands, palms up. "How so? I gave it to him, in accordance with our agreement.''

"Assuredly," Springald said, "but did you not retain a copy, perhaps?''

"I can see that, learned as you are, there are things you do not know about the priestly customs of Stygia. In all things, especially writings of ancient lore, we value the original, and abhor all copies. The copy, however faithful, may retain all writings and symbols, but is inferior. It lacks all mystical veracity. To us, such things are worthless.''

"I see," Springald said. 'Then, if you have no more to impart to us, we shall now return to our lodgings.''

"My servant will see you back to your boat," the priest said. "Without him to vouch for you, you would be killed instantly.''

Ulfilo snorted contemptuously, as if he thought little of the likelihood that mere Stygians could best him. But he said nothing aloud.

Conan remained by the window. The light within was extinguished, and minutes later the door below opened and four muffled figures exited the building. There was no need to follow now, for he knew where they were going. Now the most important thing was to get off the mainland undetected. When the street was deserted once more, he began to descend the carven wall. Despite the Cimmerian's iron strength, his fingers and toes ached with fatigue. He had to come down very carefully, as his hands were almost numb with tension. Thus it was that, just as he was passing a second-floor window, he did not react swiftly enough when a pair of huge, misshapen hands shot out from within and grasped his neck like the coils of a python.

Conan had not even time nor breath to curse as he was snatched inside. And he knew that he was in the grip of no ordinary man. The huge, powerful Cimmerian was being manhandled as easily as a ten-year-old child. With a snarl, Conan got his feet beneath him and his own hands shot out to grip the other's neck, only to discover that the creature had no neck to speak of. Its head seemed to be set squarely upon its hairy, sloping shoulders. Wasting not an instant, Conan gripped the back of the massive head with one hand, the other going beneath the backward-slanting chin. The breath whistled through his half-constricted windpipe as he began to twist the malformed head around. He was not certain whether he wrestled with a man or with an ape.

Either the creature lacked speech, or it was so confident of its strength that it scorned to raise an alarm. The two struggled in grim silence, rocking around the room, toppling furniture and spilling things. As a vase shattered on the floor, Conan knew that help would arrive for the thing all too soon even if it never called out. The knowledge added redoubled fury to his exertions. The muscles of his shoulders and arms swelled until they seemed ready to burst his skin, then something gave way beneath his hands and there was a sharp crack. The thing he held shuddered for several seconds, longer than any human being should take to die, it seemed to Conan. Then the huge hands fell away from his throat and clear, precious air rushed into his lungs. So great had been his exertion that, for a few seconds, Conan was unable to do anything save fall to his hands and knees and drag breath after breath into his tortured body.

Abruptly, the door burst open and his eyes were dazzled by a torch held high. Before him he saw the sprawled, hideous corpse of the thing he had wrestled. It was more manlike than apelike, but its low brow and prognathous, fanged jaw proclaimed its kinship to the jungle beasts, as did its overlong arms and short, bowed legs. It was all but covered with short russet hair but, manlike, it wore crude leather trunks and armbands of hammered copper.

"Cimmerian!" Now he saw that the torch was held by the priest, Sethmes. He lowered the torch. "You have slain Thog!"

"If I hadn't he'd have throttled me," Conan said, rubbing his throat. He saw the shambling shapes of at least two more apemen behind the priest. Then the torch was lowered toward his own face.

"You shall wish that he had. Were I to turn you over to our courts, they would be most pleased to know that I have taken Amra the pirate, long thought dead."

"But you won't turn me over to them," Conan growled.

"So I will not." He called over his shoulder. "Come in and bind this rogue for me."

The apemen began to shamble past their master but by this time Conan had regained his strength. He did not like the odds, for one of the apemen had been enough of a handful. He sprang to the windowsill, poised there for a second, and leapt to the street below. He took the impact on springy, bent knees and instantly began to run toward the river.

"Catch him!" shouted a voice from above as he heard the impacts of several creatures, men or apemen, landing on the street behind him. The Cimmerian laughed grimly as he ran, for he knew that the apemen with their short, bowed legs would stand no chance of catching a straight-limbed hillman running at speed. Even if the mage had human servants after him, he knew that city men were blind in dim light, which was almost as daylight to him.

At every opportunity, the Cimmerian dodged around corners, taking alleys and avoiding broad streets. His infallible sense of direction kept him headed toward the river despite these detours. At length he came out upon the river embankment. Such few pedestrians as he had passed wanted nothing to do with a huge man who seemed to be running for his life. Conan did not pause at the edge of the water wall, but rather launched himself at a full run and clove the water cleanly five paces from the river's edge. He went deep and came up swimming hard, his black cloak trailing behind him. It was a nuisance but he did not pause to take it off. When he was near the center of the river, he slowed and turned to look back toward the shore, first draping his head with a fold of his cloak, leaving only a slit to permit vision. He saw vague shapes wandering along the crest of the river wall. They seemed to be peering out toward the surface of the river, but they bore no torches, nor did they raise an outcry. It was very strange, but Conan suspected that the priest of Ma'at, whatever Ma'at might be, had no desire that the authorities should look into his activities.

After a few minutes, the shapes faded into the deeper darkness of the city. Conan turned and swam slowly back toward the island, but he did not go ashore there. Instead, he swam to the ship. The crewman left aboard as night watch all but collapsed from apoplexy as the dripping, black-cloaked Cimmerian drew himself over the gunwale.

"Conan!" the man gasped. "I'd thought you one of the river monsters, come to get me!"

The Cimmerian doffed his cloak and hung it over a yard. He shook the excess water from himself and waited for the night air to dry him.

"Why came you not in a boat, hailing like any honest man?" the crewman asked.

Conan did not deign to answer. "I sleep aboard ship tonight."

"Got into a fight on the island, eh? Well, make yourself comfortable in the rope locker. If any come asking for you I'll say I've not seen you this night."

Conan went to the locker and crawled through its low hatch. he found a spare sail and lay down upon it. He tried to think through the strange things he had seen and heard that night, but the hand of fatigue lay heavy upon him, and soon he slept soundly.

"Conan! Are you in there?" It seemed that he had just lain down, but he saw Wulfrede's face framed in the square of the hatchway, bright sunlight streaming in from behind him, making an incongruous nimbus of his red hair and beard.

"Aye, I am," Conan said. He meant to speak out but instead his voice was a hoarse croak. In the excitement of fight and flight, he had not realized how badly his throat had been savaged. When he sat up his neck pained him so that he could barely turn his head. He crawled to the hatch and thrust head and shoulders outside. "How much longer do we lie here?" he asked.

"We are ready to set sail now. I was waiting for you, cursing your tardiness, when Mahaba told me that you swam aboard last night and slept in the locker. Wherefore did you . . . Ymir! Did the law catch and hang you? Your neck is nigh as black as your hair!"

"I wrestled with a python last night," Conan said. "Is the Stygian pilot aboard?"

"Not yet. I am now ready to signal that we are ready to sail. He will row out in a few minutes."

"Then tell me when he has left the ship," Conan said, withdrawing into the darkness of the locker.

"What means all this?" demanded the shipmaster.

"Nothing I can speak of now," the Cimmerian said. "Close the hatch." Grumbling, the Van did as he was told and Conan was in darkness again. He heard the grating and thumping as the capstan was turned and the anchor broke free of the harbor mud. Then there was a scraping as the pilot boat came alongside and the pilot and his crew came aboard. The oars were run out and the ship began to drift with the current. He heard the orders of the pilot as he called instructions to the blindfolded rowers. The ship made its slow passage through the cleared channel.

In time the oars halted and he felt a slight bump go through the ship as the pilot boat drew alongside. A few minutes later the hatch opened once more.

"They're well away, Conan," said Wulfrede. "You can come out on deck now."

Stiffly, the Cimmerian made his way out through the hatch. The ship lay drifting as the crew eyed him curiously. He ignored them, staring instead behind the ship to be sure that the pilot boat was well away. Already it had entered the channel. They were well away from the great port of Khemi. Satisfied, Conan looked about and noticed that the Aquilonians were nowhere in sight.

"Are you going to tell me what this is all about?" Wulfrede asked.

"Later," Conan said. "Let's hoist sail and be away from this place."

Wulfrede began to bark orders and the sailors shipped oars and laid hands to the halyards. Conan, eager to be away, lent his own strength to the task and soon the long lateen yards were rising up the masts, their triangular sails at first hanging slack, then bellying forth with the breeze. The *Sea Tiger* began to make its way south, toward unknown shores.

Later in the same day, in the harbor of Khemi, a lean black ship made its way from the harbor on long black oars. Once free of the harbor, it raised black sails and began to cruise to the south. A golden standard was raised to the top of its foremast: a curious trident enclosed within a golden crescent.

# FIVE
## Corsairs

Theirs was not the only craft to ply the dangerous waters of the Black Coast. Each day brought sightings of sails, but the other ships did not approach. Ships avoided one another in these waters. The only exception was a strong party of five Zingaran trading vessels, confident enough in their numbers that they sailed close enough to the *Sea Tiger* for the crew to gape at the ivory tusks stacked like cordwood on the decks, the bundles of splendid feathers and heaps of exotic woods so abundant that all could not be stored in the holds. All proclaimed the richness of the southern trade for men brave enough to take chances and well enough prepared to fare forth in sufficient strength.

Other ships, though not approaching so closely, proclaimed their cargoes by way of the terrible stench that carried miles downwind. They were slavers, their holds packed with hundreds of miserable wretches confined in conditions of utmost filth and squalor. Fewer than half would survive the rigors of the voyage, but those, cleaned up and fattened it the slave markets of the civilized worlds, would fetch a decent price. The coastal chiefs sold their neighbors so cheaply that the high losses during transport were acceptable.

Progress down the coast was good. Conan was pleased with both the ship and the weather. He was not so well pleased with the men. The rough crew that had begun the voyage were in no way improved, and he did not like the look of the new men Wulfrede had hired during their stay on the Tortoise. There were a half-dozen of the newcomers, villainous-looking scoundrels whose every breath cheated the gallows. When Conan asked Wulfrede about the new men, the Van merely shrugged.

"I had to take what was available. Ordinary sailors would not ship out for a voyage as chancy as this one, and few such sailors are ever to be found at loose ends on the Tortoise. I made sure that they are all competent seamen. I could demand no more than that."

"We shall see," Conan said grimly. As to their seamanship, he was not so sure. Their hands, which never strayed far from their weapons, seemed far more apt for the wielding of arms than for the work of a ship.

Fortunately, the sailing conditions demanded little of the seamen save an occasional trimming of sail as the winds continued fair, propelling them ever southward. But almost from the first day the lookout had spotted a strange ship far behind them. The presence of the vessel troubled the Cimmerian, and on this day he like the idea of a follower even less. Making a trumpet of his hands, he hailed the lookout atop the mainmast.

"What see you?"

"That same black-sailed vessel sailing in our wake," the man called out. "Just near enough to see. I have spotted him thrice today."

"What means this?" said Ulfilo. He and the other two Aquilonians stood upon the poop deck taking the air.

"I do not know and I do not like it," Conan said.

"It may be nothing," said Wulfrede. "Word got around on the Tortoise that we were sailing toward little-visited waters.

This fellow may think that we have discovered rich trading grounds and is following us to see where they are."

"I still do not like it," Conan said. "We have enough to concern ourselves with lying straight ahead. I don't like having to worry about what's behind us."

"What is ahead?" Springald asked.

"You see those islands?" Conan pointed to a line of what looked like grayish smudges far in the distance. "Those are the Blood Isles. Any ship passing between the Blood Isles and the mainland runs a gauntlet of pirate craft. The natives have no occupation save preying upon passing ships."

"Can we not pass to seaward of the islands?" Springald asked.

"The winds and water that way are very treacherous," Wulfrede informed him. "Just to clear the isles would mean sailing out of sight of the mainland. Then a slight change in the wind could blow us far out to sea, and there is a current that would carry us out further. Closer inshore to the islands there are dangerous rocks and shoals. Believe me, there is less peril in running between the islands and the mainland."

"Then we shall look to our weapons," Ulfilo said stolidly.

"That still leaves the problem of our follower," Conan said. "I say we wait until dark, then double back and board him before he knows he has come upon us."

"Board him on the high seas without warning?" Wulfrede laughed heartily. "Why, that would be piracy!" Several sailors who had been idling about listening echoed their captain's laughter.

"What care we for that?" Conan demanded. "It is not as if he is likely to hale us into court! "

"No," Wulfrede said. "This is my ship and I say we concentrate upon the corsairs ahead of us. Whoever that is in our wake can bide his time." The shipmaster went forward to see the ship's readiness for battle while Conan fumed. Springald walked up and laid a hand upon the Cimmerian's shoulder.

"This displeases you, my friend?"

"I am displeased and puzzled both," Conan admitted.

"How so?"

"First, I think it a mistake to engage an enemy in front while another possible enemy menaces you from behind. That is only sound tactics. Secondly, I never knew a Van who was not always eager for a fight. Why is the man so reluctant to contest with this follower?"

"Perhaps he is right. Perhaps it is only a trade rival. He is a merchant skipper who has sailed these waters many times, after all. I think we should trust his judgment."

"We have little choice, short of mutiny," Conan grumbled.

"Come with me," Springald said. "My friends and I have some questions to ask of you, since it looks as if we may soon be in conflict with these seaborne raiders." He followed the man to the poop deck where Ulfilo was thumbing the edges of his massive sword.

"Should we be attacked," Ulfilo began, "what sort of fighting may we expect to see?"

"These men do not raid far from their home islands," Conan said. "Their craft are big canoes, paddled by a score of men each."

"How do they fight?" Ulfilo asked.

"Most are spearmen, although some favor big knives or short swords. They have some bows, although these are not very formidable, and the pitching of the canoes makes their archery worse. They will paddle as swiftly as they can to board and engage us hand-to-hand. They are fierce and fearless in close combat. Their hide shields are long and narrow, and none wears armor. They rarely throw their spears, but use them for thrusting."

"They do not sound very dangerous," Ulfilo said.

"A man who has no fear for his own hide is always dangerous," Conan reminded him. "I've seen such warriors happily bury their teeth in the throat of a man who's just gutted them. And be careful how you swing that sword. If we should be boarded, it will get very crowded on deck. Sailors favor short weapons for that reason. And don't try to fight as you would on land, with your feet firmly planted. Balance is the most important thing in a ship fight, for the deck never stops moving beneath your feet. Keep your knees bent and never strike when the ship's movement throws you off balance. You can't hit with full strength that way and it just further unbalances you. Defend yourself until you are firm on your feet again and *then* strike.''

Ulfilo looked as if he resented being told how to fight, but Springald was attentive. Malia was composed as always. If anything, she seemed excited by the prospect of action.

As the isles drew nearer the sailors grew tense and subdued, forgoing their customary raucous singing and coarse humor. Their eyes were always on the horizon, their fingers straying ever to their weapons, fondling a trusted hilt or thumbing an edge of steel to test its razor-keenness. They passed the first and second islands without incident. The third island was the closest to the mainland, and as they passed through the narrow strait separating the land masses the lookout cried out loudly from the masthead.

''Canoes! Canoes! The black devils are upon us!''

''Where away?'' called Wulfrede, rushing to the rail.

''Off the starboard bow, coming from behind that big rock just off the south cape of the isle!''

''How many?'' Conan yelled.

''I see three, but I think another comes even now!''

Ulfilo came on deck, buckling on a steel breast-and-back. ''How long before they get here?'' he demanded.

Wulfrede shrugged. ''It depends upon how hardy their paddlers are, and how long a chase we can lead them. If we sail fast enough we will be past them before they close the distance and they will have to chase us to catch up.''

''Can we not add speed by using our own oars?'' Springald asked as he came up the steps from below. He now wore a steel cap with pendant neckguard of mail and a shirt of light, silvered steel mesh. His basket-hilted sword was bare in his hand and on his left forearm he carried a small steel buckler.

''Nay,'' said Wulfrede, ''on this type of ship the oars are only used for maneuvering into and out of port. Otherwise, we only use them in a calm or an emergency, to keep away from rocks and so forth. Anyway, the last thing we want to do is tire out the men before the fighting even begins. There's a calculation to this sort of battle, you see. The longer they have to chase us, the wearier will be the men wielding the paddles, while our men will be rested and fresh when the fun begins.''

''Most perspicacious,'' Springald commented.

Malia came up on deck, pale but composed. ''What shall I do?'' she asked, with no quaver in her voice.

''Stay below,'' Wulfrede said. ''You'll be safe from such weapons as the blacks have in your cabin. Their canoes cannot ram and they'll not try to set fire to the ship. After all, they want to take it intact.''

''Springald and I will guard the passageway below,'' Ulfilo said. He turned to Malia. ''If you see a corsair coming down the steps, you will know I am dead.''

''I am prepared,'' she said, tapping a small jeweled object that hung from her neck on a golden chain. Conan saw that it was a tiny dagger. Clearly, she did not intend to use it on a corsair.

''As you will,'' Wulfrede said. ''You realize that if you wear armor it will drag you under, should you go into the water?''

''The only way I leave this spot is dead,'' Ulfilo said, leaning on the long hilt of his sword.

''Suit yourself,'' said the shipmaster, eyeing the long blade dubiously. ''And be careful how you swing that blade.''

''We have been told,'' Springald said.

Conan, barefooted and dressed only in his short sailor's breeks, swarmed up the mast and stood atop the yard, looking first toward the island. There were now five canoes coming for them, closing fast. Then he peered behind them. The black-sailed vessel was still there, keeping its distance. Conan muttered a curse and slid down a backstay to the deck.

''Our guests rush to meet us,'' the Cimmerian said. ''Five canoes now. We must give them a proper reception.'' He took up his weapon-belt from where it lay on the deck and girded it about his sinewy waist. He unhooked his sheathed sword from its hangars and stripped the sheath from the gleaming blade. He tossed the sheath down the stair to the lower deck.

"I'll not need that until the party's over," he told the Aquilonians. "I advise you to do the same. A dangling sheath can trip a man on footing firmer than a ship's deck." Springald followed his advice. Ulfilo ignored it.

As the canoes drew ever nearer the sailors hefted their weapons nervously and their teeth showed in wolfish grins of anticipation. Each man now held a short sword or axe and bore a small, round shield of wicker covered with hide. A few wore steel caps or light helmets made of rawhide. Sheaves of javelins and boxes of slingstones had been set at intervals along the rails. Bows and arrows were issued to men who were skilled archers.

Conan took up a bow, strung it and tested its draw. It was a cheap weapon, such as were sold by the crateload to ships at emergency stores. The arrows were likewise inferior, their points of cast iron, heavily greased, their fletching tied on with twine. The sea air would quickly loosen even high-quality glue. Conan chose a score of the straightest and thrust them beneath his belt.

"You are an archer as well as a swordsman?" Springald said.

"Aye. This is no fine Hyrcanian weapon, but then I'll not be shooting at a man a hundred paces away from the back of a galloping horse. Nor will these shafts need to pierce armor. Against naked men at close range, it is adequate."

Now they could hear the chanting of the savages as they drew nearer. It was a deep, booming sound that stirred the blood; a barbaric invitation to battle and slaughter. It proclaimed an elemental joy in the shedding of blood. It proclaimed that these warriors would not be satisfied with prisoners to sell as slaves or hold for ransom. They would slay all who came within their grasp.

The paddlers worked their paddles standing, while within the canoes stood men shaking their spears in time with the chant. The islanders were tall men, lighter of skin than the mainland blacks. Their naked bodies glistened with oil and were made gaudy by paint. They wore tall headdresses of colorful feathers that nodded in time to their chants. Their spears bore arm-long points of crudely forged iron, but they were nonetheless deadly for their roughly hammered surfaces. Their edges gleamed bright and sharp. Their short, thick hafts were of tough ebony.

With a sudden, fevered burst of paddling, the canoes surged ahead. The rhythmic chant gave way to high-pitched war cries as the blacks knew that their prey would not escape them. Arrows began to arch from the canoes, but the palmwood bows and reed arrows were not formidable, and the shafts were easily stopped by the seamen's light shields. Arrows began to fly from the ship to more telling effect, and men toppled screaming from the canoes, their bodies pierced.

Conan drew, loosed, and saw another body splash into the warm sea. He drew and loosed quickly, not bothering with careful aim, just using the packed mass of bodies as his target. The range was too short to waste good marksmanship and it was imperative to cut down the enemy's numerical superiority. Each big canoe carried perhaps forty warriors, and should all board at once, they could overwhelm the ship's company by sheer numbers. Javelins and stones now flew between the vessels as the last few paces between them dwindled.

Then came a crunching of wood as the bow of a canoe smashed into the starboard gunwale of the *Sea Tiger*. In an instant, tall black spearmen swarmed over the rail, to be met by the swords and axes of the sailors. Men screamed and cut and stabbed, bled and fell. The already uncertain footing of the deck became even more treacherous as blood and entrails turned it to a ghastly shambles.

From the poop deck, Conan shot his last arrows, then snatched up his sword and vaulted over the rail to the deck below. Another canoe slammed into the port side, and the Cimmerian sprang to the shattered rail to repel boarders. The first to try was a man who wore a short mantle of leopard skin about his shoulders and a face-frame of scarlet feathers. He raised his spear on high, but before he could strike, Conan's sword halved him at the waist. He fell back into the canoe in two pieces, both of them spilling intestines. As others sought to board the ship, Conan's sword flashed, taking off a hand here, a head there. By himself, he prevented the warriors of that canoe from gaining a foothold.

But nearby the other canoes grappled and spilled their fighting men onto the ship. They were many, but the sailors were fierce and knew that they fought for their very lives. The sound of sword and axe shearing into naked flesh made a sickening drum-roll in time to the chants of the warriors who still stood in their canoes, awaiting an opportunity to slay or be slain.

Men were not the only predators of the sea that day. Trian-gular fins cut the water as hungry sharks sped toward the strug-gling craft. The sudden abundance of blood drew every predatory fish for miles and they converged as do vultures and ravens wherever men fight upon land.

Two enterprising sailors dashed to the ship's hold and strug-gled back up carrying between them a massive boulder, a part of the ship's ballast. As comrades cleared a space for them at the rail, they cast it overboard, into the center of one of the canoes. The heavy stone crashed through the thin wood of the bottom and the canoe began to fill with water. The warriors aboard the sinking craft screamed, not for fear of being eaten by sharks but in rage at the thought of dying without a chance to slay an enemy. The sailors set up a cheer and several went below to fetch more stones.

Conan backed away from the rail to take a breather and survey the fight. Several sailors took his place at the rail as he backed away. He saw Wulfrede, who was merrily singing a Vanir war song as he hewed men down with an axe. One on one, the sailors were a match for the fierce but poorly armed corsairs. It was the numbers of the enemy that made them dangerous.

The Cimmerian sprang onto the poop deck and there found Ulfilo and Springald guarding the passageway to the cabins be-low. He saw now why Ulfilo had ignored his advice concerning his sheath. The man's feet did not move as he fought. He had chosen his place to fight and he did not budge. As he swung his great blade evading and ducking the deadly spears, his knees and body flexed fluidly, but his feet stayed exactly where he had planted them when he took up his position. His blows were powerful and well timed. It was an impressive sight. Nearby was Springald, and as Conan had surmised upon first seeing the man, he wielded his short, basket-hilted sword with skill. Conan had met scholar-warriors before and knew that learning in no way weakened a man, unless he so chose. The bookman fought, not grimly like Ulfilo, nor furiously like Conan, but artfully and with a smile upon his round, intelligent face. Conan grinned at the sight. These two needed no help from him.

With one of the canoes eliminated the sailors were not so hard-pressed. Even as he noted the fact, Conan saw a crewman thrust back from the rail by a spear that pierced his body and emerged bloodily from his back. The warrior on the other end of the spear sprang onto the rail screaming his victory cry as he withdrew his spear. He raised the weapon high and was about to spear another man when Conan's sword traced a glittering blur to shear the black warrior's head in two. The blade crunched deep into the breastbone, so that the Cimmerian had to brace a foot against the corpse in order to drag his blade free.

As the dead black fell, Conan leapt into the canoe and swung his sword with both hands, the bloody steel working in savage, horizontal half-circles, shearing flesh, bone, and entrails at every stroke, sending crimson droplets to patter into the sea like rain. Behind him, sailors hooted with glee and piled into the canoe. They fought their way from one end of the canoe to the other. The blacks fought to the last man, preferring death by steel to the teeth of the maddened sharks that by now were churning the sea to pink froth.

Conan and the others returned to the *Sea Tiger* in time to see the remaining canoes beating a retreat and no longer as crowded as they were when they attacked. The sailors sent up a savage cheer, waving their weapons overhead in triumph. For a few minutes Wulfrede went among his men, congratulating them heartily, then he returned to the task of continuing the voyage.

"Back to work!" he cried in high good humor. "Cast the dead overboard. Some of you men fetch buckets and wash the blood from the deck before it dries. The wounded, come to the poop deck for bandaging. Stow the weapons in the chests. Mind you clean and oil them first.''

The men carried out his orders jauntily, seemingly unsaddened over the shipmates they had lost. Within minutes the deck was sparkling and the ship was back on course. The ship's cook built up his fire and heated a pot of pitch to treat the worst cuts, while the sailmaker stood by with needle, thread, and palm for the wounds where stitching seemed more appropriate.

Conan climbed the mast once more and peered along their wake. The black vessel was still there, keeping its distance. Apparently, it had shortened sail while the *Sea Tiger* was engaged with the corsairs, for he now saw its main yard ascend and the great sail fill with wind. He cursed softly, unable to comprehend what the pursuer wanted. If he wished to attack, now was the time to do it, while *Sea Tiger* licked its wounds, wearied with battle. But he seemed content to keep his distance. Conan descended the mast and went to the poop, where he found the Aquilonians, who had fought without the slightest sign of distress, looking pale at the casual way the sailors disposed of their dead.

"They just throw their comrades to the sharks?" Ulfilo said, indignant. "Have they no gods, no rites for the departed? Do they not fear the spirits of the dead will pursue them?"

"Back in whatever homeland they once had," Conan said, "I've no doubt they had customs and rites for burial and appeasing the spirits of the dead. They have no nation but the sea, now. For sailors, the sea is a proper grave. If you ask them, most will tell you that the sharks are servants of the sea-gods, and it is thus that they accept the offering of the sailors' lives, and the dead now go to rest in the bed of the sea. Seamen have many beliefs, some of them passing strange, but fear of the dead is not among them. Upon the sea death is a commonplace, and staying alive is a remarkable accomplishment."

"Fascinating," Springald said. "And you, Conan? What are your beliefs in this matter?"

"Cimmeria is a landlocked country and my people have no beliefs or traditions concerning the sea. Our only god is Crom of the Mountain. Crom does little for us, alive or dead, save give us life and a fighting heart and with these we strive to battle and stay alive as long as possible. Whether we die on sea or land matters not.''

"A bleak philosophy," Springald, "for a notable gloomy people."

"Come," Ulfilo said to Springald, bored with the subject. "Let's go below to clean and tend to our weapons and harness. Nothing etches fine steel as fast as blood and I want to get the stains out of my clothing and armor."

"Ever the soldier, eh, brother-in-law?" said Malia as she came up the stair.

"What else?" said Ulfilo, immune to irony. The two men disappeared below.

"My brother-in-law is a good man," she said when they were gone, "albeit a little stiff and utterly devoid of humor." She looked the ship over with a critical eye. "One would never guess that this vessel was a bloody shambles but half an hour ago. It looks as it did before we sighted the corsairs!"

"Wulfrede keeps a trim vessel," Conan said. "And the corsairs were too bloodthirsty for crafty piracy."

"What do you mean?" she asked.

"They came aboard maddened for blood and slaying. If they had been wise, some would have been detailed to board with axes, to cut up the rigging and smash our steering gear. Then we would have lain crippled for many hours. They could have gone back to their island and returned with reinforcements to finish us off."

She shuddered at the thought. "I thank Mitra that he did not bless them with such foresight." She looked the Cimmerian over with calculation, not for the first time. "I heard you and my companions speaking just before I came on deck. It is not the first time Springald has said that the Cimmerians are famed for their gloom. And yet, you are different: moody and subject to long silences, but you laugh as loudly and boisterously as any when a better mood is upon you."

"I am unlike the rest of my race," he explained. "The Cimmerians are the greatest fighters in the world, but living among them is a great tedium, except for the fighting they delight in. They despise all luxury and soft living, and they hate to leave their own borders or live among any but kinsmen. I knew I was different from an early age."

"How so?" she asked.

"From earliest youth, I listened to the tales of traveling traders and the few Cimmerians who had fought in the wars of other lands. I longed to see the great cities and travel in far lands. I can endure hard campaigning and I fight with a red fury, in that I am like my kinsmen. But I cannot stay in one place for long before the wandering urge comes upon me. And I like fine wine and good food, and the sound of music." He looked her over as frankly as she had studied him. "And I like soft women who smell of perfume instead of peat-smoke. In that I am very unlike the other men of my nation."

She favored him with a smile. "I am very glad to hear that." With this ambiguous statement, she went back below. No sooner had her white-haired head disappeared below than Wulfrede climbed to the poop deck and the two men walked casually to the fantail. Leaning on the fantail, they conversed in low voices.

"What's the butcher's bill?" Conan asked.

"Eight slain outright," Wulfrede answered, "and two more who may not last the night."

Conan grunted noncommittally. "Not many for the slaughter we wrought among the corsairs, but each man we lose is one we cannot replace in these waters.

"Aye. We cannot afford any more such fights ere we reach our destination."

"The black ship still keeps its distance," Conan said.

"I saw. It is as I thought. He is just a trader who thinks we have discovered rich pickings. That being the case, he is going to be disappointed when he finds out where we are going." Wulfrede chuckled, but Conan kept his own counsel.

# Six

## The Coast of Bones

The sea slashed at the jagged rocks, the greenish water churning to froth until the rocks resembled the jagged teeth of a sea monster foaming at the mouth. Wulfrede was at the helm, trusting no other as the *Sea Tiger* made its way through the treacherous passage. In the bow, Conan took soundings with another skilled leadsman, each man casting his lead-weighted line to read the depth of water beneath the keel by means of the knots tied at intervals along the ropes. One cast his lead as the other reeled his in, so that there was little interval between readings.

"Two fathom" sang the man who stood next to Conan. He called melodiously, making a song of it. He was a coastal black who claimed to know these waters. They had picked up a number of such men up the coast, to replace the men lost in the fight with the corsairs, and as a hedge against the losses sure to come. These men were of the Lua tribe, a relatively peaceful folk for coastal Kushites and well known as mariners. Men of the tribe customarily hired onto vessels heading south, to be dropped off in their homeland on the return trip.

"Fathom and a half," Conan called out. The sailors stood by the rails, holding their silence. The rocks loomed near and this was a peril greater than the corsairs had been. The *Sea Tiger* drew less than a fathom of water, but even a small spur of rock thrusting within three or four feet of the surface could gut her, ripping her bottom open from bow to stern, plunging her beneath the waves in an instant. Even a strong swimmer would not be able to get himself free of the wreckage before the suction of the whirlpool created by the sinking ship dragged him under.

A shudder went through the ship. The leadline was jerked from the Lua's hand as it was caught between the hull and something below. The sailors and passengers gritted their teeth until the shuddering stopped.

"Just a sandbar," Wulfrede said. "We'd know if it was rock." His words were casual, but there was sweat upon his face and it was not from the heat of the morning.

Conan drew in his lead. "Six fathom!" he called, grinning. Everyone breathed normally again. They were past the rock barrier and in the deeper water of the lagoon. Wulfrede wiped sweat from his brow and handed the helm over to a seaman.

"I'll not make such a passage again for any man's pay!" he said.

"And yet you must make it at least once more," Springald pointed out. "How else will you leave here?"

"We'll be here some while," Wulfrede said. "I'll send out a boat to take soundings and find a safer channel out. Six inches of stone could have killed us all back there."

The lagoon was broad and quiet, bordered by a wide beach of white sand. Beyond the sand lay a wall of dense jungle, its green vegetation brilliant in the morning sunlight. A great silence lay over all, but Conan knew that was because of distance. The jungle was never silent, but was always alive with the call of birds, the buzz of insects, and the cries of victims brought down by predators. From the lagoon, though, all was quiet save for the distant murmur of the waves upon the rocks now safely behind them.

Now the Aquilonians joined Conan at the rail as he scanned the shoreline.

"I see no sign of habitation," Springald said. "No craft on the shore, no huts, not so much as a plume of smoke from the jungle."

"Do not be deceived," Conan warned. "The Borana are there, and their eyes are upon us even now. They'll have doused their fires as soon as we were sighted. They are measuring us now."

"Measuring us for what?" Malia asked.

The Cimmerian grinned at her. "For dinner."

"Most of this lot are too tough and stringy," Springald said. "Malia is surely the most toothsome."

"You are not to think of me as flesh for a cannibal," Malia said indignantly.

"It is not proper," Ulfilo agreed.

"By Ymir," Wulfrede said, "we wouldn't want to be improper, would we?"

"How do we go ashore?" Springald asked.

"We will send a boat first with some men, all heavily armed, but carrying trade goods," Wulfrede said. "They must see that we are strong, but we do not wish them to think us pirates or slave raiders."

"Will you be in the first boatload?" Ulfilo asked.

The Van shook his head. "My first duty is to my ship."

"Aye," Conan said. "This may be a hostile shore, and the shipmaster must stay with this vessel until he is assured that all is peaceful. I will take the first boat ashore."

"I would be with you," said Springald. "I wish to study these people and the land."

"As you wish," Conan said. "But be ready for trouble."

"I have been since we left Aquilonia," the scholar answered.

With the ship anchored and the crew armed and at the ready, the boat was rowed toward the beach. Still there was no sign of

the natives. In the bow of the boat Conan sat upon a chest of
trade goods, with Springald just behind him. As usual, the Aquilonian carried his satchel of books. Six hard-bitten sailors rowed
the craft, and a seventh steered. All were heavily armed.

"There is the river," Springald said, pointing to a gap in the
trees where a sluggish stream disgorged green scum into the
cove. "That water does not look inviting."

"It looks cleaner than when last I was here," Conan said.
"It was a different time of year and the water was lower. Perhaps we can drink it without having to strain it so much."

"I hope so, Conan," said the steersman. "The casks are
getting low."

When the keel touched sand, the men leapt overboard and
dragged the boat further onto the sand. There they unloaded the
chests they had brought. Conan eyed the seaweed litter on the
beach and pointed to a likely spot.

"Take everything over there," he instructed, "above the high-
water mark." The men did as bidden. When the chests were in
place they spread blankets and opened the chests. Soon the blankets displayed a sample of goods to trade: multicolored beads,
coils of copper and brass wire, ingots of iron, knives, hatchets,
hawk bells, looking glasses, paints, and bolts of cloth dyed in
vivid colors.

"Now what?" Springald asked when all was arranged.

"Now we wait," Conan said.

"I would like to do a bit of exploring," the scholar said,
eyeing the treeline hungrily.

"Not until we know exactly how we stand with the natives,"
said Conan.

The men stood nervously, fingering their weapons, as they
waited for something to happen. Conan stood with arms folded,
as calm as a statue. The wait was not a lengthy one. For a while
they could see nothing among the trees, then there was a hint
of motion all along the tree line. Men hissed in astonishment.

"Mitra!" Springald exclaimed as fully a hundred warriors

materialized, seemingly from nowhere. "Where did they come from?"

"They have been there all the time," Conan said. "I saw some of them as soon as we landed. Like Picts, they are masters of the art of using shadows and remaining absolutely still. To one not trained to the woods, they are invisible."

Where there had been only a wall of greenery, there now stood men carrying spears and long shields. These were different from the island corsairs; stocky, muscular men of medium height, very dark of skin and with shaven heads. Their bodies were painted with streaks of green and brown, to blend with the jungle. Their eyes glared with suspicion as they advanced behind their shields.

"We're dead men!" said a sailor in a strangled voice.

"Silence," Conan said. "They are curious, and they are confident in their strength. If slavers had been here recently, they'd have come screaming and throwing their spears. Let no man draw a weapon and all may go well here."

The line of warriors stopped ten paces away and a few men advanced. These were older men with many scars and an abundance of ornaments, clearly chiefs or senior warriors. They ignored the white men and went to the trade blankets, pointing to some items and talking among themselves in low voices. Conan studied the other warriors. They looked fierce, but they displayed no signs that attack was imminent. He knew that these people customarily went into an eye-rolling, teeth-baring battle frenzy just before launching an attack. Neither did they display any fear. That meant that there were many more warriors in the woods and this was just an advance party. That was all to the good as far as Conan was concerned. In the absence of fear and hostility, trade could take place and they could get on with the next stage of their expedition.

"Who speaks trade talk?" Conan said in the simplified Kushite that served the whole of the Black Coast as a trade language. The senior men came to face him.

"I do," said a man whose eyes were circled with white paint.

"I am Ashko, chief of the Green River Borana. You come to trade, not to steal or take slaves?"

"You see our goods," said Conan. "We have much more aboard our ship. If you want to trade and pledge to be peaceful, we will bring more ashore."

"What do you want in trade?" said the chief.

"You know what we want in the north," Conan said, "ivory, feathers, gold if you have any, fine pelts, gemstones, and so forth."

"Slaves?" Ashko inquired. "We have many prisoners to trade."

"Not this voyage," Conan said.

"Very well," said Ashko. He grinned, exposing teeth filed to points. "You have my pledge. We will trade in peace, so long as you offer us no violence or insult." He put out his hand and the two men gripped forearms. "We will pass the word to the nearby villages."

The warriors relaxed their vigilance a trifle and they wandered over to examine the trade goods.

"All seems to be going well," Springald said, a line of sweat glistening upon his brow.

"Aye, so far," Conan said. "You understood what was said?"

"Most of it," the scholar answered. The Aquilonians had been learning Kushite from the new sailors in preparation for their journey inland.

"Keep on your guard," The Cimmerian warned. "All can change in an instant. It could be a ruse. A pledge to a stranger means nothing on this coast. Their oath is binding only within the tribe."

"I see. So all is not well?"

"We cannot be sure just yet. We must have more evidence."

"So what do we do?" Springald asked.

"We wait some more," Conan answered.

Within an hour, people came streaming from the nearby villages. Among them were elderly people, women carrying babies, and small children who had to be restrained from snatching at the brightly colored trade goods.

"There is our evidence," Conan said. "The women and babes would not come here if there was danger of fighting." He ordered the sailors to return to the ship for more goods and men. Soon the beach was thronged and preparations were under way for a great feast. Chained prisoners, guarded by warriors, dug a fire pit in the sand. Soon flames leapt from the pit as native cooks prepared meats for roasting. Jugs of primitive wine and beer appeared, along with piles of fruit and meal-cakes.

In the last boat to come ashore were Wulfrede, Malia, and Ulfilo. The Van beamed as the saw a file of bearers emerging from the tree line, some of them staggering beneath the weight of great tusks. Others had bales balanced upon their heads. He walked over to Conan.

"I see you have things well in hand. This should be a trip of high profit even if we don't find the prodigal brother."

"We care nothing for profit," Malia said. "We must find my husband." The natives gaped at the Aquilonian woman, exclaiming over her white hair and exceedingly pale skin. Women came to stroke her skin to determine whether she wore white paint. She bore this treatment with aristocratic stoicism.

"Well, I care a great deal for profit," Wulfrede assured her.

"We must ask them about the Horns of Shushtu," Springald said.

Wulfrede shook his head. "Nay. First put them at their ease doing something they are accustomed to; trade. Later we will broach the idea of an expedition, for we must have bearers. What we do have to ask them about is a source for clean water, or we'll all be down with fever."

"I've already asked," said Conan. "An hour's paddling up the river there is a stream that flows in from nearby hills. It is clean and fresh."

"Good," said the shipmaster. "Tonight we feast with our new friends. In the morning we send a boat to fill the casks. In the afternoon, when everyone's head has stopped ringing, we hire bearers for a trek inland.'' The Van went to confer with the arriving village headmen and make preparations for the distribution of goods and the bestowal of presents for the important men.

''We must ask about my brother,'' Ulfilo said.

''Later, at the feast,'' Conan cautioned. ''Let them grow jovial with drink first. But I can tell you now that I see no sign of his ship. Your brother may have come to grief after leaving Khemi. He many not have reached the Coast of Bones.''

''He arrived here safely,'' Ulfilo maintained. ''You may take my word for that.''

''You are being cursed secretive,'' Conan said hotly. ''If you would tell me what you know, I would be better able to do that which you have hired me to do.''

''Soon, soon,'' Malia said. ''My brother-in-law is excessively gruff, be we have reasons for our caution.''

''You had better,'' Conan said. ''You risk all our lives with your secrecy. Our situation is dangerous enough without that.''

''You think we are unsafe here?'' Malia asked.

''There is no safety on the Black Coast,'' Conan assured her. ''These people are volatile at the best of times. A brawl or even an insult from one of the sailors could touch off a massacre. We are perhaps as safe as we can be upon this stretch of coast, but that is not very safe at all.''

As the sun set, trading broke off for the day and all except the slaves fell to feasting. The Aquilonians and the sailors kept casually wandering toward the fire pit, ostensibly to check on the progress of the cooking, but actually to assure themselves that they would not be served human flesh. To their relief, they saw nothing but the carcasses of pigs, goats, fowl, and game animals roasting and giving forth a luscious smell.

''Perhaps it is just a rumor after all,'' Springald said, ''that they are cannibals.''

''It may be that they eat only enemies slain in battle,'' Conan said, ''and think thereby to absorb the enemy's courage.''

''You do little for my appetite,'' Malia said. They sat upon

the ground just beneath the trees with huge leaves spread upon
the ground before them. Servers laid slabs of smoking meat and
other foods upon the leaves while slave women fanned them,
more to drive the insects away than for the sake of coolness.
The latter was an impossibility in the sultry, humid air.

Wulfrede came to sit by them. A gourd of native beer in one
hand, he picked up a roast jungle fowl with the other, biting
into it with gusto. He washed down the mouthful with a draught
and belched.

"By Ymir, but I could get rich from this voyage were I not
such an honest man," he announced.

"How is that?" Springald asked.

"One of the chiefs just offered me a hundred slaves for Malia.
They are much taken by her fairness. She is an exotic item in
these parts."

"You constantly try to provoke me," she said stonily. "I
choose to ignore it, as usual."

"You Aquilonians are a humorless folk," Wulfrede grumbled.

The evening progressed well. The chiefs and warriors were
in a good mood, for they had been successful in their warring
with neighboring peoples and had not been raided by pirates or
slavers for some time. No traders had ventured to their usually
inhospitable coast in a long time, so they had a wealth of things
to trade and a great need for the things they could not produce for
themselves. For metals and cloth and beads they were happy to
trade at a good rate, and they only lamented that the whites desired
no slaves, for they were tired of feeding their prisoners. Wulfrede
assured them jovially that, when he returned, he would direct some
reputable slavers to the Coast of Bones.

As bellies were filled and the brew continued to flow, Conan
broached the first part of their business to Ashko, who now
rejoiced in a fine necklace of pierced silver beads and a short
cloak of scarlet silk, presents from his new friends.

"Tell me, Ashko," Conan began, "know you aught of a white
man somewhat resembling Ulfilo here, who visited this coast

within the last two years? We know he was here once, and he may have returned again. He is a friend of ours, and he has been missing for some time now."

"The mad one?" said Ashko. "Had he yellow hair upon his head and face? Such a one was among us for a while, not wishing to trade or to fight, but to journey inland, saying that there was something he sought there. The first time, he fared inland with a hundred men, white and black, and all well armed. Only he and two others returned, wasted almost to ghosts. He promised to come back with many rich presents, and he sailed away with the men he had left to guard his ship."

Conan was not deceived by the Boranas' present hospitable mood. They were savages and possibly cannibals, and Marandos, the brother of Ulfilo and husband of Malia, had been wise enough to arrive with a strong band. They had let him go upon his return because he promised rich gifts.

"And he did indeed return?" Conan pressed.

"He did, with the fine gifts he hand promised. This time he had two hundred men and *bumbana*, and they disappeared inland once more. We have not seen them since."

"What are bumbana?" Conan asked, but Springald broke in hastily.

"When did you last see them, my friend Ashko?"

"Perhaps six moons ago, perhaps ten or twelve," the chief said, shrugging.

"These folk have little sense of the passage of time," Conan told them. "There are not true seasons here, just rainy seasons and dry, and often it's hard to distinguish one from the other."

"That is inconvenient," Ulfilo said, "but at least we now know that my brother reached here on his second voyage and was well when he returned inland."

"Conan," said Malia, "ask the chief why he calls Marandos a madman." Malia was not yet fluent in spoken trade language, and in any case the chief would have felt insulted to be addressed directly by a woman. The Cimmerian translated the question.

"Only the mad trek far to the east," Ashko told them. "Among us, only witch doctors who wish to gain great power fare thither. Great spirits and demons dwell beyond the eastern mountains, such as drink the blood of all who come near them. There is nothing worth seeking there. On his first trek he returned with nothing but his life, and that was much diminished. He has not returned since that time." The chief performed an expressive shrug. "He was mad."

When the feasting and revelry were over for the night, the ship's company retreated to the camp they had set up on the shore. Guards were posted, for this was not friendly country, whatever the recent appearances. Wulfrede had given stern orders that certain men were to refrain from intoxicating beverages, and these had first watch. There was grumbling among them, but they knew better than to defy their captain and were assured that they could drink their fill the next day while the others worked. Thus did the Van maintain both vigilance and peace among his crew.

Before all were bedded down, Conan sought out Ashko, who was yet just sober enough to speak.

"You are still awake and walking upright?" said the chief with a sharp-toothed grin. "Did we not feed you well enough or supply you with enough drink? Is it a woman you wish now?"

"No, my friend, your hospitality has been overwhelming. Never have I been entertained so splendidly. But, I wished to ask you about something that you said this evening."

"What was that?" asked the chief. He walked to the great cooking fire and clapped his hands. A woman came running with a pair of gourds and a wooden pitcher of palm wine.

Conan accepted one and drank to show courtesy. "You used a word which I had never heard before. You said that the madman had returned from the north with men and bumbana. What are these bumbana?"

Ashko displayed astonishment. "Have you no bumbana in the north? And yet you must, for he had half a score with him when he returned."

"Perhaps I know them by another name," Conan said. "What does this name signify to you?"

"Why, the bumbana are the beast-men, the half-apes who dwell in the mountains far to the east."

"I see. What sort of ship did he sail in?"

"Ships of the northerners are much alike to me. The first was much like yours. The ship he returned in looked like the first, except that it was all black, even the paddles and the big cloth that catches the wind."

"One last thing," Conan said. He squatted next to the fire, took a stick and began to scratch a figure upon the earth. "Have you ever seen anything like this?" In the dirt he traced a broad crescent moon with its horns pointing upward, enclosing a trident with three wavy tines.

Ashko grunted affirmatively. "There was a golden figure like that atop the great pole of the black ship."

# SEVEN

## The Trek Eastward

The next two days were taken up in trade. The Aquilonians were impatient, but both Conan and Wulfrede cautioned not to rush matters. Besides, more villagers were arriving from the interior and they might turn hostile if the traders were to pack up and leave. On the third evening, they called a meeting of chiefs. After an exchange of compliments and bestowal of presents, they got down to business.

"We wish to travel beyond the eastern mountains," Conan announced. "And we will pay handsomely for boats to take us upriver as far as we may go, and for bearers to carry our necessities where we must travel overland. We want at least fifty strong young men. As we use up stores, the bearers may return home in small groups."

Ashko shook his head. "We Borana are warriors and do not carry burdens for other men, but some of these chiefs have subjects who may do such work."

"Why not just buy slaves?" said a chief who had arrived with a chain of captives, only to be disappointed to find that the merchants wanted no human goods. "You may work them as you wish and, when they are no longer needed, you may eat them."

The Aquilonians paled, but Wulfrede broke in smoothly. "You know as well as I, my friend, that they would always be trying to escape. We cannot guard them all the time, and if they march in chains our progress must be unacceptably slow. No, we must have free, willing men."

After much palaver a chief agreed to supply them with the men they needed. "But you must understand," he said, "that they will accompany you only as far as the mountains. To climb into them is forbidden, for they are the home of spirits. You must arrange for others to carry your goods further."

Conan spoke in a low voice. "You might as well accept these terms, for you'll get no better. These are fierce people, and if they fear those mountains, no amount of bribery will tempt them. We'll have to hope that there are villagers at the foot of the range who are not so chary of the local demons."

"If we must," said Ulfilo, tight-lipped.

The bargain was struck and it was agreed that they should set out the next morning. Upriver natives had arrived in large dugout canoes loaded with ivory and other trade goods. There was ample room in these to carry the men and their belongings. The bearers they would acquire at more distant villages.

"I think," said Wulfrede when the council was at an end, "that it would be best if I and most of my crew accompany you upon this journey inland. You might not be able to find the men you need when you get to the mountains, and the loss would leave you weak, indeed."

"Would that not leave the ship vulnerable?" Ulfilo asked.

"I will leave five or six men to take care of the Sea Tiger. Ashko has agreed to see that she remains unmolested. After all, he and the other chiefs are most anxious that I return safely to send back slavers to trade for their excess stock."

"Think you that those seamen of yours will take kindly to the idea of an inland trek among the cannibals to a destination our employers are so reluctant to disclose?'' Conan asked suspiciously.

"They fear me," Wulfrede said, "and they will obey."

The next morning the Aquilonians, the Cimmerian, and a score of sour-faced, grumbling mariners filed into the big dugouts.

Conan took the lead craft, along with the Aquilonians and with his suspicions. The black follower had dropped below the horizon as soon as they had reached the Coast of Bones and had not been seen since. He had no doubt that they had not seen the last of the sinister craft or its inhabitants.

"But this river smells foul!" said Malia, twisting her face into a comical grimace as she boarded the dugout. In deference to practicality, she had exchanged her fine gown for a sailor's baggy trousers tucked into the tops of knee-high boots and a belted tunic with sleeves to the wrist. Her fair skin was further protected from the burning tropic sun by a wide straw hat with a shoulder-length veil and silken gloves. She had objected to wearing the stifling clothing in the fierce heat, but Conan had pointed out that, while they were in lowland jungle, biting serpents and stinging insects were likely to be far more dangerous than heat stroke, wild animals, or human enemies.

"Here at the shore," Springald told her, "the river deposits all it has collected for hundreds of leagues. As we go upstream, the water should grow cleaner. Am I not right, Conan?"

"Aye," said the Cimmerian. "But we'll find little clean water until we reach the mountains. We must drink only from the casks or from such clean springs as we come upon. Those will be few. As for the smell . . ."—he shrugged his massive shoulders—"a smell you will get used to. There are worse things."

"I just found one of them," Malia said, disgustedly brushing a many-legged thing from the flaring cuff of her glove. The native paddlers were much amused, for the thing was ugly but harmless, such as they ignored even when it crawled across their naked flesh.

"We will show you the deadly ones," said Umgako, the left-side bow paddler who set the pace for the others. "That one just makes a great stink if you squash it."

"Splendid!" murmured Malia. "Not only do they sting and bite, but some of them smell even worse than everything else!"

"Cast off!" Conan shouted. All were aboard now and it was time to put some distance behind them. He had little faith in the heart of the sailors for this venture. They might be brave as lions at sea, but this was not their element, and he knew that most men were likely to panic when subjected to unfamiliar surroundings. They might be tempted to rebel and go back to the ship so long as it was near to them. In the bow of the dugout behind him, the sailor Umu favored him with an ugly, humorless grin. Conan was confident that there would soon be blows exchanged between himself and the seaman.

The first day's paddling was hot and monotonous. The river was a sluggish one, much fouled by slime, and inhabited by crocodiles in extravagant numbers. In some places it widened into pools where hippos flourished. Malia clapped her gloved hands with delight at sight of the comical-looking animals and the scholar urged the paddlers closer to them for a better look, but the natives balked, eyeing the beasts warily.

"They are right," Conan said. "These are not creatures to trifle with. They frolic like puppies, but in truth they are dangerous, bad-tempered beasts, and they would overturn and crush our canoes should we annoy them. Admire them from a distance, if you will. Soon enough we shall encounter beasts that are deadly and look it."

The first night, they camped upon the low ground with smoky fires burning to drive the swarming insects away. The jungle pressed close upon them, and the dark hours were clamorous with the cries of predators and prey.

"How do men live in such a place?" Malia asked, gingerly lifting her veil to sip at a bowl of watered wine.

"Few do so by choice," Springald told her. "The weaker

peoples are pushed into jungle or desert land by the stronger, who seize the good grazing and farming land.''

"Aye," Conan said. "I'll wager when we get into the up-lands, we'll find warlike herdsmen who are numerous and well armed.'' The Cimmerian was distracted by happenings a few paces away, where the seamen had established their own fire and sat talking in low voices. He could not make out words, but he could tell from their glances and gestures that the men were discussing the lofty personages who sat at his own fire. The rumbling voice of the brutish Umu was unmistakable, and as Conan watched the man, whose glances in his direction had been unmistakably contemptuous, favored him with an evil grin.

Since coming ashore, Umu's shipboard reticence had given way to open insolence, but the man always stopped just short of giving Conan cause to call him out. Whatever Umu was say-ing, the others seemed to agree with him. Conan saw crooked teeth exposed as men thumbed the edges of their knives or stroked the shafts of the native spears some of them had ac-quired. It boded ill to come, but Conan was not sure what prod-ded them to this behavior. In this country, it was imperative that the little band stay united.

Whatever the reason, Conan intended to brook no more of it. Better a somewhat reduced company than one in which he could not turn his back on men who were expected to follow his or-ders. Perhaps a quick, brutal lesson in good manners would be best for all concerned.

The next two days took them deeper inland. Here the jungle grew down to the water line and so overhung the water that they were often in danger from venomous serpents dropping from the branches overhead. From time to time they passed small villages of circular mud huts with conical, straw-thatched roofs. Here the villagers flocked to the riverbank to stare at the strangers. Small children danced with delight to see so odd a sight. These strange, pale creatures looked like ghosts to them, but who ever heard of ghosts showing themselves in the daytime?

The end of the day brought them to a much larger village

situated at the base of a majestic waterfall. The cataract fell in multiple ribbons that coalesced into a vast, foaming spray halfway down a titanic cliff, then smashed to churning foam upon the jagged black rocks below. A rainbow seemed to hang permanently amid the mist below the fall.

"How beautiful!" Malia exclaimed.

"Aye," agreed Wulfrede, albeit wryly. " 'Tis a fine sight, but that escarpment is going to take some climbing. This is as far as we go by water."

They were helped ashore and welcomed by the villagers, who set up a joyous chant when they recognized their chief and returning warriors among those in the canoes. The all-pervading mist provided a welcome coolness as the belongings of the expedition were unloaded and carried to a great hut under the direction of the chief, who then assigned other huts for the housing of his visitors. He gave orders and people dashed about, readying a banquet.

"Not more feasting and palavering!" Ulfilo grumbled. "I want to get on with our mission."

"We have to select our bearers," Conan said, "and I want only the best. We'll need at least until tomorrow afternoon to assemble volunteers and select the ones we want. Believe me, it will save us time later on. Sick or lame men will slow us far more than a little delay here."

"We shall trust your judgment," Ulfilo said, still grumbling.

Conan saw Springald gazing at the waterfall with the look of a man enraptured.

"What see you in the water, friend?" the Cimmerian asked.

"It is the one! The Giant's Fall! See, just as the *Chronicle of the Voyage of Captain Belphormis:* it begins in white ribbons, makes a single stream as it falls and ends in mist. Even the perpetual rainbow is exactly as described!"

"Say you so?" Conan said. "And what else did this ancient captain say about this spot?"

"There was a village here at that time, but the folk were not the same as these. They were the taller, lighter people he mentions meeting near the shore, and he says that they lived in long houses made of logs, not round mud huts."

"Does this mean that we are anywhere near our destination?" Conan asked.

"There is still much distance to cover. But it means we are on the right course."

That evening they looked over the available men in the village, picking out those who looked strongest and most enduring. They found thirty good prospects while runners went to nearby villages to spread the word that the foreigners were offering rich goods to pay for bearers.

After choosing, the leaders of the expedition sat at the feast-fire, talking with the village headmen, asking many questions concerning the land at the top of the escarpment. The natives were able to give them little information, for they seldom ventured thither. The village witch doctor had made treks into the highlands but he adamantly refused to speak of what he had seen, stating that the mountains were cursed for men who had not the proper magic to protect themselves.

As they sat in conversation a strange figure emerged from the tree line. It was a very tall man who was clearly of a race different from the local natives. From shoulder to knees he was wrapped in a robelike garment of red cloth and in his hand he bore a long-handled axe. His hair was stained with ocher and built up into a crest resembling the horsehair crest of a helmet. His skin was of a coppery hue, and he walked slowly, with great dignity.

"Who is this fellow?" asked Conan as he sized the man up.

"That is Goma, a wanderer and a tribeless man." The chief spoke contemptuously. In these parts, a man without a tribe was a man without worth. "He came hither some years ago, perhaps ten years."

"A man with no tribe has lived here for many years?" Conan said. "How does such a one survive?"

"He will do no work, but he fights in the wars and raids for one chief or another. He is a great warrior, I will not deny it."

The man stopped before them and looked them over haughtily. "I am Goma. I have heard that you white men travel to the mountains. I am of a mind to go with you." He spoke trade Kushite with an accent that differed from that of the local people.

"We need bearers," said Ulfilo. "Lower your robe so we may see that you hide no illness or deformity."

The tall man laughed. "I lower my garment for no man, nor do I bear burdens like a slave or like these lowly people."

"Then be off with you," said Ulfilo, "for we need only bearers."

Springald raised a hand. "Be not so hasty. Goma, wherefore should we take you with us? As you can see, we have many doughty warriors, all well armed."

"But you have no guide. Few of these dogs have even been to the top of the escarpment. Only the old witch-man has been as far as the mountains. None of them have been beyond them."

"And you have been beyond the mountains?" Ulfilo asked.

"I have. My wanderings have taken me to many far places. I have been to those mountains, and crossed the desert beyond them, and visited the land beyond the desert."

"He lies!" hissed the witch doctor, shaking his staff so that the bones adorning its length rattled. His necklace of dried human hands flapped against his bony chest as he gesticulated. "No man can visit those lands and return!"

"And yet here I stand," said Goma, with a superior smile.

"Tell me, Goma," said Springald, "know you of a place called the Horns of Shushtu?"

"Aye. Two great peaks, one white, the other black. Between them lies a pass, a beyond the pass is a great valley."

"He knows!" Springald said, stunned. "He speaks the truth and the old books did not lie!"

"Speak no more, Goma," Ulfilo said. "You shall be our guide. What may we pay you for the service?"

The warrior surveyed the goods with the same air of contempt he bestowed upon the villagers. His features were straight and aristocratic, making him seem even haughtier. His high-cheekboned face would have been handsome, but it was adorned with numerous small, ornamental scars. More such scars decorated his arms and much of his chest as was visible. Apparently, the incisions had been rubbed with soot, for the thick scar tissue stood out like shiny black beads against the coppery skin.

"Nothing," Goma said at last. "I will go along for the joy of it." With that he turned and walked away into the forest.

"Well!" Malia said. "That is a very strange man."

"What do you think of him, Conan?" Springald asked.

"I think he knows the land where we fare," said the Cimmerian. "And I would not turn my back on him."

The next day they chose the last of their bearers and made their final preparations. The following morning they set off toward the escarpment, having seen no more of the mysterious Goma.

They set off from the village in the dim light of early morning, amid the lamentations of women who did not know when, nor if, they would see their men again. At the base of the escarpment, about a quarter mile from the waterfall, a narrow, tortuous path zigzagged up the cliff to its crest far above.

The climb was precarious, and took much of the day. Not only was the path narrow and winding, but it was seldom used, so that parts of it were overgrown with brush, while other parts were all but washed out. To Conan, raised amid rugged mountains, it was as a paved highway. The others had greater difficulty. The sailors, in particular, were unhappy. Unused to going great distances on foot, they thought the trail a great ordeal.

To the Cimmerian, any path was a good one that took them from the lowland jungle. He could endure almost anything, but the fetid swampland he found detestable. Whatever lay above, it could only be better. He fairly ran up the path, stopping often to shove aside boulders or hack away bushes with his sword. As he ascended, the vista spread beneath him widened until he could see the vast expanse of greenery all the way to a silver strip on the horizon: the sea.

At the top of the escarpment he found tall trees of a different sort from those of the lowlands. These grew farther apart, and the vines connecting treetop to treetop were fewer. The undergrowth beneath the trees was far less dense and the air smelled clean. Even as he surveyed the trees he saw a familiar form come from the shadows beneath them: Goma.

"You are hardier than your companions, man with black hair," said the guide.

"I am a hillman, accustomed to climbing," Conan answered. "They will be here presently."

While they waited Goma stood casually with his legs crossed, leaning upon the long handle of his axe like a city dweller leaning on a gold-mounted cane. Conan studied the weapon with interest. It was not the armor-smashing axe of the western lands, but rather a light weapon with a compact head bearing a crescent cutting edge on one side and a four-inch spike on the other. Its whippy, three-foot handle appeared to be made of rhinoceros horn and bore an orange-sized ball on its terminus. A leather thong connected the handle to Goma's wrist. Such an axe, he knew, could be swung with blurring swiftness and would be an excellent weapon in this land where helmets and armor were rare.

Soon the others began to arrive. First came Ulfilo, tired but too proud to show it. He was closely followed by Malia and Springald, both of them puffing unashamedly. Then came Wulfrede, with some of the sailors. The rest of the sailors were strung out along the line of bearers.

"I see our friend has joined us at last," Ulfilo said.

"And Conan looks like a courtier after a morning's stroll in a formal garden," Malia said sourly. Conan translated these comments for Goma, who seemed hugely amused.

"There will be no more climbing for many days," he assured them, "but there will be much danger and other hardship."

"Hardship even for you, Goma?" Wulfrede demanded.

The native grinned. "In the desert to come, even a man such as I may be tested to the limit."

Wulfrede glared at the Aquilonians. "He mentioned somewhat of a desert last night. You people said naught of any desert."

"They said cursed little about anything," Conan said. "I think it is time we were told more of what we are headed into. Come now," he said impatiently, "civilization is far behind us. Surely you do not expect to be overheard or spied upon here!" His broad gesture took in the primeval forest around them and the vast jungle spread like a green carpet below.

Ulfilo looked uncomfortable, then gave orders. "We rest here for an hour so all may catch their breath. Then we march."

The sailors cast themselves upon the ground and the bearers lowered their burdens. The last of the bearers had reached the plateau but a few weary sailors still straggled up from below.

"Conan, Wulfrede," Ulfilo said. "come aside with us." The two followed the three Aquilonians beneath the trees. Goma stayed where he was, staring off to the east, apparently lost in contemplation of something the rest of them could not see. In a quiet glade, the five took seats upon the ground. Springald took his satchel from his shoulder and opened it. He withdrew some books and papers and began.

"All my life I have been a scholar and a student of the great voyages of the past. Some years ago, while studying in the very strange and ancient library of the kings of Aquilonia in Tarantia, I came upon certain books concerning the explorations of mariners from the long-disappeared kingdom of Ashur. One of these had a most astonishing tale to relate: It seems that one Captain Belphormis, in the routine task of opening up a new trade route into the interior of the Black Coast, discovered numerous traces of a far more ancient civilization, one that disappeared many thousands of years ago. This was the empire of Acheron. Captain Belphormis discovered certain signs and sigils in the mountains east of here, insignia peculiar to Acheron and its gods."

"Acheron!" said Wulfrede. "It is a name from legend. But surely that land was far to the north of here, else the tales lie."

"So it did," Springald said. "I think I know as much of that ancient land as any scholar, and on some things all the stories agree: the Acheronians were close relative to the Stygians, they were rich beyond belief, and they were destroyed when the Hyborians, ancestors of ours who founded the lands of Aquilonia, Hyperboria, Nemedia, Brythunia, Koth, Argos, the Border Kingdom, and Corinthia. When after centuries the Hyorbians took the fabulous capital of Acheron, incomparable Python, the Acheronians fled in a mass to take refuge south of the Styx with their kinsmen of Stygia. They never retook their ancestral lands, and merged with the general population of Stygia.

"There grew up around this catastrophe whole cycles of tales concerning the final days of Python. Many of these are mere folktales, others are the sober accounts of officials and scholars. These agree on a signal fact: None knows what ever became of the wealth of the kings of Python."

"Royal wealth does not just disappear," said Wulfrede. "Did the king not take his treasury with him when he fled to Stygia?"

"I have read every account of those times I have been able to lay hands on," Springald said. "I think few can have escaped me. The last king to reign in Python was Ahmas the Twenty-seventh. Knowing that the long war drew to a close and that soon he must flee, he made arrangements to safeguard his treasure. He knew well that, while his royal relatives in Stygia might be only too willing to grant him asylum, he would not be among them long before his wealth drained into their own coffers."

"A wise man," Wulfrede said, nodding. "No man can be trusted, where great treasure is concerned."

"Even so," Springald said. "In the final days before the fall of Python, a great fleet sailed southward under cover of darkness. It was never heard from again from that day to this. It is believed by many historians that the fleet bore away the treasure of Python."

"And why did this King Ahmas not fetch his treasure back when he was safe?" Conan asked.

"He never had the chance," Springald said. "When the end came he was too slow to flee Python. He sent his family ahead, but undertook the defense of Python himself. Purple-towered

Python was defended street by street, and most of the city was destroyed thereby. In the final battle in the palace compound, despite the entreaties of his officers, Ahmas refused to desert his loyal guardsmen. He cast off his royal insignia so that the invaders would not try to take him prisoner and he died fighting as an ordinary trooper at the Ruby Gate of the palace enclosure.''

"That is how a king should die," pronounced Conan. Ulfilo nodded agreement.

"For a few generations his descendants lived at various courts of Stygia as pretenders. But when it became plain that the Hyborians would never be driven from the northern lands, the Stygians tired of supporting them and they lapsed into obscurity. None knows what became of the last of them.''

"And none of them knew where Ahmas had hidden his treasure?" Wulfrede asked.

"So it would seem. The fleet must have sailed under sealed orders and not a man of it returned. If Ahmas entrusted the location to an official or kinsman, that one must have died without passing it on." Wulfrede passed him a wineskin and the scholar took a drink, then continued with his tale.

"When I found the account of Captain Belphormis, I grew most excited. Clearly, the explorer did not know what he had come upon, and merely noted the signs as curiosities. Old books are very dusty and I repaired from the Royal Library to a nearby tavern to wash the dust from my throat.''

"And you took the books with you?" Conan asked.

"Ah, well, I was well-known in the library by that time, and the keepers no longer bothered to search my satchel upon leaving, and, after all, no one had touched these books for at least two hundred years, and it seemed a shame . . .''

Wulfrede laughed heartily. "Fear not, I'll not call you a thief, bookman. Go on.''

"Well, in the tavern I fell in with a young captain, a paid-off mercenary. The handsome young man seemed so gloomy, and I was so elated with my discovery, that I sat down to drink with him, and as the wine flowed I began to tell him of my findings. I learned that the young captain was Marandos, a younger son of an ancient noble house of Aquilonia. He was without employment or prospects, and like so many noble warriors he felt that mercenary work was beneath him in any case. On top of that he had . . ."—Springald glanced at Malia in some embarrassment—"a rather extravagant young wife."

"That is not true!" Malia said heatedly. "It was he that insisted upon dressing me in fine silks and giving me jewels I never demanded."

"However that may be," Wulfrede said, chuckling, "our young soldier was just the sort to find a treasure map intriguing, eh, Springald?"

"You are right. As we talked, and the wine flowed, he grew enthusiastic about going to look for the place described in such detail by Captain Belphormis. I confess that actually going in search of the treasure had not occurred to me. But then, I was a mere scholar and he was a professional adventurer. He was not in the least fazed by the thought of traveling great distances and enduring hardship in search of immense wealth, for he already did those things and got mere soldier's pay in return. What was the risk of mere pain and commonplace death, if in return one could gain the wealth of an ancient king?"

"That is understandable," Conan said. "But he went south with a ship and a crew. Surely he did not do these things on a paid-off captain's money."

"Nor did he," said Ulfilo. "He came to me, something he had not done in the years since he left home. My brother Marandos is a proud man, and would not come to me for aid unless it should promise great profit to us both. I was skeptical at first, but as Springald explained matters and showed me the many things he had found, it seemed to me not such a bad idea to risk some money on a venture of this nature."

"That was not all," Malia said. "Tell them the rest!"

Ulfilo looked uncomfortable, but he complied. "True, it was not simply a matter of helping a brother. The family had fallen upon hard times. The king of Aquilonia, Numedides, is not a friend of my family, and our lands have been eroded away over the years. Lately the harvests have been poor, and profitable wars few. This seemed a chance to recoup the family's fortunes."

"I urged that this was a fool's mission," Malia said, "but my words would not move my husband or his brother. This mad scheme came to obsess them, and they spoke incessantly of ships and men, of marches and maps."

"That was much trust to repose in a bookman who was unknown to you," Wulfrede said.

"From the first," Malia said, "Springald gave us surety of his earnestness."

"What had he to give as surety?" Conan asked. "Scholars rarely own broad lands, or fine houses or herds of livestock."

"I pledged the one poor possession I could call my own," Springald said. "I told them that, should Marandos not find all as predicted in my translations, then Ulfilo should have my head."

There was a pause. "You pledged your *head*?" Conan said with genuine wonderment.

"I'll own it seemed a passing strange item to pledge," Ulfilo said, "but a gentleman could scarcely doubt the sincerity of his oath."

Wulfrede laughed heartily. "You may all be mad, but at least you are madmen with real style!" His merriment was unforced. Indeed, the Van had been most cheerful ever since the subject of "treasure" was broached.

"Let us now hear of this letter Marandos sent you from Khemi," Conan said.

At these words the others seemed abashed.

"My brother," said Ulfilo, "did not reach the treasure on his first voyage. But before the remnants of his men forced him to turn back, he came within sight of its place of concealment. When he reached Khemi, he sought backing for another voyage. It time a

Stygian noble contacted him, a man named Sethmes. He agreed to supply a ship, a crew, and provision for another voyage.''

"I never knew a Stygian to be truly obliging where risk of money was concerned,'' said Wulfrede. "Your brother must have looked a ragged beggar when he got to Khemi. How did he persuade this Sethmes?''

"In the first place,'' said Ulfilo, "an Aquilonian nobleman's high birth is plain to another nobleman, albeit disguised in rags.''

Conan managed to keep a straight face while hearing his. He had known many ruined nobles in the mercenary armies of the world, and such men were rarely distinguished by anything save arrogance.

"But,'' Ulfilo continued, "he was able to show by certain signs that he was on the track of a great treasure, and by giving certain pledges to the man he secured the necessary resources for another voyage. During that time he sent the letter to us, urging us to follow him with a ship of our own, and good and trustworthy men, for the hardships and dangers to be overcome were formidable, but the rewards of success incalculable.''

"And what did the man pledge to this Sethmes?'' Wulfrede demanded.

"That is of no concern to you. It is between Sethmes and my family. Rest assured that your own reward will be abundant. Sethmes is in Stygia and need not concern us here.''

As to that, Conan had severe doubts. They were still holding much back. Getting information from these people was worse than breaking through the multiple doors, barriers, and traps of a royal treasury. But he was determined to discover the rest before they proceeded much further.

"Well, we have lounged here long enough,'' Ulfilo said. "I trust that, if you are now satisfied, we can proceed. We may put a league or two behind us before nightfall.''

"Aye, I am satisfied,'' said Wulfrede, "so long as there is treasure and I to have a part of it!''

Conan was not deceived by the Van's jovial tone. The man

was deeply suspicious but was content to let matters rest for the moment.

Goma grinned when the saw the foreigners return. "Are you ready now, oh white people, to see the world as Ngai created it?"

"Aye," said Conan, now eager to see a new land, whatever might befall. "Show us this wild country. I am keen to hear the wind in different trees."

Stolidly, the bearers shouldered their burdens. With Goma in the lead, they walked into the trackless wilds of an unknown land.

# EIGHT
## The Great Plain

The forest continued for many leagues, in some places relatively open and easy of traverse, in other places swampy and dense, but the general trend of the land was upward, and as they ascended the dense places grew fewer and farther apart. The wildlife was abundant, but it was primarily of the smaller species, and most of these were arboreal. There were an infinite variety of birds, monkeys, and cats. Malia exclaimed with delight over each new oddity until even this variety began to pall with sheer abundance.

There were many small forest deer and ground-dwelling fowl, so the travelers never lacked for fresh meat. The northerners refused to eat monkey, but the natives esteemed them a delicacy. Ranging ahead of the column, Conan plied bow and sling, leaving the carcasses hanging in trees for those behind to collect and clean.

Whatever the irregularities of his employment, Conan found the life very agreeable. He had been in civilized lands for too long. Always, he chafed under the strictures of city life, and none of those applied here. His natural savagery began to assert itself as he spent his days scouting the land ahead of the column. From Goma he got a sketchy description of what each day's march would be like, the land and obstacles to be traversed, and then he was on his own.

Too fine a woodsman to need a path, he could cover vast distances in a day, ranging far to both sides of the route as well as far ahead, always on the lookout for other humans, who in this land must always be considered hostile. But he found nothing save the remnants of old hunter's fires. In some spots he found neatly laid hearthstones forming a square. These he thought to be left by Marandos on one of his treks inland.

The insects did not swarm in this upland forest as in the lowland jungle, so by the third day Conan had discarded shirt and breeks, to move the more silently. Each morning, dressed only in loincloth and sandals, his sword and dirk belted to his waist, bow and arrows cased across his back, a native spear in his hand, he faded into the forest as silently as a ghost.

His companions seemed nonplussed to see the redoubtable Conan, already a hard-bitten warrior, thus transformed into a wild creature more primitive than the natives. The blacks were tribal folk who rarely went into the wild save in groups and pined when separated from their kin. Conan seemed to revel in the solitude of his new existence. Of the travelers, only Goma smiled at this metamorphosis, as if he knew something about the Cimmerian the others did not.

Conan did not notice their puzzlement, nor would he have cared greatly if he had. He felt as if he were coming alive for the first time in years. Life alone in the forest demanded the utmost alertness, and at every step he took, his senses were fully open. Knowledge of his surroundings poured in through his every faculty in a way that would have been impossible for his companions with their civilization-dulled senses. Each change of scent that came to his nostrils, each sound, every hint of movement, even the feel of the air upon his skin, told him of subtle alterations in his environment, of opportunities and possible dangers.

Civilized men learned to shut out all such sounds and smells and sensations in order to be able to concentrate more fully upon the tasks at hand, upon war or profit. Thus they rendered themselves three-quarters deaf and blind and senseless. Conan suppressed such faculties when he was among civilized men, but he never lost them. In a pause while stalking a woodland antelope he would track the flight of the birds overhead, smell an herb crushed by a passing hoof, and hear the slither of a serpent through the weeds ten paces away, all simultaneously without losing his concentration on the beast he hunted.

On the evening of the ninth day in the upland forest, Conan returned to camp, greeted by the savory smell of roasting meat. As always, the sentry jumped with fright at the Cimmerian's sudden appearance.

"By Set, Conan," said the sailor who had sentry duty, "can you not hail the camp from a little way off to let us know you are coming in? Half the bearers think you are some sort of woodland spirit disguised as a man, and I am not sure they're wrong."

"If you need a hail to stay alert, you fail in your duty," Conan answered. He found the Aquilonians seated around a fire, perusing one of Springald's maps. They looked up at his approach and he took an object from his belt-pouch and tossed it to Ulfilo. The man caught the thing and examined it by firelight. It was a small bronze buckle with a broken tongue.

"This is Zingaran work," the Aquilonian said.

"Aye," Conan answered. "Cast off when it was broken. I found it by the remains of a fire. It must have come from your brother's expedition, one of the times he passed this way."

"A native might have got it in trade," said Springald.

Conan shook his head. "A native would never have thrown away a good piece of metal. He'd have saved it to work into something else. All metal is precious here."

"Then we are still on course," Malia said. Surreptitiously,

she examined the Cimmerian by the flickering firelight. He seemed a creature entirely different from the rough-hewn adventurer they had encountered in Asgalun. This near-naked wild creature was more like one of the tawny, spotted cats she had glimpsed prowling near the camp. Massive as he was, the great muscles rolled and slid beneath his supple hide like those of a dancer, and his silent grace was akin to that of a great predator. Even the gaze of his lambent blue eyes now had the impersonal ferocity of a lion's.

"How much farther?" Springald asked. "These maps are exceedingly vague, and the written accounts are more concerned with incident than with specific detail as to distance. Here it says: 'That week we visited diverse villages and traded for ivory at a profitable rate.' But whether they traveled two leagues or a hundred in that week, whether they visited four villages or twenty, they do not say."

"Goma says that tomorrow we will come to the end of the forest," Conan said. "After that, a long stretch of savannah before we reach the desert. We still have a long way to go, and a great train of men like this travels at the speed of the slowest bearer."

"Let us hope it is not too much farther," Malia said. "The sailors grow restive. They mutter that they did not ship for an endless march."

"Say they so?" Conan said. "Would it be all of them, or just the one called Umu?"

"He is the ringleader, no doubt of that," Springald said. "I do not understand why Wulfrede does not curb the insolent dog."

"I have wondered that myself," Conan said. "But I'll not have an unreliable man behind my back in country like this. If Wulfrede will not see to this matter, then I must." He jammed his spear into the ground by its butt-spike and slid his cased bow and arrows over his head and laid them upon the ground.

"What will you do?" Malia asked apprehensively.

"I will have a few words with the sailors," said Conan. He

walked casually to the long fire at which the sailors lounged, talking among themselves in low voices. Umu sneered in his direction, saying something inaudible that brought a laugh from his sycophants. Wulfrede looked on with cool amusement.

"Greetings, brothers," Conan said. "Are all well content here?" He did not look directly at Umu. The others avoided his gaze and said nothing.

"Behold!" brayed Umu. "The naked savage deigns to speak to us! By Ishtar but this Cimmerian mountain goat has grown more a savage than the black dogs of the coast."

"You do not keep good order among your men, Wulfrede," said Conan.

Umu stood, grinning evilly. "At sea our captain's word is law, but not on land. That is the sailor's custom. And why should we owe you any respect at all, Cimmerian? You are a barbarian without land or kin. And you are a landsman, for what sailor can live in the woods like a beast?" He looked to the other sailors for support, but most of them kept silent counsel. Conan knew what he meant: they had worked and fought beside him, but this was a test of supremacy, and they would back whoever won, at least until another challenger should arise.

"And you," Conan said, "are a troublemaking ape who whispers behind my back to rouse these my comrades to treachery."

Umu's ugly face turned crimson. "I challenge you to your face this time, Cimmerian!"

"And about time," said Conan. "A stupid swine like you has no business trying to talk like a man anyway."

With an inarticulate cry Umu drew his long, heavy knife, the firelight glinting from its serpentine blade. Conan's sword was out as swiftly and the two blades flickered together so quickly that to the onlookers they were nothing but a blur. The bearers chattered excitedly and the sailors growled encouragement. All seemed pleased with this rare sport except for the Aquilonians.

"Can you not stop them, Captain?" Malia cried.

"Why should I want to do that?" Wulfrede demanded.

"When men thirst for each other's blood it is best to let them settle it."

Conan's sword was longer and somewhat lighter than Umu's knife, but the seaman's great length of arm made up for the slight disadvantage. He was also immensely strong and amazingly quick for a man so bulky. Neither man fought with great craft or fencer's learned skill. It was strength, speed, and endurance, and the two were well matched. In the end, it was balance, steel-trap reflexes, and endurance that tipped the balance in the Cimmerian's favor, especially the latter. Umu began to puff and wheeze, unused to this sort of exertion. Conan's breathing was even, his limbs working smoothly and without slowing or trembling despite the great effort demanded of them. In time Umu's blade began to wobble from its formerly lethal paths and Conan's darted under it to skewer him through the body. Conan jerked the blade free and thrust it again, this time beneath Umu's chin. The point pierced tongue, palate, and brain, and the man toppled stiffly, like a falling tree.

Conan stood looking at the sailors, blood dripping from his sword. His body shone with sweat but his breath was still steady.

"Does any wish to take up Umu's fight?" he asked.

A sailor spat on the corpse. "He was no friend of mine."

"Aye," said another. "I was cheering for you the whole time, Conan!" Others hastened to protest their loyalty to the Cimmerian.

"Good," he said. "We are all friends again. And there will be no more grumbling about your sore feet. When we return, you will all be so rich you will never have to walk again. Now drag this carrion out of here. Leave it in the bush somewhere a safe distance away. It will be gone by morning."

He strolled back to the other fire, cleaning his blade with a handful of grass. Ulfilo came up and clapped him on the shoulder, an uncharacteristically comradely gesture from the stiff nobleman.

"Superb fight, Conan," said Ulfilo.

"Aye!" said Springald excitedly. "Those rogues will be obedient now!"

"So they shall," said Conan. "Until next time. What's for dinner?"

The next day Conan came to the end of the trees. They did not thin out gradually, but stopped as abruptly as the border of an orchard. The trees grew up to the crest of a ridge line. The other side of the ridge bore nothing but long grass, and the land sloped gently away all the long distance to the horizon. The change in terrain was dramatic and total. The land was covered with long grass, and the few trees were not the vine-draped giants of the forest but for the most part low, spreading trees with oddly flat tops. There was bush, but it was not spread evenly, as it was on the forest floor. Rather, it grew in dense clumps that studded the plain infrequently, nowhere closer together than several hundred yards. But it was not the vegetation that drew the Cimmerian's enraptured attention. He stood leaning on his spear until, an hour later, Goma led the Aquilonians and the shipmaster to the crest of the ridge. For a few moments they stood gawking in silence. Malia was the first to break it.

"Mitra! Am I dreaming? This cannot be real!"

"It is real," Springald said with near-ecstasy in his voice. "I have heard many traveler's descriptions of this, but never did I think it could be so magnificent!"

What they looked upon was easily twenty thousand head of wild game. The vast herds began no more than a hundred paces away, where a few hundred spiral-horned antelope placidly cropped the grass, and the vista stretched all the way to the horizon, where the beasts looked tinier than the smallest ants.

As surprising as the sheer number of creatures was their tremendous variety. Unlike the west and north, where herd animals were all of a kind, here herds of many sorts mixed together in apparent amity. There were many varieties of antelope, from small, delicate impala with lyre-shaped horns to massive topi the size of warhorses. There were many others they had no names for, although Goma could supply the native names. Wandering among them like tall, stately trees were towering giraffes in small, family herds. Massive black buffalo with curling horns rooted around with their noses in the muddy spots while birds perched nonchalantly on their backs, picking vermin from the glossy hides.

There were several varieties of wild horse, with the dazzlingly striped zebras predominating. Others had brown foreparts and striped rumps. There were dwarf, spotted horses no bigger than mastiffs disputing passage with grotesquely snouted warthogs, and rival bands of baboons pelted on another with sticks and pebbles. Dominating them all, gigantic elephants moved placidly among them, like great boulders set in motion. Some of the old males were so massively tusked that they had to carry their heads higher than the others to keep their ivory from scraping the ground.

"So many!" Malia said. "And yet it is so quiet! It is like a great temple!" Unlike the animals of the forest, those of the plain rarely vented forth their cries and trumpets and bellows. Except for the occasional screech of an angered baboon or the call of a bird, the whole vast assemblace generated less noise than a small crowd of men in a town square.

"So many plant-eating beasts!" Ulfilo said. "Where are the predators?"

"The big cats are the great meat-eaters here," Goma said. "But most of them hunt in the early morning or just after dusk, some of them in the night. In the afternoon, you may see the cheetah, swift as lightning, chasing down his prey. But in the daytime, most of the beasts are safe to eat and drink."

By this time the rest of the column had caught up with them. The sailors exclaimed in astonishment at the amazing vista. They were mariners, accustomed to wide horizons, but not so crowded. The blacks murmured unhappily. They were jungle folk, accustomed to the closenesses and shadows of the forest. They did not like these open, exposed vastnesses populated with innumerable animals.

"Are those mountains far in the distance?" Wulfrede asked,

pointing to the eastern horizon, where a dim, blue-gray line stood just above the horizon. "By Ymir, but there are no landmarks to navigate by upon this ocean of grass!"

"Fear not, white man," said Goma. "I will guide you across this and stranger places." He favored them with another of his superior smiles. "And have no fear of the beasts, for I will protect you with my axe." He twirled the weapon around his head for effect, so swiftly that the shiny head formed a glittering circle.

Goma led off and the others followed. Wulfrede grumbled as he walked: "If we did not need that brown rogue to guide us, I would slay him on the spot of his insolence!"

"But we do need him so leave him be," Ulfilo said.

"He is a strange creature," said Malia, "unlike any of the other native folk we have encountered. And I do not speak of his color or his markings. He is a savage whose only garment is a wrapping of cloth and his only possession an axe, but his bearing is as proud as yours, brother-in-law. Prouder, even."

"It is damned impertinence," Ulfilo said, "but I suppose in his primitive way, he considers himself well born."

Springald went to speak to with the leaders, his short legs pumping to keep up with the long-striding Goma and Conan.

"Tell me, Goma," said the scholar, "what people may we think to encounter upon this plain? Indeed, it seems hard to envision humans living upon this sea of grass with its abundance of wild beasts." Even as he spoke, a family of giraffes sauntered by them, paying the tiny humans no heed. This was of a variety they had not yet seen; cream-colored and dotted all over with small spots. Unlike the short, knob-ended horns of the others, these had wide-spreading, palmate horns like those of some mighty elk.

"The Fashoda often graze their cattle upon this grass," Goma said. "They are great fighters and love to raid one another for cattle. They count their wealth only in cattle, and their god is a cattle god. They are excellent spearmen, but they have no good dances. Sometimes you will encounter the Zumba, the folk of the great shield and the short spear. They are very dark, and are hardy warriors as well. They farm the land and raise many goats. Their villages are small and mean, but they wear fine decorations, and their songs and dances are splendid.''

''Might they prove hostile to us?'' Springald asked.

''Every man's hand is against the stranger here, but if you are strong and wish to trade, they will let you pass.''

''Are they man-eaters?'' Conan asked.

Goma hawked and spat in disgust. ''No! That is an abomination everywhere except the coast. Here under the great sky in Ngai's land, men are men, not scavenging beasts!'' He pointed to a pack of skulking, spotted hyenas. ''The people of the coast are like those, beneath contempt. The men of the plains are like the lion, fierce and proud.''

''That is comforting to know,'' Springald said. 'Whereas we may be killed, at least we will not be eaten.''

''Not so,'' said Goma, grinning.

''What mean you?'' demanded Springald.

''It is true that you will not be eaten by men. But you will be eaten, like the man Conan slew yesterday. Here the bodies of the dead are not wasted by burying or burning. They are left in the bush to go back to Ngai, as food for Ngai's beasts. Beasts eat grass, men eat beasts, other beasts eat men. This is what pleases Ngai.''

''How comforting,'' Springald said.

As they marched across the endless plain, they saw much to marvel at. Comical ostriches sped before them. The birds had long, powerful legs, globular bodies, long necks, and tiny heads. Here and there columns of brown earth, hard as cement, spiked the plain like stalagmites. Malia pointed to these enigmatic objects, asking what they might be.

''Termite hills,'' Conan said. ''They are ravenous things. Plant a pole in the ground as thick as a man's thigh, and you may come back in a week and push it over with you hand. The part beneath the ground will be chewed to soft pulp.''

''This is a strange land,'' Malia said. ''It is like a land of dream. Here birds are the size of ponies and termites build castles. And look there, a monster from a nightmare crops grass by a deer so tiny I would not have believed it had someone described it to me.'' She pointed to where a huge rhinoceros, its longer nose horn a four-foot scythe, chewed on a bush beneath which grazed fearlessly a spike-horned antelope no larger than a hare, its reedlike legs terminating in hoofs smaller than a woman's smallest fingertip.

"There are many stranger things to be seen in land like this," Conan promised them. "And many things more terrible."

In the late afternoon they passed a pride of lions. The big, lazy cats lay upon the ground, yawning and scratching, gazing at the newcomers with fierce yellow eyes but uninterested in them. In time the cats rose and stalked away, not from fear but, apparently, because they found the smell of the humans disagreeable.

"Be careful where you step," Conan warned them, "especially after dark." He stooped and picked up a twig. It was studded with lethal-looking thorns six inches long. "All the trees and bushes hereabout are thorned like this. These will go through a bootsole if you come down on one squarely."

"The land itself is fierce," said Springald. "And everything in it is hostile to the stranger."

That night they built their fires on the plain, and under Goma's instruction they dragged thorny bushes together to form a protective circle, which he called a *boma*.

"Will it keep the lions out?" Wulfrede asked.

"It will keep out a sick or wounded lion," Goma answered. "That is the only kind likely to attack a man. A man is too small to make a meal for a grown lion, much less a pride of them. But one too disabled to hunt the fast runner or the strong beasts may become desperate enough to eat men. And the boma will keep out the hyenas."

"Those cowardly scavengers?" Wulfrede snorted. "A handful of rocks sends them running."

"In the daytime they are cowards," Goma said, "but at night they gain courage. They may run in and seize the arm or leg of a sleeping man. Their jaws are more powerful even than those of a lion, and they can take a leg off with a single bite.''

"A land-going shark, eh?'' Wulfrede said. "I will take your word for it.''

The night, and those after, were noisier than the days. The roars of the hunters and the cries of the hunted split the darkness with terrifying suddenness, bringing bleary-eyed men from their sleep to their feet, snatching at their weapons. In time they learned that these noises signified danger to other creatures, not to themselves, and they snored through them. Elephants sometimes walked up to the boma and peered curiously within, but they quickly lost interest and moved on.

The great abundance of game meant that there was plenty of meat, so much that soon Malia was complaining at the monotony of the diet.

"Roast antelope again?'' she cried on the evening of their tenth day on the plain.

"Not the same sort,'' Springald assured her. "This one had curly horns, unlike the others we have been eating.''

"Roast meat!'' she said plaintively. "How I long for bread and fruit. Even a dish of lentils would break the sameness.''

"You may as well wish for some wine and ale while you're at it,'' Wulfrede said. "Water is fine to sail upon, but I weary of it as a drink.''

"Just be glad that we have water,'' Conan said. "Albeit muddy and murky.''

Malia made a wry face. "What these herds of animals do to a water hole is something no gently bred lady should have to face, much less drink.'' Despite her words, the noblewoman seemed to thrive upon the life. Her step was springier and she was in all ways more assertive than when Conan had first encountered her in Asgalun. Despite her complaints, neither the food nor the water had damaged her health. On the contrary, she was stronger than ever and in the evenings seemed less tired than the men after a long day's march.

Before them the mountains loomed ever higher. They had

seemed at first but low hills, but then each day's journey seemed to bring them no closer. Eventually, their true size had become apparent. the entire crest of the range was crusted with the white of snow, revealing them to be far higher than the men would have guessed.

"Where do we get across?" Conan asked their guide.

"See you that notch?" Goma said, pointing.

"I see it," Conan said.

"We will fare thither. It is a long, hard climb, but that is a pass that will take us across the mountains."

"I see nothing that looks like the Horns of Shushtu," said Springald, wiping sweat from his brow.

"You will be able to see the Horns from the far end of that pass," promised Goma.

"Then we are getting near," Malia said.

"You just walked all the way across this plain," Conan said, "and you still think 'in sight' means 'near'?"

"It is another journey from the pass to the Horns," Goma said, "and a harder one."

"The desert?" asked Wulfrede.

"The desert," Goma concurred. They continued toward the mountains. Before they reached them, they met the first humans they had seen since climbing the escarpment.

What they saw first were not men but cattle. The beasts were rangy, long-horned creatures, colored in every hue sported by the bovine breed. There were solids as well as patched and mottled hides. In the distance, the men were barely visible, although the sun shone from spearpoints and flashed from elliptical white shields.

"What think you, Conan?" Ulfilo asked as the herdsmen caught sight of them and began trotting toward the column of strangers.

"I think they must be good warriors to keep cattle in country as wild as this. The threat of predators must be constant, and Goma says they are cattle-raiders like my own folk. That is a life to keep a man alert and handy with his weapons."

At Wulfrede's command the sailors assembled and stood on guard while the bearers piled their burdens and stood apprehensively. There were no longer as many bearers as when they had begun. Some had turned for home when the supplies they carried were consumed or used up, others when they had fallen sick or were injured, thorns being the most common cause of injury. Two had died of snake bite. One had wandered outside the boma at night and had not returned. He was presumed eaten. Another had simply dropped dead of no cause anyone could fathom. About forty remained.

"Are these the Fashoda?" Conan asked Goma.

"Aye. You will see that those that approach are all young men. Among the Fashoda the boys actually herd the cattle. The youths guard them. The older warriors guard the villages."

Conan grunted. "Young warriors are always the prime troublemakers. I hope these are not the truculent sort."

"Are they likely to be, Goma?" Springald asked, fingering the basket-hilt of his sword.

"You never know until something happens," said their guide.

Soon a line of a hundred young warriors stood before them. They were stone-faced, holding spears with exceptionally long and broad heads. They wore much paint, laid on in bizarre and imaginative designs. Their hair was grown long and bound tightly back from their faces except for a fringe across their foreheads. They were fine-featured and as lithe as panthers and they wore nothing besides their feathers, paints, and ornaments.

"These are handsome fellows," Malia said admiringly.

"For savages," Ulfilo grumbled.

"They are so much alike they might as well all be brothers," Springald pointed out. "The same features, the same color where you can see it, all built the same and not two inches difference in height between the tallest and the shortest. This is the sign of close breeding. They must never marry outside the tribe."

"Their customs are not our main concern just now," Wulfrede said. "Are they hostile or not?" The sailors fingered their weapons nervously, some of them fitting arrows to string.

"Let us have no fighting if it can be avoided!" Ulfilo barked. "Remember, we must come back this way when we return. Even if we can fight our way through here, they will be here waiting for us in strength when we come back."

"Aye," Conan said. "These are cattlemen, proud but unlikely to attack if we do not threaten them or their herds. On the other hand they are young warriors whose judgment may be limited. They will react to the slightest provocation. so do not provide it."

"You are diplomatic for a barbarian, Conan," Malia commented.

"I was a young warrior once, myself. I know how they think and act. The Cimmerian mountains or the southern plains, they are much alike when it comes to that." Conan spent this time sizing the warriors up. He was impressed by their impassivity. They did none of the dancing, whooping, and posturing favored by other tribes as preliminaries to battle. He knew that this was undoubtedly their chosen method of intimidating a possible foe, but he also knew that it meant they had a strong sense of discipline. If the young warriors were schooled early in the importance of maintaining this demeanor, they were far less likely to give way to hysteria and begin slaying without reason. He saw that many wore headdresses of lion skin and necklaces of the animal's teeth were popular trophies, displaying that these warriors were valiant in guarding the tribe's herds against the marauding cats.

One of the warriors spoke. He wore nothing they saw to distinguish him from the others. Goma translated his words.

'He wants to know who you are and what you want."

"Tell him," Ulfilo said, "that we are traders, bound for the mountains. Assure them that we mean them no harm, and that we have goods to trade, and presents for their chiefs." Goma translated. The warriors absorbed this message and said nothing more. Soon another, larger group arrived. These were mainly older warriors. They looked much like the younger ones, but they wore less paint and many of them wore cloth wraps like Goma's. Along with these were a number of unarmed men with graying hair who strode along amid massive dignity, carrying

long, intricately carved walking sticks. These were without paint
or ornament, and they were swathed in more voluminous wraps
than the others.

"The higher the rank," Springald observed, "the fewer the
ornaments."

"And the greater the clothing," said Malia.

"The warriors are allowed much vanity," Goma told them,
"and no cattle. These elders are the men who own all the cattle.
Their wealth and their honor is in their herds."

With the arrival of the chiefs, negotiations began. Bales were
opened and wares examined. Now the warriors mingled freely
with the newcomers. Toward the leaders and the sailors they
were courteous, but they treated the bearers with utter contempt.
To the warrior-herdsmen, men who carried loads for others were
nothing but beasts of burden.

"My bearers may not be mistreated," Ulfilo insisted, through
Goma.

An elder shrugged. "Would we abuse another man's cattle? They
are nothing to us. Just do not expect us to treat them as men."

The Fashoda were most interested in the iron bars, of which
the expedition still had a good supply. They also wanted cloth,
beads, and wire of copper and brass. The warriors poked at a
small box of fishhooks and asked what they might be. When the
hooks were explained to them, they laughed heartily. Fish, it
turned out, were an abomination to them and were never eaten.

Jugs of weak beer were brought out from the nearby village
and the chiefs and traders sat down to bargain. The elders were
somewhat embarrassed because they were not in the habit of
amassing trade goods like the lowland people, but they truly
wanted what the whites had to trade, especially the iron.

"These last years have been good," explained a seam-faced
old man. "The grass has been high, there has been little sick-
ness among men or cattle, and we have repelled all attacks. We
have a great many boys clamoring to be initiated as warriors,
and we must have spears for them all."

"How shall we settle this?" Wulfrede asked the others. "We

do not need cattle. but they have seen our goods and they may decide to take them by force if they cannot get them by trade.''

"We are treasure hunters, not traders,'' Conan pointed out. "What we do here is buy good will for our return journey. Tell them to take what they want. Then they can gather hides and ivory, which we will collect when we come back this way.''

"Excellent!'' Ulfilo said. "Goma, tell them our decision.''

The chiefs were greatly pleased at this face-saving solution, for the young warriors were by this time all but salivating at the sight of so much iron and copper and brass. Women, too, had come from the village and now they exclaimed happily over the abundance of multicolored beads.

"This could have turned out badly,'' Ulfilo said that evening as they drank beer from wooden bowls and ate roasted wildfowl. "But all is for the best, clearing our way before us and securing our line of return.''

"But we must find out whether these people saw Marandos. Surely he must have come this way,'' Malia said. To her delight, women had brought out milk, fruit, and flat bread cakes from the village. The change in diet pleased her greatly, but now she was worried about her husband again.

"The plain is broad,'' Goma said, "and a band like ours could easily go from the escarpment to the pass without coming near this place, but I will ask.'' For a few minutes the guide conversed with the chiefs, then he turned to Malia.

"They say that until six moons ago they dwelled in pastures far to the north of here. These people never stay in one place for long. But they say that a village about three days from here claims to have seen men like ghosts some time back. There may have been a fight, but they are not sure.''

"That is little to go on,'' said Ulfilo, disappointedly.

"It will have to do,'' Conan said.

# NINE

## The Mountain Pass

The trek to the base of the mountains went easily, for now they had an escort of the Fashoda, young warriors who regarded this duty as a sort of holiday from the drudgery of guarding the village's cattle. But nature had a most surprising delay in store for them.

It began with the appearance of a strange beast. The whites laughed when they saw it; a lone male at the head of a straggling line of its kin. The Fashoda pointed at it with their spears and chattered excitedly.

"What is it?" Ulfilo demanded.

"The warriors say we must stop," Goma translated. "For the *K'hnu* is here." The first sound in the word was a click unlike anything in any northern language.

"Stop?" said Ulfilo, mystified. "For *that* thing?" Indeed, the creature, which was now near and regarding them with profoundly stupid eyes, looked more comical than forbidding. About the size of one of the larger antelopes, it had the head, beard, and horns of a goat but the rest of it seemed to be pieces of several animals coupled together.

"Aye," Goma told them. "We may as well rest here anon. It is said that, when Ngai created the world, he had some spare parts left over, and from these he created the K'hnu: the head of a goat, the forepart of a topi, the hinder parts of a wild horse, and the wits of an ostrich. But to make up for their lack of all things handsome or wise, Ngai gifted them with one great ability, which you shall perceive shortly. Set up camp, white men, we go no farther this day."

Grumbling and mystified, they did as he advised. Within the hour, the straggling column was a great skein, thousands of animals heading north. Before sunset, the plain was carpeted with them, as far as the eye could perceive. And they were truly witless creatures, as Goma had intimated. Some would turn and head back south for no reason. Others compromised, standing in one spot and bucking up and down. Yet others ran in tight little circles until they collapsed from exhaustion.

The travelers killed a few for meat, but the companions of the luckless beasts took no slightest notice, continuing their migration northward.

"There cannot be so many beasts in all the world!" said Malia, her mind reeling at the sight.

"And yet," said Springald, "Goma tells me that this is not the only such herd. There are hundreds of them, and each year they migrate from south to north, then back again with the changing of the rainy and dry seasons."

"It is a good thing we travel afoot, not mounted," said Ulfilo. "For I'll wager horses would starve where such a herd has passed."

Conan stood near the edge of the vast herd and watched it pass. Soon he was joined by Goma. The two watched the great migration for a while, then the native spoke.

"You find this a fine sight, swordsman?"

"Aye. All my life I have been a wanderer, ever tiring of the place where I was and longing to see new things. Up north I was a-wearied of the kingdoms and their endless wars and even more tired of them when they were at peace. When the three mad ones approached me with their fool's mission they promised me great reward, but in truth I accepted not for that, but rather to see new places and new things. This"—he gestured toward the expanse of milling beasts—"is such a thing as I have never seen before. The whole plain with its great variety of beasts is another. Years ago I saw its fringes, but I did not find my way into the true interior. However things fall out, I'll not regret the journey."

Goma grinned. "That is ever the way of the adventurer. I alone of my own folk am a wanderer, and I have visited many lands and seen many sights strange to the eyes of my people, things I am glad I have seen, terrible though some of them were. But, in time, a man must return home, not so?"

"That may be," Conan said. "I have visited my own homeland since I left as a boy, but I have never stayed long. Is that what you do, Goma? Do you now return home?" He gave the tall warrior an appraising look, but got only another grin in return.

"As you say, white man, that may be."

The migration held them up for two days. The animals kept passing so endlessly that they began to suspect that the creatures were circling around them and going by over and over again. But in the end the herd became small enough that they could actually see across it, then it tapered rapidly until there was only a staggering remnant of the old, the sick, and the weak. These unfortunate beasts were perishing on their feet as the animals ahead of them devoured every scrap of grass. When the travelers set out once more it was across a plain cropped as close as it might have been by a palace gardener. It was also abundantly carpeted with dung, which would promote the next season's grass. Jackals, hyenas, vultures, and other carrion-eaters swarmed over the plain to feast upon the abundance of carcasses.

Before the mountains, though, they encountered yet another

native people. These were somewhat shorter than the Fashoda, but of a sturdier, more muscular build. Their skins were glossy and so dark as to approach true blackness, unadorned by paint. Their body-covering shields were made of cowhide with the hair left on, and the men wore short kilts of animal pelt. Bands of luxuriant monkey fur decorated their arms above the biceps and their legs below the knee.

These redoubtable warriors streamed out from a village of circular huts and formed a double line with shields almost touching.

Ulfilo sighed. "Must we do this again?"

"So it would seem," said Springald.

"Then break out the presents. Goma, what are they saying?" A grizzled warrior with a stubby chin-beard was speaking to the leader of the Fashoda escort.

"The Zumba captain says: 'Do you come to steal our cattle, our women, and our goats?' The Fashoda answers: 'Your cattle are skinny, your women are ugly, and no true warrior has anything to do with goats. We escort these white people safely to the mountains.' "

The captain now looked toward the strangers, triple ostrich plumes nodding above his head as it turned. Goma spoke.

"The captain says: 'More white people?'"

Malia gripped Ulfilo's arm. "They have seen Marandos!"

"Be ready," said Conan. "There may have been fighting between them."

But the Zumba did not seem threatening. They were more apprehensive of the Fashoda than of the pale foreigners. After a bit of palavering, a trading session was agreed to and the by now customary negotiations began. The Zumba farmed and thus were able to present a greater variety of foodstuffs to their guests. As Goma had indicated, they were far more musically inclined than their neighbors, and their complex, harmonic songs filled the evening air, interspersed with frenetic dances to the accompaniment of drum and flute. The Fashoda looked on aloof, leaning on their spears.

In the midst of the celebration, a bizarre figure appeared. At his arrival the singing tapered off to a ragged silence, the dancing slowed, then stopped and the last drum was silenced in mid-beat. He was a small man, draped all over with strings of bones, claws, feathers, and carved fetishes. He carried a staff that rattled with similar adornments. His face was painted white, with the eye pits left unpainted to give his face the aspect of a skull. The Zumba drew aside at his approach and he leveled his staff at the newcomers.

"You go across the mountains!" he said in the trade language they understood. "Only death awaits you there! Beyond is the sacred place of the gods of the land. You must not go there! I forbid the Zumba to go with you!"

"Who is this?" Ulfilo demanded.

Goma questioned the chiefs and supplied the answer. "This is Umbaso, the head witch doctor of all the Zumba tribes. He lives far from here. I do not know how he knew that we would be here."

"Has he the power to forbid these people to supply us with bearers?" Ulfilo asked.

"We shall know soon," said Goma. The shaman began to harangue the people, and their expressions changed from mere apprehension to outright fear.

"Surely these people do not have wizards of true power," Springald scoffed. "After all, they have no books. How can sorcerous knowledge be compiled, stored, and passed on by people who have not the craft of letters?"

"So long as they fear his curse," Conan said disgustedly, "that will prove sufficient. They care not if he can summon great demons or perform high magic. If they believe he can strike them blind or lame or make their parts wither and fall off, that is power enough for them."

One of the chiefs spoke rapidly to Goma, who translated: "He says that by no means can he give us men to carry our burdens, so long as Umbaso forbids it. They will not molest or hinder us, but we go on only at our peril and by ourselves."

Ulfilo glowered ominously at the shaman, gripping his hilt. "I would greatly enjoy hewing this filthy mountebank down."

"As would I," Conan said. "But I cannot advise it. We may have to go from here more lightly equipped. What of it, Goma? Will this make the balance of our journey unfeasible?"

Goma shrugged his broad shoulders. "True men can endure anything. Those who cannot make their way in the world without their comforts should not start on ventures that call for a warrior's heart."

"I believe we have just been challenged," Springald said.

"I for one need no servants to look after me on campaign," Ulfilo said, stung. "And I can bear hardship as well as any man."

"And what of the woman?" said Wulfrede.

"Have I complained thus far?" Malia said haughtily.

"Yes," Conan said. "But mainly about the insects, I'll own. Wulfrede, what of the sailors?"

"They will obey me," the shipmaster asserted. Conan had his doubts. If the piratical crew were willing to face such conditions, it could only mean that Wulfrede had revealed to them something of the treasure, and that was bad.

"We go on to the mountains," Conan said to the leader of the Fashoda escort. "Will you go with us now?"

"We do not fear this Zumba wizard or his curses," the man said. But the Cimmerian could detect his unease. The other warriors cast sidelong glances at the shaman, unwilling to show open fear of a mere Zumba, but frightened nonetheless.

Conan rose and went to confront Umbaso. "Why do you seek to hinder us from crossing the mountains?" he demanded.

The wizard smiled slyly. "I did not say you could not go. What care I what happens to strangers? The gods of that place do not need me to protect them. They will make you suffer as they will." His eyes glowed weirdly in their dark pits. "But I would not have my own folk offend them."

"Why are the gods of the mountain and of the land beyond

different from those of the plain, who do not resent us?" Conan asked.

"The powers there are not of this land, nor of its people." He rattled his staff and recited his words in a near-chant. "Long, long ago came the men and the half-men to this land, and they passed through the mountains and went beyond. They brought with them a new god, a jealous god who tolerates no others. When the men and half-men died, they were transformed into spirits to guard the land of the new god. If you meet them, they will slay you and eat your souls." Again he smiled. "But who am I to deny them their sacrifice?"

"And yet white men like us came hither, and passed beyond. And some returned, and came back yet again. That does not sound like the action of men who feared gods and spirits."

The smile became a crooked leer. "Aye, white men went thither, and a very few came back, and they were not as they had been. And now they have lured more of their fellows to the forbidden lands. Perhaps the spirits savored the taste of these souls, and crave more."

"And what is the name of this foreign god?" Conan asked.

"It is called Ma'at," said Umbaso. When he pronounced the word, the Aquilonians shifted nervously.

Conan did not like the air of wizardry, and he did not like the talk of gods and spirits and the eating of souls. But he had a powerful urge to see what lay beyond the mountains. When he had a chance, he took Springald a little aside from the others.

"The wizard called this god Ma'at. Have you heard of such a god?" Conan asked.

"Ah . . . well, yes. Ma'at is a god of Stygia, and is regarded as one of the most ancient of that land of many gods. Unlike other gods, Ma'at has no form. It is never depicted as human or animal, and is the least defined of gods. In the oldest of texts, Ma'at is said to be a judge of the dead, determining the fate of each individual. If Ma'at was pleased with the deceased, he was allowed an afterlife much like that he had enjoyed on earth, but without its sufferings and fatigues."

"And if Ma'at was not pleased?" Conan asked.

"Well, the souls of the unworthy were fed to a monster called the Devourer of Souls." He cleared his throat. "Still, one must not allow oneself to be upset by the words of an unwashed, bone-bedecked savage medicine man. What knows he beyond crude tribal superstitions and a few spells of petty power? All this may be a folktale passed around by the local natives. After all, these people are seminomadic and undoubtedly dwelled far away when Python fell." He sounded as if he spoke to reassure himself.

"Perhaps that is so," Conan said. "But this has become something other than the simple manhunt and treasure hunt it was when we began. I'll not tolerate more surprises, bookman!"

"I quite understand your indignation, my friend, and I assure you that you need have no apprehension of unpleasant revelations! Why, the very concept that an ancient and rather ill-defined pre-Stygian deity could still be guarding the treasure, not to mention its minions, who began their vigil already handicapped by the disadvantage of being dead, is absurd by all standards of knowledge and scholarship, both of the natural and the supernatural worlds!"

"Springald," Conan said ominously, "if I did not like you, I think I could kill you just for being so long-winded."

When the next morning's trek began, all were subdued except for the lowland bearers, who knew that soon they would be released to return to their homes. The others wore looks that were downcast to varying degrees, except for the always cheerful Wulfrede. Conan looked merely grim, the Aquilonians anxious. Most sullen of all were the sailors. Once again, they were scowling and muttering among themselves. Conan wondered whether another salutary killing would become necessary.

Two days later, they stood at the foot of the mountain. The great, rocky spine loomed far above them. Its lower slopes were densely carpeted with greenery, its upper reaches a forbidding series of bare crags. The bearers dug a pit in which to cache such goods as could not be carried farther. That accomplished, they turned their steps toward home, escorted by the Fashoda, who had agreed, reluctantly, to accompany the lowlanders to the edge of their territory.

Now the much reduced group eyed the mountain with grim determination.

"We accomplish nothing here," Ulfilo said. "Let us go."

"Aye," Wulfrede said. "For what need have men such as we for tents and suchlike fripperies? We wear our weapons as always, and we can carry such necessities as are called for on a venture of this sort. All else we shall find along the way." His men seemed to have no such optimistic confidence, but his glare of warning silenced any opposition.

"Lead on, Goma," Conan said.

Their guide grinned. "That I shall. Bid farewell to the easy days, for here begins a man's work." With that he led them up the slope.

The change from grassy plain to forested mountains was sudden and dramatic. The trees were not giants such as they had encountered in the lowlands, but they grew thickly and were of many strange varieties. The animals were likewise of smaller sorts; monkeys, apes, small deer, and many types of wild pig. Along with these were the expected predators to eat them. Clouded, spotted, and striped cats prowled the shadows, and great serpents glided through the leaf mold and across the branches.

Their path followed an ancient watercourse, and ascending its rocky length from boulder to boulder was not unlike climbing a titanic stairway. Before they had made an hour's progress, their legs were screaming with fatigue and Ulfilo had to order a halt.

"Is there no better way?" he demanded of Goma.

"This is not a route commonly traveled," the guide assured him. "Not even by animals. Such few men as have passed this way have left few traces. But is it not known by any wanderer that water takes the easiest path across any land?"

"That is true much of the time," Springald gasped, his thighs trembling from the effort. "But such a path, while the most direct, is not always the most efficacious for the human frame."

"And yet this is the way we must go," Goma said. "For there is no other upon the first half of this slope. Under the trees the ground is as steep, and the footing treacherous as well. Men would slip and be injured. And there are many venomous serpents there."

"We engaged him because he knows the way, Ulfilo," said Malia. "He has not guided us wrong thus far." In deference to her sex and rank, Malia bore the lightest load, and she was not as fatigued as the others. Even so, she displayed numerous scrapes and bruises from the heavy going.

"What think you, Conan?" Ulfilo asked. Unlike the others, the Cimmerian was as fresh as if he had just arisen from a restful night's sleep.

"I was raised among hills as rough as this," he said, "although they were by no means as green. Goma speaks the truth. Even so, I intend to range ahead and to both sides, as I did in the lowland and in the forest above the escarpment. It may be that I will find things of value, for we do not know whether Marandos followed this route." His piercing gaze swept the Aquilonians. "Or *do* we?"

"He speaks of the mountain," Ulfilo said, "but not of how he ascended it."

"Very well," said Conan. "I shall range ahead, beginning after this rest." He turned to Goma. "Are there good campsites on this slope?"

"None you would think comfortable, but tolerable."

"We are not concerned with comfort," said Malia. "We are concerned with getting to our destination." Something in her words gave Conan pause. She spoke of their destination, not of her husband. Was it just a slip of the tongue, or was she more interested in the treasure than in the man? If so, she would not be the first wife to arrange her priorities thus.

Without waiting for the others to regain their strength, Conan left them where they sat and faded into the forest. The relatively small trees allowed abundant sunlight to penetrate to the forest floor, allowing dense undergrowth to flourish. Brush and high grasses were everywhere, demanding that the Cimmerian proceed with great caution, for death could hide anywhere.

Twice he saw gorillas, the huge, manlike apes that legend held to be fierce, terrifying creatures. But these proved to be shy and retiring. Each time he encountered a group, an immense male glowered at him from below heavy brow-ridges until the others had fled into the brush, then the big male would turn and go as well. Conan did not confuse this antisocial flight with weakness. He knew that even the smaller females were stronger than any man, and one of the big bulls had more power in one arm than the Cimmerian had in his whole body.

Smaller apes swung through the branches overhead, distinguishable from the monkeys by their generally more manlike appearance and the absence of tails. These hooted and jabbered at the newcomer but showed no fear, as if they thought little of the ability of a ground-dwelling creature to hurt them.

Wild pigs were everywhere, and Conan knew that these beasts, if threatened, could be as dangerous as any lion. The upcurving tusks of a boar could gut a man in an instant, and the very fact of their relatively small size made them that much quicker and that much more difficult to stop. He saw none of the bigger cats although once, surprisingly, he came upon a small group of rhinos. Why these plains animals should be in the mountains escaped him, but he found traces of passing elephants, so apparently the high slopes were not utterly eschewed by the larger animals.

He was far more interested in evidence of human presence. He knew that the tiny men who hunted game with poisoned arrows lived in the forested mountains, driven there by the taller, more warlike peoples. Far more dangerous would be outlaws, cast out of the flatland tribes for transgressions and living a desperate, animallike existence in the wooded slopes. Such men could be far more difficult to handle than the usual tribesmen, for they were not bound by tribal custom, and their behavior could not be controlled by negotiating with tribal chiefs. Conan had himself been an outlaw, and he knew the breed well.

As he scouted the land, he saw no signs of organized groups of men greater than small hunting bands. There were remains of numerous campfires, most of them years old. He found broken arrow points of flint, but no sign of the passage of either of Marandos's expeditions.

When he returned to the others late in the day, they had made little progress. The climb up the steep slopes was far more strenuous than anything that had gone before. Even Wulfrede sat on the ground, wincing as he massaged the cramping muscles in his tree-trunk thighs.

"You Cimmerian mountain goat!" he called when he saw Conan. "How dare you come here looking like a boy after a morning in the cliffs hunting eiderdown!"

"Time was when the Vanir had a reputation as climbers," said Conan. "The sea cliffs of Vanaheim swarmed with men hunting birds and eggs and down."

"Aye, but twenty years on a ship's deck have robbed me of my squirrel's limbs."

"Saw you anything, Conan?" Malia asked. She was drawn but seemed to be holding up well.

"Just more rough country. No sign of men other than hunters."

"There will be few but the half-men on these lower slopes," Goma said. "Up higher, it may be different."

"Do outlaws dwell in the upper reaches?" Springald asked.

"Aye, we may encounter outlaws there. Or far worse," Goma said darkly.

That night they slept fitfully on the slanting ground, and the next morning they awoke stiff and sore. Their progress that day was even slower than the day before, but by the third day they began to grow accustomed to the brutal terrain and even the sailors began to regain their good spirits.

As they ascended the flora changed dramatically. Instead of the broad-leafed hardwood trees they began to see tree-sized ferns, and flowers of unearthly size and color. The eerie land-scape took on the aspect of a world in the process of creation, its disparate elements not yet divided into their own spheres. Here flowers seemed to spring from bare rock. Crystal forma-tions had the aspect of plants. A plant appeared that had a twenty-foot trunk covered with bark, but from its crown branched the fleshy arms and sharp spines of a cactus.

Low clouds wreathed the area, billowing about them and be-stowing a constant, fine drizzle. Their already ragged clothing began to deteriorate further and constant care was required to keep the rust from their weapons. But here, at least, they could at last leave the rocky watercourse. The ground between the strange plants and stony crags was open, covered with mossy growth that was pleasant to feet bruised by days of boulder-climbing.

"How do you stand it, Conan?" Malia asked of the Cim-merian who strode beside her. She shivered in the chilly mist of morning but he seemed not to notice it. "You now wear less than a Shadizar dancing girl, but you act as if it were a summer afternoon in Tarantia. While the rest of us groaned all night for lack of a soft spot of ground to sleep on, you just curled up on a rock and slept like a two-year-old child. We are worn down by hardship, yet you look better than when we found you in Asgalun!"

"I come of a hard land and a hard race," he told her. "What are hardships to you are the everyday conditions of living in Cimmeria."

She shivered again. "I thought I had seen some of the tough-est men in the world, soldiers and adventurers and warlords. You are an education in the real meaning of the word." She studied him frankly and saw much to her liking. His long-swinging stride made her half run to keep up, but he moved with a grace a racehorse could not match. Every part of him was in movement. When she looked at the others, nothing on them seemed in motion save their toiling legs and their puffing faces. It was as if the legs did nothing but haul along the inert mass of their bodies. Not Conan. The weeks of effort had re-moved the last traces of what little spare flesh he had carried and his skin lay paper-thin over the great rolling muscles and rippling smaller muscles that were in constant motion as he walked. Even his hair, which had grown longer, waved in the faint breeze. His skin, except for its numerous scars, was as glossy and supple as the finest leather of Kordava. In his sun-darkened face the gaze of his brilliant blue eyes was as that of an eagle.

Of the others, only Goma had anything like Conan's physical address, and the dark man was so abstracted and withdrawn that much of the time he scarcely seemed to be present. Conan, on the other hand was always, intensely *there*. His presence and his unfailing alertness made him seem ten times more alive than the others.

Once, as they climbed, she had seen a covey of pheasantlike birds fly abruptly from beneath the Cimmerian's feet. In a reflex action as swift as a steel trap Conan's hand flashed out and caught a bird by the neck, killing it instantly. As he hung the bird from his belt for later plucking and cleaning, she reflected that she would never have believed that a man could be so quick. And yet, when he was at rest he was absolutely still, never shifting or fidgeting like others. At those times such necessary movements as he made were minimal and were performed with absolute precision. She was jolted from this pleasant contem-plation when he raised a hand.

"Stop!" he said, quietly but urgently.

"What is it?" she asked. He stood frozen, his nostrils flared but his eyes scanning the far distance from one side to the other, then back again. The others began to catch up.

"What is it?" Ulfilo demanded. He was fast adapting and his breathing was regular. Springald and Wulfrede arrived along with Goma.

"Do you see it?" Conan said to their guide.

"I do," he said.

"See what?" said Springald testily.

"Sign that we may not be alone," Conan said. "We go forward slowly now, weapons out."

"Get behind us, Malia," said Ulfilo as he unsheathed his great sword. She complied amid a sound of steel sliding against wood and leather.

Conan and Goma went ahead, twenty paces upslope of the others. Their heads sweeping from side to side, they looked like hounds on a scent. They stopped at what looked like a cairn of stones and waited for the rest.

"Put up your weapons," Conan said. "They have not been here in a long time."

"Not been here? Who?" Ulfilo demanded. Then, "Mitra!"

The cairn surrounded what had been a large fire pit. Within the pit, along with the cinders and ashes, were clean-picked bones. Human bones. Other bones were scattered around the site.

"It was the gleam of bones I saw first," Conan said. "Then the stones."

"The long bones have been split to extract their marrow," Springald said shakily, his face pale. "Cannibals have feasted here."

"Not cannibals," Goma said. "Bumbana."

"What are bumbana?" Wulfrede asked.

"Half man, half ape. They haunt these mountains, seeking such prey as they can find. They have fire but no speech that a man can understand."

"That explains who did the feasting," said Springald, regaining his composure. "But who provided the feast?"

"Search for anything that might tell us who these bones belonged to," Conan ordered. "These remains are many months old. They are only here because there are no hyenas or other big scavengers this high up. Wood and cloth will have rotted, but there may be metal." All save Springald spread out to search the ground. The scholar began to examine the bones.

"Look here!" crowed a sailor, holding up something glittering. They crowded around and passed it from hand to hand. It was a jeweled brooch, figured in designs none of them recognized.

"It comes from no land I know of," Wulfrede said, excitement in his voice. "And the treasures of many lands have passed through my hands."

"These men must have come from beyond the mountains," said Ulfilo.

"They may have traveled here from there," said Springald, "but by no means did they originate there. Come here and see." They encircled the pit, where the scholar sat upon the edge of the stone cairn with a collection of bones at his feet. He held up a bowl-shaped piece. It was strangely marked, with four deep grooves forming a square. The bone thus surrounded was perhaps an inch on a side, thin and porous.

"This, as you can see, is the top of a skull, removed no doubt to get at the brain, which it seems is esteemed as a delicacy among the bumbana." He ignored a gagging sound made by Malia and went on. "This man has been trephined. That means that his skull was opened to relieve pressure on the brain caused by illness or injury. This is an operation performed only by certain very expert surgeons of Nemedia. A silken cord is dipped in diamond dust and drawn along the skull as a flexible saw, cutting out a small square of bone. This operation was a success, as it healed over many years ago. And look here." Now he held up a jawbone. There was a glint of gold at the base of some teeth.

"This fellow lost three teeth at some time, and they were replaced by a trick the Stygians use. Three teeth were extracted, probably from a slave, and their roots filed off. These were then bound together with the very finest gold wire, and the assembly similarly wired to the flanking, healthy teeth. I think that we see here the remains of some members of one of Marandos's expedition."

"But which expedition?" said Ulfilo.

"And which members?" Malia asked, distressed. "Could my husband be among these?"

"That is difficult to say," Springald mused, looking over his collection of bones. "Had Marandos any injuries or surgical procedures that might have left marks upon his bones?"

"None," she said miserably.

"These are fool's questions!" said a sailor. He was a gap-toothed sea dog with rings in both ears and a ruby stud in his nose. A faded kerchief covered his pate and a scowl decorated his ugly face. "What care we who these were? We did not sign on this voyage to deal with man-eating half-apes!" The other seamen made sounds of agreement. Conan and Ulfilo were about to draw their swords but Wulfrede brushed past them. "I'll deal with this," he muttered as he passed. He strode up to the speaker, truculent as a wolfpack king whose leadership has been challenged.

"What is this, Blamath? Would you be captain now, you ill-begotten son of a diseased mother? Think you that you can handle a ship like the *Sea Tiger* by yourself?" He laughed loud and scornfully. "You'll have her on the bottom and your mates feeding the fish before you're half a league from shore!"

"Now, chief," the man growled, "I speak no mutiny, but we are sailors, not foot-slogging soldiers. What business have we toiling over mountains at the behest of gilded Aquilonian bluebloods?"

"What business?" Wulfrede bellowed. "What business, you say?" He held the glittering brooch beneath the man's nose. "Is this not business enough for you? Would you not like to find more of this? This bauble alone is worth two years of a seaman's pay! A few such trinkets in your purses and not a man of you need ever ship before the mast again! Would that not be worth a bit of hardship and danger, eh? Is life at sea so easy and so safe that this little hike and perhaps a bit of fighting frightens you off? I never shipped cowardly dogs before, why have the sea-gods so cursed me now?" He wore a look of near-comical consternation as his men rushed to assure him that they were his men and would follow him anywhere.

"Lead us, Captain!" said a skinny Zingaran whose face was

bisected by a scar from hairline to chin. "Lead us to more treasure!"

"Aye!" said a Kushite with shark teeth in his hair. "Lead us to gold and jewels, and we will slay your enemies and drink their blood!" The one named Blamath withdrew sullenly and owned that he had spoken out of line.

"That is better," Wulfrede said expansively. "Now I think I lead men again! Now, continue searching and bring back anything that might tell us who these men were. And I'll have the hide off the back of any man who tries to conceal valuables! That is not the way of the sea! Now go." The men sprang to do his bidding as vigorously as they would have swarmed up the rigging at sea. The shipmaster returned to the group around the fire pit.

"That was masterful," said Springald admiringly.

"It went well enough," Wulfrede said. "But men like these are as changeable as children in their moods. I may have this to do over again before long."

"The treasure gets split more ways every day we travel, it seems," Ulfilo said, sourly.

Wulfrede grinned at him. "Come, my friend, did you really expect to lead these sea dogs to treasure and have them carry it back for you, and not give them a share of it? If so, you are a fool beyond the ken of any man with a head on his shoulders."

Ulfilo reddened but said nothing.

"He is right," Malia said. "We must let them have a share or fight them for all of it. And *someone* has to man the ship!"

The search turned up no more evidence, and within the hour they continued their march. The line of men, formerly straggling, was now bunched tightly and their hands never strayed far from their weapons. The ghastly remains of the feast had sobered everyone.

That night they huddled near their fires, and the sailors started at every noise. If the Aquilonians were as apprehensive, they hid it well. Conan patrolled around their campsite but found nothing and heard nothing. Even so, he slept even more lightly than usual that night.

The next day they crested the mountain and saw the pass before them. It was no mere dip in the mountain's spine. In some long-past age the mountain had split, so that sheer, almost vertical walls of stone rose to either hand. The millennia had deposited an uneven floor of dirt upon which little grew, for little sunlight penetrated the crack in the mountain.

"At last!" said Wulfrede. "A little march through this easy pass and we can start going downhill for a while!" The sailors laughed at his wit and entered the pass in good spirits. Conan and Goma ranged ahead and were as cautious as ever. The Cimmerian had lived a hard and adventure-filled life, and he knew better than to assume a passage would be easy just because it looked that way.

"I like a level way free of obstacles as well as any man," Conan said to his companion, "but I never liked any place that was cramped and narrow, where there is no room to maneuver and the only choices were to carve your way forward or turn and run straight back."

"Aye, that is wise," said Goma. "But it could be worse. Here there is room to swing an axe, or a sword."

"Aye, it's . . . what is that?" Conan pointed to something high on the rock wall. It appeared to be a carving of some sort, much weathered by the water that dripped down the sheer walls.

"A mark on the stone," Goma said, shrugging. "What of it?"

By stretching, Conan could just reach the device. Faded lichen crusted it and the once sharp edges had softened over uncounted years, but the design was plain enough: an oval frame within which was carved a wavy-bladed trident inside a crescent moon.

"What have you found?" called Springald as the rest caught up with them.

"Something that needs some explanation," Conan said hotly. "Tell me what you three were doing—" His words were cut short by a wild, inhuman howling. In his distraction over finding the carving, the approach of enemies had gone undetected.

"Bumbana!" Goma cried. A shadowy mass of hairy, near-human forms bore down upon them from the eastern end of the pass.

"The man-eaters come!" screamed a sailor. "Run!"

"Nay, there are more of the fiends behind us!" Wulfrede yelled. "We carve our way ahead or die here! Fight, you dogs!"

Conan whirled his blade through a short arc, shearing through the breast of one of the creatures. It was all muscle, fangs, and stinking breath, and even dead its charge knocked the Cimmerian back several paces while he wrenched his blade free.

Goma slew two with two swift blows of his light axe and Ulfilo plied his blade with both hands. Wulfrede began a Vanir fighting song as he worked his blade among the foe. Occasionally he would yank a sailor forward and thrust him into the front line to spell one of the leaders who was seriously engaged. Other sailors stabbed from the second rank with their spears. All were canny fighters, but they did not escape without casualties. With their massive strength and inhuman vitality, the bumbana managed to snatch some sailors from their companions and rip them apart barehanded. Of weapons, the bumbana had only crude clubs. A few clutched stones in their ill-formed paws.

Gradually, by dint of hard fighting, the human band pushed the bumbana back, a foot at a time. The reek of blood and spilled entrails was stronger even than the stink of the apemen themselves. A sailor screamed as apish hands snatched him from the band and snapping jaws buried themselves in his face. Another died silently as his neck was wrung too quickly for him to utter a sound.

In time, though, the half-men could stand no more. As one hairy creature, they turned and fled. As they went, they carried off all the dead, both their own and those of the men. Led by Conan, the humans gave chase, maddened by the fighting and by the undoubted fate of those carried off. Within minutes they burst through the pass, only to see the bumbana disappearing into a dense growth of trees that grew right up to the pass on the eastern end. A platform of stone perhaps ten paces on a side stretched from the gap in the mountain, and upon this the exhausted men cast themselves down.

Malia breathed in great, sobbing gasps. She had taken no part in the fighting, but the sheer terror of the situation had left her spent. When she had breath to speak, she glared at Wulfrede.

"You had me terrified! I thought we were trapped! But I saw no beast-men behind us."

He shrugged. "If the men had known that, they would have turned and run. I had to do something to keep them going forward."

"It is well for us that the things lacked the wit to attack from both ends of the pass," Conan said.

"Aye," agreed Ulfilo, who was methodically cleaning his gore-bedecked blade. "We might have died in there had they done so."

"Look!" shouted Springald, pointing eastward. For the first time they began to take stock of their surroundings.

From the ledge upon which they rested, the ground sloped sharply away, so sharply that they looked out over the tops of the nearest trees. Below them was the great hulk of the mountain. Beyond that stretched a huge vista of sandy brown wasteland.

"The desert," said Malia wearily.

"No!" Springald cried. "Beyond that!" Following the direction of his pointing finger they could just descry two crags of stone, almost symmetrical, the one on the left snowy white, the other a dull black. "The Horns of Shushtu!"

"Then it is true!" said Ulfilo at last.

"Did you ever doubt it?" Springald crowed. "The ancient books are always to be trusted."

"Aye," said Wulfrede, clapping the scholar on the shoulder and almost knocking him down in the process. "I never doubted you."

"It does not look very far," said Malia wistfully. "After all, we can see the Horns from here."

"Don't be deceived," said Conan. "From this high up, we can see for many days' travel. Goma, are there water holes?"

The guide nodded. "Aye, a few. None of them reliable, all of them dangerous."

"How do you mean?" asked Ulfilo.

"Some are mere depressions that catch the rare rains. These are dry much of the time and not to be relied on. Others are where small springs well to the surface, and these may be dry when we get to them. There is one large spring, with good water at all times, and that one is the most dangerous, for all the animals for many miles use it, and therefore the predators lurk nearby in great numbers."

"Lions?" Malia asked.

"Aye, and bold hyenas, and many big cats and creatures found nowhere else. The meat-eaters of the desert are fiercer than those of the plain. They are also more likely to be desperately hungry and therefore more likely to hunt men. It takes much territory to feed such a beast, so the lions and others fight to drive one another off the good hunting grounds. The losers are likely to be wounded from the fight, unable to chase down the eland or the swift oryx. Therefore he is looking for something slow, weak, and easy."

"To wit: us," Springald said.

"Even a foul-smelling human is meat to a lion with a lean belly," Goma said.

"We accomplish nothing here," said Ulfilo in his usual, matter-of-fact manner. "Has everyone regained his breath? Any serious wounds to tend?" It transpired that all were rested and none was too injured to march.

Ulfilo resheathed his sword. "Then lead on, Goma." Shouldering their packs, they set off down the mountain.

# TEN

## The Desert

The eastern slope of the mountain proved to be even steeper than that which they had ascended. Its growth was more dense as well, so that occasionally they had to chop a path with swords. The trees were far larger than those on the western slope and the growth beneath them consisted largely of bamboo, high saw-edged grasses, and thorny cactuslike bushes with flat, fibrous leaves. It made for hard going as the men took turns at the front of the column, their arms rising and falling like metronomes, their blades flashing in the shafts of sunlight that penetrated the canopy above. Their progress upset the local wildlife continually, as startled birds and indignant monkeys scolded them with raucous voices.

A sailor came back from a stint at the front, dashing sweat from his face with a rag. "What kind of land is this," he groused, "where it is harder work going downhill than up?"

"Would you rather fight plants or beast-men?" Wulfrede said. "Be joyful that the day that began so bloodily has become a pleasant outing.'' His men grumbled but obeyed. Even the prospect of great treasure could not raise their spirits greatly on such a day. They were men of the sea, and this toil in an alien element disheartened them as none of the perils of navigation could.

Conan resumed his scouting activity, roaming ahead and to both sides of the column, this time with a definite mission: he was looking for signs of a bumbana ambush. The beast-men had disappeared, but he knew that they must be somewhere near. He moved through the heavy brush without making a sound, leaving no sign of his passage. As a youth he had been schooled in Pictish woodcraft, and his skills served him as well in this exotic tropical jungle as in the heavy forest of the Pictish Wilderness.

The eastern slope of the mountain was cut up into knife-edged ravines, deeply eroded. The western slope had been rough, but this was far more treacherous. Despite the hard and unyielding look of the land, the soil was loose and crumbly, making footing doubly uncertain. Springs made brief runs along the bottoms of ravines, then swept over ledges to fall hundreds of feet in arcing cascades. At least, he thought, while they were on the mountain there was plenty of clean water.

He found some things more alarming than the likelihood of bumbana ambush. Here and there were traces left by animals unlike those they had encountered thus far. In soft soil he found a huge, handlike print that he could only interpret as the footprint of an ape larger than any gorilla. In another spot he found numerous prints reminiscent of a great bird's talons, along with leathery fragments of an eggshell that might have hatched a chick the size of a baby elephant. He did not know whether these were signs of a bird or a reptile, but either way the thing was a giant and its claws were not those of a grass-eater.

Vultures with wingspans of twenty feet or more spiraled lazily in the mountain updrafts, watching for carrion. It seemed likely that they rarely had long to wait. Even as Conan watched, a score of them settled cautiously onto something beyond a ridge line a hundred yards away and began to feed noisily. In the far distance he made out thin columns of smoke, perhaps the bum-bana preparing to feast upon the bodies they had carried off. He disliked the thought, but he had no intention of going to explore. The dead were dead and it was imperative now to preserve as many lives as possible. The numbers of his party had dwindled drastically since setting out and they were still far from their destination.

The sudden, sharp sound of a scream sent him sprinting back toward the column. Despite the burst of speed, he made no sound as he ducked, dodged, or sprang over the intervening foliage. He found the others standing on the edge of a ridge, staring into the deep, narrow ravine below.

"What has happened?" he demanded.

Wulfrede pointed to the rocks below. A shattered body lay upon them. "Bugnar tripped on a vine and fell over the edge. There was nothing we could do."

Conan studied the crew, and they were more somber-faced than ever. No more than a dozen were left of the score that had begun the trek. How many more would the mountain and the desert claim, and what lay at the Horns of Shushtu?

"From here on," Conan announced, "Goma and I will pre-cede the rest of you by no more than a score of paces, so that you can see us. We will call out to you any dangers ahead of you so that you may watch for them. If you would see the sea again, stay alert! This mountain is a fool-slayer as deadly as any." With that he turned and strode off, Goma at his side. The others glowered, but none sought to contradict him.

The descent of the mountain took another three days. There were places where they had to lower themselves by ropes, one at a time, from cliff ledge to cliff ledge. At one point they were attacked by man-sized birds for no reason they could fathom. Goma speculated that they might have strayed too near the crea-tures' nests. Once, on a well-beaten path, they stopped as a dark shape stepped from the jungle curtain onto their road. It was an ape, not so burly as a gorilla but fully nine feet tall. It glared at them with tiny red eyes, bared its teeth, and roared defiance.

They prepared to hurl their spears at the creature but it seemed satisfied that they were nothing to worry about and ambled off into the jungle on the other side of the pass. Greatly relieved, the expedition carried on, the men casting nervous glances into the dimness of the bush as they went.

It was with great joy that they reached the base of the mountain and found themselves on land that was almost level. It was green and grassy with the runoff from the mountain streams, but these quickly sank into the ground, not to reappear again. Half a day's march brought them to the edge of the arid land.

"Here the desert begins," said Goma, standing by a tiny stream that flowed into a pond that filled a stone basin no more than twenty feet across. "We must fill our waterskins here and carry as much as we can. It will be some days before we reach water again."

"How many days?" Ulfilo asked.

Goma shrugged. "Perhaps three. Perhaps five, or ten or even more. It depends upon how fast the slowest of us marches, and whether the first water hole is dry, or the second. The one that is always plentiful is about ten days from here, unless we are slowed by injured men or other misfortune."

Ulfilo studied the angle of the sun. "We rest here until morning. Use the daylight hours remaining to see to your gear and yourselves. Drink as much water as you can hold. We march at first light, with as much water as we can carry."

Wearily, they pitched camp by the water, a simple process in the absence of tents. Some foraged for firewood, others sat and mended their clothing and harness, cleaned and sharpened weapons and saw to damaged boots. Conan and Goma went hunting for fresh meat and returned before dusk with a pair of gazelles, which the hungry sailors quickly cleaned and spitted over glowing coals. At Ulfilo's urging, each man went to the pond and swallowed water repeatedly until he felt bloated. Waterlogged and full-bellied, they sprawled on the ground and slept like dead men.

Conan went to the fire, where the Aquilonians and the Van

sat conversing about the grueling journey ahead. Goma stood by himself some way off, leaning on the handle of his axe and wrapped in a brooding silence, staring toward the east as if he saw something in the far distance.

The Cimmerian sat and took a skewer of meat from the fire. As he ate he studied his companions. All were lean and drawn from the hardships of the journey. Malia was more ghostlike than ever, her huge eyes dominating a face that had lost all trace of softness. It had not lessened her beauty. The burly Wulfrede carried less belly than before, his wide belt showing a line of new holes where the shipmaster had bored them to accommodate his lessened girth. Springald was likewise reduced. Ulfilo showed the least change, having been lean and rangy to begin with.

"In the pass," Conan said, "just before the apemen attacked us, I found a carving on the wall."

"A carving?" said Springald innocently.

"Aye. Were you not expecting one? Did not Marandos see it on his first expedition?"

"How could you know that, rogue?" Ulfilo demanded indignantly. He made as if to reach for his sword, but Springald laid a restraining hand upon his wrist.

"What sign did you see, Conan?" asked the scholar.

"Aye, Conan," said Wulfrede. "What was it?"

"It was formed thus," said the Cimmerian. With the skewer he traced the design of the crescent and trident in the dirt before him.

"Ah, most interesting," Springald said.

"Aye," Conan retorted. "The chief back at the coastal village told me that the ship that bore Marandos on his second voyage carried just such a device at its masthead. And I saw its like carved above a certain doorway in Khemi!"

"You followed us, you treacherous dog!" Ulfilo leapt to his feet and this time drew his sword in truth.

Conan eyed him coldly. "Aye, and wherefore not? I never would have accepted your offer had I known what a secretive, duplicitous lot you were. Never have you told me the whole truth about our mission. What I have learned I have gained in spite of your words. If this is what your 'nobleman's honor' means I rejoice that I am a barbarian and a bandit, as you have named me!''

''I'll not be spoken to thus by a baseborn savage! Draw your weapon!''

''Oh, put your sword away,'' said Malia disgustedly. ''The man but speaks the truth. Have we played him fair? I do not blame him for following us in Khemi. I would just like to know how he did it!''

''Our Conan is a resourceful man,'' Springald commented, his eyes twinkling despite his fatigue.

Slowly, reluctantly, the noble resheathed his sword. ''I am still not satisfied,'' he muttered.

''Nor am I,'' said Conan. ''Not until I know what there is to know about our destination and our mission, and about who you have thrown in with besides us lowborn adventurers.''

''Aye, that would go well with me also,'' said Wulfrede. ''All is satisfactory to me so long as great treasure lies at the end of our journey, but I'd not blunder through the darkness when others know that which is important to me.'' All merriment was gone from his face and voice now. The icy north shone in his eyes and his hand rested upon his hilt. The sailors snored in blissful ignorance.

At Ulfilo's stubborn silence Malia broke in sharply. ''This is foolish! Brother-in-law, we might as well tell them what we know. We are on the edge of the desert a thousand leagues from home, and these are men we depend upon in a hostile land. Think you they will turn back now? Let us have an end of this! Tell them!''

Reluctantly, Ulfilo nodded. ''Very well. Springald, you are better at this than I.''

''Less miserly of his words, at any rate,'' said Wulfrede dryly.

''Where to begin?'' said Springald with a sigh.

''Begin with Marandos's visit to Khemi after the disaster of his first expedition," Conan suggested. "Give us the true account of his dealings with the priest of Ma'at."

"Very well. Somehow, with his reduced crew, Marandos managed to sail as far as Khemi, but they had a stormy passage, the vessel was an old one, and by the time they dropped anchor off the Tortoise, it was clear that it would make no more voyages. He sold the hulk for its timber and went looking for a backer for a second try at the treasure. Within a few days he was contacted by a man who claimed to represent a wealthy merchant of Khemi. He said that his master was interested in profitable ventures in the far south and wanted to hear Marandos's proposal. He brought safe conduct to the city proper and a meeting was arranged.

"When his guide took him to his destination he saw the sigil above the door. It was the same he had seen in the pass and elsewhere on his journey. He knew something was amiss but he was alone in a hostile city and he had no choice save to pass within. Thus he met Sethmes, archpriest of Ma'at. The priest was most cordial and received him with great hospitality. He listened to his account with rapt attention. To Marandos's amazement, he seemed to anticipate each step of the journey, as if he, too, were familiar with the account of Captain Belphormis.

"When he reached the place in his recitation where he and his men arrived at the Horns of Shushtu, the priest was quite unsurprised to learn that he had been unable to pass between the Horns to the valley beyond."

"Unable?" said Conan.

"Exactly. You see, the Pythonians left certain safeguards in place. It seems that they are still potent, and one must know the proper spells in order to pass safely."

"Spells?" barked Wulfrede. "You mean that there is wizardry involved here?"

"And how comes it that you did not know this before, with your long study of the matter?" Conan demanded.

"Because certain information had been removed from my books."

"Removed?" Conan said. "How is that possible?"

"You recall that I said that, about two hundred years ago, the books I had been studying were sent to Stygia for rebinding?"

"Aye," said Conan.

"Well, it seems that, at that time, a number of pages were removed from the crucial volume. When we received Marandos's letter, I examined the book in question and discovered that it was true. There was no apparent gap in the narrative. As one reads it, it seems merely that Captain Belphormis turned back after reaching the pass between the Horns and gazing into the valley beyond. Remember, he did not know that he was upon the trail of the treasure of Python. He was merely scouting new trade routes and did not recognize the significance of the signs he passed on the way."

"Then how did you know that the pages were missing?" Conan asked.

"By a bookman's trick. Here, I will show you." He held up one of the ancient books. "The bane of all lovers of old books is the bookworm. These voracious if scholarly beasts bore holes through text and binding indiscriminately. A single worm, given the time, can eat his way through an entire shelf of books. In fact, if one wishes, it is possible to arrange the books in one's library as they were originally ordered on an owner's shelf by simply lining up the wormholes on the bindings."

"The things a man learns from hearing the words of a scholar," Wulfrede groused.

"Go on," Conan said patiently.

"Likewise, even if the worm bores at an oblique angle, the holes in several adjacent pages will line up sufficiently for light to show through. I demonstrate." He opened the volume and held a half-dozen pages tightly together, then held them up to the firelight. The glare of the fire shone through a score of pin-prick holes in the pages.

"That is clear enough," Conan said.

"But," Springald continued, "when I reexamined the crucial passage, I noticed a discontinuity. Here is the page where Belphormis's party ascends to the pass between the Horns, and here is the next page, wherein they return the way they came." He held the two pages together and poised them between the fire and the observers. No light shone through. "Clearly, at the time this book was rebound, several pages were excised."

"Why not just keep the book?" Conan asked.

"Perhaps the culprits feared that the loss would be discovered. These were after all volumes from a royal library, esteemed highly enough to send all the way to Stygia for rebinding. And the royal librarians of past generations were probably more conscientious than those of this degenerate age. The removal of a few pages, on the other hand, would almost surely pass undetected."

"So this Sethmes staked Marandos to a new ship, a crew, and all that was needful for a successful expedition. It is plain that he expected profit, a great deal of it. What was the nature of their bargain, and how did they propose to bypass the safeguards in the pass?"

"True," Springald said, "I fear that disinterested kindness has very little to do with the Stygian nature. You see, the priest had in his possession all the necessary spells to pass between the Horns."

"And how came that to be?" Wulfrede inquired.

"In the days when Python fell, it was the archpriest of Ma'at who was entrusted with the royal treasure. It was the spells of that god with which the treasure was guarded."

"This makes little sense," Conan protested. "If the ancient priests of Ma'at hid the treasure, surely the current archpriest knows where it is hidden. Why should he help a stranger to go south and plunder it?"

"This archpriest is something of a . . . a renegade. For many centuries the priesthood of Ma'at has been entrusted with the location and access to the treasure, but a further spell has prevented them from taking it for themselves. It has been held in trust, you see, in anticipation of the return of the royal Python-ians and the reestablishment of the kingdom. Sethmes knows that the kingdom is gone forever. The royal line died out long ago. The priesthood of Ma'at has dwindled until, now, only he is left.''

"Nothing dies out in Stygia," Conan said.

"But Ma'at was never a part of the Stygian pantheon," Spring-gald pointed out. "The cult was tolerated while the pretenders to the throne of Python dwelt at the royal court. Without official support or worshipers, the cult of Ma'at faded into near-oblivion. As the last of his line, Sethmes feels that the treasure is right-fully his, and he wishes to enjoy its possession before he dies.''

"But he needed assistance?" Conan said. "He had to have someone else to fetch the treasure for him?"

"That is so. He was on the verge of hiring an expedition, even had a ship of his own under construction, when Marandos appeared in Khemi with his story of a journey to the Horns of Shushtu. It seemed to Sethmes fortuitous, as if Ma'at had agreed that it was time for the treasure to be given to those who had guarded its secret for so long. Why not entrust the expedition to one who already knew the waters to be sailed and the land to be crossed? After exacting certain . . . pledges, he agreed to outfit Marandos's second expedition.''

"What sort of pledges?" Wulfrede asked.

"He pledged everything!" Ulfilo said angrily. "Against the chance of recovering the treasure, he pledged our family lands, our titles, even his wife!"

Conan turned to stare at Malia. "Is this true?"

She held her chin high, but it trembled slightly. "It is. If all is not to Sethmes's satisfaction, I am to become his property."

Wulfrede snorted. "Such a pledge is neither lawful nor bind-ing, for he had no right to pledge you thus. Why did you not laugh in the Stygian's face?"

"I fear that it was not that sort of pledge," said Springald in a subdued voice. "It was a highly specialized Stygian contract, involving many gods and terrible curses. Marandos signed it with his own blood, and since he and his brother share the same blood, it was binding upon him as well.''

"What about Malia?'' Conan said. "She shares no blood with them.''

"There are, ah, ways of getting around that. Rest assured, she is equally bound.''

"What of you?'' Conan asked.

"Well, it was my doing that brought them here, so I bear a certain responsibility. And, anyway''—he shrugged expressively—''the treasure *is* there, and I want a part of it.''

"That last part I can understand,'' Wulfrede said, "albeit the rest vexes me sorely.''

"And now, if you are satisfied,'' Ulfilo said, "we have a desert to cross, and must begin early.''

"Satisfied?'' Conan said. "Far from it. But I have heard enough for now.'' With that they rolled into their blankets and slept.

The next morning, Conan awoke before the others. The night was still upon them, only a gray line in the far east promising the dawn. He rose, stretched, and enjoyed the early morning breeze. The last watchman nodded over the smoky ashes of the fire, a spear slanted over his shoulder. He looked around for Goma but did not see the man.

Within minutes, the camp began to stir. Wulfrede was up, kicking at his men to roll out of their blankets and face the day's march. When he came to greet Conan the east was a red glow with a pale blue rim.

"A good day for a trek,'' said the Van. "It is cool.''

"Only until the sun is high,'' Conan said. He looked back the way they had come, up the slope of the mountain. "We may have to . . . Crom! What is that?'' His eye had caught something at the mountain crest.

"Eh? What do you see?'' He followed the direction of Conan's gaze. Then he saw it too. "Ymir!''

It was a glitter of metal. The sun, still invisible to them, already cast its rays upon the top of the mountain, and from there it was reflected back.

"Men coming through the pass," Conan said. "Armed men on our trail."

"Natives, do you think?"

"Nay. You've seen their spears. They never polish them, just grease them against the wet and let them get foul. They never gleam like that. This is our friend of the black ship, following us still."

"The Stygian?"

"Who else? He has dogged our heels since we left Khemi, never far behind."

The Van chuckled and scratched in his beard. "A wise speculator keeps close track of his investment, but this is extreme."

"He's doing more than keep track," Conan said as more glitters announced the arrival of more armed men through the pass. "He intends to let us take all the risks and gain the treasure, then take it from us by force."

"He may be in for a surprise if he thinks that," said Wulfrede. "My crew may not be the prettiest that ever sailed, or the most obedient, but they are hard fighters."

"Aye, I own they are that, but they grow fewer all the time."

"Surely he must be suffering loss himself. He has come through the same country. Ah, Conan, perhaps we had best not tell the men of this just yet."

"Aye, that would be wise," the Cimmerian agreed.

"The Aquilonians either."

"Why not them?" Conan asked.

"You know Ulfilo by now. He is a warrior as fine as any, I'll warrant, but he has a high noble's overgrown sense of honor. If he thinks that Stygian priest has betrayed him, as surely the scum has, he'll want to charge up the mountain and fight him. We are not ready for that. We must be prepared, and in a good position, before we fight them."

"Aye, that would be the wisest thing," Conan agreed.

Wulfrede boxed him on a shoulder. "Then let us be about getting these men across the desert."

Conan watched Wulfrede's broad back as he walked back toward the fire. He was willing to abide by the man's advice for the nonce. The Van was canny and a fine leader of men, but Conan still did not trust him. He glanced up at the pass again. There was no further glitter of steel. Apparently the entire party had passed through, but he had been unable to judge its numbers. He suspected that he would find out all too soon.

They filled their skins, took a last, long drink, and set off.

"Where is Goma?" asked Ulfilo as they began. "Has that black rogue deserted us?"

"We will find him up ahead," Conan said. "He is a strange one, but for his own reasons he wants to go where we go. He'll not be far away."

"This does not look so bad," Malia said, studying the barren ground ahead and to the sides of them. "It is hard land, but it is not miserable, like the jungle, and the going is far easier than going up and down that wretched mountain." She looked fresher and more cheerful than at any time since the long march began.

"The hardships of the desert are of a different sort," Conan said. "Here it is the heat and the dryness that kill. No man can carry enough water, for you always sweat out more. You just hope it will keep you alive until the next water hole."

"I wonder whether these water bags are a futility," said Springald, who had a sizable skin slung across his back, changing his usual scurry step into a slow trudge. "For it seems to me that because of the extra weight, you sweat that much more. Why not just die of thirst in relative comfort?"

"There is Goma," said Conan, pointing ahead.

Malia squinted eastward, but the sun glared into her eyes. "I see no one."

"He's there," Conan assured her.

Minutes later they could all see him. Goma stood leaning on his axe, his ankles crossed, wrapped closely from knees to shoulders in his russet robe.

"What have you found?" Conan asked as they caught up with the guide.

"No one has passed this way for a long time. And there are no signs of a recent rain. That means the first water hole will almost certainly be dry. It is not spring-fed."

"Predators?" Ulfilo asked.

"Not here. As we near the water sources, we must be careful."

Springald looked about. "There is no cover here. How could they get close?"

Goma's grin was white in his dark face. "There is more cover here than you would think. Watch every rock you pass carefully. It could conceal a lion."

The sun rose higher, and the day grew hotter. By noon the men were gasping. In this open land they did not need to travel single file and they began to spread out, each man taking the ground that seemed easiest to him. Ulfilo called a halt and they rested, but there was no shade and the men suffered beneath the blazing sun. Stern warnings were issued to ration the water, but there was no way to keep the men from surreptitiously pulling at the waterskins as they marched.

At sunset they reached the first water hole. As Goma had predicted, it was nearly dry, only a muddy puddle in its center, the marks of lizards and snakes all around its periphery. They built a fire of dry brush and settled down for an exhausted sleep.

"And this is only the first day," said Malia. She had lost her earlier good spirits when the terrible fact of the desert heat sank in.

"Why did your Captain Belphormis cross this desert?" Conan asked. "He was merely scouting trade routes. Surely he would have turned back when he saw that he confronted such a dry land."

"Climates change over the centuries," Springald said, "although no man knows why. In Belphormis's day, this was a semiarid grassland, much like that on the other side of the mountain. For some reason the rain stopped falling here, and now it is a desert."

Conan nodded. "I have seen ruined cities in other deserts, and in swampy jungles as well. At some time, they must have been surrounded by fertile fields."

"Just so. In legend, such places always fall under the curse of some god or other. In truth, it is usually something less exciting. The land loses its fertility, or there is too much rain, or too little. Men must eat, and if the land will not support them, they must go elsewhere. All civilization depends upon cropland and grazing land. Where those do not exist, only nomads can eke out an existence."

"Are there ruined cities in this desert, Goma?" Malia asked.

"I have seen places where once there were many huts," Goma said. "Huts far larger than those of the coast, and made of stone. Of who built them and lived in them, there are not even legends."

"You see?" Springald said. "This land was once fertile. And perhaps before that it was a desert as it is now, over and over in a cycle."

"The sea stays where it is and what it is," Wulfrede said. "A man can trust the sea."

"Not necessarily," Springald said. "For the sea now rolls over storied Atlantis, and the convulsion in which that land sank changed the coastline. Why, the city of Amapur in Turan was once a port, and has the remains of huge stone wharfs, yet it lies more than a hundred leagues from the nearest—"

"Peace, Springald. Go to sleep before you talk us all to death." Ulfilo's voice was stern but not without affection. Amid the others' laughter, Springald grumbled to silence.

The next day was worse. The heat was greater, the desert was rockier, and the water was already very low in the flattened skins. The boots, shoes, and sandals the men had worn at the beginning of the trek had been deteriorating from the start, and now the hard desert floor was quickly reducing them to shreds.

Only Conan and Goma, neither of whom now wore footgear, showed no distress at this development.

"Their feet will toughen," Conan said.

"But will mine?" Springald mused. He walked as if upon hot coals, and the sensation was not far from that. His footgear was of far higher quality than that of the mariners, but his soles were growing thin and he felt the heat of the ground through them as through mere parchment.

"Try walking a little while without boots each day," Conan advised. "A little longer each time."

"Excellent idea," said Springald. "That way, when we reach the edge of the desert, and I no longer need to worry about the hot stones, I shall have feet as tough as yours."

Conan grinned. "And you'll have survived the desert and will have nothing to complain about."

Ulfilo trudged on, stoically pretending that he felt nothing. Conan knew that the man would die rather than betray the first hint of suffering. Malia was as proud, but could not help wincing when a new pain struck her. Unlike her brother-in-law, she had not been raised in a hard military school. The Cimmerian smiled grimly as he watched them. He always admired fortitude, even when he had little liking for those who displayed it.

The sailors were another matter. They grumbled and complained but Conan took little note of that. At this stage there was very little they could do save follow their leaders and trudge on. As for the other followers, he had plans for them as well, but now was not the time . . .

"Water ahead!" called Goma. He had forged ahead of them that morning and now stood atop a low ridge a hundred paces before them. The sailors broke into a shuffling trot, baying like hounds.

"Belay that!" cried Wulfrede. "You'll kill yourselves running in this heat and be there no sooner. Walk and we'll all reach water alive." The men slowed reluctantly, but their mood changed upon the instant. They smiled and even chuckled, even though their dry, swollen tongues prevented them from talking much.

As the sun lowered behind them, stretching their shadows, they reached the water hole. It was surrounded by a maze of animal tracks but all wildlife had fled at the approach of these strange creatures. When the water was in sight the sailors were impossible to restrain. They broke into a ragged run and flopped to their bellies, facedown in the water.

"Stop that, you dogs!" Wulfrede roared. "Fill your water-skins and let it settle before you drink!"

"It's no use," Conan told him. "Leave them be, and hope they suffer no more than bellyaches."

"Aye," said the shipmaster, shaking his head. "But as soon as they've drunk their fill they'll be complaining of hunger. We've reached the last of our food."

"We must stay here a day or two," said Conan.

"Wherefore?" demanded Ulfilo. "We must press on."

"The men are worn, they must repair their footwear as best they can," said Conan. "Also, we shall have to hunt if we're to have food for the rest of the journey."

Ulfilo brooded. "Very well," he said at last.

That night, as the moon rose, Conan sought out Goma. "Let's go hunting tonight," he proposed.

"For desert gazelle?" Goma asked. "They are not easy to hunt at night, when the big cats are after them. Early morning is better."

Conan smiled. "Not gazelle. Men."

"What men?" asked Goma, frowning.

"The men who have been trailing us since the trek began. Since long before that, for they were trailing us when we were still upon the sea. You have been concentrating upon the road ahead of us, my friend. I have been watching that behind." He described what he and Wulfrede had seen on the morning they left the mountain behind.

"And what will we do when we find them?" Goma asked.

"I will know when we see them. At the very least, I want to

count their numbers and learn how they are armed. We must expect attack from them sooner or later.''

Goma twirled his axe idly. ''Very well. It will break up a march that grows tedious.''

When all the others slept, replete with cool water, Conan and Goma slipped away. They glided over the path of the day's march like birds, no longer held to the speed of plodding sailors. Twice they passed little groups of gazelle, and the sensitive beasts never noticed. Keen-eyed cats saw the two and watched warily, but they were not about to attack any such unfamiliar things.

Once, they stopped for a while as something crossed the path ahead of them. It was just a dark shape in the pale moonlight, but it was ten paces long, crawling low to the ground with jagged spikes ranged along its spine. When it was safely past, they continued.

By the time the moon was at its height, they saw the light of fires on the desert to the west. Now they slowed and approached more cautiously.

''Sentries,'' Conan whispered.

''I see them,'' Goma answered. He held up his axe. ''Kill them?''

''See if we can get by them first. I must get closer. They might make noise if we kill them now.''

Silently the two crept forward. Wisely, Sethmes had stationed his sentries in pairs, to keep one another alert. Unwisely, the pairs were too far apart. The stalkers slipped between two of the pairs without notice. Conan caught the gleam of armor from the men. Sethmes had brought soldiers, or bravos willing to bear armor in the terrible heat. They drew closer to the firelight.

It was a large party, at least a hundred figures sat around the fires. There was a low babble of voices, and of sounds that were not voices at all. Goma stretched a long arm toward one of the fires. ''Bumbana! But they wear clothes and bear arms of steel!'' Even in a whisper, his astonishment was plain.

''These are a different lot from those on the mountain,'' Conan said. ''I saw their like up north, in Stygia.''

Crouched low, sometimes dropping and crawling on their bellies, the two circled the encampment. The tropic sun had turned Conan almost as brown as Goma, so that he was all but invisible in the shadows. He had blackened his spear with soot before setting out, and Goma had done the same with his axe.

Conan was looking for Sethmes. He did not think it likely that the archpriest would entrust this mission to a subordinate. Wulfrede had said that no man could be trusted where great treasure was concerned, and it was as true for Stygians as for Vanir, Aquilonians, and sea-rovers. If Sethmes truly expected to lay hands upon the treasure with this expedition, then he would lead it himself. He was using the expeditions of Marandos and Ulfilo as cat's paws. Conan was unsure why the man had made such elaborate preparations, but he suspected that the dangers were so numerous that Sethmes wanted his predecessors to spring all the traps and take all the losses, leaving the priest to walk in and collect the reward others had earned with their blood and suffering.

He found him at the central fire. The priest was unmistakable, with his great height and his somber mien. With him sat two evil-faced men who wore light armor of the finest quality. He recognized the harness as the uniform of the Great Ptah regiment, an elite guards corps. These must be officers cashiered for some villainy unacceptable even to the priest-kings of Stygia, for they wore no rank insignia.

"Master," said one of the officers, a man with a pointed chin-beard and a pockmarked face, "is it truly necessary to keep to this snail's pace? We could march at twice this speed."

"Aye," said the other, whose identical beard was dyed red. "At this rate, we will be in this accursed land far longer than necessary."

"You will be patient and follow my instructions to the letter. You and the rest of the soldiers have spent many years in Stygian service, and are accustomed to desert campaigning. Those ahead of us are not. They are seafaring scum, Aquilonian nobles, and northern savages. We must stay behind them, out of sight. And it is imperative that they reach the Horns before we do.''

"And why is that, master?" asked the first.

"It is of no . . . what is it?" At a nearby fire, one of the bumbana stood and stared out into the darkness, straining his tiny eyes in the direction where Conan and Goma lay. His head was canted slightly back on his bull neck, as if he were sniffing an unfamiliar scent on the breeze. Conan bit back a curse. The faint nighttime wind was blowing directly from him to the camp. He had taken every precaution to avoid being seen or heard, but it had not occurred to him that the priest would be accompanied by keen-nosed creatures. The apeman grunted some crude, half-formed syllables.

"He smells men!" said Sethmes. "That way!"

"How far?" asked one of the officers.

"He says not far," rejoined the priest.

"Desert nomads?" hazarded the red-bearded man.

"Possibly," said Sethmes. "I doubt those we follow have the craft to sneak near us, evading desert-trained guards. Khopshef, take some men out there and search for them." The redbeard jumped to do his bidding. "Geb, you take others and double the guard." The priest gabbled out some incomprehensible words and the apemen sprang from their fires. Spreading out, they began to fan cautiously into the darkness, snuffling the air as they went.

"We must use caution, master," said Khopshef as he hurried up with a score of armed men. "There may be more of them downwind. These may be a feint to draw us away. Keep a strong guard near you."

"You are wise," commended Sethmes. "Proceed with care."

"Time to leave," said Conan, tapping Goma on the shoulder. They rose to a crouch and began to scuttle away from the fire. Behind them the line of apemen shuffled through the skimpy, dry brush. Small night creatures fled from their path with shrill squeals.

"Men ahead," Goma whispered. A small file of soldiers were

spreading out, seeking to entrap the quarry between themselves and the bumbana.

"Flank them on the left," Conan ordered, turning his own steps that way. He knew it was their great good fortune that the enemy did not know their numbers and thought they might be desert-wise nomads. Had they known there were only two, the whole force would have turned out and fallen upon the spies in a compact mass.

It quickly became clear that they were not going to flank the pincer line before they were enclosed. They would have to attack.

"Take the two men on the end," Conan hissed urgently. "No war cries!"

Goma obeyed, but he began a quiet chant. Conan could see that the men before them were squinting into the moonlit dimness, unable as yet to see their quarry. That was all to the good. With his spear held low in his left hand, Conan drew his sword with his right. Soot-treated, it gave forth no betraying gleam.

They were upon the others like spirits of the desert night. Conan speared one in the throat above his cuirass, and hewed down another with his sword. He did not see Goma's axe strike, but he heard two impacts that came one after the other, so quickly they sounded almost as one. Then he heard the clatter of armored men falling to the hard desert ground.

The surviving soldiers began to call to one another, asking what had happened. In the confusion Conan speared another. Now the apemen were bearing down upon them, bellowing brutish battle cries, thirsty for blood.

"Don't fight the bumbana," Conan said, no longer bothering to whisper. "They are too strong and too many. Now, run!" Amid shouts and confusion, the two began to sprint the way they had come. Hearing screams and clashes, Conan risked a look back over his shoulder. In the darkness and uproar, some of the bumbana had attacked some soldiers. He laughed aloud. Ahead of them came a challenge.

"Who is that? What is happening back there?" A pair of

sentries peered toward them. More luck. The officer had not yet arrived to double the guard. Conan and Goma hewed the men down in passing and loped away into the surrounding gloom.

"None follows," said Goma after a half hour of speedy flight. The two slowed to a steady lope. Neither was sweating, nor was their breathing labored.

"That was a good fight," said Goma, his teeth reflecting the moonlight in a broad smile. "But now they know we are aware of their pursuit."

"Not so," said Conan.

"How can they not?" asked Goma. "They detected us and saw us."

"They think we might be desert nomads." Goma had not understood the conversation between Sethmes and his officers, so Conan sketched it briefly. "They know the sailors are not desert-wise, and the Aquilonians are from a fat, soft land. They think I am a mere hillman from a cold land, and they may not even know about you. Desert nomads are the only explanation for being set upon by so great a band."

"So great a band? But we are only two."

Conan laughed aloud. "When they count their dead they will never believe that two men slew so many in so short a time, then escaped. You have fought in wars, you know warriors. Every man will swear that he saw fifty of us."

"Aye! No warrior wants to think he was bested by an inferior enemy. By morning, they will even believe it."

"Exactly. So they will think that our party is still unaware of them. Let us keep it that way. As far as the rest are concerned, we went out hunting tonight. Say nothing to them about those who follow."

"Not even the yellow-bearded warrior?" Conan could feel the frown in his words. "But he is our leader."

"Aye, and I'll not betray him, but there is much about this mission that troubles me. They keep too many secrets. I will feel better holding a few secrets of my own. You are a warrior, Goma, and this may be strange to you—"

"I am no low dog of the coast, Conan," said Goma. "I know the ways of kings and nobles. Treachery and deceit are as the breath of life to them. They never trust and are always suspicious. Loyalty to a prince is usually rewarded with ruin or death."

"Aye, men of power are alike the world over. I always rejoice that I come of a people that civilized men call barbarians, that never knew a lord higher than a clan chief, and even they are a disagreeable breed."

By the time they came within sight of the awakening camp, they had a pair of plump gazelles across their shoulders.

"I think," Conan said before they reached the fringes of the camp, "that you come of a background that none of us suspects, my friend."

Goma nodded as if considering sage words. "That may well be. But whatever lies and deceits plague this mission, you know that I have not lied to you, warrior."

"That is true, by Crom," said Conan, "for you've said nothing at all!"

"And that is an excellent way to avoid lies, is it not?"

# ELEVEN
## The Horns Of Shushtu

Two more were dead. Both of them were sailors. One had failed to shake out his boots in the morning before donning them. A scorpion had taken up residence in one of the boots during the previous night, and had resented the sudden intrusion. The leg had swollen so swiftly that the screaming man was able to tug it only half off. The boot had to be slit down one side to get it the rest of the way off. The men had improvised a litter to carry him, but after a day of screaming that lapsed into babbling delirium, he had died.

The other had staggered along for the last days as they approached the final water hole. All of the men were like walking ghosts, mere wraiths dressed in rags, staggering blindly in the tracks of their leaders. Their reddened eyes saw nothing, their swollen tongues protruded from their mouths as if seeking moisture from the very air.

The man fell, his breath so weak that he seemed in danger of suffocation. The men were too weakened to carry him. Conan had squatted by the man and pressed an ear to his chest.

"He might live if we can get him to water," Conan had said. "Goma says the next water hole is near."

"Leave him," Ulfilo had said. "He is finished and we cannot be slowed. The rest are nigh as close to death as he."

"Aye," Wulfrede said. "It is foolish to risk all to save one, and he cannot be saved."

Wordlessly, Conan hoisted the man to his shoulder and set out. The others had shrugged. Springald, Goma, and Malia had regarded him with distinct approval, but he did not notice. He knew that even his great strength could not survive much more of this. But it was not in him to abandon a comrade who might live.

They had trudged on through the day, some of the men collapsing but somehow able to get up and stagger on. Someone groaned and pointed. There were small trees ahead. The water hole. No sooner had they seen it than the man Conan had been carrying most of the day had shuddered and died. The Cimmerian dropped the dead weight to the desert floor.

"A man should not give up too easily," he had said. Springald had come up and clapped him on the shoulder.

"It was his time. You did all a man could be asked to do, and far more." Springald's words came through his dry throat like the croakings of a frog, and the Cimmerian appreciated the effort they cost the schoolman.

Now they bathed in the cool, clear waters of the oasis. They drank and bathed and then drank again. Bleeding, festering wounds were washed and wrapped with the newly laundered rags of shirts and breeches.

The spring emerged from a cluster of rocks, an abundance of clear liquid that filled a large pond and flowed for another quarter mile before plunging once again beneath the sands and stones of the desert. It was surrounded by small trees, brush, and abundant grass.

"Dates!" crowed a sailor whose tongue had shrunk to its wonted size, allowing him to speak. "Ripe dates in the trees!"

They had all looked up and saw that, indeed, the trees were in fruit. Instantly, revived sailors had scrambled up the trunks and cast down fruit. To men who had survived on stringy meat for days, the luscious fruit was as the food of the gods.

"Figs!" shouted another. "Figs over here!"

"Someone has planted this place as an orchard," said Springald.

"Nomads, most likely," said Conan, "so that they can get food as well as water when they pass this way."

"Take care," called Wulfrede. "Else all this fruit and water will have your bellies griped for days!"

"Much good that will do," said Ulfilo. "Your men have no sense of moderation."

"Nor have I," said Malia, stuffing a handful of dates into her mouth, wincing at having to stretch her sore, cracked lips. The desert had robbed her of much of her beauty. She had kept covered as well as she could, but the desert sun was unavoidable and it had burned her. It did not merely stream down from above, but it reflected from the stones and sands as from a mirror. Dehydration and lack of sustaining food had reduced her slender body to fleshless bones. Her beautiful hair lay lank and dingy against her fine-boned skull, and her sunken eyes were haunted above dark circles.

"We must rest here a while," Conan announced.

"We are close to the Horns now!" Ulfilo protested. "There is no great desert trek ahead of us now. One more push and we are there!"

"Aye," Conan said. "But there is another mountain to climb before we reach the Horns. The sailors are weak, we warriors are not at our best, and your sister-in-law is likely to be dead before we reach the pass. She has been surviving by pure heart for days and is nigh as close to death as the man who died today."

"He speaks the truth, brother-in-law," she said. "One more day and I will not care whether we ever find Marandos or the treasure. I must have rest."

"Very well, then," said Ulfilo, stiffly. "We will rest here for two days."

"We will rest here as long as it takes to recover," Conan corrected him. "Else this whole weary expedition were worthless from the start."

Ulfilo glared at him. "I am the leader here, barbarian!"

"You are the employer," Conan said. "You engaged me to lead you to your brother. No other man could have served you better than I."

"You two could always fight it out," Wulfrede said idly. "But my money would be on the Cimmerian."

Indeed, by this time even Ulfilo's formidable strength was all but gone and his vigor was little more than posturing. Conan, on the other hand, was much revived by a little water and he looked more dangerous than ever. The desert had burned the last traces of civilization from him. Near-naked, his hair grown long and shaggy, burned darker than any of them save Goma, he stood with spear and sword like the very essence of savagery.

"No sense fighting one another, my friends," Springald said soothingly. "We are so close. The desert has set us all on edge. Let us rest here a while. Things will look better by and by."

Ulfilo put upon it the best face he could. "I suppose you are right. We rest here until Malia is fully recovered."

"I hate to miss a good fight," Wulfrede said. "But it is probably for the best."

They built fires, ate and drank some more, then slept. Conan awoke just after sunset and sat up alertly. No watch had been set, and all were sleeping like the dead. It did not bother him as it might at another time, for he knew that the pursuers were deliberately keeping their distance. He got to his feet, feeling better than he had since the desert trek began. With his phenomenal powers of recovery, he was almost as good as new. The rest would need days to regain ninety percent of their former strength, longer yet to recover fully.

Spear in hand, he walked along the rim of the pond. Animals came and went, needing the water but avoiding the end where the strange intruders camped. Conan did not molest them. The party needed meat but it was a bad idea to kill near a water hole, where a desert truce was observed. It would upset the wildlife and the local spirits might be angered. In such a hostile place Conan did not want to irritate even a small god.

Walking along the overflow stream, the Cimmerian heard splashing noises ahead. Instantly on guard, he proceeded stealthily to a clump of brush and parted the foliage slowly. Here water from the stream filled a small, stone-lined side pool. Something white and ghostly occupied the center of the pool, making the splashing noises. The hair at the back of Conan's scalp prickled, but he quickly cursed his foolishness. Ghosts did not swim. And there was only one thing that white for a thousand miles.

He watched as Malia scooped up water in both hands and raised it overhead to flow along her arms, spill onto her scalp, and cascade over her shoulders and breasts. She stood in water above her waist, luxuriating in the cool liquid. Conan strode to the edge of the pool.

"Do you realize how foolish it is to come out here alone?" he demanded.

She sighed. "I suppose a little privacy was too much to expect. You yourself told me that the killers do not hunt at the water holes."

"I was thinking about the sailors."

She laughed. "Them? All those men want now are water, food, and sleep. I have known marching armies and plundering armies, and I know that the basic necessities must be satisfied before the hot blood flows." She scooped up more water and poured it over her, letting it trickle down her lean flanks. Even in the moonlight, every rib was plain.

He sat upon a rock. "I am not so reduced."

She gave him a lazy, knowing smile. "So you are not. At another time I might be embarrassed and cover myself in maidenly modesty, but not now. I know that I am not a sight to excite a man's lust just at the moment. Let me fill out a bit and I will prepare to fight you off.''

"Some of us like skinny women," he teased. "And you *are* the only woman for hundreds of leagues. A man in these parts cannot be too picky.''

She giggled, sounding almost girlish. "You will ruin me with such flattery." She wrung the water from her long white hair, then ducked below the surface to soak it once more. When she reemerged, she spoke more seriously. "There are men whose attentions I would fight off more stoutly."

He spoke as seriously. "And you said no word to prevent Ulfilo and me from fighting today."

"Because I knew you would win," she said, facing him squarely standing now in shallower water that came well below her hips.

"You do not care if he dies?"

She shrugged her water-sparkled shoulders. "Only a woman without intelligence or spirit esteems a man who treats her like a beloved pet dog."

"And your husband, Marandos?"

"I lost him long ago to this mad quest for ancient treasure. I do not expect to find him alive, and if I do, what would I have found?" Her eyes now were hard and far too experienced. "If he lives, by now he is a madman, not the young captain I wed. No sane man, no man who cared for his family or his wife would have made that demon's bargain with the Stygian priest. Even if we find him alive, I could slay him for that!"

"Women have murdered husbands for less," said Conan.

"And yet I learned from my mother that a woman must have a man if she is to live in this world. If she would know wealth and comfort, it must be a strong man, one who can win that wealth, and protect both his wealth and his woman. For those who are not born to ease, safety, and comfort, it is the only way." She ran her gaze up and down his powerful frame. "I think there are few who could take from you that which you have grasped." She walked slowly forward, until the water came only to her knees. "And I assure you that, properly cared for, I look far better than this." Her invitation was as open as any he had ever seen.

Conan rose. "Aye, I know that well. But I do not trifle with other men's wives. Should we find that Marandos is dead . . ."—he paused and weighed his words—"then we must talk of this further."

He turned and walked back through the brush. Behind him he heard her tinkling laughter, then a splash as she dove out into the deeper water once more. He readied his spear for some hunting out in the desert, for he knew he would get no more sleep that night.

The days of rest did everyone unmeasured good. Everyone put on flesh with the abundant game Conan and Goma brought in and the fruit of the oasis. The sailors were able to make some repairs to their garments. More importantly, they had carried the hides of the game animals as they marched, and it was now dry enough to craft new soles for their footwear.

When all were rested and recovered, it was decided to resume the march upon the morrow. That day, Goma came to Conan.

"I saw a spy to the west when I was hunting this morning," said the guide.

"Aye," Conan said. "They must have been there for some time. That was a reason I insisted upon a long stay here. I wished to deny them this water hole as long as I could."

"That was a dangerous game," said Goma. "For if they had become desperate, they might have come and seized it by force."

"No, for they have been in no wise as hard-pressed as we. They have had it easier all along, with a large, well-organized expedition of disciplined men. We had only ourselves and some sore-footed sailors to bear water across the desert. They had the bumbana, who are far stronger than true men, and can carry far greater burdens."

"Ah, this is a deep game. So you wished to make them suffer, weaken them so that we will have a better chance should they try to attack?''

''Aye. By now, they cannot be in much better condition than we. And while the bumbana are strong, their feet are not much better for walking than those of apes. I'll wager they've lost a number of them in the desert.''

''But they are still many, and well armed.''

''We can only forge ahead. We know little of what lies before us. I will whittle away at them as I can. When the facedown comes, well''—he shrugged his broad shoulders—''I am too old a campaigner to try to foretell the outcome so soon. It shall be as always: fight when it is a good idea, run when you must.''

With their waterskins refilled and in a relatively lighthearted mood, they set off at first light. The mountain loomed ahead of them, but anything seemed preferable to the desert. It was not so great a mountain as the first they had climbed, and it was deeply cleft by the pass defined by the Horns of Shushtu.

Conan eyed the pass warily as they marched. There was magic up there, black sorcery that dated back ages. He detested all such wizardry, and he knew that it must be of great evil to have remained potent for so long. He had never sought out wizardry, and avoided it at every opportunity. Yet in his adventurous life he had fallen afoul of it more times than he could readily count. Some fate followed him, turning his steps directly toward that which he would most willingly avoid. He did not understand why this should be, but he accepted it as a part of living a life unlike that of other men.

''Now we near the end,'' said Springald, walking along beside the Cimmerian with a spring in his step Conan had not seen for a long time.

''Speak not of the end until our steps are well set upon the homeward road,'' Conan chided. ''It is bad luck to do otherwise.''

''Superstition!'' Springald scoffed.

''Perhaps,'' Conan said, ''but it pays to be cautious.'' Ulfilo strode up to them.

"I own that you were right, Conan," he said grudgingly. "The rest has done us all much good." It was not exactly an apology but Conan had expected none.

"Aye, we are ready for the mountain now," the Cimmerian answered. "Think you Marandos has taken care of the guardian spells?"

"If not, we are in deep trouble," Springald said cheerfully. "All my scholarship may avail us little in that case. We could sit outside that pass forever, unless, of course, Sethmes were to come along and help us out." He laughed merrily at this while Conan resisted the urge to tell him exactly how close he was to the real situation. It would almost be worth it, he thought, just to see the look on their faces, when they understood that, in playing their games of secrecy, they had left themselves open to the greatest betrayal of all.

"Come, let us not speak pessimistically," said Malia, linking an arm through Springald's and Ulfilo's. "The pass is in sight, the mountain is not high, and all is well. We will find my husband hale, we will have the treasure, and we will live forever."

"That is the spirit!" Springald commended.

Malia's recovery had been dramatic. Her burns had faded and her lips were no longer cracked and bleeding. Her hair shone and she was beginning to regain some of the flesh she had lost during the days of greatest privation.

Conan eyed the mountain in the near distance. Its sides were cloaked in greenery, but it looked far less dense than that upon the earlier mountain. He hoped that meant an easier ascent. It was a part of his calculations that they would make better speed for the rest at the oasis, while the Stygians would be forced to stay there longer themselves. It was his hope to gain the pass before Sethmes and his men and half-men even reached the base of the mountain.

By midday of the day following the morning when they left the oasis, they stood at the base of the final mountain. A wide path slanted to their right, ascending the slope. Far above, they could see that it cut back to the left.

"It looks strangely regular," Springald said, stroking his bearded chin. "Could it be the remains of a road built long ago?"

"It is just a washed-out old path, albeit a broad one," said Ulfilo. "There is not a paving stone to be seen."

"It would indeed be surprising if any paving were to survive after thousands of years," Springald said. "Not a stone remains of Python, famous though the city was."

"The only stones that interest me are the sort that sparkle and flame in many colors," Wulfrede said. "If they are set in crowns and rings, torcs and necklaces of gold, so much the better!"

"Our friend of Vanaheim keeps the crucial matters ever in the forefront of his mind," said Springald, chuckling.

"And we may at last find Marandos, my husband," Malia said. Conan suspected that she said this for the benefit of the other two.

"We'll find nothing at all if we don't get moving," Ulfilo told them. "Let's be off."

With that, they began to climb. The ground was uneven, but compared to what had gone before it was an easy climb. The heavy, sloshing waterskins made the going hard, but after the desert they were not about to abandon a drop of water until they found a reliable source. Despite the greenery, the mountain did not appear to be rich in springs.

The foliage consisted primarily of dense brush and stunted trees that clung to the thin soil. They saw occasional birds and small animals, but no large predators. Rocky crags thrust from the flank of the mountain, and upon some of these stood mountain goats of a stocky breed, with long, knobby horns that formed a sweeping, graceful curve. Overhead soared birds with wide wingspans but they saw none of these land. From time to time, they passed large stones of an oddly regular shape, never very far from the path.

"I could swear that those stones were cut by the hand of man," Springald said musingly.

"They look like mere chunks of rock to me," said Ulfilo.

But higher up the evidence grew unmistakable. Halfway up the mountain, they began to see flat, squarish stones atop the path. A little higher yet, these began to form a definite pavement. At some unthinkably remote date, this had been a road.

"Much good does it do us," Ulfilo grumbled. "What boots it that the Pythonians built a road here?"

"It is the first road we have encountered since we left the civilized lands," said Malia. "Let us enjoy walking on a paved road for a change."

Springald knelt and examined the paving stones carefully, frowning.

"Is aught amiss?" asked Conan.

"It is just . . . I cannot say for certain, but it seems to me that this stonework is terribly old."

"Python fell long ago," Ulfilo commented.

"No, longer even than that. And the treasure wards had no reason to build a road here. The last thing they would have wanted was a regular travel back and forth, or a road pointing the way to their hoard. This must have been here long before the Pythonians came through the pass."

"Well, what of that?" said Conan, uneasy despite his words. "The world is full of old ruins, in out-of-the-way places. If these few blocks date from the time of Atlantis it is not so great a marvel."

"Perhaps . . . perhaps you are right, my friend. It may be of no significance." He sounded like a man trying to convince himself.

They resumed their climb. Despite the easy going, all suffered from depressed spirits, except for Goma. The road was only a path of square-cut stone, but something in its very antiquity was depressing, as if it mocked the very brevity of their lives.

As they ascended, the Cimmerian from time to time left the road to climb atop a prominent crag and spy out the mountainside ahead of them, and also downslope, along the path they had already negotiated. Ulfilo was not slow to notice this behavior.

"With unknown dangers ahead of us," he said, "wherefore do you pay so much attention to that which lies behind?"

"It is never wise to think that danger can come from one direction only. I have seen many armies destroyed by an unexpected flank attack. Others have been overtaken by a pursuer thought to be far away."

"I never thought to be given military lessons by a naked savage," Ulfilo said. "And why speak of armies when we are a world away from the nearest civilization, when we have not seen so much as a village in a score of leagues?"

"You hired me to help you find your brother," the Cimmerian maintained. "I have served you well, and I will go about the task in my own fashion."

"Very well," said Ulfilo with ill grace, "but I am not satisfied with your explanation. Best I were not to learn that you have betrayal in mind."

"Do you accuse me of treachery?" said Conan, a dangerous gleam in his eye.

"Will you two cease this stupid bickering?" Malia said sharply. "We are almost at the Horns of Shushtu! Have we come all this way, enduring mountains and desert and jungle, just to have you two cut each other's throats over a few foolish words? I forbid it! We have come too far!"

"Yes, now of all times we must be united," agreed Springald. "We are near our goal but our trials are not at an end. Let us reserve our energies for the task ahead. Curb your ferocity, my friends."

Slowly, the two bristling warriors lowered their hands from their hilts. The sailors watched apprehensively and Goma watched with sardonic amusement.

"I am willing to let the matter drop," Conan said. "But it is my custom to answer such words with steel."

"For the sake of the mission, I am willing to let the matter rest here," Ulfilo said. He was about to add more but an angry glare from his sister-in-law silenced him.

"If that is settled, then let us go," Goma said. "We can be at the Horns by nightfall."

The rest of the day's march was accomplished amid a gloomy silence. Conan did not scan their backtrail again, but he was satisfied that the Stygian party was well behind them. He suspected that they still rested at the oasis and had not yet attempted the mountain.

The Horns of Shushtu loomed ominously above them, the two rugged crags all but identical except for their bizarre difference of color. Their sense of uneaze increased as they drew nearer the Horns. Clouds began to gather, and lightning flickered above the jagged crests.

"An ill place to be if a tempest comes," said Springald.

"Aye," said Conan. "A hard one could sweep us right off this mountain."

"Such storms must be why the road was obliterated on the lower slopes," Springald opined. "The torrents in the gorges must gather tremendous strength as they drain the slopes lower down, then overflow their banks with the power of—"

"Save your wind for marching," barked Ulfilo. "Pick up the pace! We must be in the pass before the storm strikes!"

They began to walk faster, then to trot. Hardened as they were by the long trek, this last burst of speed was murderous. By the time they gained the level ground between the Horns, Most of them were near collapse. Many of the sailors fell to the ground, gasping and retching, coughing their lungs out with agonizing pain. They had no time to examine their surroundings, for the storm broke upon them even as the last of the men came staggering in.

Lightning flared luridly, accompanied by simultaneous claps of deafening thunder. The travelers set their burdens on the ground and crouched low, bracing themselves against the howling wind, tensing every muscle each time the lightning flashed. The bolts made an eerie, sizzling crackle as they snaked along the valley between the Horns, and their nostrils stung with a strange, sharp scent that accompanied each brilliant discharge.

A flash of lightning brought two abrupt, brief screams that

sounded even above the thunderous blast that accompanied it. Two of the sailors were incinerated in an instant, their screams merely a reflex of bodies turned to charred skeletons in a moment's time.

A torrent of water sluiced through the narrows like a small river in full spate. They gripped rocks, dug their fingers into the ground, anything to keep from being swept back through the pass onto the steep road and the crags that awaited below.

Conan, quick-witted as always, drew his dirk an instant before the wall of water struck. He jammed the foot-long blade into the ground hilt-deep and gripped its handle with iron strength. No sooner was he braced against the torrent than something swept back against him, a flailing thing of arms and legs and a voice that screamed in terror. He recognized the slender limbs instantly and wrapped a powerful arm around the slender waist. Malia's arms went around his neck and she clung to him tightly as a barnacle, shivering with dread and with the bone-chilling cold of the water, accompanied as it was by an uncannily cold wind. Even in such dire extremity, Conan was able to appreciate the feel of Malia's body against his own.

Abruptly as it had begun, the rain and wind ceased. Within a few minutes the water drained from the pass and the survivors sat up to assess the damage.

"Who would have thought," Springald said, "that such a short time ago we were complaining about lack of water?"

Wulfrede laughed uproariously, "Aye, and about the heat as well!" His breath made a white steam before his red beard and, incredibly, a few flakes of snow drifted down upon his shoulders. The drop in temperature had been dramatically sudden and they shivered in their rags.

"Malia!" Ulfilo shouted. "Do you live?"

"I am here," the woman said, unwinding herself from the Cimmerian, who was somewhat reluctant to let go. "The water swept me away but Conan saved me."

Conan stood and tugged his dirk free of the hard-packed dirt of the pass. "How many of us are left?" A quick head count revealed that, besides the leaders of the little band, five sailors remained alive. Toward the western end of the pass they found the two lightning-struck men wedged, freakishly, between a boulder and the vertical rock wall. They made a ghoulish spectacle, little more than charred flesh over bones, with white teeth and golden earrings winking strangely from the horrid mass. Their steel weapons had melted and fused with their corpses.

"Mitra!" cried Malia, turning away and covering her face with both hands. She had seen much bloodshed and cruelty in her brief life, but this was a sight of unsurpassed horror.

Of the other sailors there was no sign. Apparently, they had been swept out of the pass and over the edge of the paved road, to lie shattered somewhere down the slope.

Conan looked in all directions. "Where is Goma?"

"Why," Ulfilo said, surprised, "the fellow was well ahead of us when the storm broke, about fifty paces before me when I last saw him. He must have been swept away as well."

"Did anyone see him go past?" Conan asked.

"Who was looking?" said Wulfrede. "We all had our own concerns with saving ourselves. It was only the greatest of luck that Malia struck you in passing. Would you have seen her otherwise?"

"You mean we no longer have a guide?" Malia said. "This is calamitous."

Ulfilo shrugged. "The man only agreed to guide us as far as the Horns, and he did that. It is unfortunate that he has not lived to collect his pay, but he may have wished to turn back here in any case."

"Perhaps he is still alive, farther up the pass," Springald said. "Let us look."

"Aye, we might as well, since we must be through the pass soon, else we freeze," said Wulfrede, clapping his arms against his shivering sides. "I am from a cold land, but it has been many years since I fared thither, and by Ymir, I never thought to see snow in the black lands!" Random flakes still drifted down, and among them all only Conan showed no sign of distress from the cold.

"I have known many mountain storms," said Conan, "and the violence of this one was in no wise strange. But its suddenness was, and we should not see such cold accompanied by snow. This mountain is not high enough for that. Is this more wizardry? Is it a part of the ancient curses left to defend the treasure of Python?" All looked to Springald for enlightenment. He was fussing with his satchel, fearful that water had entered it and damaged his books. Reassured that the satchel had remained watertight, he addressed them.

"It is quite conceivable. It is also likely, though, that the spell has lost much of its potency, for if the Pythonians had such control over the powerful forces of nature, then surely we all should have been slain. This may have been the last, feeble gasp of the ancient magic, especially since the Stygian priest entrusted Marandos with spells to neutralize the guardian curses."

"Feeble!" Malia exclaimed. "I rejoice that we did not encounter this curse at full strength!"

"This whole mad venture is cursed!" shouted one of the sailors. The eyes of all of them were wide with terror. "We will all die if we continue! We must go back!" Despite their evident exhaustion, they seemed more than ready to flee all the way back down the mountain. Ulfilo's face colored and he was about to launch into a roaring diatribe, but Wulfrede silenced him with an upheld palm. The shipmaster went to the speaker and stood before him, his thumbs hooked casually in his belt.

"I will not argue with you, Alkhat. I release all of you from your obligation to me, and to our employers." He spoke quietly, without a trace of rancor. "Be off with you now, and take my blessing."

The sailors stood, nonplussed. "But what of you, Captain?" asked one.

Wulfrede's red eyebrows went high in mock surprise. "Me? Why, I go on with the others, as I agreed to do long ago." He half turned to address Ulfilo, Springald, Malia, and Conan. "You *do* intend to continue, do you not?" They all nodded. He turned back to the sailors. "But you are free of your obligation. You may go."

"But, Captain," said the one named Alkhat, "we will die in that desert, or in the jungles if we should get so far."

Wulfrede smiled benignly. "I can see that you have been conversing with our schoolman. Already, you speak like a wise man." He turned back and began to walk up the canyon. "Come, my friends, I would be through this pass before it is fully dark." The others went with him. Hesitantly, reluctantly, the surviving sailors followed.

"There, you see? Was that not simply settled?" asked the Van. "There was no need to take a hard line with the lads. They had a right to be upset. But they understand the difference between grave danger and certain death. They have chosen the former."

"You know how to handle your men, shipmaster, I'll grant you that," Ulfilo conceded grudgingly.

"Crom's bones!" Conan said. "Look at this!" They were back at the point where they had gone to ground to weather the storm, and now they could see that the vertical stone walls to either side were covered with carvings. Line upon line, they marched up the walls as high as the eye could discern. Conan studied them in the fading light.

"Some of these look like Stygian hieroglyphs," the Cimmerian said, "but others are of a sort I have never seen."

"You are right," Springald said. He held one of his books, and looked back and forth from it to the incised figures. "The clearer marks are hieroglyphs, which have changed very little from the days of Python to now. But the others are far more worn, and see"—he pointed to a confused section of the carvings—"the Pythonian carvings were carved *over* the others!"

"They are pre-Pythonian?" Malia said. "But they must be. Are they perhaps Atlantean?"

Springald shook his head, his expression growing more alarmed by the second. "These are pre-Atlantean. By Mitra! I think they are pre*human*!"

# TWELVE

## The Valley of the Treasure

"Let us not waste time on old marks carved into stone," said Ulfilo. "If those squiggles are as ancient as you think, then surely they have lost whatever potency they may once have had."

"Aye," agreed Wulfrede. "They may not be magical. Many kings place stone carvings upon their borders, warning intruders of whose land lies beyond and praising their own greatness."

"You may be right," said Springald doubtfully. "No man now can interpret this ancient, uncanny writing, but there are hints and legends—"

"Enough," Ulfilo barked. "We must go!"

And so they set off. This time they were not in a long, straggling line, but in a compact group, all but huddling together amid the unknown perils of the pass between the Horns of Shushtu.

At one point, they encountered a block of stone that half blocked the gorge. It had fallen from a great height, but it was clearly a carved block, as huge as a base stone on one of the

Stygian pyramids. Springald measured it as three paces wide, five paces in height, and fifteen paces long. In the moonlight that now spilled into the gorge, they could just make out the rectangular hole from which it had fallen, far above them.

"Another trap for intruders," Conan said. "I'll wager we'd find flattened bones under there, were we able to lift this."

For the rest of their walk through the pass, they cast nervous glances overhead.

At the eastern end of the pass Conan called a halt, for he had seen something white upon the path just ahead. Going forward to reconnoiter, he found a heap of bones. The others came up behind him and gazed apprehensively at the mass of remains.

"Human?" asked Wulfrede.

"Not quite," Conan said, holding up a skull. Its apish, low-browed profile was unmistakable.

"Bumbana!" said Ulfilo. "Then they inhabit this mountain too?"

"Look at this," Conan said. He held up a handful of ornaments: an arm ring, a pair of wristbands, all of copper, and a silver chain with a pendant. "Stygian. This was one of Sethmes's servants, sent with Marandos's expedition. There was enough curse left to kill this one."

"It might have died naturally," Ulfilo said, "or been killed by its companions."

"Look at the condition of these bones," Conan said grimly. "Something flayed every bit of flesh off this creature."

"Scavengers . . ." Wulfrede hazarded.

"Look at them!" Conan insisted. "All in one place, exactly as it fell. Not the tiniest bone has been gnawed or scattered. And I do not think that it has lain here long enough for decay or insects to clean the bones thoroughly. Hair lasts after the flesh has been consumed, and the bumbana are covered with hair, but not one remains with these bones. They might have been polished by an artisan."

"Why just one, then?" Ulfilo mused. "Why not the whole party?"

"The curses have lost strength," Springald said. "And Marandos had counterspells. I think the pass is safe now."

"I hope you are right," Ulfilo said. Fearlessly, he strode the last few paces to the end of the pass. The others watched in suspense, but he passed through unharmed and they followed him.

The moonlight revealed a broad valley east of the mountain, but its pale light brought out no details. A gentle wind blew up the slope from below, its warmth welcome after the unnatural cold of the pass.

"I cannot tell whether there is a road on this side," Springald said. "We dare not press on through this uncertain darkness."

"Aye," Ulfilo said unwillingly. "We must abide here until daylight."

"There seems to be wood hereabout," said Wulfrede. "Shall we kindle a fire to warm our weary bones?"

"No fires," Ulfilo ordered. "We know not who abides in yonder valley, and I'd as lief not advise them of our arrival."

"That would be wisest," Conan said. "Wring the water out of what is left of your clothes and hang them on the bushes. If this breeze holds, they should be dry by morning."

They followed his advice, the sailors bemoaning their hardships, the rest stoically, then they sat or lay down to wait out the hours of darkness. One by one, they dropped off to sleep, only Conan remaining wakeful. He sat with his back against a smooth boulder, a spear slanted over his shoulder, his sword close to hand. He had cleaned it and left it bare while its sheath dried. A wise warrior took care of his weapons first.

He was not greatly wearied, and he did not wish to sleep until he knew that they were safe. In the silence he kept all his senses open and receptive, but he heard nothing save the rustlings of tiny animals, and he saw nothing save a few, flitting bats. This indicated safety to him, for there were no men or large predators nearby, even though the bright moonlight made for excellent hunting conditions. Satisfied, he nodded off to sleep, ever ready to spring to full wakefulness at first hint of danger.

The moon had fully set by the time Conan awoke. The stars still shone, but the dawn was no more than a thin gray stripe on the eastern horizon. He unwound to his full height, stretching and walking the stiffness out of his joints as the gray stripe became a rosy glow that spread upward, causing the stars to wink out in its path. He began to recognize shapes, then colors below. When it was possible to see details, he began shaking shoulders and prodding backsides.

"Get up," he said "Morning is here and you must see this."

Ulfilo sat up, rubbing his eyes. "Eh? Daylight already? Why did you not rouse me an hour ago?"

"I was asleep an hour ago," Conan growled. "and there was nothing to see then anyway, so there was no reason for any of us to be awake. Now quit complaining and look down there."

One by one they stood, then stared dumbfounded down the slope of the mountain.

"Mitra!" Springald said. "Does the climate and terrain of this land change every time one crosses a mountain range?"

Spread below them was a vision of paradise. The land to the east lay on a higher plateau than the desert to the west. The mountain sloped gently and rather briefly to a valley of surpassing greenness. It was not the dark, ominous green of the jungle, but rather the brilliant, orderly green of the more temperate lands. They could see that much of it lay under cultivation, with straight-rowed fields outside the clustered huts of villages. A number of streams flowed through the valley and herds of what appeared to be cattle drank and waded in the waters. Neat orchards were surrounded by fences or barriers of some sort. They could not make out the composition of the fences.

Much of the land was still wild, although nothing like what they had come through. Upon some of the low hills they could see small herds of wild game, including a few elephants and giraffes.

Far to the south they could just make out something that looked too large to be a mere village, but it clearly was not a natural feature.

"A city?" Malia said, wonder in her voice.

"Ruins, perhaps," said Springald, "left from the days of the Pythonians."

"We'll know soon enough," said Ulfilo. "Is everyone ready?"

By this time all had redonned their clothing and slung their weapons about them. "Then let us be on our way."

Their hearts were lighter as they began what they all hoped to be the final leg of their long, long trek. The slope promised none of the hardship they had endured thus far, and the valley below was as inviting as a lively port city.

Conan was not so sure. It looked like a fine land, but it had been his experience that the best lands were inhabited by people adept at defending their lands against all comers. A long stretch of peace could soften the dwellers in the easy lands, but such places excited envy and their borders seldom remained untroubled for long.

"Look!" said Malia when they were halfway down the mountain. She pointed at a hulking creature a few dozen paces off the trail they followed. The beast looked something like a rhinoceros, but the blunt horn of its nose forked sideways, and a pair of stubbier horns blossomed farther up its snout, just below the piggy eyes. It placidly munched a mouthful of grass and paid them no attention whatever.

"Have you ever seen its like?" Springald asked Conan.

"Never," the Cimmerian said. "I'll wager this land holds many surprises for us."

"May they all be pleasant," Springald intoned.

The path they trod bore no trace of paving, but Springald assured them, in his pedantic fashion, that this was not to be wondered at, for it was obvious that this side of the mountain got far more rain than the other, and this water would long since have obliterated any traces of man's work after so long a time.

As they reached the lower slopes of the mountain, they began to see traces of cultivation. Bushes grew in straight lines along the slopes, and vines were similarly arranged upon props. N one seemed to be tending them and monkeys frolicked freely among the foliage. They decided that these crops were not in fruit to be thus unattended.

"When will we encounter people?" Malia wondered aloud as they neared level ground. The answer to her question came almost immediately.

The man stood on a grassy sward, leaning on a long spear. He gazed up the lower slope of the mountain, and he straightened when he saw the approaching travelers. Because of the distance they could tell little about him save that he was tall and thin. He turned slightly and raised a curved object to his lips. They heard the high, piercing note of the horn, then the man resumed leaning on his spear.

"There is only one," said Springald, optimistically.

"He blew that horn for someone's ears," Ulfilo said.

"And he does not look afraid to see many armed strangers approaching," noted Wulfrede.

"Because he knows he has little to fear," said Conan. "Look."

A double score of men trotted up to the lone watcher, and their spears made a fierce glitter in the sunlight. As one, they began to run toward the newcomers. They made no warlike show, but ran silently, in an orderly, disciplined fashion.

"Keep your hands away from your weapons," Ulfilo ordered. "They are too many for us, and this valley may be full of their like. Remember, we are peaceful travelers and I'll kill any man who hints otherwise."

Minutes later the warriors were all around them. They were all tall men of light brown color, with handsome, regular features. Their hair, reddened with ocher, was worked into varying shapes, and most had patterns of tiny scars worked upon their skins. All carried broad-bladed spears and small, oval shields.

"They all look like Goma!" Malia gasped.

"I knew that rogue was hiding something from us!" Ulfilo said indignantly.

"And here we are without an interpreter," sighed Springald. "This could prove to be awkward."

All of the warriors wore white plumes in headbands of leopard skin. Most had one or two. A man stepped forward who wore three. He also wore golden armbands and anklets. He said something in a stern voice.

"This must be their officer," Conan said. "I'll try Kushite on him." He essayed a few words, but the man just stared blankly. The Cimmerian tried other tongues used sometimes in the black lands, with no greater success.

The officer barked something and gestured with his spear. The others formed a square around the newcomers and all faced in one direction.

"I think we are about to be escorted somewhere," Springald said. "I advise that we go along with them."

"That would be best," said Ulfilo. "They have not turned hostile, and have made no move to disarm us."

"Suppose they want to eat us?" said a sailor.

"You are too skinny," Wulfrede assured him. "They will want to fatten you up first."

And so, for lack of any alternative, they marched away, within the hollow square of their warrior escort. The road they took was not paved, but it was level and well tended. They began to see many people working in the fields flanking the road. These dropped their tools to come nearer and gape at the passing newcomers. These workers were both men and women, some of the latter carrying infants slung to their lithe bodies in reddish cloths. Of the men, none bore weapons. The crops they tended resembled nothing the westerners knew, but they seemed to include both grains and vegetables.

Once they passed a tiny village that contained nothing but warriors. These were identical to their escort, save they wore blue feathers in bands of lion skin. They glared malevolently, but Conan had the distinct impression that their hostility was not toward the newcomers. Rather, it was directed at the white-feathered warriors. This was a thing to be considered.

"We are headed toward that city," Springald observed.

"If city it is," said Ulfilo.

"At least," Malia said, "there is no desert here, and no jungle, and no horde of attacking apemen. I'll not complain if the place we are going turns out not to be the equal of Tarantia or Belverus."

"That's the spirit," Conan commented. "Keep your guard up, and take the good as it comes." His laugh boomed out, startling some of the escorting warriors.

The walk was lengthy, but not unpleasant, especially in comparison to their recent hardships. They passed a number of tiny villages, each consisting of no more than ten to twenty huts. The huts were beehive-shaped, covered with dense thatch. They were uncommonly clean and neatly kept for primitive settlements. The people were of a sort difficult to read, Conan thought as he walked by one village after another. They did not seem to be downtrodden, brutalized serfs, for their interest and curiosity concerning the newcomers was lively enough. But their attitude was guarded, as if they were afraid to exhibit enthusiasm. There was no laughter, and the people did not sing as they worked, unlike most people south of Stygia.

The Aquilonians seemed not to notice this, but the Cimmerian knew that aristocrats seldom noticed anything about their inferiors as long as they were not insolent or hostile. He could see that Wulfrede's sharp blue eyes noticed the oddity, though.

"I think there is trouble in this land, my friends," the Van said.

"How so?" asked Ulfilo.

"The villagers are afraid of our warrior guards."

"When are toilers not afraid of warriors?" Ulfilo said.

"The blue-feathered warriors we passed dislike them as well," Conan pointed out.

"Jealousy between regiments is common," Ulfilo said.

"I think our friends are right," Springald put in. "Something feels . . . I do not know, something feels just *wrong*. This seems a fair and bountiful land, defended by sturdy warriors and worked by diligent peasants. These are all the ingredients for a happy nation. But these folk are uncommonly subdued and it is not from fear of us, for they can see that we are few and are encompassed by their own warriors.''

"Civil unrest, perhaps?'' Stubborn and arrogant as he was, Ulfilo did not lack astuteness when it came to the exercise of power. "All people are unhappy and uncertain when it is not clear who governs.''

"That may be it,'' said Wulfrede. "I have been in lands on the verge of civil war where the air sang silently with this sort of unease.''

"No sense speculating until we know our position,'' Conan said. "But we must be on our guard.''

"I see no signs of the treasure we seek,'' said Malia.

"Aquilonia is rich,'' Ulfilo said, "but the common folk there do not go about decked in gold and jewels. The rulers here may have it hidden in vaults.''

"They may not even know of its existence,'' Springald said.

"How so?'' Wulfrede queried.

"These people much resemble those Captain Belphormis described encountering near the coast. They may have migrated hither in recent centuries. If so, they may be as ignorant of the treasure and its bearers as the people who now live where Python once stood.''

"Then the treasure may be untouched!'' Wulfrede said happily.

"It may be unfindable,'' Malia said. "Who knows what it might be buried under?''

"The instructions given by the Stygian priest to Marandos were quite explicit,'' Springald said. Conan took careful note of this. It was the first he had heard of such instructions.

Malia laughed. "Springald, it is you yourself who are always reminding us of the vast gulf of time that separates us from the fall of Python! It was the greatest city in the world, but no man now is even certain where it lay. Yet you expect all here to be as the treasure-bearers left it?''

"Well, I, ah . . ."

"I suggest," Conan said, "that we have enough to concern us at the moment. Let us see to assuring our own lives before we worry about the treasure."

"You ask a great deal," Wulfrede said, "if you ask *me* to take my mind off treasure!" At this, even his sailors raised a feeble laugh. Malia laughed louder than the others.

"You seem in good spirits, sister-in-law," said Ulfilo, as if he considered this to be a deficiency in character.

"I have not lost my sense of humor. Look at us! Ten ragged, half-starved scarecrows on a fool's errand in a savage wilderness and we speak as if we could hoist a great treasure upon our backs and walk home with it! Does no one besides me understand the folly of this?" Her voice grew ragged in speaking the final words, finishing with a near-sob.

"Now, my dear," Springald chided, "there is no need to grow so exercised. We shall find the treasure, and doubtless these simple natives will consent to furnish us with bearers. We can pay them with trinkets when they bear the treasure back to where we cached our trade goods. And, do not forget, you may soon be reunited with your husband!"

"Oh, yes," Malia said. "I must not forget that." Conan could have laughed at her tone, were their situation not so serious. He fell back a few steps and spoke to Wulfrede while the Aquilonians chattered among themselves.

"Think you these 'simple natives' will be so easy to deal with?" he asked.

"What?" said Wulfrede in mock horror. "Do you expect me to disagree with our aristocratic leaders? For shame, Conan!"

"They would consider my people to be simple savages," Conan growled. "But we would hew them down for being mad fools."

"We Vanir are a more civilized folk. We would sacrifice them to one of our lesser gods since they are worthless for anything else."

"Yet Ulfilo is a great fighting man," Conan said. "And

Springald is an amusing fellow and loyal to his friends. No, the prospect of treasure has made them mad. They want to believe that they can just walk in, find it lying somewhere convenient, and leave with it. And, wanting to believe, they do not recognize the difficulties they face.''

''Perhaps not,'' said the Van, ''but harken to my words. If that treasure is here, I shall not leave without my part of it.'' The blue eyes were frosty, and Conan knew that the shipmaster was not to be dissuaded.

He had known the Nordheimer people, the Aesir and the Vanir, from earliest youth. They were an uproarious, pleasure-loving people who reveled alike in bloodshed, feasting, fine raiment, and beautiful ships. Above all they loved gold, silver, jewels, and other precious things. Their greed at times approached madness.

Conan, a son of the dour Cimmerian race, was not quite so single-minded in his pursuit of these things. He liked them well enough, setting him apart from his mountain-bred kin. When he lived in the civilized lands, it gave him pleasure to win gold in order to live prodigally for a while. But always he had to turn back to the hard warrior's life of savage blows and cruel conditions, and these suited him as well. Wealth had never been an end in itself to Conan.

Now, amid the wonders and terrors of the black lands, the attractions of treasure seemed remote to him. Back in Asgalun, the prospect of high pay and a share in the treasure had been pleasant. Here it all seemed unreal. From the day they began their trek inland, he had shed the veneer of civilization and reverted to his origins. The wonders and splendors through which they had come had long since purged him of greed. He wanted to see more of this wondrous land. Gold would merely encumber him. Still, he had accepted this mission, and he would see it to its conclusion, no matter how foolish it had become to him. Conan had never accepted pay without rendering value.

They were unprepared for the sight that greeted them at the end of the march.

"It is a city!" Malia gasped.

Indeed, the wall that towered before them would not have disgraced one of the major cities of Aquilonia, Nemedia, or any of the other great habitations of the Hyborian nations. Beyond the wall they could see lofty towers and the rooftops of huge buildings. Upon the great wall were carved strange, arcane figures in low relief.

"Surely these village folk did not build such a place!" said Wulfrede.

"Nay," said Springald in an awed, hushed voice. "I think we look upon the architecture of ancient Python, perhaps the only example yet in existence! Think of it! The nation and city were obliterated, the Hyborian invaders leaving not so much as a stone standing upon another. Yet here, in the far reaches of the black lands, a city of that empire still stands."

"I like it not," Conan said. "If they came here to hide the royal treasure, why did they build an entire city? Look at the size of those stones!"

Now they were close enough to see what the Cimmerian meant. The masonry of the wall was indeed Cyclopean. The smallest stones were at least as large as the one that they had found fallen in the pass. Many of them were far larger.

"I judge the lintel stone above the gate to be fully twenty-five paces in length," said Ulfilo. "I'd not want to be the general assigned to reduce this place with rams and siege engines."

They were not permitted any leisure to examine the wall more closely, but were marched through the gate and into the city beyond.

"Taking this place would not be such a task after all," Conan noted. "Look at the condition of the gate."

"What gate?" Malia asked. "I see no gate."

"That is what I meant," Conan answered. "The timbers have long since rotted away and the metalwork has been scavenged."

"Aye," said Springald, pointing to a number of square holes in the uprights supporting the tremendous lintel. "See, there are where the great hinges were attached. Wood and metal do not last the way stone does. The wood is long since rotted away, and these people, or their ancestors or some other people who passed this way, took the metal to make weapons.''

"Let us hope that is all they took," Wulfrede grumbled.

Indeed, they could now see that most of the city was ruinous. Temples stood roofless and abandoned, as did other huge buildings that might have been theaters or law courts or covered markets. Smaller buildings were inhabited, incongruously roofed with thatch.

The city seemed to have a sizable population, with an unusually large proportion of warriors, all of these wearing white or black feathers. Workers in wood and metal plied their crafts beneath shades of thatch or woven fiber, and women pounded grain in large mortars with clublike pestles of hard wood. Goats, cattle, and poultry made the air noisy and fragrant. The larger animals grazed in what might once have been public parks, or the gardens and orchards of the wealthy. The scene was fairly typical of native villages in this part of the world, save for its bizarre setting amid the ruins of a great and uncanny city.

They passed a market where beasts were slaughtered and cut up on the spot and where hunters hawked the flesh of wild game. At one end of the market huge fish, half the size of a man, were strung like beads from cords passed through their gills.

"At least I see no man-meat for sale," said a sailor. "That's a comfort."

"But where do they catch such fish?" queried another. "Surely not in the streams we have passed here." The fish were not merely large, but seemed somehow misshapen. Their bulbous heads bore flat faces that seemed repellantly humanoid, and their forward pair of ventral fins bore five bony ribs, making them resemble webbed hands.

"I do not know about the rest of you," Malia said queasily, "but should we be offered fish to eat here, I think I will pass."

They had picked up a large following of town idlers, and some who had dropped their labor to see this new wonder. The

parade passed between two pedestals that had once borne colossal statues, now toppled, and entered a broad square framed
by giant, ruinous buildings. Its paving stones were a lurid red
color, and at the far end of it stood a cylindrical tower fully a
hundred feet high, its preserved condition explained by the mas-
siveness of its masonry, which was again of the Cyclopean order. A continuous belt of relief sculpture ascended the tower in
a spiral, interrupted only by occasional, narrow windows.

"How many fled Python with the treasure?" Conan asked.

"But a few shiploads," said Springald, stunned by the frag-
mentary splendors all around them.

"Then what did they use for a labor force?" the Cimmerian
demanded. "It can take all the men of a province to build a
Stygian royal tomb, and they can be a lifetime building it."

"I . . . I know not, but there must be an explanation," Springald stammered. "Perhaps they found this valley abundantly
peopled, and forced the inhabitants into slavery."

"Enough," Ulfilo said. "We have more important things to
concern us."

Their escort halted before a stone platform that extended from
the base of the tower. At intervals around the border of the
platform were man-high posts, and atop each post was a grinning skull. Some of these were bleached white, others with some
dried flesh still adhering, still others nearly fresh.

"This has a grim look," said Ulfilo.

"See you any faces that look familiar?" Wulfrede asked.
Malia shuddered at the question.

"None of the more recent ones are white," Springald said.
"As for the rest, all skulls look much alike."

There was motion visible within the doorway at the base of
the tower, and all the people in the plaza, including their escort,
fell to their faces. Each raised a right hand, palm toward the
doorway, and shouted a rhythmic chant.

The man who strode from the doorway was fully seven feet
tall. His body was roped with heavy muscle, readily visible
since he wore little save ornaments and a brief leopard skin. He

would have been handsome as well as imposing, but the decorative scarring customary with these people had been carried to an extreme in his case. Every square inch of his skin bore the scars, so that he appeared to be covered with a skintight garment of shiny black nodules.

Just behind and to one side of the giant was a tiny, wizened creature of indeterminate gender. This grotesque being opened its pink toothless mouth and screamed something. Instantly, warriors of the escort leapt to their feet, grasped the travelers by the arms, and forced them to their knees.

"I kneel to no savage!" Ulfilo shouted.

"Ordinarily, neither do I," said Wulfrede, dryly. "In this case, however, it may be advisable."

"Aye, bear with shame for now," Conan growled. "Later is the time for revenge."

Behind the giant followed a colorful entourage. Some were women of exceptional beauty who bore fans, flowers, or pots of smoking incense. Dwarfs and others with grotesque deformities capered, and a band of stalwart musicians beat upon drums, blew horns, and shrilled upon pipes. A man whose face was painted as a death mask carried a sword slanted across his shoulder. Its blade was broad and swelling, squared off at the tip. No great guesswork was required to understand that this was an executioner.

The giant said something and a man of medium height came forward. He wore a long robe striped red and blue, and a good many ornaments upon his arms and neck. To their great surprise, he addressed them in excellent Kushite.

"Who are you, and why have you come to the land of King Nabo? Strangers from beyond are forbidden to tread upon the sacred land of the valley."

"And yet you are a stranger here by the look and sound of you," said Conan. "I'll warrant your sire and dam were a Stygian and a Kushite."

The man was astonished. "I am indeed. I came here a slave, captured beyond the mountains and sold here by traders. I have risen in service to King Nabo and am now a counselor. I ask again: what is your business here?''

"We seek my brother," said Ulfilo. "His name is Marandos, and he led men hither some time back. We have reason to believe that he survived the accursed pass, and entered this kingdom.''

"And what sought he here?''

This was a delicate question, for they knew not what they faced. In the midst of a powerful and warlike people, they had agreed, it would be inadvisable to admit that they were on a looting expedition. Against such a contingency, a cover story had already been prepared.

"My brother is a merchant, and he fared hither seeking new territories in which to trade his goods: metals and cloth and other wares from the north. Have you seen aught of him?''

The man translated this. To their astonishment, the tiny, grotesque creature loosed a shrill laugh. Then it chattered something while pointing a scrawny, taloned finger at the newcomers.

"Aghla says you lie!'' furnished the translator. "She says that you are treacherous thieves, come to plunder our land.'' At least that settled the question of the creature's gender.

"Wherefore says she this?'' demanded Ulfilo, wounded in his dignity.                                          ·

"She says you come here seeking treasure, the ancient wealth of our gods.''

"But what of Marandos?'' Springald said.

At that moment, someone in the crowd of onlookers sneezed. King Nabo glanced idly in the direction from which the sound had come and Aghla pointed toward the offender, screaming something. Instantly, guards plunged into the crowd and dragged forth a trembling wretch. He was a man dressed in a kilt and wearing no ornaments. From the wood shavings adhering to his skin and clothing, he was an artisan of some sort.

The king waved casually to the skull-faced man. That worthy strode importantly to where the guards held the culprit down on his knees, with both arms behind his back. The force seemed unnecessary, for the man did not struggle, but behaved as if resigned to his fate. The executioner gripped the long handle of his glaive in both hands and commenced a whirling dance around the condemned man, accompanied by the drums of the musicians behind the king. He twirled his blade with ornate flourishes, from time to time springing in close enough to brush its edge against the skin on the back of his victim's neck.

Each time he felt the cold iron, the man winced and twisted his face in an agony of dread. His face turned grayish and spittle dripped from his slack mouth. He looked more than half dead already.

"Why will they not kill the poor fool cleanly?" Conan growled.

"I think this king has a taste for the antic," Springald said.

With a demented howl, the executioner sprang into the air, whirled around twice, and came down an arm's length from the prisoner. The broad blade made a circular flash and the victim's head went spinning toward the dais, still wearing its expression of dread. The guards released the spasming corpse and it collapsed twitching to the ground, spouting blood from the stump of its neck.

With a gobbling cry, Aghla sprang forward and seized the head. She held it high, dancing in the same manner as the executioner, unmindful of the blood that fell spattering the filthy rags she wore. She whirled her way to the dais and deposited the head upon a vacant post amid the laughter and applause of the crowd.

"I do not know what this signifies," said Springald, "save that it is inadvisable to sneeze in the presence of the king."

"I hope the rules of etiquette at this court are not numerous," Malia said.

King Nabo said something to the translator. "My king wishes to know who led you here."

"We followed the writings of an ancient traveler," Springald explained. He held up one of his books. The translator took it and displayed it to the king, showing him how the pages turned. The king looked at a few pages, then spoke.

"My king does not believe that marks on leaves can lead men across great and unknown lands. He wants to know who guided you here."

"But you do not understand," Springald insisted. "To one who knows the art, it is possible to learn even the secrets of faraway lands from writing."

"I understand this," said the translator. "I have seen many books, and can read Stygian. I will try to explain to King Nabo." For a few minutes, the translator and the king conversed, but the monarch frowned and shook his head. Aghla listened closely, and interjected in a screeching, whining voice.

"My king says that you must have had a guide to bring you through the dangers of the desert and the mountain, and Aghla says that your writing is a magic that has no power in this land."

"We do not come here to work magic," Ulfilo said impatiently, "but to search for my brother. Will you not tell us what you know of him?"

"It is not wise to press King Nabo," said the translator, nodding minutely toward the new-severed head.

"Then tell the king that our intentions are entirely benevolent," Springald said, "and that we crave his protection and hospitality in this his land, while we search for our lost kinsman."

The translator relayed these words to the king. Nabo nodded, his lips curving into a smile. Aghla broke into raucous laughter, a sound that was, if anything, even more repulsive than her enraged screeching.

"I do not like the sound of that," Malia said uncomfortably.

"What is that creature?" Wulfrede mused. "Counselor? Witch? Jester?"

Conan snorted. "She could be his mother for aught we know."

"I can believe that such a mother could produce such a son," said Malia, "for they're a pair of monsters." They fell silent as the translator turned from the two.

"My master bids you welcome. You shall stay here in his royal house, and this evening he will hold a great feast in your honor."

"We had best accept without reservation," Springald said.

"Aye," Conan affirmed, speaking Aquilonian, "Our lives hang by a thread at this moment, and if we'd get away from here, with or without the treasure, we must know more about this place and its folk."

"Agreed," said Ulfilo. Then, to the translator: "Convey our heartiest thanks to your royal master, and inform him that we are most grateful for his largesse after our long journey with its many hardships."

The king seemed to be satisfied with this answer. He spoke to the translator and to the mob of servants behind him, then he turned and walked back into the tower.

"Come with me," the translator said. "You shall abide within the house of the king during your stay."

"I'd have preferred anywhere else," Ulfilo muttered, "but there is no help for it. Come on. Conan, Wulfrede, take good note of all the exits."

The Van chuckled. "I always do, for is it not said in the *Poem of Good Advice*: 'Enter no house without finding all the doors and windows, for you may need to leave hastily, and not by the way you entered'?"

"That sounds like the sort of poem a Van would compose," said Malia, chuckling despite their situation.

"We are a practical folk. That poem is full of such good precepts."

They followed the translator into the huge stone pile. Its interior was even more vast than the exterior hinted. The design of the place was exceedingly strange, for the walls, ceilings, and floors met at odd angles. Most of the floors were partial, so that one could look up and see several levels, and there were stone stairways and catwalks that seemed to go nowhere. In addition to the ancient stonework, the natives had added partitions and ceilings of wood, bamboo, and thatch. The whole inside buzzed and echoed with activity.

"What madmen built such a place?" Conan asked.

"I—I cannot say," Springald stammered. "The quality of the stonework is very similar to early Stygian, but the design—it is like nothing I have ever seen before, save in some terribly ancient drawings, long thought to have been the work of a demented artist."

The king and his entourage disappeared into some obscure part of the maze as the translator led Conan and his companions up a ramp, and thence up a series of stairways, to a lofty suite of rooms lighted by tall, narrow windows. Its walls and ceiling had the same disturbing angles, but it was clean and the floor was strewn with fresh rushes.

"Look!" Malia cried, pointing out one of the windows. They crowded to the window and gazed out, to their amazement, upon a broad lake. Its waters were exceedingly dark and seemed unnaturally still.

"Now we know where the fish came from," Wulfrede commented.

"Fish as odd as those we saw might well come from such a lake," Springald said. "I do not like the look of it."

"Aye," said Conan uneasily. "There is something strange about it."

The lake was almost perfectly circular, and it lay, as near as the Cimmerian could make out, in the very center of the valley, at its lowest level. Apparently, all the streams of the valley seemed to empty into the lake.

"There must be an outflow somewhere," Conan said, "but I see none."

"Perhaps it drains into underground caverns," Springald hazarded.

"We have more important matters to concern us than an odd lake," Ulfilo told them. He turned away from the window and took a seat on the straw-covered floor. "Such as: why will these

people tell us nothing of Marandos? We can be sure that he
entered this valley. Why do they conceal him from us?''

''They may have slain him,'' Springald said.

''You saw how a man was butchered just for sneezing,''
Conan said. ''I do not think King Nabo is one to conceal a bit
of bloodletting.''

''Perhaps they do not know of him,'' Malia said. She still
stood by the window, gazing out over the lake.

''How could they not?'' Ulfilo demanded.

''We may have paid too much attention to the lake,'' she said.
''Look beyond it to the low hills. Do my eyes fail me or do I
see another city there?''

Once more they all crowded to the windows. Following the
direction of her pointing finger, they could indeed make out a
cluster of structures that were clearly man-made.

''Perhaps he is there!'' she said. ''It may be that more than
one tribe inhabits this valley, and it could be that the two are
rivals. That could explain the king's caution.''

Ulfilo scratched in his beard. ''Aye, that may be so. But we
have no way of knowing if yon pile of stone is even inhabited.
The distance is too great.''

''I see no smoke,'' Wulfrede said, ''but fires of dry wood
might not smoke enough to be seen at such a distance. We must
watch that place tonight. Torchlight would be visible.''

Conan turned to the translator and addressed him in Kushite.
''What is that town in the hills?''

''It is nothing,'' the man said hastily. ''Just old stones.'' There
was undeniable fear written on the translator's face.

''Do not press him,'' Ulfilo said quietly.

''What is your name?'' Conan asked.

The man looked relieved to be on safer ground. ''I am Khefi.
As you guessed, my father was a Stygian trader who kept a
compound for merchandise and slave caravans on the Zarkheba
River. My mother was his concubine, a woman of Kush. While
driving a herd of cattle to a market south of the Zarkheba, I was
captured by slavers and sold from one market to the next over

the better part of two years. In time I was sold to a band of squat, squint-eyed men of a race unknown to me. They brought me here, by way of a cavern that pierces a sheer range of craggy mountains to the north. They sold me to the father of King Nabo. First I was a herdsman, but I rose quickly in the royal service, for I am capable and know tongues other than that spoken in this valley."

"Your traders came here," Wulfrede, "and you translate for outsiders. This valley, then, is not as forbidden to outsiders as you said before."

Khefi shrugged. "No people wishes to be shut off entirely from the outside. King Nabo must have steel and cloth, and like other people, the folk here prize colorful glass beads and looking glasses. At some times they want slaves, at others they have slaves to trade. But no strangers are allowed to stay longer than necessary to transact their business."

"And how are we to be received?" Ulfilo asked.

"That is up to my master. There is no law here save the will of King Nabo. Today he entertains you. If you please him, he may send you on your way with presents. If not"—he shrugged again—"he will probably kill you all."

# THIRTEEN

## King of the Accursed Lake

They rested, managing to sleep for a while, through the late afternoon and early evening. They were awakened by the sound of drums thundering below. Serving women arrived bearing ewers of water and robes made of trade cloth. All but Conan exchanged the rags of their remaining clothing for the robes, belting their weapons over the colorful cloth.

"Thus far we are being treated hospitably," said Springald, hopefully.

"That may change at any moment," Ulfilo said. "The favor of a king is always a chancy thing, and I suspect that a savage king may be even less reliable than the civilized sort."

"These women are not uncomely," said a scar-faced sailor. "Just how hospitable be this king, do you think?"

"You will keep your hands off the womenfolk," said Ulfilo sternly. "We know too little as yet. He might take mortal offense. Wait until he indicates plainly that you may make free with them."

"That is a hard thing to ask," said the sailor. "We have been a long time wandering with no female company."

"Aye," grumbled the others.

"This king takes a man's head for sneezing in his presence," said Conan with a sardonic smile. "What do you suppose he cuts off for trifling with his female property?" The sailors looked suddenly serious and said nothing.

When the setting sun stained the waters of the lake a sinister red, Khefi entered their chambers. "The king has prepared a feast in your honor," he announced. "Be so good as to accompany me."

Ulfilo turned to Springald. "Bring the satchel of presents," he ordered. "We have a few remaining that a king will not find unsuitable." To the others he said: "I want every man to be on his best behavior. We did not come this far, and endure so much, to leave our bones in this place or go home empty-handed."

"You've no argument from me on that point," Wulfrede said fervently.

"I hope fish is not on the menu for the feast," Malia said.

"Eat what you are given and smile," Conan advised. "There are many things far worse than eating repulsive fish."

They descended the steps through the chaotic tower and were led to cushions of stuffed zebra hide, where servants fanned them while the drummers and fluters played and costumed dancers cavorted. Men in demon-masks pranced on stilts, swatting at one another with inflated bladders while near-naked women, their bodies glistened with oil, gyrated energetically to complex rhythms. Children clapped and sang melodiously in eerie, many-leveled harmonies.

The dancing and singing reached an ecstatic pitch as the king emerged from his tower with his entourage. Behind him was the hideous Aghla.

"Who is that ugly old monkey?" Wulfrede asked Khefi.

"Be careful what you say," the translator cautioned. "She can read men's hearts even if she does not understand their tongues. She is a member of the royal family, and is perhaps the king's great-great-grandmother. She is said to be more than two hundred years old, and has prolonged her life through unspeakable rites. She sniffs out witchcraft plots against the king. Any who attract her suspicion die horribly.''

''Then all must be in danger here,'' Conan said, ''for no one could have pleasant thoughts about that creature.''

The king seated himself, Aghla squatting by his side, and at his signal the newcomers were given gourds of foaming beer. Wulfrede took a long drink and smacked his lips appreciatively.

''It is not northern ale,'' he pronounced, ''but it is drinkable. Perhaps these people are not as savage as we thought.''

Fruit, meats, and flat cakes of bread were placed before them, and they all ate hungrily. To their relief, there was no fish. Between courses, Ulfilo ceremoniously presented King Nabo with his gifts: a handsome necklace of silver plaques with designs in bright enamel, and a dagger with a handle of carved crystal. The king seemed pleased, but Aghla studied them with her small, shiny black eyes and favored them with a malicious, toothless smile.

''That creature's regard does little for my appetite,'' Wulfrede grumbled.

''You seem to be doing justice by the viands,'' Malia observed.

The Van tore a gazelle leg from a steaming carcass. ''Would I insult my host? Besides, who knows when we will next eat? It is best to stock up when opportunity exists.'' He set his teeth to the savory flesh, suiting action to words.

The feast continued through the long, sultry evening, until all were replete with food and half foundered with drink. Conan ate well but he knew better than to overindulge in the grain beer and the palm wine. The company was too doubtful and the circumstances too uncertain. He noted that Ulfilo and Springald were likewise cautious. Wulfrede felt no such compunctions, but he had powerful control and seemed little the worse for all the gourds he had drained.

As the moon rose over the hills to the east, King Nabo stood and clapped his hands. The drums fell silent and slaves cleared away the litter of the feast. There was a bustle at the rear of the surrounding crowd, and a pair of guards came forward, dragging between them a young woman who wore a copper collar riveted around her neck. Her features differed from those of the valley people. Her face was round and blunt-featured and she wore no decorative scars. She was plainly terrified. The king spoke and everyone laughed. None seemed to take pity on the young woman's evident fear.

"What has this one done?" Ulfilo asked. "I heard no sneezing."

"She has done nothing," Khefi said. "She is just a slave. She is to be the night's offering to the river spirits."

At this the hair rose on the back of Conan's neck. "A sacrifice?"

"Aye. That is the main reason the folk here buy slaves, for they need few for labor. But their spirits demand sacrifice, and they find this preferable to choosing sacrifices from among themselves. At great festivals, many are sacrificed in a single day."

"This is inhuman!" Malia said, indignantly.

Wulfrede shrugged. "My own people make human sacrifices from time to time. These folk may slay each other to their heart's content for all I care."

"Aye," said a gap-toothed sailor, much the worse for the wine he had drunk. "I have sailed a-slaving on the Black Coast many times, and more of the cattle die than survive the voyage. These are worthless creatures. Pay the wench no heed."

Conan's fingers tightened upon his hilt. "I do not like slaving, and I do not like sacrifice. Most especially, I do not like foul demons that demand blood. Such things are unclean."

"I remind you," Ulfilo said steadily, "that we are few and they are many. Our royal host"—he spoke the words with utmost contempt—"does not share your feelings in the matter."

"King Nabo does restrain his more delicate sensibilities to the minimum," Springald agreed.

Now the drums resumed, this time to a slow, hypnotic beat. Women came forward and draped the neck of the slave with garlands of bright, fragrant flowers. With her hands trussed behind her, she was pushed into a line that began to form before the dais. The king stood and took a torch. Holding it high, he exhorted his people.

"The king says: We have feasted well now from the abundance of our land. Let us now in thanks feed our hungry gods, who eat not of the produce of the soil, or of the flesh of the beasts, but only the flesh and blood of men and women."

"Must we go?" said Malia, looking even paler than usual.

"To fail to do so would be an insult to the spirits," Khemi warned them. "If you would live, and continue in the king's favor, you must attend."

Perforce, they accompanied the king's party as they processed around the great tower. From the base of the tower, a long stone jetty ran a hundred paces into the lake. The air had a rank, marshy smell that was more like that of the sea than that of an upland lake. the victim now looked numb, her face wearing an expression of oxlike resignation. Before her Aghla danced, laughing madly and capering, twirling on her stick-thin legs, more like an agile child than an ancient woman. As she danced she sang, or rather screeched, in a high-pitched, whining voice, calling out ecstatically.

"One should not summon gods as if calling hogs to slop," Springald muttered.

"The gods of this land have little sense of decorum, I fear," Malia said, making a creditable effort not to display the dread and revulsion she so clearly felt.

The people were singing now. Their voices rose and fell in a complicated harmony interspersed with much clapping and frenetic drumming, much of it stirring and oddly beautiful, despite the bizarre and hideous circumstances.

The head of the procession reached the end of the jetty. In

the forefront, her toes almost at the stone lip, Aghla raised her rattling staff and called upon her gods. At first her voice continued her screeching song, but this gradually changed until she was making sounds that were not those natural to any human palate. Harsh gutturals and clickings and even stranger sounds streamed from her spittle-flecked lips, and as she chanted the water began to change.

"What is that?" Malia hissed.

She pointed to a spot of color that had appeared upon the quiet surface of the water. It was a glow of deepest crimson. Then they saw that it was not upon the surface, but rather had its origin in the deepest part of the lake. Slowly, the weirdly glowing spot grew. Whatever was making it was coming nearer the surface.

Something broke the surface, startling them. Then something else leapt from the water and splashed back. Now they could see that huge, misshapen fish were springing up, like a shoal of ocean fish fleeing a shark. Other creatures likewise leapt or disported themselves on the surface. The uncertain light made them difficult to see, but they seemed like nothing that ought to swim in fresh water. Some flailed the air with tentacles. Others flapped batlike wings. To their shock, they saw a gross fish seize a squidlike creature with what appeared to be *hands* and use them to stuff the wriggling thing into its mouth.

"This is not natural!" Malia said.

"did you expect it to be?" Springald enquired.

The Cimmerian needed all his resolution to stay in place. Sorcery and dealings with unclean beings repelled him at any time, and this promised to be surpassingly horrible.

As Aghla's chanting reached a fevered pitch, the water of the lake seemed to bulge impossibly upward, forming a domed hump that glowed with a bloody, unnatural phosphorescence. Around the bulge, the lesser creatures churned the water to froth. A hideous, unstable form took shape within the bulge, a creature of writhing flesh and knotted tentacles and many glaring eyes.

"What is this?" screamed a sailor. All of them trembled and stared at the apparition, terrified.

"You will stay where you are!" Wulfrede barked at them.

"Ikhatun!" Aghla howled. "Ikhatun! Ikhatun!"

Now the watery hump lost its tension and burst, cascading down the titanic bulk of the monstrous "god." Sparks of red fire crawled along its rough black hide and the stench that came from it was repulsive beyond belief. Aghla stepped aside and King Nabo shoved the woman forward. With sight of the abomination from beneath the lake, the woman lost her brutish resignation and her face was a mask of sheer terror. A number of the creature's eyes came to bear on her and a long, lumpy tentacle uncoiled from its shapeless carcass and snaked out toward her. The woman struggled to get away, but the king held her bound wrists in an iron grip.

The woman screamed dementedly as the tentacle neared her. It terminated in a leaf-shaped pad whose inner surface was lined with fanglike teeth. As the king stepped back, this appendage enveloped the woman's body and lifted her high. She screamed even more loudly as the thing tightened around her and began a repulsive, rhythmic, squeezing motion. The woman continued screaming for an impossibly long time.

A sailor shrieked and whirled to run away. Wulfrede reached for him but the man eluded the shipmaster's grasp. An eye of the monster tracked the motion and a tentacle snapped out, incredibly swift for so massive a member. Its tooth-lined extremity wrapped around the squalling man and whirled him back toward the thing's body. As the thing held its squirming prey high, a mouthlike orifice split open on its apex, revealing quivering, wet membranes and tissue that writhed like a knot of worms. The tentacles squeezed powerfully, and thick streams of blood poured down into the cavity, drenching the interior. The blood-red sparks writhed and crackled across the thing's rough hide with redoubled fury. At last, the tentacle-pads opened. The bodies within were but scraps of ragged flesh adhering to pulverized bone. These remains dropped into the mouth, which closed over them with a disgusting sound. The monster grumbled and hooted, then began to subside beneath the water. When it was gone, the lesser creatures followed it into the depths.

Without further ceremony, the natives turned and straggled back to their homes. The visitors stood shaken but steadfast, although the four remaining sailors looked fit to perish from fright. The king gave them a sardonic smile as he passed, and Aghla favored them with a silent, toothless laugh, as if she knew that they were to be the next victims and found the idea hugely amusing.

They were silent as they went back to their quarters. Malia was first to speak as they sought their beds upon the straw.

"What was that thing? Was it truly a god?"

"I do not think so," said Springald, tugging off his much-patched boots. "I think it was nothing so familiar."

"What do you mean?" Ulfilo asked.

"Its shape, its whole aspect, hint of gulfs far beyond our own world." His voice was haunted and had lost much of its accustomed jocularity. "I think it is not of terrestrial origin."

"But is it a god?" Wulfrede asked.

The scholar shrugged. "We know that it is powerful. But who truly knows what is a god, and what is not? It exerts a great power upon the people who live here. I think it has altered the nature of everything that lives in the lake. God or not, it wields godlike power."

"I care not what the sickening thing is," Conan said. "And I have no use for the people who worship it. I think that we must get away from here as soon as we can."

"I have no argument with that," said Ulfilo, "for we've found no trace of my brother or the treasure in this place. But where can we go?"

Conan stood by one of the windows and now he pointed out across the lake. "Look."

They rose from the straw and crowded to the window. In the hills beyond the lake, where they had seen the other town, they now saw the twinkling of a number of fires.

* * *

The next day they asked permission to go hunting.

"Why do you need to hunt?" asked the king through his interpreter. "Have I not abundant meat?"

"So you have, King Nabo," said Ulfilo, "and your hospitality is most generous. But in our land hunting is the principal amusement of nobles and we find nothing more pleasurable."

"Ah, you like to kill!" said King Nabo with a smile of comprehension. This was something he could understand. "Then by all means go and hunt. You shall have an escort of my white-plumed guardsmen."

"We need no guards," Conan protested.

"But I insist," said Nabo, smiling.

"Then of course we are honored," said Springald smoothly. "Of your goodness, sire, may we have the use of your servant, Khefi? With his aid we may speak with our escort and such others of your subjects with whom we may need to communicate."

King Nabo assented with a wave of his hand. "Good hunting, my friends." Then he laughed heartily.

"I do not like the way that savage is playing with us," said Malia as they walked from the town, spears slanted across their shoulders. The four surviving sailors walked behind the leaders, and behind them a score of white-plumed warriors marched in double file.

"But what game could he be playing?" asked Wulfrede. "He has made no demands, has scarcely even questioned us save to ask who led us here."

Conan turned to Khefi. "Why does the king think we need an escort?" He jerked a thumb back over his shoulder, indicating the stone-faced warriors who trotted on their trail.

"My master fears that you may be attacked," answered the slave.

"Attacked?" Ulfilo said. "Attacked by whom? Are there outlaws here?"

"Outlaws—yes, and, and—well, rebels." He all but whispered the last word and cast nervous glances toward their escort, despite the fact that the warriors could not understand his Kushite.

"At last we are getting someplace," said Conan. "Khefi, tell us about these rebels. Forget about the white-feathered dogs. Any who looks as if he understands a word, I will slay."

"Very well. If asked, I will say that I spoke of the land and the game you might find thereon."

"That is well enough," said Ulfilo. "Now speak."

"King Nabo had a brother. This brother was older, and he became king when their father died some years ago. This king, whose name is Cha'ak, neglected the rites of the lake god, and this made Aghla very angry."

"Why did he not kill the disgusting creature?" Springald asked.

"Even kings fear Aghla, for her magic is powerful and her curses are potent. Anyway, she spoke among the people, saying that great calamity would result from the king's lack of piety. She agitated especially among the elite white-plume warriors."

"And who was the commander of this elite unit?" asked Ulfilo with his accustomed grasp of military and political matters.

"Indeed, sir, their commander was by ancient tradition the next-younger brother of the king."

"In this case, Nabo," said Wulfrede.

"Exactly."

"Pray go on," Malia urged.

"Aghla praised Nabo as a pious and dutiful prince, a man well qualified to assume the kingship, and resume the ancient rites. He raised a rebellion and drove the rightful king from the city with the support of his warriors. The blue-feather warriors also supported him, but halfheartedly."

"And had the former king no supporters?" Ulfilo asked.

"Most of his own clan remained faithful to him, and the green-feather warriors who were his personal bodyguard. There was much fighting, all up and down the valley. The final battle took place near the forbidden pass, the one through which you entered the valley."

"Was the king slain?" asked Conan.

"He was. His young son fought be his side and was supposed to have died as well, but his body was never found."

"We have seen no warriors save those wearing the white or blue feathers. What of the others?" Springald inquired.

"They fled. And the remnants . . ." He trailed off, once again glancing nervously toward the escort.

"And the remnants now inhabit the town in the hills beyond the lake?" Conan finished for him.

"Aye. It is a town far smaller than the one by the lake, but its walls are high and strong. It is really more of a fort, like the coastal forts of the Stygians. The rebels live there and they raid the royal herds and granaries for food."

"And my husband Marandos?" Malia asked. "Tell me truthfully, now: has King Nabo done away with him?"

"I swear to you," Khefi said, "that I have not seen nor heard of such a man. Surely, had he come here, the king would have required me to translate for the strangers."

They hunted through the morning, bagging some small, plump gazelle. At midday Ulfilo called a rest and the game was dressed out and cooked over smoky coals. As they ate and passed around the wineskins, the leaders discussed plans.

"We must make a run for it," Conan said. "And the fort in the hills is our only possible place of refuge." Truthfully, the Cimmerian would have preferred to leave the valley altogether, but he had given his word that he would help them find Marandos, and he would keep faith while they were determined upon their errand.

"Aye," Ulfilo said. "If Marandos survived the pass, that is the only place he could be."

"And," Wulfrede added, "there must be some reason why that fort stands there."

"What mean you?" Malia asked.

"Think of it: the town by the lake makes sense. Those ancient

Pythonians, or perhaps somebody else, built there because it is the only reasonable town site in this valley. It is in the midst of the fertile land, it is near the lake, and that is where the valley's streams all come together. It is a natural place to serve as the king's center of rule and as a market for the villages of the valley. But why a fort nearby in the hills? Surely a border or a pass is a more sensible site for a fort, where enemies might be expected to invade.''

"Why, then?" said Malia, puzzled.

"A treasury!" exclaimed Springald, his eyes gleaming.

"Aye," the Van concurred. "Have we not seen it many a time, in other lands? Kings always like to keep their treasures near them, but they also like to keep them safe, not where greedy barons or townsmen of doubtful loyalty might lay their hands upon it."

"Aye," said Conan. "That is wise. In Nemedia, and in Corinthia and Zamora and Turan and other lands I have seen royal treasuries sited thus in a strong place near the capital. These castles are often places of refuge for the king in time of rebellion."

"This time, it seems, the opposite has happened," said Ulfilo. "If Marandos encountered the rebels upon leaving the pass, he may well have ended up there."

"Then he may have found the treasure!" said Wulfrede.

Springald turned to Khefi and addressed him Kushite. "Did anyone live in the hill fort before the rebels took over the place?"

The translator shook his head. "Nay. It was abandoned, and I do not think that anyone has lived there since the days of legend."

"It is as I thought," said Springald. "Over the centuries, many peoples have drifted through this valley, and some have taken up residence in the ruins by the lake. But none had any use for the hill fort. It may have stood abandoned since the last of the Pythonians perished, thousands of years ago."

"Then the treasure may still be intact!" Wulfrede exclaimed triumphantly.

"If so," Springald said, "then it is most likely to be hidden in sealed vaults. We may have some lengthy searching to do."

"After all we have come through, what of that?" Wulfrede cried.

"Ever the optimist!" Malia said testily. "I remind you that we are 'escorted' by a score of white-plumed guards. Look at them!" She nodded to where the guards rested a little apart. While half the men ate, their spears thrust into the ground beside them, the other half stood alert, spears in hand.

"Now look at us," she said. The five of them sat near the fire with Khefi. The four sailors, their bellies full and pleasantly tipsy with wine, snored peacefully in the warm sunlight.

"The lads are good enough fighters when they are awake," Wulfrede said. "And with such doughty swordsmen as we four"—he waved expansively toward his companions—"I think we may take care of these black rogues handily. We need merely make careful plans, and attack suddenly, when they are not expecting it."

"But they have encampments all over the valley," Ulfilo pointed out. "I'll warrant that messengers have been sent to all of them, warning them to keep an eye on us."

"It could turn into a running fight, to be sure," said the Van, his confidence unshaken. "But such men as we need not be daunted by the prospect. Think of the rewards for success!"

"When would be the best time to make the attempt?" Springald asked.

Ulfilo pondered for a while. "In the early evening, as we make our way back toward the town. Let us spend the afternoon working our way in the general direction of the hill fort. As we turn our steps back toward the town, they should relax their guard a little. That is the time to strike. In the fading light, we may stand a better chance of making the hill fort unobserved."

"That is a sound plan," said Conan. "Their spears provide reach, and their shields are large, but they wear no armor. Redbeard, tell the sailors that they must throw their spears quickly, then draw their swords and come to close grips instantly. That way they will have the advantage."

"I shall tell them. What of him?" He nodded toward Khefi. The interpreter, unable to follow the conversation in the northern tongue, had nodded off to sleep.

"He must come with us," Springald said. "We will need an interpreter to parley with the rebels."

"Are you all sure this is such a good plan?" Malia asked, assailed by doubts.

"We must do something, and soon," said Conan, "else we'll all be dinner for that ugly fish god." The rest nodded agreement.

"Then it is settled," said Ulfilo with flat finality. "We do as planned."

That afternoon they continued to hunt, but they were not serious about it, missing many an easy cast. They did much talking and laughing to set their guards at ease, all the while plotting their escape. Wulfrede pantomimed frustration at his bad hunting luck, all the while briefing his sailors on their desperate gamble for freedom. The seamen grinned wolfishly at the prospect of an open fight. They were far more afraid of the lake-monster than of the worse than two-on-one odds.

As the sun touched the crest of the western range, Ulfilo called a halt. "Tell them we will return now," he said to the interpreter. Khefi said a few words to the warriors and they turned their steps toward the town.

For a few minutes they walked, slowly, as if tired by the day's activities. As they passed through a defile between two small hills, well out of sight of the nearest village, Ulfilo called out: "Now!"

Instantly, the party of northerners whirled, hurling their short hunting spears. Three natives went down with spears through their bodies. Others were wounded or had their shields encumbered by the heavy shafts. The guard captain shouted something and the warriors sprang forward as the others ran to meet them.

Conan, his sword humming, hewed an arm from a tall guardsman even as he swayed aside to avoid the man's long, heavy war-spear. All around him he heard the loud impact of swords upon hide shields, and the ugly, meat-chopping sound of steel biting into flesh. He saw a sailor go down with a spear through his throat as he tried to tug his cutlass from a warrior's belly.

The element of surprise made up for the unfavorable odds, but at close quarters their lack of shields was a handicap. Each man had to dodge with great agility and whirl his sword swiftly to avoid injury and death. Wulfrede hacked a man from shoulder to waist with his great Vanir blade and the Aquilonians wrought slaughter with their swords, but the native warriors fought fiercely and they were expert with their weapons.

Then Malia screamed. She had been told to stay well clear of the fighting, and the Cimmerian risked a glance in her direction to see what was wrong. He saw that she was surrounded by hairy forms, and that more of them were bearing down upon the combatants.

"Bumbana!" Conan shouted, slashing a black warrior across the waist. Most of the guards were dead, but now the hairy half-men were upon them. The Cimmerian thrust his sword through one and beheaded another, but he saw Springald borne down by three of the beast-men, and Ulfilo standing back to back with the Van, assailed by a half-score.

Then Conan had no attention to spare for the others. Before him were snarling faces and knotted limbs and misshapen hands that bore crude weapons. The half-men were clumsy compared to the tigerish Cimmerian, but they were swift and powerful. He knew he must break away and run, but even as he made that decision a knotty-headed bludgeon descended on the back of his black mane and he collapsed to the grass with lights flashing before his eyes. Then the club came down again and there was only darkness.

# FOURTEEN

## A Swim in the Lake

Conan awoke to great pain in his head and a sensation of swaying. His eyelids were sticky, and he had to blink the drying blood from them before he could see his predicament. He found that he was trussed up by wrists and ankles and was slung from a pole carried by two men. He could see at least one other such improvised litter, but darkness prevented him recognizing which of his companions was thus carried.

At least the carriers were humans, although the sound of bestial gruntings and snufflings told him that the bumbana were not far away. The human part of the procession sang as they marched.

"Release me, you swine!" shouted someone. "Let me go or slay me! An Aquilonian nobleman is not to be carried like the carcass of a slain goat!" Despite his predicament, Conan had to smile.

"I adjure you to hold your tongue, my friend," said a softer voice. "There is a certain futility of haranguing men who cannot understand a word you say, not to mention the unliklihood of their heeding you even if they could understand you." So Springald was still alive, and as wordy as ever.

"Peace, both of you," said Malia disgustedly. "We are doomed."

"At least you are walking on your own feet," Ulfilo grumbled.

"Do you conceive that to be a great satisfaction to me?" she demanded. "I'd as lief have been killed back there. What I want to know is why they are keeping us alive."

"I can think of several reasons," said Springald. "None of them would you find comforting, I fear."

"Then spare me," she said. "My own imaginings are terrible enough, without any of your speculations."

"The *Poem of Good Advice*," said another voice, "tells us: 'only the fool speaks when silence is the best course.' "

"Are you a fool, then, Vanirman?" Ulfilo said hotly.

Wulfrede laughed heartily. "Our present condition scarcely proclaims us to be numbered among the wise."

"Then Conan is either wise or unconscious," Malia said, "for he says nothing."

"Perhaps he is dead," Springald said.

"If the blackhair was dead," Wulfrede said, "the bumbana would have taken him, as they did my poor sailors."

A warrior came back from the head of the procession, pointing and barking something.

"The captain says you are not to talk," said Khefi.

"Tell him," Ulfilo said, "to employ a respectful tone when he speaks to his betters. His feathers and his unbound limbs make him no less a dog."

"That would be inadvisable," Khefi cautioned.

They were distracted by the sound of singing, which grew louder by the second. Then they were amid a great crowd of torch-bearing natives. The towns people danced and made sport of the captives, holding torches close to their faces, taunting them with pantomimes of tortures sure to come.

"This is a merry crew," said Wulfrede disgustedly. "I think they deserve their king."

"Nothing can live near that accursed lake without becoming twisted," Springald said cryptically.

The procession passed through the gate of the town and through the streets, picking up more revelers as they went. The townsmen were drinking and celebrating with a good deal more enthusiasm than they had the previous night. The helpless captives were pelted with offal and beaten with sticks, although no one attacked them with weapons. There was one exception. In the abundant torch-light, Conan could see that Malia, although surrounded by guards, was not offered the slightest harm or insult.

The noise grew as they entered the open plaza before the tower. From his awkward angle, Conan could only see that the dais was crowded. There was a cacophony of noise, a deafening din raised by the mob. The trussed-up men were dropped to the pavement and the poles were withdrawn. As unobtrusively as he could, Conan worked hands and feet to restore circulation. At a signal from the king, the drums stopped and the people fell silent. Warriors grasped the Cimmerian beneath the arms and hauled him to a sitting position. He allowed his head to loll as if he were not yet fully conscious. A jar of water was emptied over his head, washing the clotting blood from his face and eyes. Now he focused his gaze upon the dais, careful to keep his expression groggy and disoriented.

On the dais, King Nabo sat on a barbaric throne draped with leopard skin. Next to him, on a folding stool, sat another man who, despite his lower chair, towered over the tall king. Between the two men squatted Aghla, her withered face split by an evil leer. The taller man stood.

"Greetings, my friends," said Sethmes, archpriest of Ma'at.

"Stygian!" Ulfilo gasped. "What means this? We left you in Khemi, months ago! How comes it that you are here?"

"The black ship that followed us," Wulfrede said, ruefully. "I warrant it was this rogue dogging us from the day we sailed from Khemi."

"But our agreement!" Springald said.

At this the priest laughed richly. "Are you children? Did you really believe that bargains made with mere outlanders have any weight among the priesthood of Stygia? From the moment you entered my temple you were doomed, although you were of some small use to me, as your errant Marandos had been. This journey of mine was foretold long ages ago, and barbarian scum have no part in it save as slaves."

"Your meaning is unclear," protested Springald.

Again the Stygian laughed. "Ever the scholar, even in extremity, eh, Aquilonian? Have no fear, all shall be made clear to you. My new friend, King Nabo, has agreed that your fate is to be in my hands."

"How can you talk to the ugly dog?" asked Conan, deliberately thickening his voice. "We've had his translator with us."

"This woman and I"—he gestured toward Aghla—"share a tongue in common. It is a language far older than your infant Hyborian speech, more venerable even than Stygian." He turned to Aghla and spoke a few words in a language unnatural to the human tongue. Conan recognized it as the language the hag had used in summoning the thing from the lake. She answered in the same language, gesturing toward the prisoners and laughing in a shrill voice.

"You see?" Sethmes said, turning back to his victims. "We are the best of friends now."

While all this talk was going on, Conan was careful to watch King Nabo. Despite the Stygian's ironic statement of friendship, the Cimmerian caught some decidedly disgruntled expressions as they flickered across the king's cruel features. He was not happy about the advent of this foreigner in his kingdom.

Conan twisted his head, as if trying to work the pain and stiffness from his neck. Actually, he was assessing the manpower situation in the town. Besides the ordinary townspeople, the king's white-feather and blue-feather warriors were present in abundance. On one side of the square stood the soldiers Conan had last seen in the desert. Seeing them for the first time in reliable light, he discerned that they were a mixed bag of Stygians, Keshanians, and men of various desert tribes. They bore a variety of uniforms and arms, but they had the bearing of disciplined professionals. In their front stood their Stygian officers: red-bearded Khopshef and black-bearded Geb. Of the bumbana there was no sign.

"So what is your will of us now?" Ulfilo demanded. "I am an Aquilonian noble, and I'll not be anyone's slave."

"Oh, you have yet your uses, and surely you would be wasted fetching water or hoeing weeds from the crops! For instance, there is the hungry deity at the bottom of the lake. After so many centuries of local food, he must be eager for a change of diet." At this Conan's scalp prickled and Malia seemed about to faint.

"Stygian swine!" Ulfilo bellowed.

Sethmes ignored him, addressing Malia instead. "You, my dear, need have no fear of being sacrificed. You have a far more important role to play."

"I am not interested in your plans, priest," she said. "I would rather share the fate of my friends."

"Your wishes are of no account. It was prophesied thousands of years ago that you would come to this place." The priest's sardonic mien slipped a little, revealing the fanatic beneath the surface. "You are known by many names: the Alabaster Woman, the Ivory Queen, the Woman of Snow, and others. It is your destiny to begin the groundwork that will raise imperial Python from the dust and restore its ancient dynasty to the throne!"

"You are mad!" she said. "I am the daughter of a homeless Hyperborean lady, tossed about by wars and feuds, married to a penniless mercenary captain, and brought here by merest happenstance. If my husband and this scholar had not met by chance in a tavern one day, none of this could have happened!"

"Where the gods are concerned," said the priest, "there are no such things as chance, accident, or happenstance. All is foreordained, and all transpires according to prophecy. When the gods want a certain person to be in a certain place, it is no great matter for them to arrange a few wars, and to cause certain men who have nothing in common to meet at the proper place and time."

Now the priest glared at Springald. "And you, scholar. Do

you think that it was mere chance that those ancient tomes came to be in the library of the kings of Aquilonia, or that they were sent to Stygia for rebinding, so that they were seen by a predecessor of mine? These things were not accidental!'' He was distracted by Aghla, who spoke a few words in an urgent voice. Sethmes answered and turned to the doomed men.

''My esteemed friend, the priestess Aghla reminds me that her god is hungry, and that I have promised an unusual meal for him. Let me see—who shall go first? I do not suppose any of you would care to volunteer?'' He glanced from one to another of them, a cruel smile upon his lips. ''No? I thought not. I will send the least amusing of you first.'' He extended a hand pointing a long, bony finger. ''You, Cimmerian. These others are merely bumbling fools, but you entered my house unbidden and slew one of my servants. What a pity it is that you are still half dazed, for you cannot properly appreciate the unique experience that awaits you.''

He spoke some words to Aghla and she screeched something to the guards who still held the Cimmerian. One stooped and slashed the bindings at Conan's ankles and wrists. His head hanging, Conan saw that the man used his own dirk. A sideways glance revealed that the warrior had his weapon-belt draped from one shoulder, complete with sheathed sword. The other guard carried only a spear.

The guard resheathed his dirk and together the two warriors hauled Conan to his feet. He let his head fall back as if he were about to relapse into unconsciousness. Sethmes stepped from the dais and slapped him forehand and backhand.

''Wake up, barbarian!'' he snarled. ''I want you to see what is coming!''

Conan spit bloody froth in the Stygian's face. ''That's for you and your foul gods!'' Then he let his head fall forward. He heard his companions chuckle with satisfaction.

''This one is half dead already,'' said Sethmes. ''But he will do for a beginning.''

Wulfrede barked a short laugh. ''Even half a Cimmerian is pure defiance.''

The drums resumed their throbbing, and the guards marched Conan around the tower with the festive procession following. He lurched and stumbled, falling first against one guard, then the other. With the guards muttering curses at what an awkward burden he was proving to be, they marched him out onto the stone jetty.

The Cimmerian ignored the festive sounds behind him as Aghla whirled out to the end of the pier. She stopped to look up at him with malicious delight, then began her weird summoning. He heard Sethmes speaking, presumably to Springald.

"The hellish lake-being!" he said, sounding awed for the first time. "It came hither from a place so far that even the greatest of Stygian sorcerers have no name for it. It flew across vast gulfs of space and at last found its resting place in this lake. See you how round the lake is? This is the crater the thing made when it fell from the stars, helpless and exhausted after its long flight. A million years it lay in the bottom of the pit it had made, weak and unable to move. In time water filled the crater and still the thing waited. Fish and other life came to inhabit the lake, but the creature exudes a power that alters all life that comes near it and the living things grew strange and twisted." All this he spoke over Aghla's demented chanting, and the red glow spread in the water.

"The serpent-men of prehistory came to this valley and reared their city beside the lake. The creature consumed them and drew strength from them for millenia, changing them into something unrecognizable, at last destroying them utterly. It waited again, for long centuries. Then came the men of fallen Python, bearing their treasure and their sorcery. They found the ruins left by the serpent-men, and they built upon them, establishing their city and their treasury. Then they waited, commencing a long, long correspondence with the noble refugees of Python who had settled in Stygia.

"They built upon the wizardy of the serpent-men, refortifying the spells that protected the pass and other accesses to the valley, so that only the royalty of Python could use them. But the god of the lake manifested itself, and the colony trafficked with it, and gradually it destroyed them. Time passed, the correspondence ceased, and the Pythonian royalty in Stygia dwindled in power and wealth until the remnants became the mere priesthood of the ancient Pythonian deity, Ma'at.''

The water creatures began their mad thrashing and the hump began to grow. Conan forced himself to seem semicomatose, but he was full of an unfamiliar sensation: dread. The jetty and the town behind him were packed with armed men. The priest raved on, his voice growing more excited by the moment.

''Before they metamorphosed into something other than truly human, the Pythonians established communications with the creature, and it was from these strange communications that the first prophecy of the New Python arose. For a hundred generations, the priests of Ma'at in Stygia received visions sent by Ma'at and other gods, enlarging upon the prophecy and bringing about a whole body of lore concerning the establishment of the Purple Throne upon which shall sit the last descendant of the ancient kings of Python. I, Sethmes, am that descendant, and I am the fulfillment of the prophecy!''

The monster was fully visible now, and its tentacles began to uncoil. Aghla laughed insanely and Sethmes screamed in ecstatic Stygian. The drums and chanting rose in volume as the creature reached forth hungrily. Conan knew it was time to make his bid for life or death. He cast off his pose of incapacity and sprang to full, ferocious life.

With his left arm, the Cimmerian lifted the guard on that side and hurled him into the water. The nearest tentacle snatched the man up even as Conan turned and smashed his knotted fist into the face of the other guard. He snatched his weapon-belt from the warrior's shoulder and hurled him likewise from the jetty, where a tentacle caught him before he could even make a splash.

Aghla screamed even more dementedly than ever, and Conan regretted that he had no time to kill the repulsive creature. With a town full of furious people behind him, there was only one place to go. The Cimmerian took a deep breath and dived into the black waters of the accursed lake.

He cut the water cleanly and plunged deep, pausing only to sling the sword across his back. He drew his dirk and gripped its heavy spine in his teeth, then swam deeper, seeking to put distance between himself and the town. With horror clawing at him, he swam toward the loathsome monster. A fishlike thing with human hands scrabbled at him, its wide mouth, lined with razor fangs, gaping to tear flesh. The Cimmerian thrust his dirk through its eye and the scent of blood brought a swarm of misshapen creatures to tear the striken thing to shreds and devour it.

Lungs afire, Conan swam on. He knew the beast was directly before him, and he had no idea how far beneath the surface its bloated body extended. If he could not swim beneath it, he was doomed.

The bloody glow ahead of him grew painfully bright. It illuminated murkily a mass of dangling growths, like a waving field of seaweed. Tiny things swam among the hanging appendages, which now appeared to be long, thin tentacles covered with thorny spines. He was sure this must be the underside of the monster. With a terrible pressure crushing his chest, Conan plunged still deeper, until he cleared the tips of the tentacles.

As he swam beneath the thing, the Cimmerian saw to his further horror that the small, tentacled things swimming among the snakelike growth were miniatures of the monster above. Were they its young? Or had the thing caused lake life to metamorphose into something identical to itself? Or were the processes one and the same for the creature that had come from another world?

Lungs bursting, Conan cleared the thorny arms and began to swim upward. He had no idea how deeply he had plunged, but he knew that he had to have air quickly or he would drown. Already, spots of black swarmed in his vision against the red glow, and unconsciousness could be only moments away.

He broke the surface abruptly and gasped in a great lungful of air, almost choking on the spray of water that came with it. For several seconds, he could do nothing save breathe and feel his body regain its strength and control. Then he turned to see what was behind him.

The first thing he saw was the humped, unstable shape of the lake monster, far too close. The red sparks crawled over its tough hide with greater violence than the night before, and he saw no fewer than six tentacles above its mouth opening, squeezing screaming victims like ripe fruit. Apparently, the thing had grown so excited that it was snatching victims at random from among the crowd on shore. Conan allowed himself a precious second to hope, ardently, that among those being wrung dry of blood were Sethmes, Aghla, and Nabo. From beyond the thing came the panic-stricken screams of the fleeing crowd. He gave a short laugh at thought of their discomfiture. He hoped that the thing would spare his companions, but when all are doomed and it is an each-for-himself situation, they would just have to take their chances.

Cursing himself for wasting time, the Cimmerian turned and struck out for the far shore. At first he used a careful breast stroke, not wishing to attract the monster's attention. It seemed happily occupied, but who could tell when a creature was so alien and had so many eyes? When he felt the distance was adequate, he broke into a steady crawl that quickly put distance between him and the monster.

The swim was a long one, and several times he felt the brush of scaly or slimy hides against his limbs. Each time he took his dirk from his teeth and braced himself for attack, but nothing molested him. At last he heard the gentle lapping of water against the gravel of the shore. Too weary to stand, the Cimmerian crawled ashore on hands and knees, gasping and shaking the water from his black mane like a wet dog. He stopped abruptly when he perceived a pair of brown feet inches before his face. Next to them was the blade of a war axe, upon which the owner of the feet leaned. Conan looked up to see a familiar face grinning down at him.

"Welcome to the rebel side of the lake, my friend," said Goma.

# FIFTEEN

## The Rebels

Conan lurched to his feet. "I thought I might find you here."

"And so you did." Goma was not alone. A dozen or more warriors stood with him, moonlight agleam on the polished steel of their spears. "We saw the great commotion from the walls of our fort and came down here for a closer look. The god of the lake is having a fine time this night."

"It was disappointed because I was to be its dinner and would not cooperate," Conan told him.

Goma laughed richly. "Even the lake god would find you too tough to stomach! Come, we will go back to the fort. There are things I would know."

"There are things *I* would have known," Conan protested. "Why did you desert us just when we needed your aid the most?"

"Mind your tongue," Goma warned. "I am the leader here, and if anyone is to demand answers, it shall be I. You see that these warriors give me their allegiance." Indeed, Conan had seen the deference with which the others treated Goma.

"Aye. And I've a good notion who you truly are. What of it? We were companions and you left us without a word of warning."

Goma chuckled. "You are a hard man to intimidate. But then, one who would defy the lake god and swim away from him is not as other men. Very well, I will explain, and then you are to make no more demands upon me." Goma's manner, always haughty, had grown even more so.

"When I took service with you and the other whites, I agreed to lead you to the Horns. This I did. I was under no further obligation. Beyond the Horns, I was nearly as much in the dark as you. I had to learn the situation here before I could take any action, and I felt certain that it would be death for you all if you were to be discovered in company with me."

Their steps had led them up a steep path that ended at the base of a high wall built of heavy, rough-hewn stone. The stonework was as massive as that of the town, but it was utterly undecorated. This, the Cimmerian surmised, was the pure work of the colonists who fled the destruction of Python, before they were distorted by the influence radiating from the lake. A heavy door of new timber had been installed in its gateway. The guards at the open portal saluted Goma as they entered and shut it behind them. The gate creaked on crudely forged iron hinges and was secured by a squared log laid across iron hasps.

Within the encircling wall was a sizable village of mud-and-thatch huts. Men and women had climbed to the walk below the parapet to view the commotion across the lake, and now they descended to inspect the newcomer. Goma said something and they faded back.

"I told them to go back to sleep," he informed Conan. "They will have plenty of time to see you after dawn, and better light to see you by."

There was a squat, square keep in the center of the fort, but Goma ignored it and led Conan into a spacious hut that was three or four times larger than the others. Within he sat on a hassock of stuffed skins and gestured for Conan to seat himself.

"You have had a strenuous night, northerner," Goma said. "Have you had aught to eat or drink?"

"By Crom, I've had nothing since midday, and I've been fighting, struggling, or swimming ever since. I'm nigh famished."

Goma clapped his hands and serving women brought platters of food and foaming gourds of beer. Goma waved the servers away and sat in silence while his guest restored himself with meat, fruit, and bread, emptying several gourds to wash it all down. When he was replete, the Cimmerian wiped his mouth with the back of his hand and sat back against a cushion.

"When we were taken before King Nabo," Conan said, "he was most anxious to learn who had led us hither, and he was very dissatisfied with our answers. Then we pumped the translator for information."

"Translator?" said Goma. "Is that the slave Khefi? He was my father's herdsman but he became attached to the court because he could talk with the foreign traders."

"He is the one. He spoke of the civil war, but he was afraid to say too much even though the guards could not understand him. He said that there were rebels still in the valley. He said also that after the battle in which the old king was slain, the body of his young son was never found."

Goma smiled. "You miss little, my friend. Aye, I am that son, and I was able to prove it to these rebels. I have spent many years in my wandering, learning of other peoples, other ways of fighting, and giving the folk here plenty of time to grow sick of my uncle Nabo."

"I do not think they love him, for what that is worth," Conan said. "But they fear him and they fear the ugly old woman, Aghla."

"Aghla!" Goma spat at the name. "That ancient, evil creature has been the curse of my family for generations. She never dies; she enslaves the people to the lake god. They think that it somehow shares power with her.''

''Do you believe that it does?'' Conan asked.

''I did when I was a boy, but as a wandering warrior I encountered many witch doctors, and I saw how easily they duped people into believing their great powers. Some of them had small powers that came from spells, and some could call upon the spirits of the jungle, but most had nothing but conjurer's tricks. I no longer even think that the thing in the lake is a god. I have seen the sea and the great creatures that swim therein. The lake-thing may not even be a thinking creature. If it is a god, why is it imprisoned in the lake? Why must it have people to feed it with the blood it craves?''

''You have gained wisdom in your travels,'' Conan commended.

''When a man must live by his own wits he must learn to think for himself. I found myself without a tribe and its traditions, and I took no other man's word as truth until the truth was apparent to me. Now I have returned, and I find that many of the things my people have always believed without question are foolish. I do not think that the lake monster can be killed, but I see no reason why we must feed it.''

''Khefi said your father neglected the sacrifices,'' Conan said.

''And thereby he earned the enmity of Aghla.'' Goma spat again.

''Slay her and half of your problems are solved.''

''I intend to. And I will kill my uncle, and take my kingdom back.''

''If it is to be war,'' said the Cimmerian, ''you may count me in.''

''It is not your fight,'' Goma said.

''I am a warrior. Besides, Nabo still holds my companions, if they were not slain tonight. I undertook their service until I found the errant Marandos, and I have not done that as yet, so I am bound to fight for their freedom.''

"You have a strong sense of obligation," Goma said. "That is a good and a rare thing."

"It can be a burden. I'd as lief take spear and sword and be away from here on my own. But I undertook this task and I will see it out."

"Very well. When we march against Nabo, you shall be at my side."

"Excellent. Speaking of the mysterious Marandos, have you any idea where he might be?"

"In the morning you shall see," Goma said. "For now, get some sleep."

"I could use it," said Conan. "A long day topped off by food and beer is wearying even to a warrior of Cimmeria. It is a good thing that I reencountered you, my friend. I might have had difficulty speaking with these rebels otherwise."

Goma clapped his hands and spoke instructions to the youthful warrior who entered. "This young man will take you to a vacant hut. Sleep well, my friend. We have much to do in coming days."

Gratefully, Conan followed the youth, who in turn eyed this outlandish apparition with amazement. The hut Conan entered was like all the others, enclosing a tiny, circular room with piercings in the walls for ventilation. With his hilt close to hand, the Cimmerian drifted off to a dreamless sleep.

The morning dawned bright save for a thin mist rising from the lake. Conan emerged from his hut and stretched. The village was awakening as well, its inhabitants blinking in the sunlight, then blinking harder when they saw the Cimmerian. Chattering and gesticulating, they crowded around him, the children touching his strange-colored skin, the women fingering his long straight hair. Their curiosity lacked the hostile, cruel edge of the town people's. Since they were the same tribe, he attributed the difference to the baleful influence of the lake.

When Conan came to the entrance of Goma's large hut, a warrior on guard called inside, and Goma emerged. He spoke to the crowd at some length. Then, at a clap of his hands, they dispersed.

"I told them that you are my friend from beyond the mountains," he informed Conan, "and that we have fought side by side against enemies. I told them that you are from far to the north, a cold, cloudy country where lack of sun has bleached men white and made their eyes blue. You are to receive the same respect they would accord one of my senior commanders."

"I thank you," Conan said.

"Now, come with me. I must inspect my warriors, and we will talk as I do so."

As the rebel king made his inspection of the guard posts and his military encampments, Conan explained the situation he had left in the town. Goma hissed when Conan spoke of Sethmes and his small army.

"The Stygian! Think you he has any real sorcerous powers?"

"The wizards of Stygia are reputed to be the most powerful in the world, and I have reason to believe this is true. But this priest is something very unusual, a descendant of the ancient kings of Python. Whether that makes him more or less powerful I know not. What I have seen of him thus far shows that he is a schemer and plotter, not a fell wizard."

"And his men. Are they a considerable force in the field?"

"They look like seasoned professionals to me. As such, they should not be underestimated. They will fight in ranks, with shield, spear, and sword."

"That is no way to fight," Goma said contemptuously. "My warriors will fall screaming upon them and wet their spears in Stygian blood."

"Discipline can be overwhelmed by ferocity," Conan said. "But you will lose many men thereby."

"Warriors are born to die fighting. That is as it should be."

"I did not see the bumbana after we entered the town," Conan said. "They will probably fight like the ones we met in the pass—fiercely and stupidly."

"My uncle probably would not allow them in the city. Beast men are too low even for him."

"They were carrying our dead," Conan said grimly. "I think they were given the slain for their dinner."

"We will kill them all," Goma said confidently.

They inspected warriors who wore yellow, red, and green feathers. The men were fierce and eager for the fight. After years as exiles and outlaws, they lusted for the blood of their enemies. Goma had been among them no more than three days, yet they seemed to invest him with perfect confidence. The Cimmerian remarked upon this.

"For all these years," Goma explained, "they nourished themselves upon the hope of my return. Had I not returned a true warrior they might have doubted, but I am and that is enough for them. The leaders of the regiments regarded me with suspicion at first, but I slew one who questioned me and the others agreed that I am their rightful leader."

"That is the simple way of settling things," Conan said. "How do your numbers compare with Nabo's?"

"He has more men, perhaps a fourth more than I have. But the support of the blue-feather warriors is lukewarm. If we prevail early in the fighting, I think they will come over to my side."

"And the people of the countryside?" Conan asked.

Goma shrugged. "That is unimportant. The toilers will toil no matter who rules over them. Only warriors count."

The Cimmerian had no argument with this primitive order of things, which prevailed in most parts of the world. Those who would not fight for what they had, deserved to have nothing. They should be grateful to be allowed to live and eat. A son of a great warrior race, Conan had little sympathy for those who chose the passive life.

"You said last night that you would tell me of Marandos," he prodded.

"Aye, so I did. Come with me."

The Cimmerian followed Goma into the stone keep. Like the

surrounding wall, the structure was plain, undecorated, and functional. At ground level it had a single entrance; a low, narrow doorway that had long since lost its wooden door. The entrance made a virtual tunnel through the thick wall, debouching into a single room no more than six paces on a side. Illumination was provided by six small windows that pierced the walls about ten feet up. A stone stair gave access to a room or rooms above. In the center of the room a man sat upon a thick slab of stone. He wore little but rags, and his body was reduced to skeletal emaciation, but his eyes burned with luminous intensity. He looked up and glared from one to the other of them as they entered.

"You are a northerner!" he said as Conan approached.

"You are not blind," said the Cimmerian. "That is a good sign."

"Have you come with my brother? Did you bring men to bear away the treasure?" His skeletal face was alive with eagerness and greed. Conan could see that this had once been a fine-looking man, with a strong resemblance to Ulfilo.

"Aye, I came with him. As to bearing anything away, that must wait." At these words the man lapsed into despondency.

"How long has he been prisoner here?" he asked Goma.

"Prisoner? No man detains him here. You saw yourself that there is neither door nor guard to this place. Some months ago he came here, raving mad. He walked straight into this old rockpile and embraced that slab as if it were his mother. My people respect the mad. He seemed harmless enough, so they merely took his weapons and left him to his own devices. The women leave him food and drink at the entrance, but he takes little. Folk passing by hear him raving, but no one understood his words. I have not had leisure to do anything about it. It must be the white woman's husband, but I think she was well rid of him."

"What happened?" Conan asked the wraith who had been a captain of mercenaries. "Where are the men you brought hither on your second expedition?"

The man seemed to collect his thoughts. "Men? Yes, I had men. Men and half-men, what the jungle people called bumbana. They were to help me bear away the treasure, but they did not." He grinned slyly. "They are gone, and the treasure is mine now." He patted the stone slab upon which he sat.

"But what happened to them?" Conan asked patiently.

"Oh, some died in the jungle, and some on the mountains. We lost many fighting the wild bumbana in the hills. Then there was the desert—" His eyes grew haunted. "Many died there. The bumbana saw no reason why they should perish of hunger and thirst when the flesh and blood of men would serve them." He was silent for a while. "But they never threatened me."

"And the curses in the Horns?" Conan asked, masking his revulsion.

"The great storm struck. Lightning slew men and bumbana alike. I had one man left to me when the great stone fell." He looked up at Conan, his eyes full of grief. "And yet the spell should have prevented it! Could it be that the priest lied to me?"

"Could a sane man believe him?" Conan demanded.

The madman ignored him. "But I have the treasure now." He continued to pat the stone slab.

"It is under that stone?" Conan said.

"It must be, but the stone is too heavy for me to lift."

"You mean, you have not seen it?" Conan said, astonished.

"But it can be no other place!" Marandos all but screamed.

"I've been among madmen since Asgalun," Conan muttered, turning away from the man. "I should have known I'd find another at the end of the trail."

"You see that he is out of his head. We waste time here, Conan. There is much to do. My presence here will not remain secret for long, and when he knows, Nabo will march against me."

They turned and walked from the chamber. Behind them, the madman crooned songs to his putative treasure.

"Why has Nabo not crushed the rebels ere this?" Conan asked when they were once more in the clear sunlight.

"Because they held this fort. It is not a way my people like to fight, but it allows the few to stand against the many. Nabo would have almost certainly prevailed, but his losses would have been far too great to bear. Some subchief would have taken advantage of the popular discontent and deposed him. Nabo does not love his lake god so well that he wishes to be eaten by it. People will make great sacrifices for their true king. But Nabo is a tyrant and a usurper. As such, he must have only swift, easy, and cheap victories, or his followers will turn on him."

"It is that way everywhere I have been," said Conan, "and I have traveled farther than most men. Will you fight him in the open field, away from this place?"

"I must. It sickens the heart of a warrior to fight defensively, behind walls. And more than royal blood is necessary to bind the loyalty of men. To be a king is a thing of spirit, almost of magic. I must stand before my army and challenge the usurper openly, then crush him in hand-to-hand combat."

"And yet it will be a costly victory," Conan warned.

"I know that well. I fought in many wars in my years of wandering. I know so much more of war than does Nabo that I could crush him here without great difficulty. But my kingship would be tainted. Always, there would be those who whispered that King Goma is no true warrior, that he defeated Nabo with craft, not with courage. Among warriors such as these, those words would in time accomplish their work, and I would spend my reign putting down petty rebellions."

"You come to kingcraft with a serious mind," Conan said.

"I shrink from no battle, hard or easy. Will you march immediately?"

"First we must establish our situation exactly. But we cannot wait long. Come, I have called a meeting of my chiefs. We must know how lies the strength of my uncle. Only a fool fights blind."

They walked to the open yard before Goma's hut. There they found gathered a double score of men who bore the look of senior warriors. These had many scars and some were grizzled of hair and chin-beard, and all bore the look of lions. Besides the colored feathers that identified their regiments, they wore armbands and kneebands of long fur, variously colored. Their shields were snow-white. They raised their arms and shouted a greeting to their king.

"Stand by me," Goma told Conan as he seated himself on a folding stool draped with leopard skin. Others stood beside or behind the king, and these few wore black ostrich plumes in their headdresses. Conan assumed that the black feathers marked the king's personal guard.

Goma spoke a few words and with great speed and dexterity the men assembled a map of the valley. The skull of a cow became the city by the lake, that of a lion, the fortress. A spread of river-mussel shells was the lake itself. Black stones marked the villages, and ovals made of antelope ribs were the encampments of Nabo's warriors. The river and streams were marked out in blue-tinted sand, and a fence of spears, thrust into the ground by their butt-spikes, became the encircling mountains. Conan was impressed. This was sophisticated war-making. A Nemedian general could not have asked for better.

For better than an hour, Goma conferred with his chiefs in language the Cimmerian could not understand. From their tones and gesticulations, he could tell that some were urging immediate actions, others wanted more caution. He noticed that younger warriors were not invited to speak.

While this parley went on, Conan made a careful study of the map. He had seen many fine armies go down in bloody ruin because their leaders did not know the terrain amid which they campaigned. He saw that the lake town was situated near the southern end of the valley, and that was where the bulk of Nabo's forces were concentrated. The rest were spread northward in small military encampments. He and the other foreigners had passed a number of such encampments on their march down the valley to the lake.

Goma turned to Conan. "I know that you could not follow this, Conan. Have you any questions?"

"The outlying military camps," he said, "are they just to defend against rebel raids?"

"They are there partly to defend against cattle-raids by *royal forces*." He emphasized the last words sternly. "And partly because it is our ancient tradition to send the newly made young warriors to live in units by themselves for a number of years, guarding the cattle and entering the town and the villages only on special days, for dances and ceremonies. But his main reason is to keep the countryside pacified."

"He has made no move to call them in, to concentrate his forces near the town?"

"Not as yet. That is another reason why I must strike swiftly."

Conan smiled. "What say you to a plan that gives your men a good blooding, some quick, easy victories, and cripples Nabo badly at the same time?"

"I will listen to such a plan," Goma said.

Conan took a spear from the encircling fence. With its butt-spike he scratched his battle plan into the dirt of the map. As he spoke, Goma translated his words for the others.

"First, you must divide your forces. This is always risky in the presence of the enemy, but it is worth the risk. While keeping the bulk of the forces with you, the smaller unit, one third or perhaps only one quarter, will make a quick forced march northward, along the foothills of the eastern mountain range." His spike traced a long path to the northern end of the valley.

"This march should be completed at night, for the sake of secrecy. The men must be young and very fit, for they will get little or no sleep. At dawn, they must move south, sweeping the whole valley. They must fight at a run, eating up the military encampments piecemeal, giving them no chance to rally or to spread warning. For this reason, specially picked runners must run ahead of the main body, to kill any messengers trying to spread warning to other camps."

"This sounds very good so far," Goma said. "Continue."

"On the morning of the day chosen," Conan said, "but not too early, you must lead the greater part of your force against Nabo. If you are well spread out, making great noise and show, he should believe that you are in full strength. As you position yourself before the city, drawing in and tightening your lines"— he drew a series of lines before the cow skull—"the fleeing enemy from the encampments will appear in your rear. You may stand where you are, but for the sake of confusing Nabo I suggest you about-face your men and march away from the city. The fleeing warriors will be crushed between the two forces." Conan knelt in the dust and clapped his hands together dramatically, scattering twigs and pebbles in a powdery cloud. He got to his feet.

"Then, reinforced by the rest of your army, you about-face again, march up to the city, and issue your challenge. Now, if my estimate of his numbers is correct, you are of about equal strength. You may be even a little the stronger. Plus, *your* men are fresh from an easy victory, while *he* he still stuck with those blue-feather warriors who, by that time, are having second thoughts about who they wish to follow."

Through this recital the chiefs listened carefully. Some showed enthusiasm, others showed doubts but, when it was over, none spoke for or against it. All looked to their king, with whom the decision rested.

"It is a good plan, and I shall use it," he said at last. "But I shall make one change: *I* shall lead, personally, the force that sweeps the valley."

Conan frowned. "That is unwise. The king should not put himself at such personal risk in a battle fought in his name."

"That may be how it is done in the north, my friend, but not here. My warriors will expect it. Any of my senior chiefs is capable of handling the larger force."

"As you will," Conan said. "When do you propose to make your move?"

"There is nothing to be gained by waiting. The striking force marches out at dusk this evening!"

"You are a man of quick decision," Conan said approvingly. "What would you have me do?"

Goma grinned. "Will you accompany me? We old warhounds can show the young warriors what real fighting is like."

"Aye, I'm with you."

"Excellent. Keep that spear. You will need it. And I have something else for you." He called back over his shoulder and a woman appeared from his hut, carrying something in her hands. The king took it from her and handed it to Conan. The Cimmerian studied it. It was a circlet of copper, and from its forepeak and temples sprang three glossy, black ostrich feathers.

"This signifies that you are one of the king's trusted companions," Goma said. "All warriors will give way to you while you wear this."

Conan adjusted the headband to his liking. "Tomorrow will be a good day to wet our spears," he said. Goma translated and the words roused a great, bloodthirsty cheer from the encircling warriors.

# Sixteen
## Blood in the Valley

Dusk washed the valley in a purple light as the warriors of the flying force assembled. For this mission Goma had chosen the red-feather regiment. This contained the greatest number of young warriors, eager to make a name for themselves and well fit for the grueling task before them. Goma had commanded that they spend the day resting, not an easy order to obey, for most were going into their first fight. They had eaten well, and they would carry nothing save their weapons, for there would be nothing for them save marching and fighting until their king was restored to his throne or else he, and they, were slain.

As the first stars twinkled overhead, Goma issued his final orders, and these he translated for Conan: "There is to be no singing, and no loud chanting while we march. If a man falls, he is to fall silently, then pick himself up if he can and march on. If a serpent bites, the one bitten will suffer and die in silence." These orders were issued, and received, sternly.

"It is time," Goma said. "Let us go."

Conan stood ready. He had been given a breechclout of leopard skin and bands of long monkey fur. With his new feathers, the only things distinguishing him from the other warriors were his alien features and his long sword. He carried no shield, knowing that if he should need one, he could always take one from a dead man.

The long file of red-feather warriors made its way through the assembled host. By the king's order there was no cheering and no loud salutes, but encouragements were barked out in low, beastlike growls that were more warlike than any amount of extravagant adulation.

When they were in the open the pace of the march picked up, first a quick march, then a double-quick, finally a trot that devoured the miles. In the forefront were a number of the youngest warriors, youths who knew this land well from their numerous cattle-raids. Next came King Goma and his black-feather guard, including Conan. After them came the greater body of warriors, running to a chant that was not far above a whisper.

The moon rose, flooding the valley with pale light. To the surefooted young men, who hd spent much of their young lives standing night watch over their cattle, it was almost as good as daylight. In the brush, the great predators kept their distance, lying belly-down as this strange spectacle made its way up the valley. Instinctively, they knew that there would be no full bellies to be had from this band of steel-bristling men. The stupid, near-blind rhinos snorted and trotted away, not liking anything unfamiliar.

Goma called no halts. The night was cool but soon they were streaming with sweat and the whispered chanting grew windy. But no man faltered. It was for this reason that Goma had chosen the regiment of younger men. As the night wore on and the moon made its accustomed crossing of the firmament, some of them began to stagger, but no man fell out of the march. Their breathing grew labored, then agonized, but to fail would be unendurable disgrace.

Even the strongest were at the end of their strength when they reached the northern end of the valley. In a broad meadow the king called a halt and the men cast themselves down upon the grass, gasping. Neither Goma nor Conan were breathing especially hard, and their taut-muscled bodies merely glistened with a sheen of sweat. The king wore no decoration whatever. In his left hand he bore a small, round shield of hippo hide. In his right he idly twirled his inseparable axe.

"The sun rises," Goma said, contemplating the thin band of pale light over the eastern mountain range. "Soon she will show her face. Before that happens, we must be killing. This is the last dawn of Nabo's kingship. The sun shall set upon the true king of the valley."

"I'd not want to be king of such a valley," Conan said. "It is a fine and fair land, but that lake blights it."

"That is so. I have seen many lands in my time of wandering, and I am of a mind to lead my people away from here, away from the thing in the lake. We can find another land as good as this, with rich soil for tilling and pastures where our cattle will fatten."

"Such lands are usually claimed," Conan pointed out.

"That is the way of life. I encountered no warriors as fine as my people in my wanderings. When we find a land that is right for us, we shall drive away its people and take it for ourselves. Riches are the reward of the strong and the brave. That is how it has always been."

"Aye, that it has. It is almost time now. I can see for a good half-mile."

"Aye. Let us begin slaying." Goma shouted a command and the young warriors flew to their feet. Their teeth glistened in their scowling faces as they prepared for battle. With a final war cry, Goma pointed down the valley with his axe and set out a run. Bellowing the same cry, the warriors set off behind their king.

Conan ran beside Goma, his long legs carrying him as effortlessly as those of a trained racehorse. Within minutes they sighted the first camp. It was situated by a small stream. A few men were awake, building up fires, and they goggled in amazement at the horrifying spectacle that bore down upon them from nowhere save the realms of nightmare. They sprang to their feet and cried out. Men scrambled from their huts, half blind from sleep, groping for their weapons, but the red-feather warriors were upon them before more than a handful were armed.

It was not battle, but slaughter. The king did not bother to ply his axe. Instead, he stood aside and allowed his warriors to bloody their spears. Conan, likewise, took no part. It was grim but necessary work, of a sort for which he had no taste. When all the enemy warriors were dead, they set out once more. There had been enough blood to rouse the young men to a high pitch of excitement. Those who had no chance to participate were eager for kills of their own.

The next camp was awake and the warriors spotted the attackers in time to arm themselves and form a battle line. They were quickly overwhelmed, but they fought fiercely. Conan saw Goma kill two with swift, flicking blows of his axe, easily batting aside their spear-thrusts with his small shield.

A tall, white-feathered warrior rushed at Conan, his body all but invisible behind a long shield. The Cimmerian held his sword in his right hand, his spear in his left. With his spear he parried that of his foe, sweeping the shield aside with a smashing sword-blow. Serpent-quick, his spear thrust through the unprotected man's body. He looked for another to kill and saw that the fight was all but over. The white-feather warriors were being finished off, but a few red-feathers lay dead or wounded.

"Let us go," Goma said, shaking blood and brains from his axe. "The morning is just beginning."

"It begins well," said Conan.

The next camp was occupied by men of the blue-feather regiment. They formed their line, looking most confused. Goma halted his men and harangued the blues. "I gave them a choice," he told Conan. "Join me and kill the whites, or die where they stand. They have the space of twenty breaths to make their decision."

A few voices jabbered among the blues, then a wild cheering broke out. With their spears held point downward, they rushed to join the reds and their new king. These more than made up the casualties of the earlier fight. Thus reinforced, the war band continued its run down the valley.

And so the morning went. There were short, ferocious skirmishes and the camps of the whites. When the blues saw so many of their fellows among the attackers, they no longer hesitated, but came to join before Goma even called a halt. Singing and raising war cries, the party picked up strength as it went, leaving bloody devastation in its wake.

By the time they sighted the city, every spear streamed with blood. They had suffered slight losses and dealt out devastating punishment. The last few camps had seen the now large party bearing down upon them from a distance sufficient to allow them to take to their heels, and the growing mob of white-feather warriors let out a collective gasp of despair when they saw that there was a far larger force of enemies between themselves and the safety of the city.

As one man, the lines of warriors facing the city whirled about, presenting their shields and their spearpoints to the fleeing, panic-stricken warriors from the encampments. With the despair of the doomed, the whites plowed desperately into the serried ranks, even as the pursuers fell upon them from behind. Spears plunged amid screams and war cries, and blood reddened the grassy plain before the city.

Conan's spear thrust and his sword slashed, making no distinction between a fleeing man and one who faced him. This butchery had to be accomplished quickly, lest Nabo take advantage of the confusion to launch an attack of his own. A few minutes of frenzied action made a gory shambles of the field. When the slaying was over, Goma issued his orders and the lines reformed.

"I have placed the yellow feathers in front," he explained to Conan. "They are the strongest regiment. Next are the greens. It is smaller, but has many older warriors. They are steady and will not panic should the first line have to retire upon them. Last are the reds, for they are near exhaustion. Our blues I have placed on the far left flank. They are to call their brethren to come join them there.''

Conan scanned the city walls. Many people lined the parapet, but he saw no signs of his companions. It seemed that Nabo was going to make no attempt to defend the city, for there were no warriors upon the wall, and no one labored to barricade the gateway. Above the gateway stood Nabo himself, surveying the unexpected spectacle. To his right was the withered figure of Aghla. The ancient witch spat imprecations that went unheard amid the uproar. At his left hand was the towering form of Sethmes.

When the preparations were complete Goma turned to Conan. ''I will go now and challenge my uncle. He will claim that I am an imposter, and I will prove that I am not. I will claim the right of single combat and he will decline. Then the armies will fight and we shall destroy them. Slay all you can. No man who fights for Nabo can be allowed to live. But you must not attack Nabo himself. Only a king may slay a king.''

''But he is not a king,'' said Conan. ''He is a usurper.''

''Nonetheless, he is mine. I must slay him and all must see me slay him.''

''As you will, but if he comes at me I'll not be responsible. No man who attacks me with weapons escapes with his life.''

''Then avoid him,'' Goma said grimly.

When all was ready King Goma strode out before his army. They raised an earthshaking cheer, pounding the backs of their shields with their spear-butts, their cheers coalescing into an ecstatic chant of adulation. White-feather warriors boiled out through the gateway and formed their battleline before the city. Behind them came the blue-feather regiment. Conan made a quick assessment of the relative numbers. Combined, the white and blue warriors almost matched Goma's strength. With the soldiers of Sethmes, the numbers would be about equal. Much would depend upon which way the blues jumped. Already, the blues on Goma's flank were calling out to their brethren, who stood stone-faced.

Goma raised his axe and the men fell silent. He approached almost within spear range of the enemy and harangued the little group above the gate. Nabo was silent, but Aghla called out something, raising a laugh from the townspeople who lined the walls. Then Goma lowered his tight-wrapped red cloth, baring himself to the waist. Conan could not see what was thus revealed, but a gasp rose from the townspeople, cutting off their laughter. Now Goma shook his axe and called out to Nabo. The usurper answered haughtily. Conan knew that the challenge to single combat and been given and rejected. He saw that the warriors facing them looked unhappy, most especially the blues, and he deduced that a king was expected to accept a challenge to a duel for the throne. Their king's refusal had hurt their morale, which was all to the good.

The Stygian soldiers came out and formed a compact mass before the city gate. He saw no sign of the bumbana. All of them, warriors and soldiers, waited in a nervous silence for the serious, bloody work of the day to begin.

Goma turned his back on the king and began to walk back to his lines. Behind him, a Stygian soldier raised something to his shoulder. Conan was in motion before the crossbowman could depress the trigger of his weapon. The Cimmerian grasped the king's arm and jerked him aside as something hummed past. There came a thud and a loud grunt. In the front rank, a warrior plucked at the feathered bolt that pierced his chest. A neat hole marked the spot where the missile had passed through his hide shield.

Goma scowled. "They would use coward's weapons against an anointed king?"

"Those are mercenaries," Conan said, "and one of them saw a chance to kill the enemy leader." He favored Goma with a steely smile. "I have been a mercenary. I'd have done it myself."

Nabo screamed something and one of his warriors whirled

and hurled his spear through the body of the crossbowman. Sethmes frowned as the usurper castigated him.

"Dissension between the allies up there," Conan remarked. "All the better for us down here."

"Enough of this," Goma said. "It is time to begin. I long to sit in the chair of my ancestors." He whirled his axe high and brought it down with its stained head pointing toward the enemy. With a howl, the yellow-feather warriors sprang forward. Conan and Goma charged with them, straight for the center, and the battle for the valley was begun.

There was no art or subtlety to the combat. It was brute force against brute force. Spear thudded on shield or sank into flesh with a sickening sound. War clubs smashed skulls and short swords lopped off limbs and the scent of fresh-spilled blood began to pervade the air. Some men sang, others screamed, others chanted. The townsmen atop the wall shouted abuse or encouragement, and the people from the outlying villages crowded the nearby hills to view the unprecedented battle.

Conan slashed and stabbed in a scarlet frenzy, the battle-madness of his ancestors rising in him like a tide. After killing many, the shaft of his spear snapped when he thrust the weapon against a heavy shield. Taking his sword in both hands, the Cimmerian swung it with redoubled strength to shear through shields at a single blow, never needing more than a second blow to halve the body behind the shield.

Near the Cimmerian, Goma swung his axe in wide arcs, blocking efficiently with his small shield. Before him the enemy warriors were half defeated even before he stuck, so awed were they by his royal lineage. All around the two of them, the elite guard of black-feather warriors made themselves felt.

In the frenzy of slaying the lines lost all cohesion and began to break up into battling mobs. When the fight reached this stage, one of Goma's chiefs shouted an order and the second line of green-feather warriors joined the fray. The whites were desperate now but no man tried the futile gesture of surrender. There was to be no mercy this day.

When the battle entered this second stage, the commander of the blues made up his mind. He proved himself a crafty man, for the did not order his regiment into the general battle, where the confusion would guarantee that they would be fighting both sides. Instead, at his command, the blues turned and launched a sudden attack against the Stygian mercenaries who blocked the gate. Howling their delight, the blues of Goma's flank rushed to join them.

Thus two separate battles developed: the whites against Goma's multicolored regiments, and the blues against the Stygians. Immediately, the blues began to suffer heavy casualties. The undisciplined ferocity of the warriors met the cool, methodical discipline of the civilized soldiers. As usually happened in such instances, the soldiers' discipline more than made up for their lack of numbers. In close ranks with each man protected not only by his own shield but by those of his companions to either side, he could concentrate upon killing the warrior before him. With their superior armor, it was difficult for the warriors to inflict much damage upon the soldiers. The wall and the gateway made it impossible to flank or surround them. The battle front became a sausage-machine where naked flesh was hurled against unyielding steel, and the blues lost five men for every Stygian they put out of action.

The other battle was drawing to a close. Abandoned by the blues, their Stygian allies preoccupied, the whites were being overwhelmed. Hopeless now, some of them broke away and tried to flee. The red-feather warriors, now somewhat rested, chased those men down and slew them without thought of mercy. The slaughter was total.

Goma turned from the fight, satisfied that there was nothing left but mopping up. He found Conan standing with his sword-point on the ground, leaning on his pommel. His arms were bloodied to the shoulders, the rest of his near-naked body liberally bespattered. He still wore his copper circlet, but his three black plumes had been shorn away by near misses. He was catching his breath, eyeing the grim struggle at the gate.

"I can see that you have been busy," Goma said.

"I have," agreed the Cimmerian. "But the fight's not over. Those fellows are having a hard time of it."

"Aye, the blues are paying in blood for supporting Nabo. It is sufficient. The survivors will stand high in my favor." He shook his head. "That is no way for warriors to fight."

"Those are not warriors but soldiers, and their loyalty is not to king or general but to their paymaster. Your enemies will not always oblige you be fighting the way you like to fight."

"How may we resolve this?" Goma asked.

"Stop fighting along the whole line. You just waste your strength that way. Mass your men and charge directly against the center. The men in front will suffer, but that way you will break their ranks. Then you may roll them up as your warriors pour through."

"That sounds wise. Let us see what we can accomplish." Goma called his officers to him, and with the Cimmerian they went among the struggling blues. Making frenzied savages break off from a fight was no easy task, and from time to time Goma had to swat a man with the flat of his axe, but soon they had the blues pulled back and a lull fell over the battlefield.

With Conan's direction, Goma formed up his army in a great wedge with its point directed straight at the Stygian line.

The blues formed the point of the wedge, once more to prove their loyalty with their blood. The rest crowded in without regard to affiliation, for this was not to be a fight of battle lines but a furious, spasmodic struggle in a confined space to exterminate the last resistance to the king.

Upon the wall, the townsmen waited in silent dread. Nabo surveyed the butchered bodies of his warriors with a look of maniacal fury, and Aghla danced about screaming, to all appearances near to death from apoplexy. Of Sethmes there was no sign.

Conan and Goma stood to one side of the wedge. They had done far more than their share of the slaying, and this final stage would be left to the warriors, for it would be a matter of weight and momentum, rather than of individual prowess. The Cimmerian saw the two officers standing at the right and left ends of the front line. They looked grim but determined. They had survived many a hard-fought battle, and were not about to give way to despair when they were fighting mere savages.

At Goma's command, the wedge surged forward, first at a quick walk, then at a trot, finally at a dead run. The point smashed into the center of the Stygian line. The line bent, then buckled as men of both sides fell and charging savages leaped over their bodies. A ghastly pileup developed in the center, as bodies were pierced and blood made the footing treacherous. The first warriors to break through were immediately cut down. With their flanks wide open, effective defense was impossible. But as more men surged into the breach they were able to turn and face the enemy to both sides. The pressure against the Stygian force became intolerable, and the soldiers were broken up into smaller and yet smaller groups. Now discipline meant nothing and the soldiers, expert though they might be, were no match for the horde of maddened, long-limbed spearmen. The remnants of the Stygian formation were swept aside and the warriors poured into the city.

As soon as the gate was cleared, Conan followed Goma through. The warriors were maddened by slaughter and the townsmen fled before them. The warriors did not seem to distinguish between fighting men and noncombatants, but speared both indiscriminately.

"You had better get your men in hand," Conan cautioned, "or you will have no people to rule over."

Goma shrugged. "The town folk supported Nabo. The killing will stop soon. One thing every ruler learns, my friend: The slain are never irreplaceable. More people are born every day."

To this brutal philosophy Conan had no answer. Gentle philosophies were rare in Conan's experience and Goma's was not even to be numbered among the worst. In truth, after the first minutes of frenzy the victorious warriors calmed and the murderous fury ceased. Goma instructed his commanders to institute a systematic sweep of the town. He wanted Nabo, Aghla, and Sethmes, preferably alive. On no account was Nabo to be killed.

Conan searched among the dead mercenaries and found no sigh of their officers: the red-bearded Khopshef and black-bearded Geb. Somehow, the two had fought free and fled into the city. Were they with Sethmes, wherever he was?

As Goma's men stretched out and combed the city, they flushed out a few Stygian mercenaries, along with a number of well-known supporters of Nabo, subchiefs who had profited from the usurpation and death of Goma's father. These were exterminated without mercy. At last, they crowded into the plaza before the stone tower. As the victorious warriors cheered ec-statically, Goma strode forward. He mounted the dais and ac-knowledged the plaudits of the people. He shouted something, then, once again, he lowered his garment, baring himself to the waist. Again there came the awed hush as the people bowed and raised their hands, palms outward.

Now the Cimmerian saw that which Goma revealed. Carved into the flesh of his body was a design in shiny black scar tissue: a wavy-bladed trident enclosed in a crescent. Goma signaled for Conan to join him upon the dias.

"I have shown the people the mark of my legitimacy. For a hundred generations, the king's heir has had carved upon his body the mark of the ancient guardian of the pass."

"I have seen its like," Conan acknowledged.

"Now I shall challenge Nabo again to single combat. This time he must accept, having nothing to lose. I want you to watch for treachery."

"If you wish. But you have won the throne by battle. Why risk losing it?"

"Nabo has been a king, although a usurper. Only a king may slay a king."

"Then have your men drag him forth so that you may hew his head from his shoulders," Conan urged. "Be sensible, man You have not slept. You marched all night and fought at a ru all morning, then fought in the battle before the city. In that time he had done nothing save watch other men die.''

''Nonetheless, it is the custom. The people must see me defeat and slay Nabo, else I will never sit easy on the throne.'' Goma said these words sternly, and as sternly he turned and shouted out his challenge to the man in the tower. There was a long, tense wait, then came a stirring from within the building. A train of royal servants began to emerge: the dancers and serving women and entertainers Conan had seen before, then the skull-faced headsman. Last of all came Nabo himself, stalking with the pride of a doomed lion. Nowhere did he see Aghla. He caught sight of Khefi, and beckoned to the translator to stand by his side.

''You must tell me what is said,'' he told the slave.

''Will you speak to the new king on my behalf?'' Khefi said, dread in his face and voice.

''Aye, you served me well. Serve me well now and I will urge to Goma that you merely did a slave's duty, no more. I think he will grant you favor. He has already slain Nabo's important supporters.''

''I thank you, master,'' said Khefi with great relief.

''Now, tell me: what of my friends?''

''Both Sethmes and the king were most wroth when you so cleverly escaped. Aghla screamed that they must be fed to the lake god at once, but the Stygian priest said that the white woman must be spared, at least. Nabo protested that the lake god was beyond control and must be allowed to sink beneath the surface and grow calm again.

''Last night, the three men were brought forth to be sacrificed, but the god would not come, for all Aghla's summoning. This made her furious beyond her usual state, and she wanted to kill them forthwith, but Nabo said, no, save them for tomorrow night. Now I think he will not live to see that night.''

''Nor do I,'' Conan said. 'Where is Aghla?''

''I know not. Since the king returned from viewing the battle, we servants have all been cowering in the great hall to learn our fate. She came back with the king, the she disappeared into the tower somewhere.''

''And the priest?''

''He came back even before the king. Two of his officers were with him. I saw them running toward the storeroom where the prisoners were kept, then I saw none of them any more.''

''Crom curse the man! What is he up to?'' Conan longed to go within to determine what had happened to his companions, but he had first to determine what was to happen here. The two kings were going through an elaborate ritual that was almost like a dance, circling one another and chanting. Conan asked what was going on.

''The kings challenge one another and sing out their lineage. Since they are uncle and nephew, these are virtually the same. Nabo claims the throne is his and Goma claims likewise. This is for the sake of form, since it is clear to everyone that Goma is truly who he claims to be.''

''And if Nabo should win?'' Conan said. ''What then?''

''Then the people must swear their allegiance to him,'' Khefi said.

''What?'' Conan said, scandalized. ''After all this bloodshed, Nabo could get the throne back by winning a single fight?''

''Of course. It means the gods want him to be our king. the rebels could hold out thinking that the old king's son was still alive and would return. If he dies now, they have no one to replace him.''

Conan shook his head. ''I will never understand these people.''

The ritual ended and a servant handed Nabo his weapons: a small shield like Goma's and a short, stabbing spear. Its haft was less than two feet long, its blade as long as a man's forearm and as wide as two palms held together, needle-pointed and viciously edged.

All voices were silenced as the fight began. The two faced one another, then raised their shields. At this gesture, the drummers began a frenetic beat. There was no other sound save the drums. The two men circled warily, their small shields held well before them. Nabo held his spear low, its point directed toward his opponent's belly. Goma held his axe almost casually, as if it were resting across his shoulder. But the Cimmerian could see that the haft of the weapon did not actually touch his shoulder, and that Goma was as tense as a strung bow.

With a howl, Nabo darted in, thrusting at Goma's midsection. The challenger batted the weapon aside with his shield and sent three swift blows in return. The axe flicked out more swiftly than seemed possible, moving mainly from the wrist. By frantic dodging and skillful use of his shield, Nabo managed to save himself. Sweat sprang out on his scar-decorated brow and he showed his white teeth in a ferocious scowl.

Feinting toward Goma's face with his shield, Nabo slashed at this opponent's legs, using the spear like a short sword. Goma sprang over the first slash and jumped back from the return blow, but the spear's tip drew a long cut in his right thigh. Now Nabo grinned and called out something.

"He claims victory already," Khefi whispered.

"Too soon for that," Conan muttered. "It's a trifling wound."

Goma seemed not to notice the damage. He threw another swift series of cuts at Nabo's head and knees, alternating high and low to draw Nabo's defense away from his body. After a cut with his edge carried well past his opponent, Goma swept in with the back-spike of his weapon. Nabo interposed his shield at the last instant and the spike sunk deep into the hippo hide. Gripping his axe in both hands, Goma jumped back and hauled on it with all his strength. The great surge almost tugged Nabo off his feet, but the shield-strap gave way and Goma had to tear the encumbrance free of his weapon, giving Nabo an instant to regain his balance.

Nabo now took his spear-shaft in both hands and slashed wildly at Goma, driving him back and keeping him too occupied to formulate an attack. Conan knew that the usurper was at a severe disadvantage against the long-handled axe with shield, and Nabo knew that just as well. With a scream, he gripped

Goma's right wrist in his left hand and aimed a gutting thrust at his belly.

Goma brought his shield down just in time to preserve himself, then dropped it to grapple with Nabo. Now each held the wrist of his opponent's weapon hand and each sought to hold that weapon well away from his own body. It was a struggle of brute strength against brute strength, and Conan feared that Goma must be near exhaustion. Then a movement caught his eye. The skull-painted headsman was edging around behind Goma.

Conan saw that Nabo was aware of his henchman's maneuver, and was wrestling Goma so that his back would be toward the executioner. Conan could see theat Nabo's strength was failing. This desperation move must have been planned beforehand. Apparently, Nabo's respect for tradition was not quite total.

The headsman darted forward, his weapon raised. He was quick, but Conan was swift as a tiger. He leapt forward and his sword described a glittering circle, shearing away the arm that held the beheading sword. A second blow sheared off the skull-painted head, sending it spinning into the crowd, where a warrior caught it neatly and waved it above his own head, grinning. The crowd gasped at this lapse of protocol.

Now it was Goma who grinned as he forced Nabo back toward the edge of the dais. The usurper's face displayed rage, then anguish, then stark terror, his eyes rolling and foamy spittle dripping from his twisted lips. With a surge, Goma wrenched down with his left hand, twisting Nabo's right. Audible above the pounding of the drums was the snapping of Nabo's arm as Goma twisted it inward, ramming the usurper's own spear into his side.

Goma released his grip and stood back as Nabo kept his feet, his face knotted in agony. With a howl of pure, triumphant rage, Goma took his axe once more in both hands and whirled it in a great circle, bringing it down with all his strength, shearing down through Nabo's head, splitting scalp and skull, crashing through teeth, jaw, and neck, splitting the breastbone, stopping only when it was halfway to the usurper's waist. The tall corpse tottered for a moment, then fell to the dais, scattering blood and entrails over a wide area.

Goma waved his gore-spattered weapon aloft. A pandemonium of adulation broke out among the audience, dwarfing all that had gone before. The dancers broke into a spontaneous dance and all the musicians began to play at once. All the chiefs and captains surged forward to throw themselves at Goma's feet, knocking their brows against the bloody stones in an extravagant display of obeisance.

The valley had a new, undisputed king.

# SEVENTEEN

## The Treasure of Python

"**C**rom take it!" Conan swore. He had run all through the tower and had found no trace of his companions. "Where are they?" Outside, Goma still received the plaudits of his subjects. Cursing impatiently, he ran out a rear door, onto a terrace overlooking the lake. Far out upon its watery surface, he saw a small object. His keen eyes told him that it was a fishing boat, and he could well guess who was in it. It was headed straight toward the fortress on the opposite side of the lake. He scanned the shore and saw that the fleeing Stygian had not thought to destroy the other boats.

He ran back into the tower and found a great commotion. Goma had entered, and with him came an ecstatic crowd of worshipful subjects. Women brought him clean clothes and ewers of water. While he conversed with his chiefs, the women washed the sweat and blood of battle from their new king. He looked up and grinned at Conan's approach.

"Was that not a fine fight, my friend?"

"It was," Conan acknowledged.

"I have been told of how you slew the headsman, although I had no attention to spare for it at the time. It was the sort of cowardly act I expected from Nabo, which is why I wanted you near me. I am grateful. Name your reward."

"No time for that. The Stygian has escaped and even now is upon the lake, headed for the fortress and the treasure. He has my companions with him."

Goma shrugged. "I will send men to round them up, by and by. Let us relax and savor our victory."

"Not until this is finished," Conan said. "Aghla is with them, and who knows what mischief that ancient hag may be up to?"

Goma frowned. "Aghla! I wanted her dead almost as much as Nabo! Aye, we must do something about this."

"Who mans the fort now?" Conan asked.

"Every warrior of mine above the age of fourteen came hither to fight. We left only women, children, and the aged in the fort, and most of those must be on their way hither even now. I would guess that the place is deserted. There are matters I must attend to here."

"Then give me strong men to row a boat and I will chase them down."

"Very well." Goma spoke and a score of young men sprang forward. Conan picked six, then he turned to Khefi.

"Come you with me. I may have need of your skills."

"Upon the lake?" the slave said, queasily.

"Aye. The thing does not come up save at night, does it? Else how would men fish the lake?" Through Khefi he gave the six young warriors their orders.

"Good hunting, Conan," said the new king. "Bring back Aghla's ugly head and your reward shall be even richer."

Conan ran outside and down the long stairway to the lake. By the jetty were ranged a half-score of long fishing boats, their nets spread out nearby to dry. Conan pointed to one he deemed the sturdiest and the warriors pushed it out into the water, then scrambled into the craft and snatched up paddles. Conan and

Khefi did likewise. The paddles flashed and they were off toward the center of the lake.

Despite his confident words to Khefi, it made the Cimmerian's scalp crawl to be out upon the lake once more. Daylight or dark, it was an evil place, and the thing was down there somewhere. Only the urgent need for haste drove him to venture out onto the thing's domain in a frail fisherman's craft. To pass the time while they crossed the lake, he began to dip his sword into the water to cleanse it, but he stopped himself at the last instant. For all he knew, the taste of blood in the water might draw the monster like a shark.

The Cimmerian tried to descry the boat ahead of them, but a thin mist began to rise from the lake, obscuring any distant object. It was a strange time of day for such a mist, and his apprehensions redoubled. Things began to thrash upon the surface. Ahead of them, a tangle of thin tentacles snapped like whips.

"This is not right," Khefi said, his eyes rolling at the creatures that appeared on all sides. "The lake should be quiet at this time." The warriors were visibly upset. Bravery in battle was one thing. This was something else entirely.

"Paddle harder!" Conan urged. "The sooner we reach shore, the sooner we will be off this accursed lake!"

The color of the water seemed to be deepening, but the far shore was now just a short distance away. The paddlers went into a water-churning frenzy, leaving froth in their wake as they sought the safety of the shore. Now Conan could see why they were so beset. The tiny, withered figure of Aghla stood at the waterside, dancing and screaming. She was calling the lake creatures to deal with her enemies.

The warriors screamed as something like a bloated octopus hulked up near the boat, all but overturning it. A fat tentacle reached out and pulled a man from where he stood at the gunwale. A circular opening appeared in the thing's body, revealing a snapping, parrotlike beak. As the beak snapped shut on the screaming man, his companions cast spears deep into the gross carcass. The thing's dripping beak opened and it hissed, vomited blood, and sank beneath the surface.

Khefi grabbed the dead man's paddle and plied it with little skill but great energy. Yet more nightmarish, unstable forms began to appear around them. A sharklike monster broke the surface and completely vaulted the boat, catching another warrior and splashing into the water on the other side with the unfortunate, struggling man clasped in jaws lined with long, needlelike fangs.

The bow of the craft crunched onto the shore and the Cimmerian cleared the stem, landing on dry ground in a single bound. The others were close behind, all but sobbing in terror. Disgusting things flopped out of the lake in pursuit, but out of their element the warriors speared them easily, mutilating the unnatural bodies in a fear-induced frenzy.

Up the slope before them, Conan saw Aghla sprinting her way to safety. Her speed and energy belied her multitudinous years. Conan ran in pursuit, longing to hew the ancient, evil creature asunder. It had been a long, hard two days, with no sleep and much fighting, but Conan had endured far worse in his adventurous life. His iron frame and constitution were proof against exertions that would be the death of a civilized man. Surely, he thought, he could catch a fleeing old woman before she could think to get away from him.

Thus he thought, but events proved him wrong. While he was still twenty strides from the entrance of the fort the ancient hag disappeared through its gateway. The Cimmerian bounded through the portal, his spear raised for a killing cast, but he saw no target in which to wet its needle point and razor edges. The huts stood deserted and the old woman was nowhere to be seen.

A few minutes later, the others caught up with him. The four young warriors were little the worse for their efforts, but Khefi, accustomed to the easy if precarious life of the court, was gasping like a bellows.

"Is she slain?" asked the translator.

"No, Crom curse her, she got away. We must hunt her down

before she works another mischief with her spells. I suspect she has fled to the tower. That is where we will find the others.''

''How do you know that?'' Khefi asked.

''Trust me. I have no time to talk.''

The warriors said something to Khefi. ''They want to know if there will be men to fight this time.''

''There will be men for them to slay,'' Conan assured them. The warriors grinned at his words. Away from the things of the lake their courage returned. They feared nothing that walked.

The Cimmerian led them toward the tower, over which reigned an ominous silence. Its doorway gaped open, unguarded. Cautiously, sword and spear in hand, Conan entered. The entrance tunnel was dark and ominous. He heard no sounds from ahead, but that meant nothing. Successful ambushes were always silent. The last few feet he covered at a run, diving into the central room, rolling as he hit, and coming up with weapons ready. The room was deserted.

''It is safe,'' he called. ''Come on in.'' The others walked into the room, looking about curiously.

The chamber was exactly as Conan had last seen it, but for two exceptions: Marandos was no longer there, and the great slab the madman had caressed so lovingly now stood tilted on one end, revealing a stairway that led into the bowels of the earth beneath the fortress. What had moved it, the strength of the men or the magic of Sethmes?

''We must go down there,'' Conan said. The warriors eyed the dark stairwell dubiously. Once more, they were on unfamiliar territory. ''Go outside and fetch torches,'' he ordered Khefi.

Grateful to have instructions to obey, the slave ran outside, where fires still smoked before the deserted huts. Minutes later he returned with a bundle of torches under one arm and another flaming in his hand.

Sheathing his sword, Conan took one, as did each of the warriors. With the flaming brand held before him, the Cimmerian began his descent.

Instantly, he saw that this passageway differed from the fort above. It had been hewn from the solid stone beneath the fort, lovingly smoothed and ablaze with exotic decoration. Walls and ceiling were covered with paintings that had something of the Stygian about them, yet differed noticeably. Conan knew that this was Pythonian art, the ancestor of Stygian. The warriors pointed and exclaimed at the strange, colorful figures that ran riot over every available surface. Gods, kings, and mythological beings acted out unknown legends and the rituals of forgotten religion. Some creatures had the bodies of men and the heads of animals, or vice versa. There were scenes of banquet and battle, but most activities were utterly incomprehensible and many of them thoroughly repellent.

The stair turned out to be far longer than Conan had expected, and it did not follow a straight course, but instead took odd, unexplained turns, stopped at seemingly purposeless landings, only to continue down a few paces on. Everywhere, the riotous paintings overwhelmed and wearied the eye.

A warrior exclaimed something. "Look at the torches!" The flames fluttered in a breeze that could only originate ahead of them.

"Somebody is going to be very disappointed if this is naught but an escape tunnel." Then he chuckled. "Serve the lot of them right, though."

Now they could hear strange sounds ahead of them. There were screechings and squealings, much distorted by distance and the echoing walls. Over all, though, was a rhythmic, booming sound so low in pitch that it was more felt than heard. It was not the sound of drums, but it had a deep, oceanic beat that was like the throbbing heart of a world.

Ahead of them, they saw a strange glow that did not flicker like natural firelight. It was yellow with a faint, greenish tinge and there was a coldness to it that was not of the familiar world. It came from a portal where the stairs ended. Conan dropped his torch and drew his sword.

The room they entered was a vast, echoing chamber, so large that Conan was unable to make out whether it was a man-made place or a natural cavern. The wall through which he had just entered was smooth, and upon it were painted more Pythonian figures, these colossal in size. The farther walls were a mystery to him, for the radiance did not illumine them. It was more like a glowing fog than light spreading from a single source. In what seemed to be the center of the chamber, a vast, irregular heap of something glittered, and near this heap he saw a number of figures moving.

"Prepare to do some slaying," Conan said, "but you are not to attack the woman, the small man, the big man whose beard is yellow, or the man with the full red beard." Khefi relayed the orders, but Conan had his doubts, having seen how frenzied these men became when their blood was up. His companions would just have to look out for themselves if the warriors got too excited.

They began to stalk toward the glitter. As they drew nearer, Conan saw that the strange light flashed from jewels and gold, and that much of this precious material was formed into instruments of exotic design, rather than ornaments. At their approach, the tallest figure turned.

"Welcome, Cimmerian. My colleague, Aghla, has told me of your imminent arrival."

"To your misfortune," Conan said. He saw that, just beyond the treasure hoard, the floor of the chamber and an expanse of water stretched into the obscuring gloom. It splashed upon the floor in sluggish wavelets, and it was from this uncanny, subterranean lake that the deep throbbing came.

"Conan! Can you truly be alive?" It was Springald, looking haggard but excited. By him stood Ulfilo, wearing his perpetual look of offended dignity. Near them was Wulfrede, who seemed slyly amused. All three wore their weapons.

"How did you come to be here with this liar?" said Conan, pointing at the priest.

"When he let us out of the dungeon and gave us the choice of following him rather than feeding the lake-thing," Ulfilo said, "we were willing to set aside our differences for the nonce."

"Where is Malia?" Conan demanded.

"You speak of the White Queen," said Sethmes. Now Conan

saw that the two Stygian officers stood behind the priest, their hands upon their weapons. "You are not to speak of her as of an ordinary woman. She is now beyond your ken."

"Where is she, damn you?" Conan strode near the man, raising his sword. Geb and Khopshef stepped before their master, drawing their weapons.

"If you would see her," Sethmes said, "you need only look up."

Conan gazed up the glittering slope, which seemed to be made up of pearls, rods, and crystals, an occasional book, many complex objects dedicated to purposes at which he could not guess. Atop the heap was a structure of gold and silver glittering with jewels, in the shape of a great throne. Upon this sat Malia. The woman did not look at him or seem aware of him in any way. She wore a crown that spread over her brow in a towering fan. Great ropes of pearls and jewels hung from her neck and circles of precious metals clasped her limbs. She wore nothing else, and her full attention was directed toward the water. Beside her crouched Aghla, chanting and beating a tiny drum. It was made of skin stretched over a human skull.

"What is this?" Conan demanded. "What are you doing to her?"

"Ask him, blackhair." It was Wulfrede who spoke. He pointed to a ragged creature who sat upon the flank of the treasure heap, digging his fingers and toes into the glittering wealth.

"I see you have what you suffered so long for, Marandos," said Conan. "But you do not seem happily reunited with your loving wife."

"Wife?" The man blinked. "Oh, her. She was a part of the bargain."

"What bargain, curse you?" Beside Conan the young warriors stared at this spectacle, so far beyond their comprehension that they had forgotten that they were there to kill.

"The Stygian. He promised to lead me to the treasure, if I would lure Malia hither as well. He wanted her for something. So I agreed."

"And the others?" Conan asked.

"Well, she couldn't very well get here by herself, could she?"
He looked offended at such a foolish question. Conan turned to
Ulfilo.

"So this is the brother you crossed the world to find?"

Ulfilo spat. "Think you I set out upon such a venture for the
sake of my worthless brother? From birth he was a fool and a
wastrel. It was the treasure I wanted, to restore my family's
fortunes. As for his woman, what is she to me? She is just some
slut he found in his wanderings, no more than a horse or a
hunting dog that took his eye. If the priest needs her for his
purposes, what is that compared to establishing my family as
the greatest in Aquilonia?"

"Your honor comes cheap, nobleman," Conan said.

"You dare to speak of honor to me, barbarian!" He tore his
long blade free of its sheath.

"I did not come here to kill you," Conan growled. "We have
been companions. Let's not fight when enemies stand near."

"They are not my enemies," said Ulfilo.

"You make me regret that I came here," Conan said. "It was
to get you free of Nabo and Sethmes that I helped Goma to take
the city."

"That was most noble of you, my friend," said Springald.
"And we thank you most heartily. There is no need for us to
quarrel. Join forces with us. This is no mere treasure hunt.
There are forces at work here, things so ancient and so powerful
that the course of the world will be changed by the events of
these days in this valley. Compared to such historic happenings,
what are a few lives, or one woman, more or less?"

"Join forces with this lying, conniving priest?" Conan was
incredulous. "You have all gone as mad as Marandos! The Stygian will share nothing with you!"

"Pythonian, if you please, barbarian. I am not Stygian, but
of the pure, royal blood of imperial Python. This day I unite the
ancient crown and treasure of that nation with the immeasurable
power of the thing from beyond the stars we know. With such
power harnessed to my will, I shall raise ancient Python from

the dust and shards, restoring it as it once was, ruling it with power such as the old kings never dreamed of!'' His black eyes shone with fanatic light.

''Power?'' Conan said, aghast. ''That thing is too weak to raise itself from the hole it made when it fell to Earth. It is so helpless that it needs fearful tribesmen to feed it!''

''See you this great heap of gold and jewels, barbarian? Know you what it is?''

''It is the treasure of Python, for which certain fools have marched and fought their way across half the world.''

''Have you noticed how little of it is made up of gauds and ornaments, and how much of instruments and tomes?''

''It is plain enough.''

''This represents the concentrated magical power of the Pythonian empire! As the Hyborian tribesmen won victory after victory, the emperor called in all the sages and wizards and gathered their most precious, powerful devices into one place, the greatest ingathering of sorcerous power in history!''

''Much good did it do him,'' Conan said contemptuously. ''The Hybori watered their horses in the canals of Python. They warmed themselves by the fires of its burning palaces.''

''The stars were Python's enemies,'' Sethmes said. ''In the year of the Fall of Python, they formed a conjunction of such malignancy as is not seen in ten thousand years. But the creature in the lake sensed the power gathered in the treasury of Python, and it began to draw that power toward itself. It was not by accident that the commander of the expedition made his way across trackless waste to this valley, and erected his treasury by this lake! It was no common urge for security that kept the workmen driving their passage downward and ever downward. Each time the supervisor of the work decided that it was time to hew out a treasure chamber, some nameless impulse caused him to order further digging, until at last they broke into this cavern.''

Conan turned to the Aquilonians and the Van. ''This treasure represents his sorcerous power. Will he share this with you? You cannot be that foolish!''

''If he meant to gull us,'' Ulfilo demanded, ''wherefore did he release us from the dungeon and restore to us our arms? Wherefore bring us hither?''

At this Conan laughed heartily. ''Fools! He released you because he needed someone to paddle his boat across the lake, before Goma's men could storm into the city. He brought you here to the treasury because he did not know what he would find. There might have been guards to fight. You are alive now because he has only those two Stygian sellswords to fight for him. But you will not outlive his first exercise of this power he expects to draw from the lake-thing.''

''Must we listen to this savage, master?'' demanded the red-bearded Khopshef. ''Let me slay him for you.''

''Not yet, my friend,'' said Sethmes, a faint uneasiness showing in his eyes. ''In fact, this might be a good time for our mighty Ulfilo to display his loyalty. Aquilonian, if you would be the greatest among my nobles, slay this black-haired northerner for me.''

Ulfilo lost a bit of his arrogant self-assurance. ''Would you have it thus? The man is no danger to the lot of us. He is only a single sword. Lowborn and outlandish as he is, he was a brave and faithful ally upon the long road hither.''

''I fear you may lack the steel spine of a Pythonian duke,'' said Sethmes in mock sadness.

''I can be as hard as any man!'' Ulfilo roared. He drew his long sword. ''No foreign savage stands between me and the glory of my house!''

''Cease this!'' Springald hissed. ''This is childish!'' But his friend was past all reason. All he saw before before him was the power of his family slipping away, and an enemy who wanted to keep him from reversing that fall.

The two long swords rang together and the Cimmerian was fighting desperately for his life. Gone was any thought that he and this man had been companions, of a sort. Ulfilo was as strong and expert a swordsman as he had ever faced and Conan granted no concessions to those who drew steel on him. The blades wove a blurring net of steel around both men as they attacked and gave ground.

The onlookers watched tensely. Springald was distressed to see two friends trying to kill one another. Wulfrede looked on with his usual cool, sardonic amusement. The young warriors chattered excitedly to see this novel form of combat. Marandos ignored all but the treasure. Geb and Khopshef fingered their hilts, eager to plunge a blade into an unsuspecting back. Malia was oblivious. Aghla and Sethmes watched the water.

Ulfilo aimed a mighty blow that would have cleft the Cimmerian's skull, but Conan interposed his own blade, stopping the edge just as it touched his hair. With a powerful wrench of his wrists he caught Ulfilo's blade between blade and crossguard of his own weapon. The two stood for a few seconds in a trial of strength, than Conan jerked Ulfilo's sword aside and disengaged it from his own. His return blow was a short, powerful chop that split the Aquilonian's chest from armpit to breastbone.

Sethmes said something and his two captains jerked their blades out. They rushed at Conan's back, their points aimed between his shoulderblades, snarling. Khefi screamed a warning and Conan whirled, jerking his blade free of Ulfilo's body just in time to beat Khopshef's sword aside. The four young warriors attacked, howling.

In the wild melee that ensued, Conan was for a moment puzzled as to who was fighting whom. Swords and spears whirled and flickered. Blood sprayed the fetid, lake-smelling air, and there seemed to be too many swords in motion at once. The Cimmerian halved Khopshef at the waist, and he turned to see Geb pierced by a spear even as the Stygian gutted a warrior with his sword. At his feet lay another warrior who had failed to allow for the fact that his enemy wore armor. At a pair of surprised screams, Conan whirled in time to see the remaining two warriors fall. Over them stood Wulfrede, his blade stained to the hilt.

"Why did you do that?" Conan demanded.

"I was just clearing some possible obstacles out of the way, Conan," Wulfrede said. Behind him, the Cimmerian could see Springald stretched out upon the floor, senseless. Another obstacle eliminated.

"I should have taken your words more to heart, redbeard," Conan said.

"Aye, blackhair. *No man is to be trusted where great treasure is concerned!* That is from the *Poem of Good Advice.* I have ever heeded its teachings."

"It was you who roused the sailors against me on the voyage and the journey inland!"

"At last you acquire wisdom, albeit far too late."

"You are as foolish as the rest! How will you carry more than a packload of this wealth from here? Even if the priest would allow you to have it." This caused Conan to wonder where Sethmes had gone. Then he saw the man atop the treasure heap, standing behind Malia, his hands upon her shoulders. There was a stirring in the waters they faced.

"A packload would finance a well-equipped expedition to come back here and clean up the rest," Wulfrede said. "But that is not necessary. Even now, the priest's beast-men come hither. King Nabo would not allow them within his city, nor could they encamp near it, so Sethmes sent them into the hills nearby. They come to join him now, and it is they who will carry this treasure away."

"Then it will be his treasure, not yours," Conan said. "He will have his bumbana kill you."

"I think not. You see, he will need both ships to bear the treasure back, and who is to command the *Sea Tiger* if not I? She will have only a few skilled mariners to man her. He needs a fine seaman to con her back north. Whatever his plans for me—" He shrugged. "Many things can happen at sea, my friend." With that, the Van lunged. Their blades locked, he laughed in Conan's face. "And I think you must be very tired from your recent exertions!"

Indeed, Conan was bone-weary. The constant fighting had

taken a toll even upon his iron strength. The Van was a huge, powerful man and he used his strength to force the Cimmerian back. Conan was able to do little save parry the redbeard's swift blows and give ground. His chest heaved and sweat drenched his body as he backed away. Then he was aware that he was standing in water. The Van had forced him back into the lake inlet. The water glowed and bubbled around his knees and Conan felt a thrill of horror.

"You blackhairs were ever a hard lot to kill," Wulfrede cried, puffing already from the effort of keeping his sword in constant motion. It was the only way to keep his enemy's deadly blade occupied.

"And you Vanir were ever a race of traitors!" Conan gasped. "I should never have believed you my friend!" The Van's next blow almost split his skull. He blocked it in time to keep the damage to a scalp cut.

"Alas, how true. Farewell, Cimmerian!" His blade knocked Conan's aside and went back for a body-cleaving blow. Then his eyes widened in surprised horror. Something thick and rubbery had wrapped itself around his waist.

Now, horrified, Conan saw the tremendous bulk of the lake-thing. It towered behind the Van, filling the whole watery end of the subterranean cave. The stench that came from it defied comprehension. The tentacles raised the redbeard high and began to squeeze. Amid inhuman screams, Conan stumbled from the water. He began to run for the stair, then saw that Springald rolled upon the floor, groaning. Wulfrede had but knocked him on the head with his pommel. The Cimmerian stooped and began to drag him along.

Springald's eyes opened and he looked about him, taking in the terrifying spectacle. "Save Malia!" he gasped. "She does not deserve this!"

Conan looked up the glittering slope and saw that the priest still stood behind the throne where the woman sat, her eyes wide with fear, apparently paralyzed. Aghla danced and capered in ecstasy as the monster hulked ever nearer, reaching with its multitude of arms.

"Crom curse me for a fool!" Conan released Springald and began to climb up the treasure heap. The enigmatic crystals and wands and instruments shifted beneath him as he made his way upward. From time to time he risked a glance at the ever-nearing monster. It was now enclosed in a continuous net of red lightning.

"Now!" cried Sethmes triumphantly. "Now, I have completed the spell, fulfilling the prophecy! The power of the lake-creature and the power of ancient Python are joined!"

A thin tentacle whipped out and snatched Aghla in mid-whirl. The ancient hag squealed in shrill terror as she was raised high. Then the tentacle snapped out, casting her spinning through the air to smash against a far wall.

Conan shoved the priest aside and hauled the woman from the throne.

"No!" screamed Sethmes. "The White Queen must be joined with the being from beyond the stars! It is prophesied!"

"Find another," Conan growled. "I am taking this one."

Sethmes stooped and raised a crystal-tipped wand. Fire began to coruscate along its length as he pointed it toward the Cimmerian's chest.

"The treasure is mine!" shrieked Marandos, diving upon the priest. Lightning seemed to spread all over the madman as the two wrestled atop the heap of gold.

With Malia slung across his shoulder, the Cimmerian trudged down the glittering pile. He was anxious to be away, but he dared not stumble. When he reached the base, he found Springald weaving on his feet. With a brawny arm thrust beneath the schoolman's, Conan began to drag them all toward the stairway.

As they reached the stair portal, they were joined by Khefi. The slave had come running from some obscure corner of the cavern and he carried something in one hand. For unknown reasons, he was grinning and laughing.

"Help me!" Conan ordered. Khefi grabbed Springald and began to tug him up the stairs.

The hellish noise behind him caused Conan to turn for a last look. The monster was out of the water now, and its tentacles reached out to embrace the treasure hoard. Two human figures still struggled atop it, oblivious of the thing that loomed over them. Then the vast bulk came down crushing them and covering the entire golden hill. The red lightning that covered it winked out, and it began to glow from within. Then, in a manner not to be described in any human language, it began to *change*.

Conan whirled and charged up the steps. His fatigue was great, and carrying the woman over his shoulder did not help, but the thing behind them gave him redoubled strength and energy. By the time they were near the top of the stair, he legs felt as if they were made of molten metal. Still he toiled on. Then he heard a rumbling from behind them, a sound of rushing waters that drew ever closer.

"Climb, damn you!" he shouted. Khefi and Springald were staggering, almost at the end of their powers.

Abruptly, water surged around the Cimmerian's ankles. He could just see the light of the doorway above. Then the water rose to his knees, coming up the stairwell faster than he could ascend it. The water was at his waist as he reached the upper landing, and he was swimming when he made it into the tower chamber in a rush of bubbling, glowing water.

The gasping Cimmerian was washed out through the tower's doorway and into the courtyard beyond, where the unconfined water spread out and deposited him and his burden to the pavement. He lay there, catching his breath, stars of exhaustion dancing before his eyes. Nearby he heard someone laughing. With what energy he had left, the Cimmerian sat up. Nearby, Springald lay sprawled, vomiting water onto the pavement. Standing by Springald was Khefi. It was he who laughed, admiring something that he gripped in one hand.

"What in the name of all devils are you laughing about?" Conan demanded. "And what is that you bore away from the chamber? Did you get away with some of the treasure?"

"Much better than that," said Khefi. "King Goma will reward me richly when I bring him this!" He held out a small,
round object. It was the hideous head of Aghla. It wore the
expression of inhuman terror it had acquired when the hag's god
had seized her.

"At least someone was keeping his wits about him down
there," Conan said.

They had no more than a few minutes to recuperate when the
barbarian's keen ears detected sounds from downslope.

"The bumbana!" he groaned. "I had forgotten them!" With
Khefi, he staggered to the parapet of the fortress wall. Far below
them, the lake roiled and glowed eerily. Springald managed to
stagger up beside them. Malia lay where she was, unconscious.
Up the slope, still near the lake, came the shambling forms of
the bumbana.

"We must be away from here!" Springald cried.

"Where will we run?" Conan said. "We would be visible
for miles on these slopes, and we cannot go fast if we carry
Malia."

"Perhaps we can barricade ourselves in the tower—"

"Look!" Khefi shouted, pointing.

The center of the lake began to bulge upward, as it had when the
monster came to feed, but this time there was a difference. This was
beneath the sun of late afternoon, and the water did not glow sullen,
bloody red, but rather it shone almost white. The dull-witted bumbana turned to see what was happening behind them.

Abruptly, with a hissing, thunderous roar, the surface of the
lake burst open and something erupted from it. So blindingly
bright was the light that it was as if the sun had risen from
beneath the lake. Within the great glow was something tran-
scendantly strange and bright. It roared upward until it disappeared into the clouds overhead, illuminating them from within,
briefly. Then it was gone.

The waters of the lake burst from their banks and tumbled
up the slopes, knocking the bumbana from their feet and tum-
bling them like bits of straw. Then the waters lost their impetus

and flowed back down the slopes into the bed of the lake. There was no trace left of the apemen.

"It has gone back whence it came," said Springald. "Or continued on the journey interrupted so long ago. Who knows? Perhaps its stay here was a trifling delay to such a creature. And who knows how much of human history it influenced? Did the Hybori destroy Python because it needed this power? Did the royal house of Python dwell obscurely in Stygia for a hundred generations so that Sethmes could devise the spells to unlock that power for its use? Surely, Sethmes thought to bend the thing to his own will, while he was acting according to its will all the time."

"Springald," Conan said, rubbing a hand across his weary brow, "ere now, out of friendship, I have avoided saying this. But you talk too much."

Together, they carried Malia to a deserted hut and Conan ordered Springald to rest and watch over her. Then he turned to Khefi.

"You have had an easy time of it today. I want you to go to King Goma. Tell him I am ready to claim my reward. Tell him to send men to carry my friends."

"I am half dead with weariness," Khefi said, "but I shall do as you say. Perhaps I will return a free man, as part of *my* reward."

When Khefi was gone Conan found another deserted hut and crawled inside. Laying his weapons within easy reach, he stretched out upon his back and instantly slept like a dead man.

"Is this truly what you want?" Goma asked the Cimmerian. "Just to provide your friends with a strong escort to the coast? The valley is clean now, with the thing gone." He swept an arm to indicate the lake. Its waters now sparkled, clean as a mountain tarn. "Abide here. I will give you many wives and herds of fat cattle."

"I thank you, but it would be too dull for my taste. We have slain all the interesting people."

Goma threw back his head and laughed. "My wanderings are at

an end, but I think you have a long road to tread ere your heart finds peace. I am not without gold. Let me fill a purse for you.''

Conan shook his head. ''It would just slow me down. I would travel light. When I get near civilization once more, I shall find gold. When there is gold to be had, I never have much trouble filling my purse.''

''Farewell, then. You are the strangest of the many strangers I have met.''

The Cimmerian went to make his farewells to his companions. Malia was healthy, but she wore a haunted look, and she had not spoken since the ordeal of the cavern.

''I wish you would come with us, my friend,'' said Springald.

''You have no need of me. I said I would lead you to Marandos, and so I did. Nothing calls me to the coast. Goma will give you a strong party of warriors and bearers, so you need fear nothing. The men Wulfrede left with the *Sea Tiger* should be able to work the ship back up the coast.''

Springald took his hand. ''It is the library for me, then. Set take my bones if I ever try to make a voyage of my own again!'' And so they parted.

Two days of leisurely walking brought the Cimmerian through a narrow defile in the mountains to the east of Goma's valley. The slopes below him were carpeted with a dense growth of forest. The forest stretched away to the horizon, an awesome vista of the vast life-force of the Black Lands. Among the trees he could see moving many strange, huge animals. The savage land called to Conan, as strange places always called to him.

For now, treasure was nothing. Civilization was less than nothing. Near-naked, with only his weapons, his wits, his great strength, and his unending lust for adventure, he had all he could ever want. In himself he embodied the savage spirit of the wilderness.                     •

He paused for a few moments at the edge of the great darkness beneath the trees. Then, silent as a spirit of the forest, he disappeared within.